THE UNWANTED

Han Xiu

Translated by Katherine Lu and Jeffrey Buczacki

THE UNWANTED

English translation Copyright 2020 by Katherine Lu and Jeffrey Buczacki

Cover design and art by the Chi-Shun Yang Design Studio, Taipei, Taiwan

Print ISBN: 978-0-578-65433-1
Book design and layout by Booknook.biz
Originally published as 多餘的人

Map of China is a public domain publication of the Central Intelligence Agency

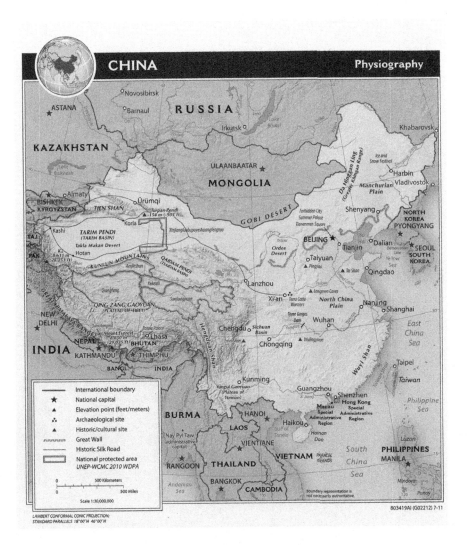

CHINA

Physiography

ASTANA

Novosibirsk

Barnaul

RUSSIA

Irkutsk

Lake Baikal

Khabarovsk

KAZAKHSTAN

Lake Balkhash

ULAANBAATAR

MONGOLIA

Da Hinggan Ling (Greater Khingan Range)

Ice and Snow Festival

Harbin

Vladivostok

Manchurian Plain

Almaty

BISHKEK

KYRGYZSTAN

TIEN SHAN

Ürümqi

Turpan Pendi
-154 m (-505 ft)

Korla

Kashi

TARIM PENDI
(TARIM BASIN)

GOBI DESERT

Forbidden City
Summer Palace
Tiananmen Square

Shenyang

NORTH
KOREA

PYONGYANG

Takla Makan Desert

Xinjiangtukubupoyeshiangfengtao

Yellow

BEIJING

Tianjin

Dalian

Demarcation
Line

SEOUL

SOUTH
KOREA

TAJ.

PAK.

K2 8,611 m
(28,251 ft)

Hotan

KUNLUN MOUNTAINS

Aerjinshan

QAIDAM PENDI
(TSAIDAM BASIN)

Ordos
Desert

Taiyuan

Pingyao

Tai Shan

Yellow
Sea

Qingdao

Qiangtang

Sanjiangyuan

Lanzhou

Xi'an

Terra Cotta
Warriors

Longmen Caves

North China
Plain

Nanjing

Shanghai

QING ZANG GAOYUAN
(PLATEAU OF TIBET)

Fekexili

Three Gorges
Dam

Wuhan

East
China
Sea

NEW
DELHI

Damolongma
Mount Everest
8,850 m
(29,035 ft)

Potala Palace

Lhasa

Chengdu

Sichuan
Basin

Ermeishan

Yangtze

Chongqing

Wulingyuan

Wuyi Shan

INDIA

NEPAL

KATHMANDU

BHUTAN

THIMPHU

Hengduan Shan

Taipei

BANGL.

INDIA

Kunming

Yungui Gaoyuan
(Plateau of
Yunnan)

Xi (Jiang)

Guangzhou

Shenzhen

Taiwan

Hong Kong

Philippine
Sea

BURMA

HANOI

LAOS

Haikou

Gulf of
Tonkin

Macau
Special
Administrative
Region

Special
Administrative
Region

Nay Pyi Taw
(administrative
capital)

VIENTIANE

Hainan
Dao

Luzon

PHILIPPINES

MANILA

RANGOON

THAILAND

VIETNAM

PARACEL
ISLANDS

South
China
Sea

Andaman
Sea

BANGKOK

CAMBODIA

Boundary representation is
not necessarily authoritative.

Mindoro

Panay

Legend

- International boundary
- ★ National capital
- ▲ Elevation point (feet/meters)
- ⁂ Archaeological site
- ▲ Historic/cultural site
- Great Wall
- Historic Silk Road
- National protected area
  UNEP-WCMC 2010 WDPA

0   500 Kilometers

0   500 Miles

Scale 1:30,000,000

803419AI (G02212) 7-11

LAMBERT CONFORMAL CONIC PROJECTION;
STANDARD PARALLELS 18°00'N 46°00'N

CHAPTER 1

IN THE CEMETERY

Whenever I think of him, Dr. D's face slowly takes shape in my imagination, not my memory. He was a German doctor, an orthopedic specialist. When my maternal grandfather was a young man, he took my grandmother with him to study in Japan, the first time out of China for both of them. They met Dr. D in Tokyo in the early 1920s. Later, Dr. D moved to Shanghai, where he set up the first of his two practices in the Xuhui district. When grandfather died in 1937, Dr. D was among the mourners in his funeral procession, and, in the early spring of 1949, my two-and-one-half-year-old self became his last patient there.

My grandmother later told me that, amidst the turmoil of a political order on the brink of change, he was the only doctor she trusted. I had slipped while walking shoeless in a pair of woolen socks on the highly polished parquet floor of our elegant house on Shanghai's Sinan Road. Hearing the thump of my fall, Sister Yang, a nun set adrift when her convent dissolved in the social chaos and now our maid, came running and, grabbing my right arm, yanked me upright. The sudden pain in my elbow caused me to burst into tears. Grandma later recalled that this was the only time in the sixteen years we lived together that she heard me cry. I do not remember ever crying out loud again. What's the point if no one is listening or cares? Since then, I have shed rivers of silent tears but never the noisy sobs of that day.

At the sound of my bawling, Grandma, then a 52-year-old professional woman, click-clacked down the stairs as fast as she could in her short heels and winter qipao of dark-coffee colored wool. Scooping me up in her arms, she headed for the door, calling out to Sister Yang to hail a taxi. Sister Yang, no doubt seeing herself as the cause of the emergency, charged out the door and flagged down a passing rickshaw.

A short while later, Grandma, with me in her arms, was standing in the empty waiting room of Dr. D's clinic. Dr. D was dressed to go out, wearing a coat and tie, hat planted squarely on his head, black medical bag in hand.

"Your arm was dangling from the elbow. Dr. D immediately put down his medical bag, took you from my arms, and placed you on the examining table."

Grandma told me this story many times during our years together, and it never failed to warm my heart. Every time I returned to Beijing from far-off places, aching in every bodily joint and muscle - except for that right elbow, which remained strong and pain-free, Grandma would smile and tell the story again. As she spoke, my aches and pains would melt away.

"Dr. D first gave you a shot of local anesthesia to numb the right half of your body. Then he took a stainless-steel nail and drove it into your elbow. He said it should be good for twenty-five years. That was acceptable. Given the uncertainty of the times, who knew what might happen in twenty-five years?" I had great confidence in that nail and never gave a thought to it failing.

I often asked Grandma, "What did Dr. D look like?" And she would reply, "Like an ordinary Westerner: ruddy face; graying beard and hair, slightly bald; gray eyes that could be serious or warm, depending on the patient's condition." Many years later, when I at last arrived in Hong Kong, I saw in <u>Time</u> magazine a photograph of a smiling department store Santa Claus emerging from a coffee shop onto New York's Fifth Avenue. That photograph perfectly captured my mental image of Dr. D, the man who almost changed my life.

"Maybe I should have let him take you back then."

I was almost ten years old and had come home with a bloody face. Grandma was telling me this story as she wiped off the blood with a warm wet towel. My silent tears disappeared into the towel as well.

"There you were, your right arm bandaged up in a wooden splint, lying there staring at him with wide open eyes. He was stroking your curly hair back on your sweaty forehead when he stopped and said to me very seriously, 'Let me take her with me. This child will be unwanted in this place.'"

Silent tears streamed down my face. When I stopped crying, I asked, "Where did Dr. D go?"

"First he was going to Hong Kong, then probably back to Germany." She thought for a moment and seemed to decide to put this subject to rest once and for all by explaining exactly what went through her mind that day.

"Dr. D was a very good person. But Germany and Japan lost the war, and we won."

As I listened to her words, my nose throbbed. When I started tripping and falling down for no apparent reason at the age of four or five, an eye doctor discovered that my left eye was an almost useless "lazy eye." In order to make the lazy eye improve, he made me a pair of glasses. That day a schoolmate had hit me in the face and broken my glasses, leaving a tiny fragment of glass lodged in the bridge of my nose very close to my lazy eye. I still have a small scar there.

As the warm wet towel moved soothingly over my face, I made a big decision: I would no longer wear glasses. I would never give anyone another chance to bloody my face. I memorized the characters on the eye test chart and managed to fake a gradual improvement of vision in my left eye. When I was alone, I would cover my right eye with my hand in order to exercise the left eye. Even though the left eye was almost useless, I wanted it to look natural and coordinated with my good eye. With much practice, I learned to judge distances so that the left eye would not steer me into objects or cause me to trip.

No one knew my secret except for Grandma and Master Mei Lanfang, a famous Beijing opera actor who taught me the technique, which served me very well. When I returned to the United States, I had to learn to drive a car. The optometrist worried that I would have trouble seeing the road's center line with my lazy eye. I was able to tell him honestly that I could judge distances with no difficulty. I can still see the look of disbelief on his face.

Every morning and evening as I washed my face, I would brush my fingertip over the scar on my nose and feel again the confidence which sustained me through many setbacks in life. I didn't think about the story of Dr. D often, preferring to savor it, examine it, and even embellish it in moments when my spirits were especially high. Dr. D was a rare touch of warmth and hope in my childhood.

"Really? Do you really think so?" My friend Maddie narrowed her bottomless pitch-black eyes, eyelashes pointing to the ground. Her body stiffened. I knew she was about to come out with something surprising. She lowered herself onto the cemetery lawn, her dark-red skirt flaring around her in a circle on the green grass, as if at the center of a bonfire. She sat there in an expressionless regal pose. It was a weekend afternoon in midsummer 1978 at Arlington National Cemetery. Maddie's golden skin shone flawless in the bright sunlight. Relaxed, she took her time before speaking.

I was in no hurry either. I had finished giving Joe a language lesson at noon and had his tutoring fee -- a crisp, new $20 bill -- in my pocket. That morning, he had timidly read a poem he had translated from English into Chinese. His Chinese was actually quite good. He could translate at sight Orwell's *Animal Farm* better than some professional translators, yet he insisted on taking lessons. This young man appeared at my apartment every weekend morning at ten o'clock sharp. Sitting ramrod straight, he would translate into almost accent-free Chinese excerpts from plays, poems, and novels. He was not interested in earning any college degree; he just followed his interests, an indulgence his family's wealth allowed him to pursue. At the end of every lesson, he would hand me a brand new $20 bill, as clean and crisp as his white shirt and spotless shoes.

"Why don't you consider marrying my father?" he blurted out one day. "He's a nice guy and rich, too. In all the years since Mother died, he has never invited a woman to dinner at home. Beautiful women have come and gone through his life, but none of them has interested him. Most importantly, you wouldn't have to work so hard. You could live with us; our home would be your home...." His voice trailed off, and so passed the only time his emotions ever got the better of his self-control.

"Good use of idiomatic expressions in that sentence," I commented encouragingly in my language instructor role. I preferred that role to the role of stepmother. Joe self-consciously returned to our translation lesson and never raised the subject again. He could barely conceal his disappointment. For him, failing to bring his language teacher into his home pointed inevitably to an eventual parting of the ways, which was what he hoped to avoid.

Joe was the best of all the students I tutored. His family's wealth enabled him to take whatever courses he pleased. Only after he started taking lessons from me did he settle down in his father's home, taking two or three hours of classes on weekends at Georgetown University. After a few months, Joe's father invited me to his house for dinner to thank me for keeping his son close to home.

"Joe is my only child, and I really miss him when he's away. How I love to be able to hear his footsteps in the daytime and to know that he is fast asleep in his room at night. It's been four full months now, and he seems content to live at home. You must be quite a teacher, so here's to you," he concluded, raising his glass. He was graceful in movement and tastefully dressed, not at all elderly. His elegant cufflinks bore a carved initial M, the first letter of the family name. We did not use the long table in the dining room but rather a charming round table in a small octagonal sun room with windows on six sides overlooking a colorful, well-kept garden. I believe he wished to convey a sense of informality and coziness.

"This was Joe's mother's favorite room," he told me. "She used to host afternoon tea here for her friends. You could do the same if you wished."

"Why not?" Maddie casually asked after learning that I had brushed off such a delicately offered proposition. "A good-natured, well-to-do, elderly gentleman; even his only son likes you and isn't worried about protecting his inheritance. What could be more perfect?" The honest question lacked her usual acerbic cynicism.

My response to Joe's father at the time was to carefully examine the room around us, eventually focusing on the shiny oak floor with its long strips of carefully fitted and well-kept wood.

"This floor is darker than the one in my grandmother's house in Shanghai. That was a parquet floor in a herringbone pattern. Before

1950 of course. I slipped on it once as a child, as my grandmother told me on many occasions. That is why it sticks in my memory."

"She is welcome to live here if she pleases; the house certainly has enough rooms." Joe's father did not give up easily. He did not shy away from the subject but returned to it even more persuasively.

"If she has trouble understanding English, you and Joe could help her out in Chinese, couldn't you?"

"Grandma accompanied Grandfather when he went to Japan to study. As far as I can remember, she once spoke Japanese with a German doctor when I slipped on her wooden floor and broke my arm. She wouldn't move here though; learning English in her seventies would be too difficult." My lame response didn't really address his question, but I had to say so.

"How is it now, your arm?" His apparent concern made me doubt the wisdom of declining his proposal.

"It is stronger and more reliable than the uninjured left arm," I said with a smile, returning my gaze to the wooden floor. "Grandma bought a traditional courtyard house in Beijing after we moved there. It had rooms on three sides and an old wooden floor so beat up that no one would ever slip on it. During the Cultural Revolution, fanatics pried up the wooden floor, exposing the cold cement underneath. They were looking for treasure or incriminating material."

Joe's father did not respond. He picked up a crystal water jug and carefully poured mineral water into my glass, a simple act that allowed him to regroup feelings that were probably rarely expressed. Many years later, I was sorry to learn that he lived the rest of his life alone. But at that time, I only wanted to talk about the wooden floor. My apartment at the time had wall-to-wall carpeting, and I missed a wooden floor. Now that a well-kept wooden floor was right under my feet, I could not help but find it beguiling. I also learned something useful that afternoon: a different usage of a familiar word that came in handy much later.

The wide rectangular opening in the wall between this bright little sunroom and the adjoining formal living room was framed in wood covered with carved designs. The floors in both rooms were of the same material and color, but under the rectangular opening and just as wide ran a piece of darker wood, not raised but visually separating the two floors.

"What is this, may I ask?"

"This is a cappuccino strip," Joe's father replied.

Seeing my confused look, he patiently explained. "It's jargon used by interior decorators." Floor design, it seemed, could be used to define space. As he preferred simplicity, he chose to achieve this purpose by creating a simple line in the floor. The decorator had suggested a strip of cappuccino-colored wood. "At the time I didn't understand what cappuccino had to do with floors until the decorator showed me a drawing." Joe's father tactfully answered my unspoken question without embarrassing me.

Twenty-five years later, when my husband and I replaced the beige carpeting in our home's adjoining living and dining areas with oak flooring, the decorator asked, "How would you like to separate the two areas?" "A cappuccino strip," I blurted out. The decorator raised his eyebrows and beamed a look of approval. "Good idea," he said. My husband had no idea what we were talking about.

Oh, what an amazing feeling! I replaced the wall-to-wall carpet with natural oak flooring thanks to the proceeds from a book and covered the floor of the entry hall with tiles of a similar color. My husband often remarked to our guests that they were walking on more than one hundred thousand words; the proceeds from my book *Conversations with Apollo* paid for this simple yet elegant beauty, including a "cappuccino" strip. My husband mischievously enjoyed reliving his initial surprise through our guests' reactions to the revelation.

Ignoring my merry mood, Maddie noted frostily, "You must be too caught up in earning a living to pay attention to the news." Spurning a comfortable lifestyle through marriage, what choice did I have but to work hard? She was right; I listened on.

"There's a Jewish doctor, a female gynecologist by the name of Perry, an Auschwitz survivor. She emigrated to the United States after she was allowed to leave Germany in 1945. Do you know where she worked in 1946?" Maddie slightly widened her eyes, her expression deadpan. When I didn't react, she slowly and quietly answered her own question:

"Manhattan East Park Hospital." I felt as though I had been hit in the head by a hammer. Maddie had my total attention. She knew that I had been born in that hospital.

"Dr. Perry could very possibly have been the first person you saw in this world." Maddie smiled mysteriously. "Do you know who this doctor bumped into on the busy streets of Manhattan?"

This time I knew where she was headed. As expected, she started to test me. "She literally bumped into an immaculately dressed gentleman who politely doffed his hat to apologize. Dr. Perry fled from the encounter, terrified; she recognized the doctor who had murdered many in Auschwitz. He was the very person who had forced her to perform abortions on Jewish women, eliminating the possibility of more unwanted lives. Rumor had it that he had escaped from Europe before the collapse of the Third Reich. For him to appear in New York in 1946 seems plausible, doesn't it?"

A chill swept over me as the sun suddenly lost its warmth, becoming a mere yellow ball in the sky. Even the grass felt cold. I managed to ask, "You don't think it could be the same doctor who treated me in Shanghai in 1949, do you?"

"Why not? Being recognized by Dr. Perry could not have been a welcome surprise. Of course he had to leave New York. It would be hard for a person to hide from his past by staying in small cities or suburbs, especially for a foreigner. Americans in rural areas would certainly be curious enough to want to know all about him." Maddie's eyes crinkled in mirth at my stunned amazement.

"So, you're saying that, after being recognized, he hurriedly left Manhattan and eventually wound up in chaotic Shanghai, reopened his clinic, reconnected with his former friends, such as my grandmother, treated my broken arm on the eve of the Communist takeover, and then left Shanghai again?" My dry lips seemed about to crack open.

"Don't you think that two years is plenty of time to do all that?" Rubbing her skirt with her fingers, Maddie flashed a charmingly tender smile.

I probably looked terribly grim, so her smile disappeared, and she continued seriously. "Take it easy. The fact that both stories use the same word – 'unwanted' – gave me a few ideas, totally unfounded thoughts most likely."

"And your wild speculation has completely ruined my sweet memory of Dr. D. Do you know how much warmth that memory has given me over the years? I cultivated the memory of him. For someone who lived for years on the brink of desperation, his memory was a spur to live on." I must have sounded angry.

"I think I'd trust your grandmother's intuition." Her sparkling eyes had become deep pools. "Unless I am mistaken, it's obvious that Dr. D left Shanghai to escape the Communists. He probably would have passed through Hong Kong on his way to somewhere else, maybe South America, definitely not Germany. He could well have been heading to my country, Brazil, or Japan, a place he was familiar with. If he had taken you with him, your life's story would have been rewritten, though it still would have been that of a wanderer. Declining Dr. D's offer to take you away was probably one of the many wise decisions your grandmother made."

My fixed stare brought Maddie's chatter to a halt. As her eyes followed mine, her face turned ashen. I sat quietly, watching the interaction of the two people in front of me. One appeared to be a well-groomed, middle-aged man. Hands in trouser pockets and swaying slightly, he was speaking softly, apparently saying something entertaining because the woman beside him was smiling. A pair of well-proportioned legs in panty hose emerged below the hem of her light lotus-root colored suit. Matching shoes and scarf completed her outfit. She held a few blue irises tied together with a beige ribbon like a cloud wrapping the flowers. A perfectly made-up face gave no indication of her age.

Wearing smiles and nodding their heads, the pair strolled by us. The man said hello to me. I smiled back. The woman was calm and friendly toward me but hardly looked at Maddie. Her elegant attire and modest offering of irises somehow outshone Maddie's flamboyant apparel and the colorful supermarket bouquet she had placed in front of her father's headstone.

The tip of the woman's shoes stopped less than an inch away from Maddie's skirt. Clasping his hands, the man stood reverently gazing at the white stone. The woman stooped to lean the bouquet of irises against the headstone, saying not a word about the other bouquet there. They bowed their heads as if to say a brief prayer. As they left, the woman smiled and nodded at me while the man politely said, "Have a good day."

"You, too," I replied.

They left just as they had come, at an even pace, chatting and laughing. Without the flowers, the woman held on to the man's arm.

During all this time, Maddie sat pale and motionless. Now she hurriedly scooped up her colorful, capacious bag and slung it over her shoulder. Pride and reserve dissipated, she managed a terse "See you next week" before walking away in a different direction from the couple, shoulders slumped in contrast to the woman in beige. A sense of sadness washed over me.

I remained sitting quietly for a while. Old Tom, a cemetery employee, drew near, pushing a cart full of flowers.

"Red tulips as usual?" he asked with a friendly smile.

"Red tulips as usual," I replied with a matching smile.

"There are veins of gold in them, really pretty," said the old man, handing me the flowers while handily picking up the wilted ones and depositing them into a small trash can underneath the cart. They were the flowers Maddie had brought. I felt a void open in my heart.

As the old caretaker continued on his rounds, I started walking toward a section of the cemetery I passed through every week. On this grass carpet lined with neat rows of white marble headstones, my feet moved me toward my relative. The sun shone on his grave, which had no weeds or withered flowers. I squatted down to place the brightly colored flowers in front of the headstone, whispering to myself, "I am here to see you. A while back my friend Maddie from my English class and I were sitting over there on the grass. She brought flowers to visit her father, too. But her flowers have been thrown away. Her father's lawful wife came with fresh irises, too. I am here to see you, alone. I don't want any company. I want to talk to you alone, just us. I miss you."

Words tumbled from my mouth, English and Chinese together. The flowers stood starkly colorful against the dazzling white marble of the headstone. The bluest sky overspread grass and leaves of the most vibrant green. An eerie peace came over me. Tears on my cheeks snapped me back to reality in this rigidly uniform place.

I walked a few steps away into the empty cemetery and then stopped to look back at the grave with its colorful flowers just to reassure myself that I was very near to him. Just then I saw a tall, lanky man walking purposefully toward me. It was Joe! Heavens, could he be heading toward the same grave? Indeed he was, and he reverently placed a white posy on the same grave. I called out, "Joe, what are you doing here?" Seeing me, Joe's face brightened, and he walked towards me.

"Who are you bringing these flowers for?" My throat was burning.

"My mother's friend," he replied immediately.

"Friend? What kind of friend?" I grabbed his arm and shook it vigorously.

"Hold it!" He laughed heartily. "What kind of friend? How should I know? Is it so important? Okay, but don't grab my arm so tightly, all right?" I looked at him intently, insisting on an answer.

Apparently unconcerned and still smiling, he said, "It's like this. When my mother died, she left me a notebook with instructions: send flowers to a certain place on certain days, buy chocolates for someone, mail a check to a certain school, that kind of thing. I just do whatever the instructions say. I don't know why the instructions say what they say. My mother had a large circle of friends, so there are quite a few things to take care of. Sometimes I have trouble keeping up. Just like today. I'm supposed to bring flowers here on Thursday, but I procrastinated. Good thing someone else brought him flowers – he's not lonely."

Typical Joe.

Frowning, I asked, "What did your mother write about this man in her instructions?"

Realizing that this was not an idle question, Joe was cagey enough to ask, "Excuse me, is this man related to you?"

"He is my father," I told him directly.

"Oh, so that's it," Joe replied gravely. "My mother requested that I bring a bouquet of white flowers to him on the first Thursday of July every year. He was her friend before she got married."

"Her first love," I suggested with a smile.

"No. Her first love is someone else; the one I send chocolates to. This man was probably a friend," Joe replied seriously.

"Why white tulips then?" I pressed, as blue irises swayed before my eyes. I was almost panting.

"I don't know. I really don't know. Perhaps he liked white tulips, or perhaps my mother once hoped to receive white tulips from him. Ancient history. No one can even guess." Joe spread his hands in the universal gesture of helplessness.

I turned my head. The red flowers were a burning flame, but the white ones completely blended into the headstone. I suddenly seemed to understand the feelings of Joe's mother. I was touched that she had cared about him.

"Let me treat you to dinner. A nice little place…" Joe clearly did not want to linger over the subject. Holding my arm, he led the way out of the cemetery. Old Tom, flowers in hand, waved at us.

CHAPTER 2

LITTLE DOG PELE

Joe smiled. "Our situations are so different. I mean our attitudes towards things."

"How are we different?" I asked without raising my head. Today's lesson is an ancient classic, *The Book of Odes*, which can be quite challenging to translate. I couldn't focus on it while chatting with him.

"If I knew my father had loved a particular woman other than my mother or vice versa, I would probably brood over it despite our casual father-son relationship." So, he was still mulling over what had happened at the cemetery the other day.

"What particular woman?" I was at a loss.

Joe pulled a black-and-white photo from his document folder. It showed the face of a woman with movie-star looks and an air of aristocratic affluence. She had to be Joe's mother. When I visited Joe's father the other day, I had not seen any photos of women; probably put away temporarily so as not to raise any questions. I appreciated the thoughtfulness of Joe's father.

I tried to imagine how it would look if my tall, handsome father were standing beside this lady. The thought prompted an involuntary smile.

Joe felt cheerful, too. "You almost became my older sister. At least our respective mothers fell in love with the same man." He actually rubbed his hands in satisfaction at the thought.

After sending Joe off, I curled up on the sofa, motionless and thinking. Joe, you are, after all, a pampered young man who never had to deal with life's storms. Your mother, the aristocratic-looking woman in the photo, probably did like my father. They could have been neighbors;

their families could have shared vacations at the beach; they could even have met at some upscale bookstore. For her part, another woman – my mother - simply needed to comply with certain formalities – a bridge – to open a door that would enable her to come to the United States before I was born. She never needed a child. Once her goal was achieved, she could wall up the door, forget the formalities, bomb the bridge. The only problem was that this child, whom she considered to be a thorn in her flesh, would stubbornly survive in spite of her purposeful negligence. Her efforts to erase this inconvenient reminder that she had a husband whom she wished so much to deny did not succeed. This husband was an unpleasant fact that was blocking the possibility of a brilliant career for her in Communist China, and this child was his daughter, tall and beautiful just like him. Even more unbearable was the fact that the child was devoted to her father against all persuasion.

My puppy, Pele, had been quietly sitting by the door while Joe and I went through the lesson. He had picked up his leash and was ready for his walk. Seeing me motionless on the sofa, he dropped the leash and quietly trotted over to stare at me. I must have looked more relaxed by then for he jumped lightly onto the sofa, placing his front leg on my arm. I gently cupped his head with both hands to look into his black eyes, and he returned the most considerate and selfless look in the world. We rubbed noses. I fished his ball out from under the sofa, picked him up, and headed out the door. I was ready for a walk, too.

When Pele first opened his eyes, he found himself lying with four siblings in a wicker basket lined with an old towel. According to the Colonel, one of my Defense Department students, the pups were taken from their mother as soon as they were born. The Colonel sadly referred to this as his "failed experiment."

Pele's mother was a pure-bred dachshund: blonde hair, well-proportioned, and dignified. The Colonel took her to upstate New York where an old friend and former colleague had a similar male dachshund. "That was one handsome male dog," the Colonel recalled. The two dogs did what came naturally, much to the Colonel's satisfaction, and soon he found out that his dog was pregnant. Of course, the father had to be his friend's male dachshund.

"The whole family was excited, couldn't wait for the new arrivals," the Colonel told me. "I looked at the litter of five puppies in the basket – none of which was blonde and none of which looked much like a dachshund. They were mostly black and yellow. The liveliest one was completely black. We were really disappointed. Then we noticed the black dog next door anxiously peering through the fence. That's when we realized that our "Sweetheart" was already expecting when we took her up to New York. What a waste of time that turned out to be!"

The Colonel decided to give away all five puppies because they were not purebred. Not only did he take the puppies away from their parents, he also decided to move to a house with a better fence so that "Sweetheart" could no longer be wooed by just any passing swain. So it was that the puppies were adopted and taken away before they even had a chance to taste their mother's milk.

I had just finished placing a strawberry cream cake on the picnic table. The box was still in my hand. Children were carrying colorful baskets nearby as they searched for Easter eggs in the grass, shrieking every now and then to announce a discovery. The black puppy turned toward the noise with curiosity, pushing its little paws backwards, ready to climb out of the basket to face a new life.

"Absolutely healthy, not a bad one," the Colonel pronounced. I picked it up, and the Colonel put a wash cloth into my cake box. As soon as the puppy was placed in the box, he began emitting a humming sound and turning in circles. He must have smelled the cream. Was he hungry then? I was so preoccupied with the little black puppy that I lost all interest in the picnic. I slipped from the garden into the parking lot, nodding and greeting people on the way.

To a puppy, a car must seem a huge new world. Mine seemed intent on locating the source of the aroma, poking at his towel again and again. As I drove, I lifted a corner of the towel. Right there by the edge was a little dab of cream. Emitting happy sounds, he stretched out his pink tongue to lick the cream. Before long, he was sound asleep, probably from exhaustion.

Thus, Pele came into my life to keep me company. I named him after the Brazilian soccer star for good reason, for he was a born ball player. I believe that talent came from his father. No dachshund could somersault as splendidly as he could. As soon as a ball was thrown to him, Pele was able to head it, keeping it off the ground for as long as he chose. When he decided to stop, he would let the ball slide down his body onto his paws, ending the performance.

I was walking Pele on the sidewalk along Route 50, where high-rise buildings dotted with plaza lawns and walkways have sprung up over four square miles. Pele found walking on cement a bit difficult, so I let him walk on the grass instead. He cheerfully kept pace with me.

Suddenly the leather leash pulled taut as Pele darted straight ahead. What caused him to sprint away like that? Did he see one of his siblings? As I was wondering, Pele approached a huge, fluffy, white dog, barking in a friendly manner and jumping up and down around his new acquaintance. He even tried to mount the white snowball. I was stunned and red-faced. The owner of the huge dog was an elderly gentleman who greeted me with a smile while trying to control his dog by tightening the leash. The two canines were rubbing noses by now. Perhaps the big dog appreciated Pele's courage? Or was it love at first sight? What was Pele doing? Wooing? I was sweating with embarrassment. The big dog was white as snow, without one hair of another color - very dignified looking. What should I do? I was anxious, trying hard to tighten Pele's leash to control his impulsive behavior.

"Don't worry. Our beautiful Mary has a lot of suitors. This isn't unusual," the elderly gentlemen assured me in a friendly tone. "What is this brave guy's name?"

"Pele."

"Well, no wonder. What courage." He smiled and bent down to stroke Pele's head. Pele, seemingly flattered by the attention, wiggled his head.

This scene ended with goodbyes. As if on a fashion show runway, Mary minced away with her fluffy tail swaying gently. Sitting on the grass, Pele stared after her, completely charmed. When Mary was far away, Pele gave me a meaningful look, which I interpreted as "I'm hungry and thirsty," so I took him home. Trotting cheerfully all the way, he quickly and practically abandoned the plaintive look of farewell he had cast after Mary.

My heart ached every time I watched Pele finish the fresh milk in his dish. He had been deprived of parents and siblings at birth and, although I loved him, I was totally inexperienced with dogs. As a result, Pele's growth and development were in large part experimental rather than planned. He ate mostly Chinese food and was totally uninterested in the fancy dog food sold in supermarkets. He adored my kitchen. He would sit patiently by the kitchen door, sniffing appreciatively as I cooked. He knew that some of the hot food was destined for his bowl. His favorite dish was Sichuan-style green beans with ground pork. After eating this dish, his face would take on a look of happiness approaching intoxication. I was always deeply touched. It was so easy to satisfy my loyal friend.

That night, after a full meal, I decided to have a serious talk with Pele. Placing him on my lap and holding his head with both hands while peering into his round, black eyes, I told him, "You are only five months old, still a puppy. You should not be chasing girls in broad daylight. This is very impolite." I spoke softly but couldn't even convince myself that I was serious. Pele's black eyes radiated innocence as he watched me attentively and rubbed his soft nose against mine. His warm little body leaned close to mine, resting comfortably on my shoulder. When I moved him onto my lap from my shoulder, he closed his eyes ever so naturally.

In this quiet moment, there was only the exhausted me and this little life that had brought me much happiness – and a little trouble. I suddenly felt sorry for him. He was a dog and far away from his kind; he lived with a human instead, a human who left home early in the morning and returned after dark. He was cooped up all day in this tiny apartment. A small, old carpet covered with newspaper by the door was his toilet. He had taught himself to roll up the paper and flatten it after relieving himself.

His human would show up in the evening, sometimes after midnight. Hearing at last footsteps on the stairs outside, Pele would bark happily and wag his tail and jump up and down with unaffected joy to welcome her home. When she took off her high heels and put on casual shoes to walk him, all she had to do to tidy the place up was pick up the newspaper and toss it in the trash. Although only five months old, Pele was already very thoughtful. Stroking his warm little body filled my heart with a tenderness that replaced the tension produced at work.

Pele never had many chances to play with other dogs, let alone fall in love. My admonition was unreasonable and outrageous. I suddenly realized that, while Pele had gained someone to feed and care for him, he had lost his freedom. Did he crave freedom? At least he had displayed a different side of his nature that day – his admiration and passion for Mary, which was rudely disrupted by two humans. But instead of harboring resentment, he remained his loyal and cuddly self.

He was still young after all, and now he was really tired. Our ball game didn't last long before he staggered toward my bed. I picked him up and placed him on a corner of the bed. He lay down comfortably, his little red member standing up like a firecracker. No doubt dreams of Mary filled his head. Pele smiled in his sleep, and I smiled along with him. Everything was all right. He would certainly have other opportunities for romance, although probably not with Mary.

That night I recalled a crimson skirt I wore once at age sixteen. It had milky white tulips with stems and leaves of the same color. It was a mid-length skirt, exposing no more than three inches of calf between the hem and the white socks I wore.

That was in the summer of 1962, following my first year of high school. I was wearing a white, short-sleeved shirt with black slacks that afternoon. I told my grandmother that I was going to visit a friend but didn't feel like wearing a black or blue skirt. In fact, those were the only colors I had for skirts. I had never owned a patterned blouse or skirt. I was just venting, knowing full well that Grandma couldn't do anything about it, for her daughter always expected me to "work hard and live plainly." My ideological molding began long before outside forces came into play. Grandma noticed that I had said I was going to visit a friend and not a schoolmate. Smiling, she asked, "Is this friend a boy or girl?"

I knew she loved me, and I also knew that, if there was one person I could confide in, she was the one, so I told her the truth.

"This is a male friend whose parents work as engineers in factories out of town while he and his grandmother live in Beijing. He just graduated from a technical high school this year and is waiting to be assigned a job. I met him at the Xinhua bookstore on Wangfujing Street. I was looking for a book of poems. It was placed on the top shelf of the bookshelf, and I couldn't reach it. He was reading a book there. He got a stool and took down the book for me - Heine's collected poems. I like Heine and so does he, so we started talking. He said he has a lot of books at home in his parents' library. I want to take a look. Perhaps I can borrow one I haven't read before."

Still smiling, Grandma nodded, put down her wine cup, and led me away to rummage through the chests and boxes stored in a small room between her bedroom and the bathroom. The storage room was a long, narrow one, with camphor-wood chests on the floor against the wall and leather suitcases piled in a pyramid on top of them. A square wooden table occupied the center of the room. Grandma had me pull out a leather suitcase and put it on the table. From the suitcase she extracted the skirt.

"The size is just right," I said, holding it up against my waist. I had never imagined myself wearing such a beautiful skirt. My joy was indescribable. I thanked Grandma, put on the skirt, and left home with a smile on my face.

That day everything seemed fine. However, when my new friend's grandmother saw me, she seemed somewhat taken aback. She drew him off to one side and without lowering her voice she asked, "How come you brought a foreigner home? Should your parents find out...." My friend soothed her. "Don't worry. She's a student at the Beijing University High School. I'll tell Mom and Dad when I write to them."

Being considered a "foreigner" was nothing new to me. On the contrary, I was quite accustomed to it. My friend's home certainly had a decent collection of books, almost as big as my grandmother's, including poetry collections and books in foreign languages. There were many different translations of Shakespeare and Pushkin. Uncle Ge Baoquan, a well-known translator of Russian literature, had the largest collection I knew of Russian literary works, but this collection was good, too. I admired the fact that a professional engineer could collect so much literature, since I aspired to become an engineer and a collector as well. My friend and I talked for a long time about books and our future professions. On leaving, I borrowed a Chinese translation of T.S. Eliot's *The Waste Land*.

I was so happy that day to have found a friend I could talk to that I did not take off that pretty skirt. My mother came home before dinnertime and saw me wearing it. Her face turned livid, and she flew into a rage.

"No dinner!"

I stood in our main room and watched her cut the lovely skirt to shreds with a pair of scissors. Only then did I perceive the graceful beauty of the tulips as they stood tall and dignified and that beauty imprinted itself on my mind. I did not know at the time that my father's ancestors were from Holland, famous for its tulips. I could not foresee that only sixteen years later I would be seeing real tulips in Washington, D.C.; even less that a few years after that I would be growing more than four hundred tulips around my house. I could never have imagined myself walking through an ocean of tulips in Holland one day.

Nothing. There was nothing. I stood there, barely sixteen, in a white shirt and shorts, watching all the innocent tulips reduced to shreds. My mother then ordered me to pick up the shreds and throw them in the trash. I was also instructed to write a self-criticism filled with the usual banalities about "infatuation with the corrupt bourgeois way of life" and "blind worship of everything foreign," the latter because the skirt had been made in the United States of America. This was how I found out that the beautiful skirt and I came from the same place. My heart lifted in exultation, and I smiled.

Looking sternly at my mother and the jade green, figure-hugging qipao she was wearing, Grandma stubbed out her cigarette and asked, "You liked flashy, showy dresses at sixteen. Did you dress in black and blue then?" Grandma had given me my most important Chinese language lessons, and I knew that in her vocabulary "flashy" and "showy" were terms of contempt.

That night, the three generations of women in our family were quiet. My mother was writing in her room, making continuous rustling sounds. She wanted me to write another self-criticism. I understood that the self-criticism had nothing to do with me, but, for the sake of Grandma's peace, I had to do it. I finished it in ten minutes and tossed it aside. Grandma spread out a thin, white, woolen pad to go under a sheet of writing paper while I opened the wooden box holding an ink stone.

I carefully rubbed a black ink stick on it and asked, "What shall I write today?"

"Mr. Wu Liu (Five Willows)," Grandma replied at once. So, in the dark of night, characters were written on the paper:

No one knows who Mr. Wu Liu is, nor what his name is.
There are five willows by his house;
He is quiet, with few words, oblivious to vanity and profit.

I recited as I wrote the characters. My favorite lines followed:

He loves to read but does not dwell on meaning.
Whenever something moves his heart, his joy makes him forget to eat.

I had written about two hundred characters when Grandma said, "Write 'Quiet with few words, oblivious to vanity and profit' a few more times." After I had done so, she would always ask, "How about a few more times?" and I always complied. She knew that calligraphy raised my spirits, and this was her way of encouraging me. But after our calligraphy session, when I went to bed, my mind was circling around the line "No one knows who Mr. Wu Liu is, nor what his name is." I could not use my father's surname, so I had adopted my mother's. Grandma tried to comfort me, saying, "You share your name with your grandfather, a righteous man." She also gave me a business card handed to her in 1944 by my father. The card had his name in English as well as the Chinese name he used in Chongqing. "His Chinese name was 'Han,' the same character as in the Chinese name for Korea; it was also the surname of Han Yu, a famous Chinese poet," Grandma pointed out. Before falling asleep, I promised myself that someday I would use "Han" as my surname.

We were all sound asleep except for my mother. She was still writing intently in her brightly lit room.

Summer vacation came and went. Only then did I discover the potency, after a period of fermentation, of the words she was writing. They prompted my school and the management of our residential building to intercept letters sent to me by my friend. Suddenly it was arranged that he would enlist in the navy's South Sea Fleet. I didn't get a chance to return *The Waste Land* to him before he left. Holding his letters in her hand, my teacher, Ms. Ying Xiya, solemnly told me, "His parents work in security organizations that require secrecy. Yet you used the excuse of reading his books to go to their home, attracting unnecessary attention. What are you up to? You even wore an American-made skirt. Are you trying to corrupt him?"

I never got to read those letters. The young man who barely escaped being corrupted was joining the military and would never send me letters again. Congratulations all around. A conspiracy to corrupt a young person in order to discover national secrets had been foiled before any harm was done. Everyone else was happy, including my teachers and schoolmates. One toady in my class even approached me with a book of Heine's poetry, wanting to "discuss" it. I said nothing. "Quiet with few words."

My mother was exceptionally happy after this, positively radiating energy. She went out dancing more often at the club run by the association of former Chinese students in America and Europe. Informing and denouncing apparently suited her, while burning away any chance for me to find friendship, not to mention love. It changed my life. I became taciturn. Seeing me cover my unhappiness with reticence seemed to give her great pleasure. In fact, I was fond of the boy, but our new friendship had not had time to mature into anything deeper. But I learned my lesson: informing and frame-ups would always follow me like a shadow. I started to spend more time at school. I no longer went home on Saturdays. On Sundays, I walked the long way to Xizhimen to catch the bus home and then took the bus back to school after lunch. This was Year Three of the Great Famine (1962), and Grandma had been tireless in her efforts to find me enough food. All along she had been preparing me for a life much more difficult than other persons'.

Fourteen years later, I got to see carbon copies of those words my mother was so busily writing, words that changed my life, stacked up in a great pile. I wasn't the only person denounced in those documents. They covered fourteen years, a period longer than the Cultural Revolution. There were probably more after that which I had no chance to see. The damage they wrought increased over the years as my mother became more adept at the sinister art of framing and informing.

For the remaining days of our short-lived, almost-first love, my friend and I learned to be smart. We passed notes to each other by hand, not through the post office. I had destroyed all his letters after reading them because I didn't have a safe hiding place for them. However, he had saved my letters to him at his home. These contained a touch of intimacy and some joy but mostly a superficial interpretation of Dante. His father took those letters to my school. All my mother had to do was add some fuel to the flames to bring about the capitulation of my friend.

Throughout this incident, I discovered that everyone was only interested in saving my friend. He was writing a self-criticism, expressing his wish to repent and remold his thinking. People ignored me. Suddenly I felt like a leper, avoided by everyone, with poison rooted deeply in my blood.

Between the spring and summer of 1964, the college entrance examinations were held. My exam came back, unscored, with the notation "This student is never to be accepted." I thought at the time that I might be the only student bludgeoned by this club because it was followed by a carrot: "Why don't you write about two hundred words saying that your father is a servile follower of capitalism, an enemy of the Chinese people, and that you want to draw a clear line of separation between you and him," I was told. "Write that and the doors of Beijing University or Qinghua University will be open to you." I did not write the desired words and, as a result, my residence was moved from Beijing to a village in the southern part of Shanxi Province. It was not until the spring of 2009 that I read in "China Through the Ages" (Yanhuang Chunqiu) magazine that "never to be accepted" had blocked many other people from the chance to get a college education. The article referred to cases in 1965, a year after my graduation, in Chongqing city, among other places, so obviously this heavy club was swung nationwide. The article reported that almost one million students with questionable class backgrounds were affected, and this was before the Cultural Revolution. I can't speak for the others, but, for my part, I have spent a lifetime enduring the ache of educational deprivation.

When I was sent to the countryside in 1964, I looked strong and healthy, but I could feel that a part of me was dying. One day after harvesting wheat, water was released into the field. We all rolled up our trouser legs, sank our feet in the muddy water, and continued to work. Suddenly one of our team leaders, a young man from Beijing, pointed at me and called out, "Your legs are too white; better let down your trouser legs." The members of the commune, who saw nothing wrong with my legs, chuckled at this preposterous comment while the other Beijing youths in our team, seeing white skin as un-Chinese, just glared at me. Self-conscious as most teenagers are, from then on, I always wore long trousers with the legs let down all the way to my instep, in mud and in water. As a result, my legs grew even whiter.

"Sent-down" youths marrying leading cadres, marrying poor and borderline-poor peasants, marrying each other, I was indifferent to it all. Black, blue, heather-hued shapeless trousers washed clean with patches neatly mended became my daily outfit, worn day in and day out, year after year. Later on, I heard about something called hormones that existed in all animals and humans and could affect natural instincts. I didn't think that the hormones in my body were doing anything, having been nipped in the bud. I was forty years old before I began to understand them. My first pimple appeared on my face after I turned fifty.

When I became Joe's teacher in 1978, that part of my being still lay dormant. I was a sexually neutral creature. Yet Joe viewed me just like any other woman. One evening when he dropped by, he noticed Pele's erect penis. He picked Pele up and let him loose outside the apartment door without a word. Pele only had his collar around his neck. I thought of Mary and panicked.

"What if Pele does something wrong?"

"Do what wrong?" a perplexed Joe asked, staring at me. "Pele is a healthy dog. He has the right to pursue what limited happiness he can."

Joe's stare made me nervous. I muttered, "He's so small. He might be bullied by bigger dogs...."

Joe looked me squarely in the eye. "Trust me: the cruelty dogs inflict on each other is nothing compared to what humans do."

Yes, I was the one who was unhealthy and skeptical, I sadly decided after Joe left.

"What have you gone through anyway?" Joe's inquiring look still hung before my eyes.

As I watched Pele soundly sleeping, I wondered aloud, "What did you find this evening?" He was so tired that he did not even hear my question.

CHAPTER 3

ROSSLYN ROSE GARDEN

Rosslyn is a neighborhood in northern Virginia, separated from Washington D.C. and the Kennedy Center for the Performing Arts by a bridge over the Potomac River. It teemed with high-rise buildings but grew no roses.

My classroom was located in a grayish high-rise building guarded by a large, pleasant fellow who tried to answer seriously the many strange questions I asked him. It was April 1978. I was still struggling to emerge from eight months of nonstop interrogations at the hands of Chinese security officers in Beijing. The doctor examining my gaunt body weighing less than one hundred pounds, flat-chested and crooked of spine, shook his head and said gently, "Eat whatever you want," as if to say that my days were numbered so diet didn't matter.

I went to work on the first day with mixed feelings. Noon came. I had an hour and a half for lunch. I walked down the stairs, saw the guard and announced, "I'm starving." Almost automatically he raised his arm and pointed to a building marked with a big yellow "M." I walked toward the sign one block away. A restaurant occupied the ground floor of the building. As the odor of hot grease touched my nostrils, I rushed in.

An hour later, I walked out of the restaurant totally refreshed and filled with gratitude, grateful that the world had such a wonderful place. The fish sandwich and French fries were unbelievably delicious. A cup of hot coffee and an apple turnover served in a small paper sleeve transported me to paradise. My empty, damaged stomach accepted these delectable offerings with trembling delight.

The building guard smiled when he saw me return. I thanked him for his recommendation, and he replied, "Anytime." It struck me that he really meant it, a stranger who was willing to point the way for me, to solve my problem. What a wonderful place this world was! In doubtful wonderment, I accepted his kindness.

My afternoon class was over. That evening I had scheduled a female student who wanted to practice her Mandarin for an hour. In between, I was sitting after dinner in a booth with Maddie, a cup of coffee in front of me.

"What's wrong with saying 'Are you ready to leave?'" Maddie asked. Her hands were shaking. Her boss had been promoted and reassigned to head a branch office in Pennsylvania. At the office's farewell party for him, Maddie has asked him this question, and now she regretted it.

"I asked him that because I thought we got along well and that he might miss us. His face got this funny look, and he said that 'to leave means to die.'"

Maddie grabbed my hand and asked, "What's the right word to use if not 'leave'?"

"'Are you ready to go to Pennsylvania?' would do, but trust me, your question did not imply dying at all. Your boss was just giving you a hard time." After answering Maddie's question, my hands began shaking as well. I knew that she would never again use the word "leave" for the rest of her life. Even if she was referring to the leaves on a tree, she probably would try to use some other word.

I was as disheartened as Maddie because I could understand how she felt disadvantaged in the face of the language barrier. Neither of us had the skill to defend ourselves verbally in English. Besides Portuguese, Maddie knew Spanish, Italian, and some French. I had studied Russian all through high school, learning English only after returning to the United States as an adult. The language never came as naturally to us as it does to a young child learning its mother tongue.

"Don't give up, Maddie," I screamed in silence as I watched her walk out the door. I could not just watch her, so I ran after her. "Don't give up, Maddie," I said. She turned and looked at me and smiled. A ray of sunset shone on her teary face.

I walked up a small, but steep, hill in high heels. "Sorry, I'm ten minutes early," I said to my student. She was young: a PhD in economics from Brown University, blonde with blue eyes, the manager of a small company.

"Learning Chinese is my hobby," she had told me. Her former teacher was from southern China, but she preferred a teacher with northern pronunciation, so I was recommended to her by the State Department's Foreign Service Institute. I consulted her.

"Is there anything wrong with saying 'Are you ready to leave'?"

She smiled. "English-speakers from different places may express themselves in different ways, but there is nothing wrong with that sentence; it shows concern."

I found reassurance in her explanation; at least I had not misled Maddie. I then started to tell her Maddie's story of a girl from a foreign country encountering such criticism in public.

"Thank goodness this is her former boss," my student commented. "He doesn't sound easy to deal with."

I started then to tell her another story, my own story.

A month after I returned to the United States, a helpful official in the Department of State recommended me to the Chinese language section of the Foreign Service Institute (FSI), the division of the Department that, among other things, teaches foreign languages to American diplomats being posted abroad. "Dr. Swift, the dean of the language school, must hire you," the official told me.

My student asked with a smile if the official had really used the word "must." "Oh yes, it's true" I responded. "He actually used that word." My student giggled. "I'd bet Dr. Swift would not have cared for that phrasing."

Indeed he did not, which was why he did not refer me to the personnel department for an interview. He wanted to meet me in person, to find out what kind of person was this woman he "must" employ. I was clueless as I mechanically followed his secretary, a middle-aged woman wearing a business suit and a professional smile, through corridor after corridor to the Dean's office. On that day, I wore a white blouse and beige pants. As I did not have much money, I could not afford to dress smartly, but I had ironed my outfit nicely. The creases in my pants were so sharp that I could almost peel carrots with them. I stood up straight in front of the Dean and greeted him in simple English.

The Dean had a head of white hair and a healthy complexion. He had gold-rimmed glasses and wore a well-tailored, three-piece beige suit and a brown and white striped tie embellished with a gold tie pin. We stood facing each other. He suddenly took off his glasses, revealing a face bathed in tears.

Something went "bang!" in my brain. Was my English so awful? Awful enough to make the Dean cry? Despair swept over me. My God, I had been studying English for a month and a half. Couldn't I even manage a simple greeting? This should have been my mother tongue. I felt so sad, so ashamed, that I wished for a hole I could crawl into to hide.

My student covered her mouth with both hands, tears welling in her eyes. I must have impressed her with my use of idioms such as "a hole I could crawl into to hide" and words such as "despair."

"I recognize you, but you don't remember me," the Dean said in a soft voice. "I'm the one who took you to China thirty years ago. During those months on the ship, you called me 'Daddy.'" The Dean's Chinese was quite clear.

Surprise overwhelmed any other emotion I might have felt at this revelation, but I nevertheless teared up for just a moment.

My student's reaction was more pronounced. She jumped up and then turned around to wipe away tears and noisily blow her nose before staring at me blankly. She must have thought that I was cold-blooded.

In fact, I had mostly felt stupid for having once called the Dean "Daddy." Before I could ask, he started to explain.

"My wife Gladys and I and our four-year-old son John went to China to bring her parents - missionaries there - back to the United States. We were students living in an apartment. It was not convenient to bring our son along but, as there was no one we could leave him with, we had to take him along. We were surprised when your mother asked us to take you with us and hand you over to her mother. Hearing John call us 'Mommy' and 'Daddy', you just followed suit. It was a naval vessel, only we four were civilians."

"This news struck a blow to my heart," I told my student. "That I had no 'Mommy' or 'Daddy' of my own so I just imitated John. Tears spilled from my eyes in front of the Dean."

My student was smart. She grasped the image of a heart being struck and understood how tears could not just drop but spill.

"That's right, just like they're drawn in cartoons," I nodded, appreciating her perception. She was happy for me.

"The secretary must have been surprised to learn that you and the Dean were old friends," my student commented. "You'd have no problem getting in to see him in the future. Moreover," she solemnly pointed out, "you had a perfect interview. Of course, the Dean had to hire you. You started working right away, and it's been smooth sailing ever since."

This time I was the one who did not understand. My student's Chinese was correct, but where did her certainty come from? Yes, I started working right away, but my smooth sailing afterward had nothing to do with my friendship with the Dean, so I wouldn't have used the term "moreover." I suddenly lost the desire to nitpick her Chinese. I smiled blandly and changed the subject, reviewing some basic terms that she already grasped and finishing the lesson.

I walked to the bus stop under high, dim streetlights. Rosslyn was dead and dark at night. I cast a long shadow as I stood alone under the bus stop sign.

I had learned the English word "must" in Hong Kong. In late January 1978, after I crossed the Luohu Bridge from China into Hong Kong, people from the American Consulate General there took me in hand. Everything, from meals to medical examinations, took place on the grounds of the consulate. A consular officer told a local airline employee, "Here is $450 for a ticket. You must take her safely from Hong Kong to the United States tomorrow." The employee promptly wrote out the ticket and handed it over.

"I'll take you to the airport tomorrow," the consular officer considerately told me.

"So much money. Where is it from?" I was worried, but I knew that I could ask him about anything I did not understand, and he would explain it candidly.

"This is a loan from the American government. There is no interest or payment deadline. Just pay it back to the government when you can. There is no hurry."

"I will work hard when I return to the United States, and I will pay it back as soon as I can," I promised.

"There is no hurry," he repeated. "After you get back, settle down, see a doctor and regain your health, then you can think about work." There was pity in his voice. I recalled the words of the consulate general's doctor: "You need to nurse yourself back to health. You are far too thin, and there is too much inflammation in your body."

The bus arrived, and the door opened. The African-American driver greeted me cordially. There were only a few passengers on the bus. The driver chatted with me about the weather. As I was getting off, he offered a friendly, "Good night and sweet dreams."

Pele was the only one with sweet dreams that night. I stared at the ceiling as I rewound memories of days long gone.

"As soon as you get on the plane, hand this letter to the flight attendant." The consular officer selected one of the several letters in his hand, all unsealed, and handed it to me. I noted down the titles and addresses in Chinese: Customs officer in Seattle, Washington D.C. airport police officer, taxi driver, U.S. State Department security officer.

"If you run into any problem, hand this letter to any policeman." The consular officer solemnly handed me the last letter in his hand.

I knew that my destination was the U.S. Department of State, where officials were working tirelessly to bring home American citizens stranded in China. Now I was on my way home, but it was a home where I could not speak the language. At that moment, a sharp pain pierced my heart, and the orders that had barred me from studying English in school fully revealed their vile visage. Their sole purpose had been to make it impossible for me to go home.

No matter how much I yearned for freedom, the language barrier would always be a ball and chain around my leg. I had to break down the barrier. I took out the last letter, opened it, and looked at the consular officer. "Please point out the most important terms," I asked.

Instantly grasping my predicament, he told me that many Americans did not know the complete, formal name of the U.S. government agency that was helping me. I appreciated his effort to ease my mental distress. I had to know where my home was or where I could settle down. He used a pencil to underline and read out "United States Department of State." It's "State Department" for short and just "State" among diplomats. But many American civilians have no idea what this organization does. They would ask, "Which state?" The consular officer explained it to me clearly, and I listened attentively, trying to soak up his words like a sponge. So "State" had at least two meanings.

My first English-Chinese dictionary was the one compiled by Liang Shiqiu. My first English-language learning materials were letters from an American diplomatic mission. My study method was to look up every new word I encountered in the dictionary and copy every sentence repeatedly until I knew it by heart. This redundant, yet effective, way of learning started on my long flight to the United States. I could not postpone this study process because it was something I must and should do – know the language of my country.

A pretty flight attendant bent down and softly spoke to me. I could not understand a word. A look of understanding passed over her smiling face, and she presented two glasses on a tray. I recognized orange juice and apple juice. With an embarrassed smile I pointed to the orange juice. Still smiling, her blue eyes filled with cheerfulness, she said softly and clearly, "orange juice." I repeated the words. She seemed pleased and placed a small paper container with those two words printed on it on my tray. This was my first lesson about beverages. "Thank you," I said from the bottom of my heart to the pleasant flight attendant, my first English teacher. She found me an industrious student, soaking up pronunciation, grammar, and spelling all at the same time. I literally gobbled up the next set of teaching materials, which included bread, butter, vegetables, Coca Cola, and water. I also learned how to ask the flight attendants for water, coffee, or tea.

After that, every English speaker became my teacher, the most helpful being postal workers, who patiently taught me how to buy stamps, even writing down sentences in my notebook. My favorite television programs were the weather reports because they displayed pictures, making the words easier to learn.

My struggles with English started in earnest at the language center established by the Arlington County government. Sylvia, a beautiful African-American diplomat from the State Department's China Desk, led me into a classroom where thirty students of all ages and races were gathered. "No one can speak Chinese here," she explained. "This is an ocean of English." I walked in, impelled by a nudge from Sylvia. I felt like a baby moving her limbs vigorously in the ocean, trying to stay afloat. Before I had time to feel fear, I was enveloped in a world of friendliness and warmth. Two teachers, a Czech woman and a Swedish man, took turns leading the class in reading, conversation, pronunciation, and grammar drills. This was a disorderly world, yet, with a little effort, I was able to blend in. After about fifteen minutes, I was no longer an observer but an active participant. I opened my mouth, accepting unconditionally correction and guidance from the teachers. An hour and a half later, I was soaked in sweat, but I was really excited. I knew that I would improve quickly.

The language center provided us with text and exercise books. After class, I went home to review and practice all that I had learned as well as to prepare for what would be taught in the next class. After a month and a half, I left the language center to continue my studies at a community college.

The German language teachers at the Foreign Service Institute were all from what was then West Germany. They were always neatly and appropriately dressed in business attire. I would come across them every morning as I reached my floor. We always smiled and greeted each other. One day, after our usual greeting, one of the German teachers took me aside for a moment. Although getting on in years, with silver hair coiled into a bun, she looked quite elegant. Below her long wool skirt showed a pair of shoes made of some exquisite material. "Beautiful shoes," I couldn't help but say. She smiled and, lightly holding my hands, told me that in a nearby building Apple Computer was experimenting with software to teach English composition. The office was open on weekends as well, and I might find the instruction useful. "It's free, and there are technicians around to help," she told me. These were two important points for me. I thanked her and walked into my classroom to begin teaching.

At five in the afternoon, I left my building with the crowd and walked to another building where signs in front of the elevator pointed to the Apple Computer language laboratory. The language lab was all white, spotless and brightly lit. Only a few people were there, working in front of computers; most of the stations were empty and quiet. A young lady walked up to me with a broad, calming smile.

"I'm sorry. I have never used a computer, and my English is limited," I attempted to explain. "I cannot express myself in complete sentences."

My honesty must have touched her because she brought me to a desk and had me sit down. She touched "Start" and the screen lit up showing a smiling face and the word "welcome." The young lady told me to type in a three-letter password, explaining, "The next time you come in you can use any of the computers, and your progress will be tracked."

I keyed in "HAN," whereupon the computer immediately asked me to make a sentence. After I made one, the computer responded, "OK," but commented that the sentence could be improved. It showed two examples, which I copied down in my notebook. And so it continued as I lost all sense of time communing quietly with the computer.

"We close at seven, and it's already eight." The lady walked over and bent down to remind me, still smiling. I apologized with what must have been barely coherent awkwardness as she showed me how to shut down the computer. We turned off the lights, shared an elevator downstairs, and walked together to the bus stop. Along the way I told her a lot about myself. She quietly listened, finally responding thoughtfully, "What monstrous government would forbid students from learning a language? Learning is a natural right for everyone!"

I had difficulty understanding what she said, so I asked her to write it down in my notebook, and she neatly printed the words for me. On the bus, I opened my English-Chinese dictionary and looked up every word. I have never forgotten that last sentence.

I stayed up late that night. After that day in November 1978, my first encounter with a computer, the machine became my English instructor, teaching me spelling, grammar, and syntax. The Apple computer enhanced the learning process considerably in terms of both quality and speed. I opened my notebook, conscientiously copying all the model sentences shown by the computer. Tears fell onto the paper as I wrote, a 32-year-old doing the assignment of a grade-school pupil. And I had always been an "A" student.

My memory flashed back to a scene in one of the exclusive apartments reserved for employees of the Xiehe Hospital in Beijing. Zhang Zhengping, whose parents had been educated in America, was my classmate in junior high school. Sometimes I would visit her in the gloomy, high-ceilinged Western-style apartment where she lived. One day while we were trading novels there, her mother came home. She saw me, frowned, and said something in a foreign language. We had been practicing speaking in Russian, but she also spoke English at home, so I figured that she and her mother were conversing in English. Although only thirteen, I could hear the animosity in her mother's tone. I stood up, shouldered my backpack, and politely said goodbye. Zhengping didn't say a word as she closed the door gently behind me. That was the last time I ever visited that stately building.

When I got home, I told Grandma that I should learn English. She thought a bit before replying. "It wouldn't be impossible to find you a teacher. But if you do, it will raise people's suspicions and that will make your already difficult position even worse. You'll have a chance sooner or later." She spoke with a bitter smile that hinted there was much more to say, but she said no more.

That night in 1978, I wrote a letter to Grandma, who was still living in Beijing. I told her that today I had met two good teachers: the computer and the computer operator. My English, I continued, would improve by leaps and bounds.

At that time, I could not foresee that it would only be in 2001 that I would start writing in Chinese using a computer. In my brain, Chinese and English occupied separate spaces and performed separate functions with different temperaments, each opening and closing on its own schedule – impossible to unify.

Until late on this winter night, as the wind howled outside, I sat at my desk writing repeatedly "Learning is a natural right for everyone!"

Joe listened in silence to the account of my fledgling ventures in the English language. His Chinese was so good that I had few occasions to speak English with him. When I timidly showed him my English composition, he pulled out a red pen and quietly made corrections. He never critiqued my efforts or sought to assume the role of teacher, for he did not wish our relationship to move beyond that of student and teacher. Once, after he had made drastic corrections to one of my book reports, I timidly suggested that it would be unfair for me to take money for teaching him. He frowned, replying that he preferred to regard his actions as simply helping someone. His correcting my assignment was no big deal, just as post office employees would write a sentence in my notebook without my buying any stamps. Joe solemnly placed the money for the lesson on the desk and watched me put it away. He said, "Don't mention this again," and I knew that if I wanted to keep him as a friend I should not.

I had told Joe about my miraculous reunion with Dr. Swift. He listened attentively then asked, "Well, what happened next? Did you ever meet John again?"

I did meet him again, at the Swifts' home. I told Joe that John was not at all like his cosmopolitan parents. He came across as a typical blue-collar worker. He had asked his father jokingly, "Why did you hire her instead of me? I can speak Spanish." Dr. Swift had just smiled. As I sat there watching John, only two years older than I, smoking non-stop, I was suddenly reminded of the scar on my leg.

"That was a cigarette burn. They are white people, and that boy is the son of white people. Of course he despises you. Getting burned by a cigarette butt left behind by adults is nothing. Let me tell you how bad racial discrimination in America can be. Yours is an insignificant example. It is stupid of you to harbor false hopes about America." So said my mother, emphasizing her point by poking my forehead with a nicotine-stained yellow finger. Grandma was the one who replied though. "I have seen that boy. He was clinging tightly to his mother as they got off the ship. His grandfather, Rev. Hubbard, was overjoyed to see him and lovingly bent down to talk to him."

Of course, John was now grown and no longer shy. Sticking out his hand to shake mine he said, "My parents tell me that we spent a few months together in a car and on a ship. Now I'm an auto mechanic in a small town where the air is clean and the people are simple, unlike Washington." His stubbly-bearded face wore a sincere smile. I, for my part, was a bit uneasy and offered a polite, restrained greeting.

Dr. and Mrs. Swift were puzzled by their son. "He actually likes it there. He likes his work, and he is happy, so it's all good." I didn't say anything. John was living the life he wanted, which did not require any explanation.

Dr. Swift added, "We have another son who was born in Sichuan. After you, your grandmother, and that other lady left, Gladys and I, together with John and my in-laws, traveled to Nanjing. While we were trying to persuade Gladys' parents to return to America with us, we were detained by the new Communist government and sent to a concentration camp for foreigners in Sichuan. That's where George, our younger son, was born. When the Korean War ended and we were allowed to leave China, George was already two years old, the same age you were when you arrived in China. George likes to work with his hands, too. He works in a factory that manufactures machines. He's married and has two children." Nothing more was said about the camp in Sichuan.

Just then, the sturdily-built John and his mother were standing by a grove of bamboo in the backyard. She was worried about the bamboo's rapid growth, which was drawing complaints from the neighbors. John suggested uprooting them. The breeze carried their conversation to Dr. Swift, who offered no comment. Instead, he asked about the woman who had accompanied my grandmother to meet me at the dock in Shanghai. I told him, "Her name is Zhao Qingge. She's a distant relative of my grandmother's. Grandma can speak Japanese but not English, so she brought Zhao Qingge along to translate. It was a surprise to find that you and your wife could speak fluent Chinese. Of course, your father-in-law, Rev. Hubbard, was a sinologist." Dr. Swift chuckled. "In 1948, when we met you for the first time in Manhattan, you were speaking Japanese, too. You were playing with your nanny's daughter, and when she called her grandmother "Ah Ba San," you copied her."

True, the girl had a grandmother, and at the time I did not. I wonder if the girl had pointed to my curly hair and accused me of misappropriating her "Ah Ba San." Dr. Swift told me, "Your father saved that elderly Japanese couple from an internment camp by hiring them to work as his housekeepers. After you were born, the woman cared for you while her husband, a skilled gardener, kept the garden beautifully."

"What internment camp?" I wondered.

Dr. Swift saw my puzzlement. "Oh, that was a dumb policy. When war with Japan broke out, the American government was concerned that Japanese-Americans and Japanese citizens with permanent U.S. residency might provide assistance to Japan. The government constructed camps west of the Mississippi to house these people where the government could watch them. After the war, those camps were dismantled and the former inmates remained in this country. That's not what happened in China. In the 1950s, those who were detained in the Chongqing camp all left China. That elderly Japanese couple has a son and daughter-in-law in the United States. They had no family left in Japan. That was why your father hired them to work in his house." Before I could digest the differences between internment and concentration camps, a shiver tingled down my spine.

"You've been to my father's home in Manhattan?"

"Of course," he replied with a smile. "I went there to pick you up. Your father was stationed in New Zealand. Your mother lived in New Haven and rarely went back to Manhattan. She wanted us to take you to China, so she gave us the address of your father's house in Manhattan. When we got there, that elderly Japanese couple greeted us."

At that point Gladys and John walked in. Hearing the conversation, Gladys added casually, "Your mother said she couldn't pay your traveling expenses, so she gave me a coat instead."

"That must have been some coat," John said with a laugh.

"Oh, that coat was light and soft. It served as your blanket in the camp in Sichuan. By the time we left China, it was worn, torn, and full of holes." Gladys gazed at her son with deep affection. John's laugh took on a bashful tone, and he seemed to look at me with a new tenderness, as though these childhood memories connected us.

Later on, Gladys showed me some old photographs. There was one of her alone, bundled up in layers of clothing, squatting over a rock in a creek scrubbing a blanket with a glum look on her face. The background was ordinary countryside, lacking any defining feature. The photo must have been taken in the camp in Sichuan.

I analyzed for Joe. "They had their second child there, indicating that they were together, and they even had a camera, so not all their possessions were confiscated."

Joe responded slowly. "I'm surprised how easily you just went off with strangers. The Japanese lady cared for you after you were born. Before the age of two, you went off with Dr. Swift, who didn't speak Japanese, far away from the house with the beautiful garden and the Japanese-speaking playmate."

I had a photo of myself with another little girl, standing in the driveway of my father's house. We wore similar light-colored coats and dark plaid skirts, but my light, curly hair contrasted sharply with the Japanese girl's straight, dark hair and little-girl's haircut. According to Dr. Swift, "that girl was a year older than you, but you were half a head taller."

When I related this to Joe, he pointed out that "familiar surroundings, language, and playmate couldn't tie you down. After a few months of travel, I'll bet you were speaking English like a native with John, your new playmate. In Shanghai, you were met by your grandmother. You didn't even know what a grandmother was, even less understand her Wuxi dialect. Yet you just walked away with her. You must be a born wanderer."

"But the scar from the cigarette burn was not John's doing or the result of racial discrimination," I told Joe. "Dr. Swift said that the Japanese grandmother gave him a small jar of ointment to treat the burn on my leg. She also told him that I tripped easily as a result of losing sight in one eye due to a high fever. How had all this happened? Dr. Swift didn't have time to find out. He was just relieved to know that my sight returned and my burn healed. Gladys even remembered that the ointment was quite effective."

I recalled the pensive look on John's face as his parents recounted their fragmented memories of the distant past. As he drove me home later that evening, he suddenly became very courteous, saying, "I hope I was nice to you when we were together in the car and on the ship." I just smiled, for I had no memory of how the four-year-old John had treated the two-year-old me. For no particular reason, I didn't mention this to Joe.

Joe, however, would not let go of the subject. "But who burned you with the cigarette? And who stopped the Japanese couple from taking you to a doctor?" I think the fact that my father had taken the Japanese couple home from the internment camp and entrusted his home to them and their coming up with the effective ointment convinced Joe that they were my guardians in Manhattan. Indeed, I had seen photos of that couple – the wife with a hairnet and the husband with wrinkles all over his face.

Other than my mother, I couldn't think of anyone else. I remembered that nicotine-stained finger that used to poke my forehead, those words of malice blurted out, and Grandma's unintelligible muttering. I was speechless but still happy, for I knew it had nothing to do with racial discrimination; it was just maternal hostility towards me. I smiled with relief, surprising Joe. The more puzzled he grew, the happier I felt. Finally, we both burst out laughing.

"Dr. Swift is a kind man," I told Joe frankly. He said that, on the ship, he had told Gladys, "This child's mother doesn't seem to want her anymore." Gladys had agreed. "We decided then that if we could not find your grandmother, we would adopt you." I looked at Joe earnestly, willing him to share my feeling of warmth.

Joe was unmoved. "I think Gladys must have felt relieved to see two Chinese women waiting for you as you were disembarking from the ship." His words continued to ring in my ears after he had left. No doubt he was right.

I took from my closet shelf a blue purse wrapped in layers of plastic. Inside one of the compartments was my very first passport. A little girl with curly hair and round eyes gazed seriously at the camera lens. This green-covered passport was issued by the State Department in Washington D.C. on July 29, 1948. I was not yet two years old. Signing the passport in my place was none other than Gladys Swift. In the column headed "Relationship" she had filled in the word "granddaughter." There had been no better way to describe the relationship between us at the time – total strangers. After only a few months back in the United States, I could read printed characters and also some cursive script. Just when my spirits were starting to rise, I thought of John. At that time, he was four years old, probably not able to sign his name in his passport either. In the "relationship" column Gladys of course would have written "son." The son was four and the granddaughter was two. The passport issuer must have turned a blind eye to the inconsistency.

A number of speculations became hard facts as I flipped through the pages of the old passport. On page 9 appeared the first visa, issued on August 26 by the Philippine Consulate in San Francisco. On page 10, a Philippine immigration officer named G. Bautista recorded my date of arrival in the country: September 15. On page 11 appeared a Hong Kong immigration stamp dated September 18. It indicated that the ship was berthed in the colony but that I did not disembark. Perhaps I saw the lights of Hong Kong harbor from the deck. All the other pages were blank.

When did I arrive in Shanghai? The passport held no answer. Shanghai fell to the Communists on May 24, 1949. Had the port's customs and immigration controls collapsed by mid-September 1948? One thing at least was clear: I lived my first two years in the Free World.

For one whole month, how did I get from New York to Washington, D.C. and then cross the country to San Francisco? No one ever told me. What a ship we must have had to carry us across the Pacific Ocean in a little over half a month!

After that, there were no entries in the passport. But in 1977, the diplomats stationed in the U.S. Liaison Office in Beijing did not care whether my passport documented my arrival in China. They only cared that it showed I was "born in the United States, which makes you an American citizen, and there is no evidence that you ever renounced your American citizenship." To those intrepid diplomats, that was enough proof to fight for my right to return home.

Accompanying a family of three strangers speaking a different language across the Pacific and not yet two years old. I put the passport back with my other documents in the closet. I sat on the bed and held Pele, a sense of warmth enfolding me.

July 27, 1976, the day of the great Tangshan earthquake, was my first day of work at a small clothing factory in Beijing after my return from nine years in the Xinjiang Uyghur Autonomous Region, that vast, sparsely populated territory in Chinese central Asia. After the sky had fallen and the earth sunk, apprentices and masters alike were transfixed with horror and fear of what might come next. Their homes in ruins, they were still expected to keep 24-hour watch at the factory. I told the factory manager that my mother had not been in the stricken area and my grandmother was safe in a small but sturdy house. I volunteered to stay in the factory at night so that everyone else could go care for their families. I also gave up my allocation from the factory of wood and canvas for tents so that others could have more.

I did as I promised. I stayed at the factory at night, sleeping on the pattern-cutting table and going home to see my grandmother only when others reported for work during the day.

Sometime after the disaster had passed, the factory's Communist Party secretary told me that I had performed good service for the factory. He wondered whether there was anything he, as a leader, could do for me. I knew that a connection to an American passport and birth certificate could mean real trouble for this good man. I also realized that someone in his position was my only hope of recovering those documents, seized by Red Guards in 1966. So, I mentioned that Red Guards had taken some old documents from my home. The party secretary was the third generation of a working-class family. At the beginning of the Cultural Revolution, he had been repeatedly denounced and publicly criticized as a capitalist holding a position of authority. Merely mentioning Red Guards got him angry. Striking his chest for emphasis, he undertook to retrieve my documents.

On December 28, 1976, an official from the Ministry of Public Security in Beijing came to our factory and, in front of the party secretary, returned to me my old passport and three copies of my U.S. birth certificate. "It didn't take long to find these; they've been sitting in a safe at the ministry for the past ten years. Now they are yours again to keep as souvenirs," the official commented. Little did he or anyone else know that from that moment on my world was no longer the same. A ray of hope glimmered through the clouds; what came of it would depend on my wits and courage. Today, this passport really is a souvenir, commemorating my childhood journey as well as my desperate struggle as an adult.

CHAPTER 4

GRANDMA

After hauling a basketful of dirty laundry down the stairs to the laundry room, I was sweating from the pain in my back. Sunday mornings were for washing and ironing, no procrastination allowed. I turned on the TV news as I ironed my work clothes. It was pouring rain outside. Washington's constant humidity wasn't good for my back, which hurt whether I moved or not. Tears of pain dripped down my cheeks.

Through a film of tears, I spotted a book, *The Injustice to Dou E*, by Yuan dynasty playwright Guan Hanqing. A student at the Foreign Service Institute had written his doctoral dissertation on Yuan dynasty plays, which got me thinking of Joe, whose grasp of Chinese was certainly strong enough for him to appreciate such material. After I mentioned this in a letter to my grandmother in Beijing, she sent me this book along with a letter in which she said that "this book was seized in a house search during the Cultural Revolution and later returned in tatters. I did my best to mend it and added a cover, but, without tools and with my hands hurting, this was the best I could do. The idea was to keep it from falling apart in your student's hands." Her letter, like her speech, was simple and concise, without frills.

I put away my clothes, glanced out the window, and wondered if Joe would brave the weather to come for his lesson.

The pages of the old book were soft and the edges frayed, yet the printed characters had the solidity of characters carved in stone. As I leafed through the pages, a medicated plaster fell out. I quickly rummaged through my kitchen drawers to find a candle. Slowly I warmed the plaster over the candle flame. Grandma knew that, although my life had stabilized, my back pain persisted. My cheerful letters couldn't fool her. The plaster turned black, giving off the pleasant aroma of Chinese herbal medicine. Applying the plaster to my back and gritting my teeth against the heat, I took short breaths. As the heat gradually banished the pain, tears of pain turned to tears of relief. Testing the result, I stood up and found the pain much diminished. I hurriedly straightened up the apartment. Wouldn't it be nice to have a neat home even if Joe did not come?

The doorbell rang, and Joe appeared at the door with a big smile. He shook the water off his big umbrella before slipping it into a cover and stepping in onto the doormat. He took off his shoes, which were encased in rubber overshoes. Underneath, his shoes looked brand new. I marveled at the rubber overshoes. "I never knew such practical things existed!" I gushed. Joe chuckled at my amazement. "These are old-fashioned and black. Most young people today don't care for them, but I think they're practical and cheap. How could I walk on your clean carpet with wet shoes?"

Even as he chatted and laughed, Joe noticed my wet cheeks. Wordlessly, he looked me up and down. I dredged up an explanation that did not disclose my pain.

"I just got a letter from my grandmother, along with a book. We can use both as your next lesson texts. You should learn to read cursive characters as well as printed ones, and Yuan dynasty verse is something you could appreciate." I placed the letter and the book on the table in front of him.

Grandma's handwriting was beautiful and elegant, with clean, clear strokes. Joe rubbed his hands. He picked up the letter and began to read smoothly. Then he put down the letter and picked up the book, caressing the crude but solid cover. White threads went through the front cover and all the pages to the back cover. The tattered book was on the road to restoration. The holes through which the threads passed seemed large, probably pierced by an awl used for making the soles of shoes, I explained. "Wooden stapling machines were destroyed by Red Guards at the beginning of the Cultural Revolution. The book was hand-stitched by Grandma's arthritic hands. Fortunately, it's a thin book." Unconsciously,

I had adopted Grandma's short and terse speech pattern, omitting much context.

Joe carefully placed the folded letter between the pages of the book, which he put down reverently on the table. Pressing down on the cover with his large hand, he said, "I'll do Yuan verse and this precious letter for my homework. For today's lesson, can you tell me your grandmother's story?" His eyes had a look of burning interest that invited me to pour out my heart. It's been said that stories have lives; if they are not told, they will die and disappear. This was a story that deserved to live.

On the edge of Lake Tai, south of the Yangtze River, sits the small town of Caoqiao, part of the rich, fertile area of abundance that is Wujin County in Jiangsu Province. My Grandma was born into the Xie family there in 1898, in the waning years of the Qing Dynasty. Her father, my great-grandfather, had six wives. Grandma's mother was wife number six, and she bore him a son and a daughter. Grandma had many siblings, but only this one brother shared the same mother with her. They remained close throughout their lives.

Joe's eyes were wide open, probably wondering why Mr. Xie had to have six wives. When I asked Grandma the same question, she just shook her head and smiled, saying, "I don't know. His first wife bore him two sons within three years, so perpetuating the family name was obviously not one of the considerations." Two glasses of wine later, Grandma's eyes crinkled into a smile as she added, "Perhaps he just liked different kinds of women."

Wouldn't such a large family invite a host of tragedies? After all, writers - Ba Jin for example - have depicted such households as riddled with evil. Not at all. This large family lived together peacefully, exhibiting neither tragedy nor comedy. The Xie family owned considerable farmland and fish ponds and enjoyed an affluent lifestyle. Each wife had her own courtyard in the family mansion. Just outside the walls was a large fish pond around which geese, ducks, and even mandarin ducks wandered and swam between lotus leaves. Plum and some sixty mulberry trees grew around the pond.

The wives took turns preparing a day's meals of breakfast, lunch, dinner, plus a midnight snack sometimes, for the whole family. All Grandma's mother had to do was oversee the kitchen staff who did the actual work of preparing the meals. When Grandma taught me the word "home-making," she stressed that the housewife who swept, dusted, and cooked herself was doing housework, which was not the same as "homemaking."

Grandma recalled that her mother kept busy overseeing a number of workers who cared for the mulberry trees and the silkworms that fed on their leaves. After the moths emerged, she would bring the cocoons to a mill where the silk fibers were unwound and spun into thread. The mill could dye the silk thread whatever color the customer desired. Grandma's mother would draw and cut patterns out of paper and transfer them onto plain silk fabric which she then embroidered using the colorful silk thread she brought home from the mill. Her designs included tall, elegant lotus flowers, undulating lily pads, butterflies, and dragonflies. She didn't do this to amuse herself. Her exquisite embroidery graced the living room curtains, clothing, and shoes for older members of the family.

"'Cat's whiskers' require the most care to embroider. One gray silk thread has to be divided into twelve silk filaments as does another undyed thread. Then the strands of the two colors are twisted together into a single thread, according to the desired pattern. Only in this way will the whiskers appear vivid and lively," Grandma told me with a smile. "My mother's embroidery was the best in the family."

Joe's expression was one of admiration. I went on to tell him that my grandmother's special skill was restoring old books, a skill that had been passed down in her family for more than one hundred years. No matter how damaged or tattered a book was, she could bring it back to life. Her dowry had included a stitching machine made of rosewood, and she used it to restore numerous books. Since old Chinese books contain neither punctuation nor page numbers, a prerequisite for ordering the pages correctly is the ability to understand and punctuate sentences, which in turn requires knowledge of classical Chinese. For relaxation, her mother loved to sit in a comfortable chair with eyes closed and recite poetry. Embroidery and book repair both demanded good eyesight. "That's why our rooms were always brightly lit, even at night," Grandma explained.

Book repair tools were passed down from generation to generation. Grandma's mother also knew how to make new tools from bamboo, tools for separating pages and repairing frayed corners. Her tools were kept in a silk wrapper decorated with colorful embroidery; when unrolled and spread out, they looked like a collection of surgical instruments. Grandma said that, starting when she was little, she enjoyed watching her mother restore books, and her father enjoyed watching, too. The work required total concentration. "My brother and I knew that book repair was important, so absolutely no interruptions." Dinner time in the Xie household was fixed, not to be altered lightly. "One of the exceptions to this was when my mother was repairing a book. My father, brother, and I would quietly wait for her to place the restored book on a square table, under a smooth, gray brick wrapped in a coarse, white cloth. Then she would raise her head, smile at Father, and dinner would be served. Those were my favorite times, when Father would eat with us in our living room, just the four of us. It was wonderful. Father usually ate dinner in his first wife's rooms." Grandma's face always wore a smile as she recounted this.

"After dinner, Father would stay on, sipping tea and swapping stories about books with mother. He was always pleasant. I only saw him sad and disappointed on two occasions." Tears welled in Grandma's eyes at the recollection.

The first occasion had to do with learning to write Chinese characters. Grandma's older brother had a tutor who came to the house to teach him. Tables and chairs were prepared and arranged in the living room for the lesson. As the tutor went through the lessons with her brother, Grandma would position herself behind the door curtain in the kitchen silently memorizing. Her big brother learned to write using a brush, ink, paper, and ink slab. Grandma's mother spread a thick layer of ashes on the kitchen's brick floor and drew in thin lines to make squares. Grandma would kneel on the floor to excitedly practice writing characters with kindling wood. One day, without any warning, her father abruptly lifted the door curtain, picked Grandma up, and washed the dust off her hands. He sat her down at the table and started to teach her how to grind ink onto the ink slab and trace characters in red ink with a brush.

"Father solemnly looked Mother in the eye. Mother calmly cleaned up the ashes on the floor and then turned around to do her embroidery. That night, Mother whispered, 'Now that your father has started you on the path of learning, you can study openly. I could not initiate this process – only your father could.' Mother was extremely pleased, I know." Tears were in her eyes.

The second occasion had to do with foot-binding. When Grandma was five years old, her mother started to bind her feet. Grandma was surprised at the strength in her mother's hands and at the excruciating pain in her little feet. Her mother forbade her to cry, lest this elicit scorn from others. The binding was so painful that Grandma's face was covered with drops of sweat the size of peas. As she struggled against the urge to cry, tears and sweat rolled down her face. She thought she must be dying.

Grandma guessed that her big brother informed her father what was going on. The day after her foot-binding, her father rushed into the courtyard crying out in a pained voice, "Little Xiu, where are you?" In excruciating pain, Grandma cried out, "Daddy!" Following her voice, her father rushed into the bedroom and, with shaking hands, cut the bloody white cloths off her feet with a pair of scissors.

He mother stood nearby with a stern look on her face, her perfect three-inch feet peeking out from beneath her skirt.

"Who will marry her when she grows up?" she asked in a voice hard enough to hammer nails into wood.

"There will always be open-minded people who oppose the evil custom of foot-binding," her father replied firmly.

"That was when I knew that the agony of the past twenty-four hours was truly over. I grew so relaxed that I lost consciousness. When I woke up, I was in Father's study. Seeing me awake, he said that his Little Xiu would never have bound feet because she would travel far and walk long distances. Thank goodness Father saved my feet. Otherwise, I would have felt humiliated years later when I went to Japan, where the women all had healthy, normal feet." Grandma put down her wine cup and lit a cigarette, letting the smoke drift over her facial expression.

"I wonder what this did to your grandmother's mother's self-image, with her tiny, bound feet that were admired by so many. Yet her husband totally rejected the tradition, and her daughter would not grow up with bound feet. How would she have felt?" Joe had tears in his eyes, as though he knew the answer.

"Heartache. From that day on she lived with a pain in her heart. The house was always filled with the scent of Chinese herbal medicine." When Grandma related this to me, her tears finally began to fall.

People in those days were different. The days passed without analysis or explanation. On the surface, nothing changed, but underneath changes were occurring. Grandma said that her mother's temperament was no longer the same. Formerly gentle with her daughter, she became much stricter with her children after the aborted foot-binding. She taught her daughter embroidery, book repair, and how to raise silkworms. Her standards were extremely high, and her smiles became scarce. Only when Grandma had performed to her satisfaction would she smile.

"I enjoyed writing most of all," I told Joe. "Grandma taught me how to grind an ink stick with water on a stone ink slab to make ink. When I could not keep my characters within the squares printed on the paper, I became frustrated and anxious. Grandma smiled and told me that, when she was little, she practiced by holding an egg in the palm that held a brush with a coin balanced on top. When the coin remained steadily on the brush, a second coin would be added, and then a third. She claimed that while her brother's egg often cracked, hers never did; it just got warm. This made me think: I'm just holding a brush – no egg, no coin – so calm down. Sure enough, soon the brush no longer strayed outside the squares, and my writing improved daily."

The story apparently captured Joe's imagination. He declared that he would use the same method to practice writing characters. I hastened to tell him that there was no set method for practicing Chinese calligraphy. Pu Xuezhai, for example, a prince of the Qing Dynasty, would attach one end of a cord to his wrist and the other end to a brick while writing. Author Lao She strove to first achieve a state of calm, which was reflected in his clear, straight writing style.

Joe abruptly interrupted, urging me to continue with Grandma's story.

Not surprisingly, Grandma's father had everything planned early on. He arranged to marry Grandma to the son of an old friend in nearby Yixing County. No one knew how they reached this decision. Grandma's new family would be the Zhaos, a rich, influential family in that county.

The elder Mr. Zhao was a progressive country squire who was not content to just own land; he wanted his sons to go into business, industry, and finance. Such a man was not looking for a daughter-in-law with tiny, bound feet.

The marriage of a daughter of the Xie family was an important event. Her dowry included a house on Lake Tai in Wuxi, which was confiscated by the new Communist government in 1949 and turned into a hospital. Grandma never lived in it despite being the titular owner. Another dowry item was a wooden chest with explicit sexual scenes painted on the four inside bottom corners. "That was how a girl received her sex education from her mother. No words, just pictures." Grandma continued, "Sexual activity only brings happiness in the proper circumstances. Shameful sexual activity that must be carried out furtively will not bring happiness." Grandma seemed very sad. Since, for all practical purposes, I grew up without a mother, the job of guiding me into adulthood fell to her. Of course, when I was growing up, "sexual activity" was merely a phrase to me; I never imagined what it actually meant.

Also included in the dowry, at the bottom of the chest, were book repair tools. They were rolled up in a blue cloth bag that Grandma's mother had sewn with fine, tiny stitches. Grandma used it for many years, so it was a familiar item at home. When Red Guards ravaged our home, they threw the blue cloth bag and the tools inside onto a pyre of burning books, reducing everything to a pile of ashes as Grandma watched impassively.

The dowry chest also held instruments for embroidery. One of these was a silver thimble, an essential aid in the making of our shoes and clothing. It escaped the Red Guards and has traveled the world with me, even to America.

Joe couldn't picture what the thimble looked like, so I put it on my middle finger and used it as I sewed a button onto a shirt. When I had finished, Joe held it carefully in his open palm as he examined the lion's head decoration that wound around it. He asked softly, "Isn't such a thimble a rarity today, even in China?"

"China has more than a billion people, and half of them are women. Thimbles are indispensable to daily life, although most are not so exquisite," I replied and then continued Grandma's story.

At eighteen, Grandma was married into the Zhao family. She had never met any member of the family where she would be spending the rest of her life, including her husband-to-be. During the wedding ceremony, she was able to look downward through her heavily veiled headdress and see, to her great relief, that the man with whom she bowed to heaven and earth had normal hands and feet. Later, when they were alone and he lifted her veil, she saw a handsome young man smiling at her. "Thank goodness," she exclaimed in her heart.

"Was he good looking, your grandfather?" Joe asked curiously.

"Yes, indeed. I've seen a marvelous photo of him in Beijing opera costume posing with one bent leg raised off the ground." I tried to demonstrate the pose as I explained.

"What happened then?"

"Later on, the elder Mr. Zhao wanted his son to study in Japan. The son insisted on taking his wife along, arguing that he preferred to have his wife, rather than a Japanese maid, tending to his daily needs. His father readily agreed and my grandparents began studying Japanese at home in preparation for studying economics in Japan. A Japanese couple came to their house to teach them the language, with the husband teaching Grandfather and the wife teaching Grandma. Six months later, they left home for Tokyo, where they settled in as students. Back in 1918, not only did Grandma study herself, she also helped her husband with his studies.

"Three years later, they returned to Shanghai, where Grandma took a management position at a bank jointly funded by private interests and the national government. Grandfather mainly stayed home, occupying himself with calligraphy and singing in Beijing operas. They often entertained, and Grandfather, as an amateur Beijing opera singer, would perform arias from various operas. He took his singing seriously, receiving lessons from Master Ma Lianliang and even appearing on stage with Master Mei Lanfang, two famous professional performers." Seeing that Joe was clueless about the finer points of Beijing opera, I moved on to another aspect of Grandma's life.

"Grandma was the only woman in the office. Not unlike men of today, men in those days liked to drink. One day at a banquet, her colleagues were egging each other on to drink more. Grandma took up the challenge, matching them drink for drink. By the end of the evening, she was the only one still sober. After that evening, her colleagues in the office addressed her as 'Mr. Xie' or, behind her back, as 'Wine Fairy.' In the early 1950s, I heard visiting friends address her using both terms."

"So, your grandfather didn't really work," Joe observed. I sensed that he was interested in Grandma's perception of such a man.

"You have to remember that they lived in a different era. Grandma considered him the best man in the world: he didn't use opium and never took a concubine. How splendid!" Joe laughed heartily. It suddenly occurred to me that Joe himself didn't work either, so I chose my next words carefully. "Not only was Grandfather a good man; he also lived a good life. In 1937, at the age of forty-three, he contracted tuberculosis and died. Grandma would say thankfully that "Your grandfather was the most blessed person on earth. He did not live to see the Japanese invasion or that mob of ignorant parasites that appeared after 1949."

Joe, a bright fellow, instantly understood. He said, "I'll bet your Grandma boycotted Japanese imports after the invasion. She probably also refused to recognize the Communist rule."

"Bravo," I responded. "Indeed, those were her two deepest convictions, and with good reason when it came to the second one."

"After Grandfather passed away, Grandma was reluctant to stay with the Zhao family with her sixteen-year-old daughter. She also decided to leave her job at the bank where her husband's family was a major shareholder. So she transferred her savings to the First National City Bank of New York. With her knowledge and experience in finance, she passed the civil service examination and became a government employee in the Department of Statistics. In 1949, far from her hometown, she was nevertheless labeled a 'small landowner' by the new regime because, although she never received one grain of rice from any property, some land was still in her name. This label was less damaging than that of 'class enemy.' According to the Communists' system of categorization, her daughter's class background was 'old employee,' the 'old' denoting that her parents had worked for the former Kuomintang (KMT) government. My class background was 'employee' because my mother worked in a theater company. The label 'dregs of American imperialism' did not appear on any document but hung in the air around me like haze."

Joe listened with total concentration to my description of the categories into which people were consigned. Hearing about this from someone who had lived it enabled him to feel the reality of the barriers and confinement that the policy produced.

Not only had Grandma worked for the KMT government, but she had moved with it to the temporary capital of Chongqing during the war with Japan, a journey that involved trekking over mountains on foot. One of the names from that trek that stuck in my mind was Jiujiang, a port on the Yangtze River in Jiangxi Province, where she boarded a ship.

"People used to say how difficult life was during the Japanese invasion, but Grandma spoke of it as a time of high spirits. It was nothing like the famine of the early 1960s. During the early 1940s, the entire country was united in resisting the occupation. The people of the nation were focused on one goal: expelling the Japanese."

About that time, Grandma started getting migraine headaches. According to her, when she embarked at Jiujiang, so many people crammed into the ship that she was forced to spend the night standing in the chilly wind at the ship's bow. She attributed the migraines to that night. When I was growing up, the only time she would remove her wool cap was during the height of summer. By then, the migraine headaches had become a useful pretext to avoid working for the Communist government, which had urged her to rejoin the work force. Although claiming that migraines and advanced age – in fact she was only in her early fifties – kept her from working, in her heart she was determined to remain loyal to one man in her life and one government as well. She told me, "A man with feet in two boats will sooner or later fall into the water." This saying stayed with me, especially as I witnessed over the years a number of employees of the former government strive to help the new government, only to fall into the water, suffering persecution and terrible tortures.

"Wait a second. There are gaps in the story. First of all, your parents met in Chongqing. What happened after that? Second, how did your Grandmother wind up moving from Nanjing to Beijing?" Joe wanted all the details.

Grandma and my father met once in Chongqing. Grandma said that my father's job at that time was to facilitate the transport of supplies from Burma to Yunnan. Wearing his uniform, he stood in front of Grandma near the end of the war. He respectfully handed her his name card. Printed vertically on the Chinese side of the card were characters that identified him as a major in the U.S. Army Transportation Corps, stationed in Chongqing. His name in Chinese was Han. The other side of the card, printed in English, bore the additional handwritten address of his duty station in Chongqing. He also presented Grandma a small photograph of himself in uniform; in it he wore a solemn expression and gazed straight at the camera. On the back of the photo was the seal of the Great Wall Studio in Chongqing, where the photo was taken, and the studio's address: 38 Xinsheng Road.

My father told Grandma that he was from New York. As a military officer, he said, he would be sent to serve in different places, adding an element of uncertainty to life. Nevertheless, he promised to "try my very best to give your daughter stability." His candor and evident sincerity impressed Grandma. She knew that she would not have many opportunities to see him in the future, so she replied with equal candor. "I believe my daughter only wants to go to the United States," she told him bluntly. "He smiled gently and indicated that he was willing to help her just the same," Grandma recalled. She added that their conversation was carried on in Chinese. "Mr. Han's Chinese was okay; he was able to express himself."

I had seen that gentle smile in another photo, one showing him sitting with my mother on the deck of a ship with a pipe in his hand. The war had ended, and they were on their way to the United States. Those are my parents, I told myself.

After they left China, Grandma went back to Nanjing with the KMT government. Civil war was raging. During the eight-year Japanese occupation, while the KMT national government struggled to defend the country, the Communists had conserved their strength and infiltrated their spies into the government. As the tide began to turn against the KMT, some infiltrators began to surface while others remained under cover and even followed the KMT in its retreat to Taiwan. Today, decades later, this is common knowledge. In the 1950s, however, when Grandma was telling me this, I knew immediately that I must keep it secret because it ran counter to the new regime's public stance, and disaster awaited anyone who said otherwise.

As a government employee in 1948, Grandma was preparing to follow the KMT to Taiwan. That summer, she received a telegram from New York informing her that I was en route to China with Rev. Hubbard's daughter and son-in-law and would soon arrive in Shanghai. Grandma stayed to await my arrival, losing her opportunity to leave the Mainland. As she waited, Grandma considered her options. She knew that the Communists would ferret out KMT supporters in Nanjing, as it was the capital of the former regime. This meant that Nanjing and Shanghai were no longer safe places to stay. She also knew that the First National City Bank of New York would soon move its operations to Hong Kong. So she went to the bank and withdrew all her savings in the form of gold bars known as large or small "yellow fish." As the gold was handed over, the bank teller told her, "The times are unstable; please take good care of yourself." Grandma decided to head north with me as soon as I arrived.

She also paid a visit to Rev. Hubbard, who was residing in Nanjing at the time. In fluent Chinese, he declared that he would never abandon his Chinese flock. His daughter and son-in-law had tried to persuade him to leave China before being struck by the Communist scourge. Failing in that, they were traveling to China to take him home. Rev. Hubbard confidently asserted that "Scourges like the Flood don't scare me. Didn't we have Noah's ark?" Grandma, an atheist, smiled but did not reply. She told him that she was waiting for her granddaughter. Rev. Hubbard happily noted that his daughter and son-in-law were arriving on the same ship, and they arranged to meet again at the dock.

"No wonder the First National City Bank of New York is your favorite bank," Joe laughed.

Indeed, it was. The first time I received my salary from the Foreign Service Institute, the clerk in the payroll office directed me to a bank downstairs in the same building. "Where is the First National City Bank of New York?" I asked. "In New York," she replied. Seeing me transfixed with indecision, she added, "They have branches here, too, but the nearest is three blocks away. Look for the sign that says 'Citibank.'" Amazing. In 1948, Grandma withdrew her savings from the First National City Bank of New York in Shanghai as the bank prepared to evacuate to Hong Kong. Thirty years later, I walked into one of its branches in northern Virginia and handed my first U.S. salary check to a young teller with blonde hair and blue eyes.

"This is my first check. I will be making deposits every two weeks from now on."

The young man smiled and asked, "What made you choose us?" Looking around, I could see banks all around the neighborhood, yet I had chosen what looked like the smallest one. I tried my best to explain the events of thirty years earlier. He solemnly took my check and opened two accounts for me: a savings account and a checking account. He gave me three blank checks that I could use before my printed checks arrived in the mail. "From now on, you're one of our valued customers. I'll do my best to give the same dependable service that my predecessors in Shanghai gave your grandmother."

I walked back to the Foreign Service Institute under the mid-day sun feeling so warm. So much money in just two weeks! And the bank was guarding it for me. Clutching the blank checks tightly, I walked into the administrative office and told an elderly clerk that I wanted to pay back the $450 airfare lent to me by the federal government in Hong Kong.

"My God! Your first pay check and here you are paying back the loan! Plenty of Americans wouldn't think of ever repaying the government," he mumbled. "Good girl, you are such a good girl." I wrote the check and handed it over, and, as I did, a sigh of relief escaped my lips. As a Citibank check, it could be cashed right away. How nice! I told Grandma about this in a letter, and I could see her smiling thousands of miles away.

It was not until I had received salaries and checks from, among others, National Geographic magazine, The Johns Hopkins University's School of Advanced International Studies, the Washington Post, and the ABC television network that I realized that my salary at the Foreign Service Institute was not all that generous. But what did that matter? I had been earning between 26 and 32 renminbi -- about four dollars -- a month in

China. My current income was 500-600 times more than that, so I was perfectly content.

Grandma took me to Beijing in the early 1950s. There she bought a small house on Rice Market Street with rooms on three sides of a courtyard. After the purchase, she still had enough "yellow fish" from the bank that she could afford not to work. Mrs. Xu, the lady who acted as go-between in Grandma's purchase of the courtyard house, was also from Wujin County. Her husband used to own a small workshop employing a few master binders of traditional thread-bound Chinese books. Watching land reform unfold in rural areas in the years following the Communist takeover, Mr. Xu became uncomfortable with keeping employees because an accusation of exploitation could lead to prosecution. He quietly let his workers go and sold off the equipment in his workshop, retaining only a single stitching machine, which he and his wife used personally to earn their living. Grandma bought one of the stitching machines from his workshop. Although a far cry from the work of art that her rosewood machine was, it was efficient and cute. A flatbed tricycle rickshaw carried the device the short distance from Wuliang Daren Alley, where Mr. Xu lived, to our house on Rice Market Street. Thanks to introductions from Mr. Xu, flatbed rickshaws from bookstores all over the city often pulled up in front of our house carrying gunnysacks of volumes in need of repair.

On a large, flat, wooden table Grandma would spread out a canvas on which she would separate and arrange the damaged pieces of paper. The blue cloth bag would be unrolled and, sitting on a high stool, I would quietly watch her restore the pages to book form, one by one. A shallow blue dish held the translucent powdered lotus root paste whose mild fragrance perfumed the air. Using a thin, flat bamboo tool, Grandma would scrape a tiny dab of paste between the two halves of pages that had separated, page after page, until all were back together. Heavier paper with the look of dark fabric was used for the front and back covers. Then I would hear the gentle sound of the stitching machine. After stitching, Grandma would paste a strip of high-quality white Xuan paper from the town of Xuancheng in Anhui Province on the cover; then she would wrap the book in a white cloth and place a green brick on top. When all was done, Grandma would pick me up from the stool and take my hand, and we would go outside, usually to the grocery store to buy oil, wine, and sugar, three of the most important items in our pantry. Despite living in Beijing for thirty-six years, Grandma never lost some of her southern customs. One was putting some sugar in her stir-fried vegetables; another was speaking in her southern dialect. In the early 1950s, when I was four or five years old, whenever we walked into the grocery store the manager would sit me on the counter so I could translate for him. Soon, though, my fluency in the southern dialect declined, replaced by standard Mandarin. However, I could always understand Grandma when she spoke the southern dialect and she, in turn, always understood my Mandarin.

Returning home, Grandma would put down the grocery basket and wash her hands. Then she would light some incense, place the now-flattened book on the desk, and drip a few drops of clean water onto an ink slab. Choosing an appropriate brush, she would write the title of the book on the strip of Xuan paper on the cover. This completed the restoration.

Mr. and Mrs. Xu often came to visit and discuss technical problems of book restoration. A frequent topic of discussion was the stiff, blue-cloth-covered board cases that held two or more volumes of thread-bound books. Two ribbons were carefully threaded between the boards to make it possible to neatly tie up the case, creating a real thing of beauty. Mr. Xu made the cases himself. Sometimes they would bring over pieces of books to discuss with Grandma. They never came empty-handed, always bringing a bottle of wine, a carton of cigarettes, a bag of candies, or some other gift. Grandma would always say, "You are too kind," and I would say, "Thank you Great-uncle Xu and Great-Auntie Xu." Grandma always invited them to stay for dinner, which would feature dishes from their southern roots, and they would eat and chat and laugh. They never talked about people or events that were taking place in their native county in my presence.

When a few volumes had been restored, Grandma would wrap them in cloth, and we would take a pedicab to the Chinese bookstore in Qianmenwai. The clerks there were unfailingly polite, always inviting Grandma to sit down for a cup of tea. She would unwrap the restored books for them to examine while they drank tea and chatted about books.

After receiving cash from the store's bookkeeper, Grandma would walk around the store's sales floor where her restored books were on display with price tags in a glass-fronted cabinet. She always bought some books for me to study, including, on one occasion, a thread-bound edition of the venerable *The Origin of Classical Poetry*. In 1964, when I left Beijing to go to Shanxi Province, I left this book at home with our other books. During the Cultural Revolution, our home was searched by Red Guards and the books confiscated, but not burned. After the Cultural Revolution, this book was one of the few items returned to us. When I left China, Grandma wanted me to take this book with me to the United States.

Some of her restored books also served as my textbooks, but these were rare because they earned money for us: money for the salary of Mrs. Li, our household helper; groceries; fabric; money that enabled me to wear a new padded cotton jacket at the beginning of every new year when I was little. All those restored books kept us going without having to use any of Grandma's "yellow fish." This was very fortunate because, during the three-year Great Famine, these bought the food that kept us alive. In the end, I never got to keep one book that Grandma had brought back to life.

Joe held *The Origin of Classical Poetry* with both hands before slowly untying the stiff brown paper case's cloth ribbons. Opening the case, four slim volumes appeared.

"This is called a six-sided case. It fully encloses the volumes inside. The top cover is square and simple with cloth ties to close the case." I picked up a volume to show Joe. "This is an ordinary four-pinprick thread-bound book with grayish woven paper for the front and back covers. This black 'fish tail' design on page edges serves as a sort of table of contents. Chapter and page numbers are printed in square brackets, simple and tasteful."

Opening the book, Joe pointed to one page and asked, "What is this?"

Next to three elegantly written Chinese characters was a round red ink stamp featuring a red star surrounded by characters that read "Horse Stable Branch of the Revolutionary Committee of the Beijing City Yongdingmen Tree Farm Labor Union." On top of this stamp was a government stamp that simply read "cancelled." The first page of the other three volumes that comprised the book all bore the same two stamps.

"These stamps showed that, after Red Guards confiscated the book during the Cultural Revolution, it somehow became the property of Horse Stable leftists. After the Cultural Revolution, China's new leaders implemented a policy that aimed at returning confiscated property, so the book came back to its owner: my Grandma."

Frowning, Joe asked, "Weren't Red Guards all students? Wouldn't those people in the Horse Stable be workers?"

"The rise of the Red Guards during the Cultural Revolution soon led to People's Liberation Army (PLA) and workers' propaganda teams wielding ultimate power over people's lives and property." As I spoke to Joe, my mind wandered back to January 1978, when I was leaving China. At the border with Hong Kong, Chinese customs officers inspected and confiscated every picture and every bit of writing, even my diary, except for those impressed with the government seals; perhaps they were just accustomed to seeing them.

Joe picked up the first volume and, carefully opening it to the first page, asked, "Was this book really printed in the summer of the seventeenth year of the reign of the Emperor Guang Xu as it says on the second page?" The page displayed two vertical rows of printed characters that read "Reprinted by the Sixian Bookstore in Hunan in the summer of the seventeenth year of the reign of Guang Xu."

Sadness showed on Joe's face. I assumed that he was sad to see ugly red seals defacing the elegant antique books. I was able to comfort him on that point. "Grandma believed this set was reprinted by an unknown bookseller because the paper used is quite different from that of other Sixian printings. So, although the books were nicely reprinted, they are far from being antiques."

Joe grumbled that anything older than fifty years in the United States was considered an antique. It seemed my explanation had not made him feel better.

Opening the book, I began to talk about its compiler, Shen Deqian, who lived from 1673 to 1769 in Changzhou, which today is called

Suzhou. Joe abruptly stopped me. "I can do this research on my own." He put together the volumes of *The Origin of Classical Poetry* and the ragged *Dou E Yuan*. Placing them side by side, he gravely asked, "What happened to your Grandma's hands?"

"Arthritis," I answered unhesitatingly.

"Are the joints swollen and contorted?" I was starting to wonder about Joe's persistent questioning.

"No. The joints of her fingers were not swollen. In the early spring of 1967, when I fled from Shanxi to Xinjiang, I detoured from Datong to Beijing to visit Grandma. I discovered that her fingers were badly contorted. Was this caused by arthritis? I couldn't be sure. In 1976, after I was sent back to Beijing, I spent every day with Grandma for more than a year. I always carried or moved anything heavy, and I never thought to examine her hands, usually hidden in her sleeves, except for one time, the night of the big Tangshan earthquake. When the shaking started, I picked her up from her bed, together with the cotton blankets, and placed her under a solid desk pushed into a corner next to a wardrobe. It seemed a safer place for a 78-year-old woman than outside with the crowd. The space under the desk was only big enough for one person, and Grandma grabbed me, saying, 'How about you?' I gently detached her slender fingers one by one from my arm only to find that they were all skewed in one direction. I held her cold hands between mine under the blanket as I sat on the floor holding on to her tightly. Only my arms were under the desk; the rest of my body was exposed. Our whole house shook, and the rumbling sound of the ground blended with the screams of people outside. I sat there holding on to Grandma, not at all frightened."

Joe was silent, seemingly living through the event in his mind, perhaps coming up with some more questions. Then he remembered. With flashing eyes, he asked, "About land reform. You mentioned that your grandmother and Mr. and Mrs. Xu didn't talk about their hometown. Did your grandmother talk about it with you after you grew up?"

"One hundred fourteen," I answered huskily, staring into his eyes. "In 1963, Grandma's older brother by the same parents came to Beijing from Shanghai to visit her. That was the first time since 1949 and also the last time they met. They talked in front of me about everything that had happened in their hometown. I didn't know Grandma's family, their names and relationships, but I remember this figure clearly. During land reform and the Elimination of Counterrevolutionaries movement, between the Zhao and Xie families 114 people were killed. From six-month-old babies to 90-year old men, no one who stayed behind was spared. Great-uncle held a low-level job at the Bank of Communications and lived hand-to-mouth without party affiliation. He never took one grain of rice from his family's land rents. This saved him from the fate that befell so many of his relatives." The words poured out of me in a single breath. My hands and feet felt ice-cold. Joe was silent, stunned, with tears welling up in his eyes. He asked no more questions, just quietly left with the books and Grandma's letter.

With rain pattering against the window, I heated water and made myself some coffee to warm up. As I wrapped my hands around the mug, I decided to write Grandma a letter asking about her hands. Listening to the rain, my mind was still churning over the number: 114. I did not want to dwell on the grim statistic, so I opened *The Origin of Classical Poetry* and started reading. *Poetry reached its pinnacle during the Tang Dynasty, but the pinnacle was not the same as the origin....* Punctuation here was really not necessary. As my mind focused on the book's words, I gradually calmed down.

That day, I wrote to Grandma asking about her hands. I didn't get an answer until the end of 1983, when my husband and I were in Beijing. One day, when she suffered chest pain, we took her to Capital Hospital. There, the doctor told us that the chest pain was caused by badly mended ribs. While I went to the pharmacy, Grandma quietly told my husband the story. In 1966, someone had denounced her, alleging that she had worked for the KMT government's intelligence service. One of the neighborhood revolutionary groups, together with a fellow named Dai Jinde, the head of the local revolutionary cultural unit, arrested her. They tied her hands tightly together and hung her up to force a confession. They also beat her, breaking three of her ribs. She was saved by Old Mister Wang, who worked at the nearby police station on Yenyue Alley. He had known her for more than ten years, and he rushed over as soon as he heard of her plight. He told the torturers that the old lady was almost 70 years old and that what they were doing could kill her. As the local police officer, he could have been held responsible in the event of a fatality. He saved her from the torturers but had no authority to send her to a hospital, so the ribs were left to heal on their own.

"I just have to live with deformed fingers," Grandma said stoically, trying to comfort my husband with a smile, gently patting his hand with her crooked fingers. "I couldn't tell my granddaughter about this; she'd likely go out and kill them." Grandma laughed cheerily. "Anyway, I've outlived all those who tortured and beat me, especially that Dai Jinde. He died dirty."

My observant husband remembered the sentence "He died dirty," which he did not understand at the time. He then asked the question he really wanted an answer to: "Who denounced you? Is he dead?" Grandma's smile faded. "Ours is a simple family; you can guess." And she gently patted his hand again.

Later that day, we took Grandma home. We made sure that she would take her prescribed medicine by writing down for her maid the times and dosages of each medication. We then returned to our temporary accommodations at the Jianguo Hotel. That evening, as we sat in the hotel's bustling restaurant, my husband repeated Grandma's words. I told him that "died dirty" meant that the torturer had suffered from incontinence during his last years, so he "died dirty." He thought for a while and then carefully said, "The denouncer must be your grandmother's daughter. She said yours was a 'simple family.' You were in Shanxi at the time, so the only person living with your grandmother was your mother; it had to be her."

I was speechless.

In 1980, I actually believed that woman's lies. She swore that everything she had done during those years was because the system forced her. I believed her when she said that everything she had done to me was coerced as well. I even took her into my home in the United States. During her first week in this country, while I was at work during the day, she spent most of her time at the Chinese embassy. I knew nothing of this until an FBI agent came to my house to ask her what she was doing at the Chinese embassy. Her reply was "Seeing friends." Asked why she was staying there so long, she replied, "Taking a nap." The FBI agent walked over to my telephone and, turning over, discovered a "bug." At a loss for words, she turned to look out the window. I told her, "You will leave my house first thing in the morning. I never want to see you again." Those were the last words I ever spoke to her. My husband had heard this story from me, so when Grandma hinted that her denouncer was a family member, he was quick to connect the dots.

Remorse filled my heart. If I had only known earlier that she had falsely accused her own mother, as well as her daughter, all doubts about her character would have been erased, and I never would have let her into my home. I agonized that evening, wondering why Grandma had not warned me about her. Carefully choosing his words, my husband later told me, "Your mother came with a mission. You could not have stopped her even if your grandmother had warned you. Even if you hadn't petitioned for her entry into this country, the Chinese government would have found a way to get her here." I realized this was true, but it didn't make me feel any better.

Forty years earlier, Grandma had warned my father about her, but hadn't he taken her to New York anyway? Most of us shrink from thinking ill of other people, especially those we love, always hoping that they will do the right thing in the end. But evil exists; wishful thinking does not make it go away. When did she become a tool of the Communist regime? My husband had no doubts. "Long ago. Before the Cultural Revolution, even before you were sent off to the countryside in 1964."

On that rainy day in 1978, there was still so much that I did not know about my own family. In my letter to Grandma, I expressed concern about her hands. By 1983, when I had collected more pieces of the story, I thought of Joe, whose instincts led him to discover so much from a raggedly bound old book.

CHAPTER 5

MY STORY

It was a morning in February 1979. The sky was bluer than blue, and the capital lay under a blanket of snow. My internal alarm clock went off at 5 a.m. I switched on the TV news where a reporter was announcing through lips bluish with cold that large numbers of farmers in trucks and tractors were descending on the city to protest low farm product prices. As a result, the reporter continued, all the roads and bridges in the Washington, D.C. area were heavily congested. The video showed long lines of cars mixed in with gigantic trucks and tractors, none of them moving. The huge farm machines made the cars seem tiny, an effect that was almost comical – unless you were stuck in traffic. Even more important for me was that public buses were not running on time. The reporter helpfully suggested that commuters take the subway or "just stay comfortably at home unless it was absolutely necessary to go to work."

School closings had nothing to do with me. Students at the Foreign Service Institute, unlike college students, were used to taking risks. I decided that not only did I have to go to work, but that I should go in early. How to go? Walking to the subway station closest to my apartment took about as much time as walking to work. With buses running irregularly, I decided to go on foot. I bundled up in a down coat and warm scarf, tucked my pants legs into a pair of warm boots, made sure Pele had food and water, and out I went.

The sidewalk by the apartment complex had not been shoveled, but people walking to the bus stop had beaten a narrow path. The snow plows hadn't yet come either. Route 50 was clogged with traffic, but everywhere else was an expanse of whiteness. I braced myself to walk over the virgin snow. With no other pedestrians around, I was moving faster than the motorists sitting in their cars.

As I trod along, a gigantic vehicle came into view. With wheels taller than I was, it reminded me of the combines introduced by the USSR a long time ago. I had worked with something similar in Xinjiang. This one was even bigger, though, with blue paint glistening in the sunlight. I looked up at the driver and saw a man with a reddish face in a sleeveless undershirt. In fact, he appeared to be sweating on one of the coldest days of the year, with temperatures near zero. Inside the vehicle's cab it must have been as warm as summer. Awestruck, I watched the giant inch along the crowded highway. Through the steam-fogged windows of the trailer behind it, a strong-looking young woman was just picking up a baby from a bath tub and wrapping it up with a large towel. The baby was waving its limbs happily. My goodness! The behemoth was carrying its own steam bath! Who were these people? This was really something!

Suddenly I heard someone calling my name from a car idling behind the giant vehicle. It was Mr. Xia, a sonar navigation specialist and my first student of the day, beckoning me to get into his car. As I joined him inside, he smiled and said, "You are really something, walking to work!" Just then, an idea struck me. "These cars are barely moving. Why don't we have our class right now?" Mr. Xia chuckled. "I was thinking that at this rate I'd get to school just in time for my class to be over. What a nice surprise, my teacher dropping in on me. This must be my lucky day."

Mr. Xia was in an advanced tutorial class. He had a solid foundation in Chinese to begin with and just needed the specialized vocabulary relating to sonar navigation. For his tutorial, I had bought a military dictionary from Hong Kong and subscribed to a military magazine so I could compile interesting teaching materials devoted to sonar navigation. He enjoyed his class, coming every morning for an hour before going to work at the Defense Department.

Glancing at the briefcase lying by my feet, Mr. Xia said hesitantly, "My class materials are in my briefcase. Should I take them out?" "That won't be necessary," I replied. "I have everything we need in my head. Just drive slowly when we start drilling." I could tell that this answer pleased him.

It took a whole hour for us to make our way to downtown Rosslyn. By the time we got there, I told Mr. Xia that he had satisfactorily completed his class for the day. "You don't have to drive to the Foreign Service Institute; just drop me off at the next light." He was happy to comply. Just before I got out of the car I asked, "That gigantic vehicle in front of us can't be a freight truck, can it?"

"Only farmers use those vehicles. You can see they are equipped with every convenience," Mr. Xia explained. He was able to use several Chinese idioms fluently in his answer, which clearly made him very happy. Bidding me a warm farewell, he continued his commute to the nearby Pentagon.

It must have been unusually cold - the door to the building where I taught was tightly closed. As I pushed open the door, the guard was surprised to see me.

"You're really something! You're the first teacher to arrive."

Hearing this made me feel relieved. I described to him what I had seen on the way in. Seeing my interest in those house-like vehicles, he readily expounded. "Good heavens, those farmers' trailers are equipped with kitchens, baths, beds, and even refrigerators." I was baffled. "If they live such comfortable lives, why are they demonstrating?" The guard looked at me solemnly and replied, "I wouldn't say that. People have the right to appeal wherever they see injustice and inequality. In a democratic society, voices from all sides need to be heard."

The snow kept a few students away from class - the ones who lived far away where the plows could not remove the snow in time for ordinary cars to use the roads.

Mr. Lei arrived in time in his big Mercedes Benz. He told me that his car not only had more horsepower than most cars; it also had four-wheel drive instead of the usual rear-wheel drive. Snowy roads weren't a problem for him. Mr. Lei, a senior official in the Department of Agriculture, was a student in my advanced class. His focus was on matters agricultural, so we did not have much time to talk about wheels and engines. At the end of class, I wanted to raise a question that had been on my mind: would the farmers' demands be met since they had taken so much trouble to come to the capital?

Mr. Lei seemed to have been expecting my question. Rubbing his hands, he explained in a thoughtful voice that American agriculture was marvelously productive, so bountiful that, if the land were exploited to its limit, the country could feed half the world's population.

"But, like people, the land needs to rest sometimes, too," I interjected. Nodding, he continued. "On one hand, the land needs to rest; on the other hand, the farmers need crops in order to live. So, the government provides subsidies to farmers to enable them to let some land lie fallow. In other words, some farmers receive government subsidies for not producing anything. However, no policy is perfect. Some farmers are dissatisfied with the current policy, so it's good that they come to the capital to get the government's attention. We should listen to their side of the story. Of course, the enactment of any law or policy must go through review." Mr. Lei's broad smile revealed that he was delighted to have used correctly the idiom for "through review."

Just then, the department head, Dr. Yates, knocked at the open door, greeted Mr. Lei, and announced that all federal government offices would be closed that afternoon. All teachers and students could go home at the conclusion of class. He cautioned us to drive safely. After Dr. Yates left, Mr. Lei courteously offered to give me a ride home. I thanked him but declined, telling him I would take advantage of the free time in the afternoon to prepare some special teaching materials for a few students in the advanced classes. As he left, Mr. Lei warned me, "Don't stay more than two hours. The roads will get more slippery as the day wears on."

I was hardly in a mood to prepare teaching materials. I was awash with memories and turbulent thoughts. What I really wanted was to be alone to think.

Although I was living in Washington D.C. at the beginning of 1979, my heart was still linked with the abased and abused Chinese farm workers in that impoverished land. Only three years earlier, I had been in Xinjiang, China's far west. During the day, farm workers used shovels and the heavy-headed, short-handled hoes peculiar to Xinjiang to repair endless columns of narrow ditches in the barren fields in preparation for spring irrigation. The sharp edges of the shovels only made white streaks on the frozen soil. The hoes made lovely silvery arcs in the air as they came down, hitting the ground with a metallic clang, only to loosen a few shards of soil. Every shovelful of earth caused scarred and bloody hands wrapped in rags to shake with pain. We all knew the effort was futile. As spring arrived, the frozen soil thawed and was then used to repair the many gaps in the irrigation canals. Nevertheless, over the long winter season farm workers still had to toil in the frozen fields or else "study politics," "fight selfishness and repudiate revisionism," and "draw out revolution from the depth of the soul," which were more painful than drilling holes in one's heart.

Returning at night to the humid, subterranean dungeon that was my assigned dwelling, I hurriedly stuffed some sticks of firewood picked up on the way back from the fields into the adobe stove. Lighting the fire, I pasted my body against the stove wall, willing the meager heat to chase away the chill that had penetrated my bones. The dinner bell rang, announcing the time to grab my rice bowl and line up. Salty boiled cabbage was not very appetizing, but my empty stomach demanded something. I just tightened my belt and lived with the pangs of hunger.

The annual mass "push" to clean silt from the huge irrigation canal that channeled the spring runoff from the mountains always took place in winter, since there was no water in the canal then. A few companies of our Xinjiang Production and Construction Corps would march all day to Longkou, about thirty miles away, where the canal began. On those excursions, we lacked even the luxury of subterranean dungeons at night. The bitter cold of December nights froze our blankets into stiff cylinders. After emerging from the cylinder in the morning, I had to let the sun shine on it all day before I could climb into it again in the evening.

We farm workers were paid 32 renminbi per month in these harsh conditions. More importantly, we each received thirty jin (about 33 pounds) of grain a month. The Xinjiang Production and Construction Corps was charged with opening up wasteland and garrisoning the frontier. The central government sent a million Han Chinese to Xinjiang to carry out this "strategic mission," so that no one in China would starve. What it actually accomplished was to expand desertification at a time of famine.

One year, there was a major flood in Henan Province. The United Nations sent shipments of corn for disaster relief. Instead of helping the afflicted areas of Henan, however, the Chinese government sent the gunnysacks of corn to southern Xinjiang – life-saving provisions for members of the Xinjiang Production and Construction Corps. Seeing those plump corn kernels, even the normally anti-American political cadres couldn't keep from voicing their praise. "It's from the United States, after all; even their corn kernels are bigger than ours." Tractors roared day and night powering the machines that ground the kernels into flour. The aroma of steaming cornbread had every face in the troop wreathed in smiles. When the lid of the steamer was removed, we were surprised to see that the loaves had fallen apart. We had to put the bread in bowls and scoop it up with spoons.

The lack of a glutinous element in American corn puzzled us until an agricultural technician in the troop offered an explanation. Corn, he said, was a seed. In order to prevent its top-quality corn from being planted abroad after exporting, the United States removed a part of the kernel essential for the seed to grow. In other words, the corn could be used for food or feed but not for planting.

The technician had had his "rightist" label removed, but the "revolutionary crowd" could always re-label him. He, therefore, was usually quiet, only answering questions from his leader when necessary. Speaking so much this time made his face turn red. Seeing that the group leaders were irritated by his explanation, he added, "This is a kind of protectionism on the part of American capitalism."

"Protect what?" the political commissar asked heatedly, his face an angry mask.

"To protect America's own agriculture," the technician answered nervously.

While the crowd was busy cursing American protectionism, I keenly savored each spoonful of America's corn, every morsel entering my mouth ever so warmly and fragrantly, sliding gently down my throat to soothe my empty stomach. And it got me thinking: America was trying to help others while protecting its own agricultural technology and farmers. That seemed a sensible thing to do. I also thought about those farmers, young and old, in flood-ravaged Henan. Without this corn, what were they going to do?

My musings suddenly ended when loud sounds of reproach reached my ears. The wife of the political commissar was yelling at her husband. "What makes you so proud? If you don't like the look of that steamed bread, don't eat it! Go ahead and starve!"

That shut them up. Everyone knew that the steamed cornbread, in whatever form, was a godsend. We enjoyed it for six months. Since it had come as donated aid, we workers only had to pay about half of what we had been paying before for steamed bread. Everyone was getting used to it. Afterward, whenever the kitchen made steamed cornbread using local corn, people would complain, "What is this? It tastes sour and smells rotten!" To which the cook would riposte, "Still thinking of American cornbread? Take a look in the mirror. What makes you think you deserve such a comfortable life?" The cook came from three generations of poor peasants, so he always had the last word in arguments of this sort. Moreover, those of us with some education knew that he was right. As members of the Production and Construction Corps, we ate immeasurably better than we would have back home. The cook himself had joined the Corps to escape starvation in his village in Gansu.

Midnight on the edge of the desert was usually the hardest time of day. The wall next to the fire was ice cold. Our meager dinners had long been digested. The front and back of one's body seemed to stick together. "Cold and hunger intertwined" was the best description of how we felt, but no one wanted to say it. Lying in the bone-chilling cold with open eyes was no way to spend the night, so I got up.

The kitchen was partially open to the outside. The cook had already lit the fire to prepare cornmeal porridge for breakfast. I walked over to the stove and started to feed red willow branches into the opening. "Don't sit too close. You'll be in big trouble if your clothes catch fire," the cook smilingly cautioned me. He chattered freely about the bitterly difficult lives of Gansu's farmers. That was why, even though he was classified as a "poor peasant," the political commissar never asked him to testify at the mass rallies about his suffering in the old society and his happiness under the new regime.

"The worst year was 1960 after all the grass roots and tree bark had been eaten. Village after village showed no trace of life." He told his story in a hoarse voice as he chopped the outer leaves of cabbages. I listened to him quietly even though I had heard the story many times already. I had been "sent down" to the countryside in the southern part of Shanxi Province where cotton and wheat were abundant. It had been difficult during the years of the Great Famine but nothing like the starvation in Gansu. Only after arriving in Xinjiang and listening to the workers who had fled those famine-stricken areas did I learn about the real misery and abuse endured by China's bitterly poor peasants. They would talk at length with tears in their eyes about their hometowns in Sichuan, Gansu, Ningxia, Shaanxi, Henan, or wherever. Their fingers were all short, rough, and could not be closed to make a fist. They explained, "This is the result of scraping food from the soil day in and day out."

The rumbling sound of the heating system coming on in the empty FSI building interrupted my reverie and brought me back from faraway Xinjiang. I felt that I had to learn more about American farmers. Weren't they staging their protest in the streets in front of the Capitol? I wanted to see how they mounted their protest. I also wanted to see if they were all like the farmer I had seen through the tractor window.

With my coat buttoned up to my chin and my things in my handbag, I headed over the skywalk towards the Rosslyn subway station. Only a few passengers on the platform were headed towards downtown Washington, while quite a few were waiting to head further into the Virginia suburbs. People were eager to get home.

A train slid up to the other side of the platform. A few passengers got off, but many more boarded. It must be warm inside the train because disembarking passengers were buttoning up their coats and hats and wrapping scarves around their necks, ready to face the cold. A tall, grayish shadow detached itself from the stream of people and walked towards me. It was Joe. He took off his hat and smiled.

"What are you doing here in Rosslyn?" I asked, surprised.

"I live here. Or, more precisely, I have a small apartment here. If the weather is bad, like it has been these last two days, I'll stay here overnight. Also, when friends visit and I don't feel like introducing them to my father, we'll meet here to chat, play chess, or have a beer." He asked me where I was going.

"I want to see the farmers' demonstration."

Joe smiled. "The demonstrators aren't poor farmers who till some-one else's land. They're landowners. Many of them own large mechanized farms, orchards, or ranches. Some even have their own agricultural research institutes."

"So they're farm owners. My goodness! I've been calling them farmers and nobody corrected me before now," I said, unsettled by the contrast between American farmers and the downtrodden tillers of the soil in China.

Joe smiled. "When I heard the news, I started wondering how I could translate it accurately into Chinese. I checked with the Library of Congress, and this term 'farm owners' came up - very proper, to my mind."

"You keep saying 'own,'" I said, still trying to process these revelations that were forcing me to rethink how I thought of farmers and landowners. Other than the virtues of being able to endure hardship and unremitting hard labor, Chinese farmers possessed absolutely nothing. The small plots they received through early land reform after the Communist takeover were gradually taken away in a series of "cooperation" movements and turned into collectively owned farms no longer owned by farmers.

Seeing me in a kind of trance, Joe could tell that my thoughts were undergoing some major re-assessments. His smile disappeared, and he asked seriously, "Do you still want to see what the farmers are up to in town?"

I now knew that American farm owners driving their own vehicles to the capital and Chinese farmers had almost nothing in common. Nevertheless, I wanted to know more, so I nodded saying, "Yes, I'd like to take a look."

A train heading downtown arrived, and Joe and I got on. There were few passengers. As we sat down on a long bench, Joe quietly commented, "I figure that they are barbecuing."

"Outdoors? In such cold weather? I doubt it."

"They have to eat, too, don't they," Joe said reasonably.

As we approached the station serving the Smithsonian museums, Joe said, "Between here and Capitol Hill is where the activity is. We can see it if we get off here."

At the top of the escalator leading out of the station, we encountered two young men, who looked to be of high-school age, distributing flyers and speaking in a southern accent. Joe and I each got a flyer, which we stuck in our coat pockets as we kept walking.

Was this a protest demonstration? It looked more like a carnival.

The soft harmonies of country music floated through the air. I could hear guitars and drums. Along the National Mall, tractors and trailers were neatly lined up. In the middle of the grand matrix formed by the parked farm machines, an area cleared of snow dispersed smoke carrying tantalizing aromas from what must have been upwards of one hundred barbecue grills arranged into a large rectangle. Behind the grills stood robust, contented-looking men wearing plaid shirts over white T-shirts. With huge spatulas they turned thick steaks, meaty pork chops, and oversized green peppers, onions, and ears of corn on the grills. Even the chickens turning slowly on rotisseries, their fat dripping into the charcoal fire producing a burnt fragrance, seemed unusually large.

They really were barbecuing! The tantalizing, smoky aromas reminded me that the cereal I had eaten that morning was by now completely digested.

"Miss," Joe nudged me so I would turn and notice a husky fellow smiling at me. Beer can in hand, he asked, "Would you care for something? Steak? Lamb chop? Half a chicken?" I could see other local people chatting, eating, and drinking with the visitors. Joe popped open a beer someone handed him. Feeling a bit uncomfortable, I asked shyly, "May I have a drumstick and half an ear of corn?" "Sure, sure." The smiling man put down his beer. He wrapped a drumstick in a piece of aluminum foil and placed it on a paper plate along with a perfectly grilled ear of corn. He handed me the plate and a couple of napkins.

I thanked the man, the fragrance of the corn in my hand filling my nostrils. A first, tentative bite filled my mouth with the sweet juice of young corn. I couldn't help but think of the times I had eaten American corn in Xinjiang, and I was suddenly immersed in a roiling cauldron of conflicting emotions. I heard the soft voice of the husky barbeque master saying, "Take a few more home with you, if you like." Holding back tears, I forced a smile and thanked him profusely. He handed me a plastic bag holding three ears of corn – grilled, young, American corn with unmodified kernels. I thanked him again and turned to look for Joe. I found him sitting cross-legged nearby working on a steak with a plastic knife and fork. A sturdy man was talking earnestly to him, and it looked as though worldly Joe and he had a lot to talk about. As I walked towards Joe, the sturdy man whipped out another round stool, as if by magic.

So, there I was, comfortably seated near Joe and nibbling on a tender drumstick. Looking around, I saw robust women taking meat and vegetables from a number of white freezers. An orderly chain of young girls shuttled the food between the freezers and the grills amid singing, music, and laughter.

The sturdy man took the empty plates from our hands and put them in a huge trash can. Then he removed the two stools. His warm, big hands grasped ours as we said goodbye.

Walking back to the subway station, we saw farmers bringing food to policemen clad in heavy coats who were keeping watch over the event. No matter how much the policemen declined, the farmers kept urging them to eat something. The officers were not accustomed to such warm and friendly "demonstrators." Eventually, though, they uneasily accepted plates piled with food. I saw the sturdy man who had been our host handing a policeman a soda.

"Policemen can't drink alcohol while on duty," Joe pointed out.

"Of course not," I nodded, feeling warm at heart.

In the subway station, I couldn't resist asking Joe how he and the farmer could strike up such an animated conversation. Joe smiled and said that his father was in the alcohol business. Be it wine, beer, liquor or cooking sherry, they all involved agricultural products. Now I understood. I thought of Joe's father's stately, art-filled house, with its elegant furniture and gorgeous garden. It all came from alcohol which, in turn, had everything to do with grain and fruit. Joe said that his father's company was in California. "My mother is also buried in California," he added. His father enjoyed the different seasons, which was why he lived on the east coast.

It dawned on me then that there were people who did not have to live where they earned their livelihoods. They could choose a place to live that had nothing to do with their work or even their relatives. They could live where they liked. Such people seemed to live on a different planet from the people with whom I had lived for the past thirty years. Noting my silence, Joe suggested that we go to his apartment for a cup of hot tea before I went home. We boarded a train that had just pulled in.

It was a very short trip. I had worked here for almost a year among the high-rise buildings without realizing the existence of such beautiful apartment complexes with neat little balconies. Looking out from there over the Washington area must be pleasing to the eye. Joe told me that these were not rental apartments but rather condominiums. Residents owned their apartments and shared ownership of the land, lawns, fountains, trees, exercise rooms, swimming pools, and other facilities inside and around the building.

"In other words, this little apartment is all yours. Should you decide to sell or rent it out in the future, it's all up to you." I couldn't help admiring the beauty of the word "ownership," and I exclaimed, "Long live private ownership!"

Joe was happy. "Private ownership also means 'Long live taxes.' Not only do condo owners have to pay property tax; they also have to pay management fees. All that beautiful scenery and those common facilities have to be maintained, right? That is why rights and responsibility go hand-in-hand. We can't have one without the other."

"Chinese farmers have responsibilities but no rights," I pointed out.

"The problem is in the system. Communism definitely has its problems," Joe said in a low but firm voice. He reminded me of a Chinese saying: "One who is in the right need not raise his voice." I smiled approvingly.

As soon as we arrived at the top of the steps leading into the building, the door was swung open by a man standing inside. He wore a long coat and hat with gold and red trimming, and his face glowed with ruddy health. He courteously addressed Joe as "sir" while Joe called him "Tom." Tom pushed the button by the elevator and, when the elevator door opened, pressed the button PH 20 inside. He stood attentively by as the elevator door slowly closed, smiling all the while.

Joe said softly, "Tom is one of the doormen in this condo. Ours are different from doormen at department stores or restaurants. Ours see everything, hear everything, and know everything and everybody. If you get along with them, you're fine. If you don't, you'd better move somewhere else." It looked as though Joe and Tom got along just fine. I took note of the importance of a condo doorman. Seven years later, when I moved into a stylish condo on New York City's Upper East Side, the things I learned from Joe that day came in handy.

"Excuse, me, but what does 'PH' mean," I asked, knowing that Joe would not mind my ignorance.

"'PH' stands for penthouse. Not the adult magazine that you sometimes see at newsstands with plain brown paper over its cover. This is the kind of penthouse people live in, the top floor of a building with a wide terrace outside. In the summer, I host small parties there. I'll invite you up to see the fireworks on Independence Day," Joe explained as he pulled out his door key.

My impression of a penthouse, gained from books and films, was that it was like an attic: a low space where adults could not stand upright and where children found interesting objects in storage. But in this penthouse, the ceiling was high, and the living room, dining room, and kitchen shared an open area painted light gray. I saw furniture with clean, straight lines, modern art on the walls, and a top-of-the-line music system, all revealing a hitherto unknown side of Joe. The hall closet held coats of various types in different materials, patterns, and lengths, all in shades of gray. Joe hung my coat in the closet and invited me to sit down on the leather sofa in the living room. Then he walked into the kitchen and filled a kettle with water. Holding a tin of tea in one hand, Joe used his other hand to push a button as he walked towards me. Immediately the fireplace blossomed into a cozy fire.

Seeing my surprised look, Joe explained, "This is a gas fireplace. It saves a lot of trouble." Opening the lid of the tea tin, he asked, "How about some Ceylon red?" The tea leaves diffused a strong fragrance totally unlike the jasmine or Dragon Well tea I was familiar with. I nodded.

With Joe busy with the tea, I walked towards a large window facing east. The Washington Monument glimmered in the distance. Closer, the Potomac River presented a serene blue mirror. Even closer stood the building housing the Foreign Service Institute where I taught. Good Lord! I worked right under Joe's nose!

Placing a tray on the coffee table, Joe casually remarked, "I bought this place two years ago, before you came to Washington." This made me think of Dr. Yates, who had introduced me to Joe.

"Colonel Yates and my father were colleagues in the Air Force. They even spent time in the same military hospital early in the Vietnam war. After leaving the military, Colonel Yates went back to school to become a linguist, while my father returned to the family business and became a businessman. They are still close friends. All my Chinese teachers before you were mediocre. Not long after you arrived at the Foreign Service Institute, Dr. Yates recommended you to my father as a teacher. That's the whole story," he concluded with a smile.

"What a small world," I marveled, and this got me thinking. Dr. Yates had recommended me as a language tutor to his good friend's only son but had never asked me how my pupil was progressing. In fact, he had recommended my services to a number of people and companies in need of a teacher or a translator, helping me to establish my new life here, and had never asked how the jobs turned out. I realized now how much confidence he had in me. I also realized how much of the warmth I had experienced in the United States emanated from the Foreign Service Institute and from my department head, Dr. Yates.

As I looked around, I was drawn to the floor-to-ceiling bookcases flanking the fireplace. I had never seen such exquisite books in any house since arriving in the United States. Leather-bound books! Could I touch them?

"Go ahead and examine them," Joe offered, opening the glass front of the bookcase. I pulled out a small book in German. I knew it was German because every day I passed by the beautiful bulletin board displays maintained by the Foreign Service Institute's German language section. Now I savored the elegantly engraved design on the book cover, the delicate illustrations, and the golden edges on each page. I saw an illustration showing God and the Devil in a dialogue, which reminded me of *Faust*. Could this be Goethe's famous poem?

From behind me came Joe's voice. "I tried my best to read the original. For Goethe, I studied German. For Dante, I studied Italian. For Diderot, I studied French. For Wang Wei, I studied Chinese."

Joe's words made me suddenly aware of a huge void in my life. I was studying English for survival, not for Shakespeare. As if sensing my distress, Joe looked me in the eye as I replaced the book on the shelf and gently closed the bookcase door saying, "I have my regrets, too: after all, I didn't study Russian for Pushkin."

I had studied Russian for six years, but not for Pushkin, either. In junior high school, I had to study Russian while my classmates could choose either Russian or English. The authorities were determined that I should give up the idea of ever going home. However, as one door closed on me, another door opened up. Russian class was rigid and boring. It wasn't that the teachers were poor; on the contrary, they wanted to be interesting, but the teaching materials were terrible. We did not learn how to say "drink a glass of milk" or "eat a piece of bread." Rather, the texts we used had us saying things like "Marxism and Leninism," "socialism," and "dictatorship of the proletariat." By the time I graduated from high school, our command of Russian enabled us to translate the Chinese Communist Party's weighty and painfully dry "Nine articles criticizing Nikita Khrushchev's revisionism."

But language is a fascinating thing. Once I figured out the grammar, with the help of a Russian-Chinese dictionary, I was able to read Pushkin's poetry.

At one party around a campfire, as I recited *The Story of the Fisherman and the Golden Fish*, author Lao She, or Grandpa Shu, as I called him, stood with his cane watching me, an approving and encouraging smile wreathing his features. For as long as I had known him, I had never seen him smile so warmly. This smile was neither bitter nor forced but rather pensive. When we last saw each other, I read Pushkin's poem *Happiness* to him. That was in 1964, just before I was sent from Beijing to the countryside. Grandpa Shu could not do anything for me. As I bid him farewell, his parting four words were "Eat enough, dress warmly." Two years later, sadly, he drowned himself in a lake. For the next twelve years, I tried to eat enough and dress warmly but failed miserably.

In front of me was a rectangular tray. Underneath its transparent surface glaze lay an elegant grayish textile in a pattern of dark gray leaves and stems and a lighter shade of gray flowers. On the tray sat a Japanese-style copper teapot plated in silver and mugs that were used as teacups, as well as a sugar bowl, creamer, and even a honey bowl. Drinking green tea had never been so complicated, and I ran out of energy to ask more questions as culture shock set in. The person in front of me was born with the proverbial silver spoon in his mouth. Eating enough and dressing warmly were never problems. He did not have to earn a living with blood, sweat, or tears. The beautiful objects on the beautiful tray suddenly created a gap a thousand miles wide between us.

Noticing my silence, Joe enthusiastically added sugar cubes and cream to my tea. "Chinese books are always at my bedside," he told me, explaining the lack of Chinese books on those lovely bookshelves. I smiled, relieved that he did not perceive the real reason behind my silence.

I picked up a very heavy spoon. It had to be silver, and it stood out against the grayish tea set. I stirred my tea and then laid it on the saucer, which was also a part of the tea set.

"In a country with a healthy financial system, anyone can buy and sell stocks and bonds from home. Long-term bonds are safer than short-term ones, which carry greater risk. Although trading stocks does not constitute actual production, the circulation of funds definitely promotes production. In this area, I am blessed with a particular talent." Joe was the first person to talk to me about trading stocks. Grandma was, of course, an expert in this field. But I was born at the wrong time, a time when life was extremely difficult for everyone, and in a country without a market-based financial system. It would have been useless for her to pass on to me the tricks of the trade, and we never touched on the subject during our many talks over the years. Even after I was granted permission to leave China, she didn't raise the subject; perhaps she felt that the game of finance was way beyond my reach.

But on this cold winter night in Joe's elegant residence, he casually opened a window for me. I learned that anyone could participate in the Wall Street game. Always wandering through the halls of world literature,

Joe was not completely dependent on his wealthy father for money; he spent part of his time playing the market. This gave him freedom, freedom to choose his lifestyle and place of residence. Looking around, I remarked, "I figure there are only two principles to follow: scarcity equals value, and buy low, sell high."

"You'll be invincible one day if you put your mind to it," Joe pronounced.

"It's getting late," I said, cupping the warm mug of tea with both hands. Joe rose immediately to phone Tom downstairs for a cab.

"What is it the Chinese say?" Joe was not really asking me but searching for his own answer. "Better walk ten miles than take one risky step." In this bitter cold with slippery roads, calling a cab was naturally a practical step to avoid risk. I could imagine Joe calling a cab on bad weather days. In a minute, Tom called to say that a cab was waiting at the door.

Taking the elevator down, I noticed how respectful Tom was. He opened the car door for me and then did the same for Joe. He stood there in the freezing rain even as the cab started to pull away.

The taxi was much faster than the bus. I stepped out of the car and started to walk towards the door of my apartment building. The cab did not move. Only when I was inside the door did the cab slowly drive away. It dawned on me that I was witnessing something I had never experienced during my growing years: good manners that came from respect. Through my curtain, I could see the flickering red tail lights of the cab carefully moving onto Route 50. At that moment, I felt the closeness of Joe. Every day I spent in the United States shrank the distance between us.

Cute little Pele came up to me. He was hungry, but he didn't press his claim. Instead, he rubbed his head against my hand. I took a plump ear of corn from the box; cold, it still smelled appetizing. Pele sniffed it and turned away. I opened the refrigerator, took out the milk, and poured some into his bowl. Pele trotted over enthusiastically, wagging his tail. I heated leftover stir-fried green beans from the day before. The aroma brought Pele to his food bowl, waiting for dinner. That evening Pele had milk and Chinese food while I had instant coffee and corn on the cob.

Suddenly I started to notice my movements. Coffee melted instantly as I poured boiling water into the tall mug. With a stainless-steel spoon I scooped a spoonful of powdered creamer into the coffee and then added a spoonful of sugar as well. The spoon was short, so I picked up a brown plastic stirrer from McDonald's. It was perfect for stirring coffee and also often served as a bookmark. I sometimes carried it to the office. Clean and dry, it quietly stayed between the pages. I smiled, thinking of Joe's misty tea set.

A year earlier, in 1978, I had walked into the State Department and handed the guard in the lobby a letter from the consulate general in Hong Kong. The guard had politely asked me to take a seat, then picked up the phone and held a brief conversation. After hanging up, he broke into a broad smile and told me that the officials on the China Desk were waiting for me. I had known of these people before I knew the word "desk." "China Desk" was the unofficial name of the office officially known as the "Office of Chinese Affairs." There were quite a few China experts who were waiting for me, an American rescued from China and returned to the United States.

A beautiful African-American woman soon entered the lobby at a quick pace. She smiled, extending her warm hands. Carrying my small suitcase, I followed her upstairs. As the office door opened, the most heart-warming expressions in Chinese greeted me:

"Good heavens, you're finally here!"

"You must be hungry."

"Did the stewardess on the plane take good care of you?"

I couldn't stop tears rolling down my cheeks, but I finally calmed down and sat. The office director who talked to me was Mr. Roy. The lovely African-American woman was Sylvia.

Mr. Roy asked me, "What do you most want to do right now?"

Without hesitation I replied, "Learn English. Find a job."

Smiling, Mr. Roy softly asked, "Do you have any money?"

The Chinese renminbi I took with me had been converted into Hong Kong dollars, which I had used to buy a dictionary, some clothing, and American dollars, which I had used for the taxi fare from the airport to the State Department. Searching my pocket, I triumphantly pulled out one American dollar, worth about eight renminbi. For many years in China, I never had eight renminbi in my pocket, so I did not feel embarrassed or poor at all.

"Find her some money," Mr. Roy immediately ordered his staff. After everyone else had left, he asked, "This country is huge. Where would you like to live?"

I took out my father's photo from an inner jacket pocket. That two-inch picture had accompanied me to Shanxi, to Xinjiang, to Hong Kong, and to Washington. It was creased and the edges were dog-eared. I had shown it to the Consul General in Hong Kong.

"General H was the highest-ranking American military representative in Panama. He fell ill with equatorial fever there and died on his way back to Washington at the age of fifty-six. I could tell from Mr. Roy's calm demeanor as he informed me of my father's death that he had really been waiting for me. I learned that my father had been a general. It sounded plausible that a field officer in the 1940s could be a general in the 1960s. I also noticed that Mr. Roy used the formal term "fell ill" used in written communications.

So, he was gone, and we are forever separated. Perhaps that was for the best. From then on, nothing, not even language, could separate us. When did he die? In 1968. I had been in Xinjiang, on the verge of death myself. Where was he buried? Arlington National Cemetery.

"I'd like to live in Arlington, to be close to him," I told Mr. Roy, my mouth completely dry.

Watching complicated emotions pass across my face, Mr. Roy quietly prompted, "We can help you find some relatives. Perhaps your father has siblings in America."

My finger touched the dollar bill in my pocket, and suddenly I could feel the limitation it represented. This person gave me life, gave me a strong will to live; I had refused to turn my back on him even if it meant my life. What did his siblings have to do with me? I was a stranger to them, perhaps an undesirable one or an unexpected burden. As these thoughts ran through my mind, I smiled and said, "Thank you for your suggestions, but I'd rather be on my own."

Mr. Roy wasn't ready to give up. "Perhaps they'd be willing to help you." I thought perhaps the opposite was true. My present relationship with my father was perfect. I had found out what I needed to know, which was good. I wanted to keep things simple, without the baggage that might come with an unknown family: pity, charity, indifference, displeasure, hypocrisy. This could be torture - much worse than hard work and thrifty living.

My face must have shown the uncertain calculations racing through my mind. Mr. Roy remained silent, waiting for me to speak. I smiled and asked, "What language do people speak in Panama?"

"Spanish," Mr. Roy answered. We were both relieved.

At that moment, Sylvia reappeared. Holding a paper, she announced, "Good news! The Arlington County government has a fund established by some kind-hearted person specifically for use by American citizens returning after being stranded abroad for many years and who cannot speak English. Money from the fund can be used in any amount but only during the first three months after the citizen's return. The fund has been sitting earning interest for more than twenty years and, until now, no one has met its requirements. So, let's go to the Arlington County government offices now. There's a lot of work to do."

I was stunned. What luck – money sitting unused for twenty years, waiting for me to come "home" and use it.

Mr. Roy was really pleased. "Sylvia will help you with the details. Call me directly if there are any problems." He formally handed me his business card, which I accepted equally formally. Thanking him, I left.

Sylvia and I left the State Department in an official car. I later found out that on that same day the American government was pressing the Chinese government to give an accounting of all the American citizens still detained in China, demanding that the Chinese issue them exit visas as soon as possible, allow them to contact American officials in China, and provide them with transportation and travel documents so that they could leave China without delay.

So many demands! The American government was doing everything possible to facilitate its citizens' long-overdue return. My return proved that China's solemn assertions in more than a hundred meetings in Warsaw over fifteen years that no Americans were detained in China were just bald-faced lies. I also had no idea that on that day officials on the China Desk worked late into the night on my behalf. I found myself flustered in a beautiful new world of material civilization. Suddenly I discovered "I have everything now."

"I'm Linda," a blonde woman with a ruddy complexion greeted us as she descended the steps of the Arlington County government building. She stretched out her hand, not to shake mine, but to embrace me. I smiled, my thin body comfortable in her embrace. Linda dismissed our driver, saying that she would take Sylvia and me to our destination. Once again, I picked up my small suitcase and said goodbye to the driver, who drove away in the State Department car.

"Please sign here. Then we'll go buy some necessities for you." Linda showed Sylvia a document. After scanning the document, Sylvia smiled and nodded, and I signed the paper.

Linda drove. On the way, she told us that, while waiting for us, she had found me an apartment close to a bus stop. "This is very important, at least until you learn to drive. You can move after three months if you don't like the place. We have signed a three-month lease and the rent is already paid." Overwhelmed, I couldn't speak - only nod.

Was this a furniture store? I couldn't even see the back of the store. What Linda had done was quite an eye-opener for me. She held in her hand a list of everything necessary to furnish a living room, dining room, bedroom, and study. The store manager came to greet us as soon as we walked in. Examining Linda's list, he asked what colors we had in mind. All three of them looked at me expectantly. I told Sylvia, "I prefer warm colors such as beige and light brown – something with a sunny feel." What I did not say was that, as someone who had lived in a dank underground dungeon for nine years, what I craved most was sunlight and fresh air. The store manager nodded and led the way. As we followed, I quietly asked Sylvia, "I really have a study?"

Linda explained it all to me in detail. "A one-bedroom apartment's monthly rent is $200. For another $20 a month, you can add a study, which could serve as a small bedroom." My God! Two hundred-twenty dollars a month is equivalent to 1760 renminbi. What kind of palace would I be living in that cost so much? Seeing my consternation, Sylvia pressed my hand reassuringly and said, "Don't worry. The rent is cheap. Trust me."

We looked at a double bed, two night stands, and a tall chest of drawers, all in a natural wood color. The mattress was a Simmons. Why did I need a double bed? I had never slept in a double bed. My head was swimming. "Relax," Linda said. "You'll soon get used to it."

The rectangular dining table was light brown with stripes and came with six matching chairs. As I touched it, a tear rolled down my cheek. The beautiful table felt firm yet gentle under my hand. The living room suite consisted of a large sofa and two upholstered chairs, all in a light brown floral design. The manager pointed out that the large sofa was actually a sofa bed that opened up into a double bed. "This will be handy when you have visitors," Sylvia told me. Feeling a bit dizzy, I couldn't say a word. Three small coffee tables and one large one, a floor lamp, and two table lamps? Why did I need so many lamps? I opened my mouth, but no sound came out.

A desk with four drawers and a matching chair, a wide bookcase, and a desk lamp with a green shade were selected. I had seen this kind of lamp on Uncle Pan's desk in his apartment in the Chinese Academy of Science compound in Zhongguan Village. I told Sylvia, "I like this lamp very much." The store manager was happy to hear that and said that he personally liked that set of oak furniture – it was cozy and reliable.

"Have we missed anything?" Sylvia and Linda double checked the list and added a few more lamps.

The chosen pieces were swiftly wrapped and moved out. Linda told me that the furniture would be placed in my apartment while we continued to shop. "You'll spend your first night in America in your own apartment."

The store manager presented the bill, and Linda extracted a checkbook from her briefcase. "This is the second check," she said. "The first was for the apartment rent." Remarking the amount, I haltingly said, "I hope I haven't spent all the money. I'd like to keep some for others like me." Linda gently patted my hand. "We're actually quite frugal. Everything we've bought is necessary. You haven't spent a fraction of the money available."

Next door to the furniture store was a department store. Bags of bed linens, a few sets of towels, many boxes of pots and pans – Sylvia and Linda were shopping with gusto. I suggested buying a sewing kit and a pair of scissors, after which I just stood around with nothing to do.

Looking around, I noticed rows of colorful women's clothing. I couldn't help walking over to touch them, gorgeous blackish greens, so soft and of such fine workmanship, with the waist slightly tucked and a soft waistband. I knew from my experience at the garment factory that these garments were simple but well-tailored.

As a saleslady approached me with a friendly smile, I hurriedly retracted my hand. Sylvia appeared at my side and said a few words to the saleslady, who then took out a measuring tape from her pocket to take my measurements. Sylvia explained that I could only wear a size 6 or 8 at present, but suggested getting a size 8 or 10 since I was so tall. "You'll look so much prettier when your figure fills out," she said.

Sylvia and Linda enthusiastically selected a pile of clothing for me. In the fitting room, I found not only outerwear, but underwear as well. From the other side of the fitting room door, Sylvia asked if there was any problem. "How can I try on the underwear?" I asked. "What if it doesn't fit?"

"No problem," Sylvia replied. You have to try them on to find out." Really! They fit! And they were lovely! Underwear, pantyhose, blouses, pants, skirts, long coats, short jackets, and even that blackish-green dress all took their place on the cashier's counter.

"Sleepwear! I almost forgot!" Linda cheerfully exclaimed. My face turned red when I saw the sexy sleepwear. It seemed fit only for goddesses. Instead, I insisted on buying two sets of pajamas – one sky blue and one white with tiny pink flowers. Linda and Sylvia did not try to talk me out of my choice. All this clothing, together with some bottles of unknown substances, glasses, a small television from the electrical appliance department, a radio, toaster, iron, and vacuum cleaner were sent to "my" apartment after Linda wrote another check.

"I'm starving. Let's go eat and then visit the supermarket for groceries and drinks," Linda suggested.

Noticing me handle a knife and fork with no difficulty, Linda expressed surprise. I told her that, during the 1950s, I had opportunities to eat at the Moscow restaurant in the Soviet Exhibition Hall in the western part of Beijing. My companions laughed, and I continued, "It's now called the Beijing Exhibition Hall, but they still serve Western dishes such as borsch and Hungarian goulash." In this relaxed atmosphere, we talked about anything that came to mind. I was surprised to find that we were all born in 1946, just after World War II – part of the Baby Boom generation. "A generation that cherishes life and believes in positive thinking," they said, and I agreed.

I noticed that they treated me to dinner but split the bill between themselves. "Going Dutch" they called it. I was filled with gratitude and respect for these people who, as part of their jobs, were spending so much time and effort on me without touching the checkbook. I hoped that one day soon I could treat them to a dinner. Later, I learned that "going Dutch" meant that all the diners split the bill evenly. So, in this case, two people splitting the bill for three persons could not be considered "going Dutch." Still, I was grateful to them for introducing me to the idiom "going Dutch," the meaning of which I could never have guessed.

The supermarket was close to my new apartment. "You can walk to buy groceries if you want," Linda told me.

This supermarket was gigantic! Besides milk, eggs, bread, fresh produce, fruit, meat, juice, and other foodstuffs, I discovered soy sauce, vinegar, peppercorn salt, barbecue sauce, and instant noodles. Seeing labels with Chinese characters, such as Xin Dong Yang, Lee Kum Kee, and Wei Chuan, was like seeing family members. What most surprised me was that I now owned a two-wheeled shopping cart with a laundry basket that I could use to haul my groceries home. "The laundry room is in the basement of your building. This basket is indispensable," Linda thoughtfully informed me. The trunk of her car was packed with groceries and various odds-and-ends.

My apartment complex was brightly lit. The manger, a gray-haired woman, warmly greeted us, mentioning that the department store delivery truck had just left. As we opened the door of the apartment, a soft light from within spread onto the landing.

So, this would be my home. The furniture had been placed exactly where I would have placed it. It already gave the impression of having always been where it was. The soft, light-brown carpet blended harmoniously with the furniture. Before I knew it, we had stowed food, drinks, plates, pots, and pans in the capacious refrigerator and numerous kitchen cabinets. Linda adjusted the thermostat and hooked up the television and radio. Sylvia filled a kettle with water and placed it on the stove.

"This is a gas stove. Don't forget to turn it off when you are done using it." She carefully demonstrated how to operate the stove. I paid close attention, trying hard to remember everything she said.

The manager told me how to get to her office and then handed me two keys saying, "I'm Sue. Please come to see me tomorrow whenever you can. I hope you'll like this apartment."

As she wished me good night, the kettle on the stove started to whistle. I carefully removed the kettle from the burner, turned off the gas, and asked my two new friends, "The water is ready. Would you like tea or coffee?" They both applauded this milestone and said, "We'll help you make the bed, and then we'll have to go."

I stood watching them fit the thick, white bed pad over the mattress. A fitted bed sheet went snugly over the padding, followed by a matching top sheet. A soft, beige bedspread was placed on top. Pillow cases the same color as the sheets covered the two pillows. In this light, I noticed that they were not solid white, but featured a delicate design of blooming roses woven into the fabric.

Sylvia and Linda marched into the living room and unfolded the sofa bed. Sylvia held the bed linens in her hands while she explained that they were specifically designed for sofa beds and that they were different from regular bed linens. This time I helped them make the bed and fold it back into the sofa.

"Go to bed soon. I'll pick you up at 9:30 tomorrow morning for your medical check-up at the hospital." Again, Linda embraced me and then left with Sylvia. My watch read midnight as I closed the apartment door, but before launching into an examination of my feelings about the day's adventures, I took out my English-Chinese dictionary, notebook, and pen and jotted down the key words on all the labels and their meanings in Chinese.

All the things we bought that day seemed to have been swallowed up by cabinets and drawers. The apartment possessed an amazingly large capacity. I finally walked into my new bathroom, unwrapped a new bar of soap, and took a deep breath. Then I opened all the jars and bottles.

Each had a different fragrance. With the help of a dictionary, I soon learned that one was shampoo, another was facial lotion to be applied in the morning, and yet another was facial lotion to be used before bedtime. The last bottle was hand lotion.

After taking a bath and washing my hair, I wrapped myself in a big towel. In front of the mirror right behind the bathroom door, I tried on my first US-bought bra – a white, lacy, 34B. I could feel the difference right away. While my cotton bra from China flattened the breasts, this one gently followed my natural contours. Whatever fabric it was made of, it straightened my posture. Turning sideways, I was pleasantly surprised to see the beautiful curve running from my breasts to my lower abdomen.

I put on my new white pajamas and walked into my study. At the age of thirty-two, I finally had a study of my own. From my small suitcase I extracted my library: two volumes of *Gu Wen Guan Zhi* (ancient essays) in book jackets, a thread-bound edition of *Gu Shi Yuan* (ancient poetry) in a slipcover, a copy of *Wen Xin Diao Long* (ancient literary theory), Eliot's *Waste Land*, Romain Rolland's *Jean-Christophe* in four dilapidated volumes, one Russian-Chinese dictionary, *Selected Poems of Pushkin*, and a paperback Dante's *Inferno* with enough wear to argue convincingly that it had itself passed through hell. They all fit on my brand-new bookshelf. I then placed the English-Chinese dictionary, exercise book, and a pen on the desktop. Sitting down, I turned on the desk lamp and started reviewing the close to one hundred new vocabulary words that I had learned that day. Before I knew it, it was four o'clock in the morning. I told myself that I could still get four hours of sleep, so I turned off the lights and went to bed. I was asleep the moment my head hit the pillow.

I opened my eyes at exactly eight o'clock, feeling totally rejuvenated. Making a note to myself that four hours of sleep were plenty, I jumped out of bed to embrace the second day of my life in the United States.

As I made the bed, I realized that I had slept near the edge, leaving two-thirds of the bed undisturbed. I reminded myself that this bed was mine, that I didn't have to worry about people chasing me out of it in the middle of the night or being rousted to attend some urgent gathering. I really could sleep until dawn without a worry. This I told myself, yet over the following decades worry-free sleep proved elusive. When I thought I had slept well, the doctor said my sleep was light, like that of a bird that could be startled by the mere twang of a bow, ready to flee at any moment.

I finished making the bed and donned my new blouse and pants, neatly pressed and wrinkle-free. The classical music station was playing Dvorak's *New World* symphony, which perfectly matched my mood.

I had to take a blood test that day, so I could not eat breakfast. This left time to explore and look for ways to improve my new home. Venetian blinds on the two windows between the living and dining areas had been pulled down to block light from outside. Raising the blinds, I saw a large paved parking area downstairs surrounded by several four-story brick buildings. They were collectively known as "Lee Gardens." I also discovered a shiny rod mounted in the wall, probably for curtains. I got to thinking: wouldn't it be pretty to hang ivory-colored lace curtains? As I was pondering this, I saw Linda getting out of a car in the parking area. I grabbed my handbag, locked the door, and walked downstairs to meet her.

The doctors and nurses at the hospital were very pleasant. With much gesturing, I underwent a battery of tests, including an eye examination and a dental checkup with x-rays and cleaning. By noon, Linda and I were sitting in the empty waiting room waiting for the test results. Sylvia joined us with a thick English-Chinese medical dictionary.

The doctor who spoke to us wore a solemn expression. With the help of the dictionary, I learned my physical condition: underweight, seriously anemic, extremely low blood pressure, arrythmia, leaky mitral valve, occasional heart palpitations, serious rheumatoid arthritis, congenital cracked and bent vertebra, serious inflammation of rib cartilage, chronic kidney infection that had progressed into acute infection, stomach ulcer, a left eye that was almost legally blind, serious iodine deficiency, serious periodontitis.... Was I still alive? I broke out laughing. The doctor looked up from the thick pile of lab reports to gaze at me through his glasses with the expression of one looking at a dying person. Sylvia and Linda naturally grasped the doctor's concern. They calmly asked for his advice.

I could imagine, even without translation, what the doctor had to say about me: that my days were numbered. "Do whatever you want to do and eat whatever you want to eat" were his words. "Most people cannot last very long in such a condition," he told Sylvia and Linda.

But I was not "most people." I had charged out of the inferno.

With a smile on my face, I thumbed my nose at Fate and screamed at the top of my lungs, "You have already taken my father! You threw me on a trash heap at the end of the earth to die and be forgotten! And now you're rushing to send me somewhere else? No way! I haven't lived yet! I want to stay around and live a decent life for a while!"

Fate was oblivious to me. I decided to save myself.

Now it was my turn to comfort my two new friends. I smiled and through body language let them know that I was ready to face my physical problems with all the determination I could muster.

With Sylvia's help, I calmly asked the doctor to help me fight the kidney infection and correct my bent vertebra. The doctor seemed surprised. He told me that those two problems could probably be resolved with appropriate medication and a metal back brace. The back brace was not as heavy as I had expected, and it did wonders in alleviating my back pain.

Medications in hand, I said goodbye to the doctor. Wearing a more relaxed look than earlier, he replied, "See you in two months, if you're willing." I told him I definitely would.

My upbeat attitude also seemed to hearten Sylvia and Linda, neither of whom looked as worried as before. On our way back, Linda handed me a month's living expenses plus monthly passes for the bus and subway. I asked them for help in arranging English lessons and then said cheerfully that I would like to buy some fabric to make curtains. They exchanged happy looks and drove me to a store right in front of a bus stop. Sylvia said that if I took the bus for two stops, I would see my apartment complex.

The fabric store was descriptively, if unimaginatively, named the G Street Fabric Store. At the time, I didn't know that it was famous. The main store was situated on G Street in downtown Washington, D.C. On my second day in the United States, I entered this store with a thick envelope in my bag and a new back brace that made me forget about my pain. Inside I found myself surrounded by an ocean of fabrics. My work experience in a Beijing clothing factory had given me eyes as sharp as a ruler when it came to estimating how much fabric a given project would require. For less than twenty dollars, I bought a lacy, ivory-colored fabric. What drew me to this fabric was its large, elegant tulips.

I navigated home on the bus with no trouble at all. In the manager's office, Sue warmly greeted me and handed me a map, a printed card with the Lee Gardens address, and a bus route map and timetable. She also marked my address on both maps lest I get lost. I figured that if I could find my way from Xinjiang to Washington D.C., I could certainly find my way to Lee Gardens from anywhere.

After thanking Sue, I went home in a cheerful mood and cooked myself a bowl of noodles with some spinach and two slices of ham and two poached eggs. I turned on my color television and watched the weather report while I ate dinner. For the longest time, I found television graphics very helpful in increasing my vocabulary.

After dinner, I made myself a cup of coffee, spread out the fabric, and started to cut and sew. The apartment took on a much cozier look with the new curtains. I ran outside to look up at my windows on the second floor; they sure looked pretty.

Curtain project completed, I took out paper and pen to write a letter to Grandma, telling her about my new apartment, the convenient public transit system, and all the amenities that my apartment contained. Regarding my medical examination, I told her about the back brace and antibiotics and that all was well. I introduced my new friends, Sylvia and Linda, and described the tulip pattern on my curtains. I did not mention my father; instead, I wrote about the help I had received from the American government in settling down. I excitedly informed her about soon starting English language classes at a language center. I mentioned all the good news but steered clear of forbidden subjects. I knew that the letter would be thoroughly inspected by the Chinese government before reaching Grandma's hands. I carefully checked every word before sealing and addressing the envelope. It was very satisfying to see my return address in beautiful handwritten letters in English.

Next, I opened the map Sue had given me and looked for Arlington National Cemetery. It was not far away. "I'll come to visit you quietly, all by myself," I promised.

A cold night in early 1979 found me sitting at the same light brown dining table reminiscing about the eventful days surrounding my arrival one year earlier. Now all my windows sported curtains. Bookshelves were filled with books. I had built a whole wall of books using boards and metal L-brackets. I made time in my busy schedule to visit friends. Now I understood that what Linda had procured for me were in fact the most basic necessities. I also realized that Sylvia was absolutely right: the monthly rent on my apartment, which cost only one-seventh of my monthly salary, was reasonable indeed. I was extremely comfortable living here. Before three months were up, I signed a one-year rental agreement. Since the lease was for a longer period, the rent was ten dollars a month less, much to my surprise. The sofa bed had been pulled out for Maddie, who would curl up on it while muttering, "This place is paradise."

After two months in paradise, my bra size had grown to 36B. When I went back to the doctor who had warned me that my days were numbered, he didn't recognize me. After telling him my name, he asked what I had been eating. I told him everything, proudly adding that I was especially fond of McDonalds. "My God!" he gasped. I could see that he was brimming with advice and exhortations, but seeing the English-Chinese medical dictionary in my hand, he contented himself with urging me to see him again in two months before waving goodbye.

I was wearing size 12 and 38C bras when Joe met me for the first time. I stayed at this size for many years.

Now, recalling those well-equipped tractors in downtown Washington and Joe's almost too-elegant-to-believe condo, I broke out in happy laughter. It would come, just like in the movie *Lenin in October,* where Lenin's chief bodyguard, Vassily, comforts his wife, saying, "There will be bread; there will be milk, too." I had my doubts about Vassily's promise, but I was confident that I had bid farewell to starvation, both physical and intellectual.

Three years later, when my husband and I had just gotten married, he admitted that he had little faith in the stock market, since his father had hardly made a profit in a lifetime of investing. When I made no comment, he continued, "Now we have some spare cash, and we should be investing in stocks, but I don't know what to buy." I opened the window and asked smilingly, "What do you see out there?" Surprised, he peered outside before replying, "Cars. Lots of cars." Leading him along my line of thought, I said, "Cars need gasoline, which means profits for oil companies." "But which one?" he asked. "There are so many." I gazed at the distant neon lights and confidently suggested, "Why not Exxon?" And it turned out to be an excellent investment for us.

Joe had laughingly remarked once that there was no direct correlation between knowledge of economics and successful investment. But I clearly remembered that, back in 1979, he predicted that I would be successful if I decided to invest.

For years afterward, I never saw a tea tray as gorgeous as Joe's, not even in New York City. I tried describing it to a long line of gift shop managers and clerks: transparent, insulated material over a textile base. They showed me many elegant tea trays, but none that resembled Joe's. It was not until 1996, seventeen years later, in Athens, that I spotted the beautiful tray from a Paris maker. I immediately bought three: one large, one small, and one medium, and they have never failed to attract admiring eyes at tea parties ever since.

Of course, neither did I ever expect to have the opportunity to carry on companionable conversations with Apollo at Delphi during a three-year posting in Athens. I confided to this most-approachable god that in 1978 I had been railing mightily against my fate. Apollo shook his head and sighed. "Oh, you mustn't do that. No one can argue with Fate. Even I am subject to its dictates. Your path has switched from one full of dangers to a much safer one, and you avoided meeting Hades too soon. This is probably the working of Fate, rather than the result of your strong will to survive."

After a while, the all-knowing Apollo added softly, "To be honest, Fate has treated you well." I nodded in agreement, and Apollo smiled tenderly.

On this cold night in 1979, I could not have foreseen all the beautiful things that lay ahead. But what Joe said to me that night filled me with self-confidence. On this freezing cold evening, I knew that there was no distance between Joe, who was sitting by his gas fireplace holding a leather-bound book, and myself, sitting at the dinner table with a stirrer from McDonalds in my hand. We seemed so close.

CHAPTER 6

DR. YATES

D r. Yates, the director of FSI's East Asian languages program, was a very smart man. Whether making requests or issuing directions, he was always calm and friendly. I knew from Joe that he had a military background, and his bearing confirmed it. He wore a suit every day and always looked neat and composed. At the Chinese section's faculty meetings at the end of the day, only he and I never appeared rumpled and worn out.

Late one Friday afternoon, after making xerox copies of materials for my advanced students, I entered the conference room where the other teachers sat discussing their weekend plans. Dr. Yates asked about a few students' progress and listened to the reports of the teachers responsible for those students. Business concluded, Dr. Yates turned to me and asked, "Your blouse still looks fresh at the end of the day. What's it made of?" I was wearing a white blouse I had purchased in Hong Kong.

"Silk," I replied.

Ms. D, one of the teachers, smirked, "You've been here more than six months, and you're still wearing the clothes you arrived in?" Ignoring her, Dr. Yates asked me, "Your silk blouses, do you wash and iron them yourself?" Before I could reply, Ms. O, another teacher, simpered, "No one washes and irons their own silk clothes these days." Ms. C chimed in, "Maybe. Dry cleaning isn't cheap. If you don't have the money, you have to do it yourself." With my focus on Dr. Yates and my students' schedules, I hardly heard the words issuing from their heavily made-up faces.

"Yes," I told Dr. Yates. "I take care of my own clothes. People have been cleaning silk clothing for thousands of years, long before dry cleaning existed."

D, O, and C looked at each other expectantly.

Dr. Yates smiled. "Great," he said. "There's a women's clothing company that is planning to promote a line of silk blouses. Market research showed that many American women like the blouses but are concerned about the cost of dry cleaning them after every wearing. The company has asked us for help. They want to know if we have anyone who can and is willing to demonstrate on TV how to wash and iron silk. I think you can handle this." Smiles froze on the faces of the Gang of Three. Dr. Yates bounced up from his chair cheerfully and looked at his watch. "The company is sending a car to pick you up. Gather your things and meet them downstairs." It was an hour and a half before quitting time when Dr. Yates sent me off on this mission that no one else could or wanted to undertake.

"You think I can go on American television?" I asked him quietly.

"You'll be fine," he replied with a warm smile.

"I'll be on my way then. See you Monday."

Back in my classroom, I packed my tote bag, turned off the lights, and walked into the hallway. The doors of the other teachers' classrooms were closed and the hallway empty. The only sound was the tap-tap-tapping of my heels on the linoleum floor. I took the elevator down to the lobby. A friendly security guard walked over, saying that Dr. Yates had instructed him to see that I got into the car.

Friendly faces welcomed me as I climbed into the clothing company's car. A van from a local TV station was behind us. A woman from the clothing company sat with me in the back seat. "After working all day, your blouse still looks great," she commented. Her expression told me that she was speaking sincerely. After half an hour's drive, we arrived at the TV station. In the studio, a shiny, white, square laundry tub sat below a wall shelf filled with a variety of detergents and soaps. I could take my pick. I asked David, one of the station employees, if they had any Ivory soap. Everyone looked at me, surprise written all over their faces.

"It's what I use," I told him. His expression showed disbelief. "You really use Ivory soap on silk?" he asked. I nodded, surprised by the jubilant expressions of the onlookers, especially the clothing company's representative.

"Great."

"Magic!"

"Wonderful!"

I didn't grasp the reason for their delight. I only knew that Ivory soap was very reliable. It even removed ink stains.

Waiting for David to bring the Ivory soap, I examined the blouse I was going to wash. It hung on a hanger beside the laundry tub. The color? Turquoise. Pure silk. The collar had yellowed, and the front held ketchup and coffee stains. I took a ballpoint pen from David and confidently added a long line on the sleeve of the blouse. David's small, knowing smile disappeared, replaced by a very serious look. The clothing company's representative looked aghast.

I ran lukewarm water into the laundry tub and placed the soiled blouse in the water. "Water is best for silk. We'll let the blouse soak for ten minutes."

"While we're waiting, let's get a close-up of your blouse, the one you've been wearing all day," David said. I stood still while the camera focused on my blouse. Ten minutes later, there was a fresh bar of Ivory soap by the laundry tub. I rubbed a little water on the soap and carefully soaped the stained areas of the blouse. Then I gently rubbed the stained areas against each other. The ketchup and coffee stains quickly disappeared and the yellow on the collar faded considerably. The line of ink on the sleeve was much shorter. Confidently, I immersed the blouse in the water again, re-soaped the still-soiled areas, and repeated the gentle rubbing. Holding it up to the light, I was pleased to see that all the stains were gone. The onlookers applauded.

After rinsing the blouse twice in warm, clean water, I pressed it between my palms to remove excess water. I hung it up still dripping and gently tugged on the collar and down the front to help prevent wrinkles. "We'll have to wait quite a while before we can iron it," I announced. No sooner had I spoken than a white electric fan on a side table started turning quietly. In a few minutes the blouse was no longer wet, just damp. "That's enough," I told David. "Silk's easiest to iron when damp."

An ironing board was already set up. On it was a fine, snow-white cloth. There was even a metal stand on one end of the board for resting the iron. The iron's weight was just right. I turned the blouse inside out and started to iron. The skill I had developed through trial and error at the clothing factory in China was barely exercised by the mere ironing of a blouse. I turned the blouse right side out and picked up the white cloth. Placing it between the iron and the blouse, I ironed the tips of the collars, the cuffs, the lapels, and especially the button holes and the areas around the buttons until there wasn't a single wrinkle to be seen. I hung this splendid-looking blouse on a hanger amid applause and cheers.

"Absolutely brilliant! In your hands, the iron is an instrument that achieves perfection: from left hand to right hand and from your right hand back to your left. I'm totally dazzled," David gushed. He sprayed more mist on the blouse, returning it to a semi-dry state. "Now please slow down and do it one more time."

The image of gentle and decorous Master Li teaching me how to iron a dress suit appeared before my eyes. She demonstrated every movement with perfect precision, everything clean and neat. In the factory, we had a daily quota to meet. One could not leave work until the quota was met. I only worked in the clothing factory for a year and a half, with the last eight months under constant police surveillance, so I never had an apprentice of my own or any chance to demonstrate my skills. Most unexpectedly, I found in America that these skills won considerable praise. I steadied myself and carefully started to iron again, making sure that every movement was scrupulously accurate. When the filming of this television program was completed, enthusiastic applause broke out.

To my great surprise, a well-dressed gentleman, one of the managers of the women's clothing company sponsoring the program, approached me after the filming. Handing me an envelope containing payment for my demonstration, he said, "It seems to me that you really like this iron. Would you like to keep it, and the ironing board as well? They seem to come alive in your hands."

The same car and the same lady who had picked me up earlier took me home after the filming.

"Your movements were so graceful, so quick and precise. Where did you learn how to do that?"

It was in a clothing factory in Beijing, where, every twenty-six minutes, a pair of blue jeans would have to be sewn and the ironing time could not exceed two minutes.

The lady's eyes filled with tears.

"Pardon me for mentioning it, but Dr. Yates told us something of your background. We were shocked to learn of such cruelty."

I smiled and patted her hand lightly. Then I asked, "Why were you all so happy when I wanted to use Ivory soap today?"

She smiled, too. "It's almost embarrassing to admit, but Ivory soap is the cheapest soap in America. Nobody would have guessed that it could be used to wash silk. We all expected you to use something more expensive. Your demonstration will make consumers very happy."

After she dropped me off at home, I took the check from the envelope and stared at it. It amounted to more than two months of my rent. I vaguely realized that, whereas manual work in China was considered punishment, in America it was actually respected and carried nice rewards. As I touched the iron through its insulated bag and the folded ironing board, I felt a pang of heartache thinking of the skilled workers in China who worked the clothing factories' sewing machines until they almost went blind. What rewards did their dexterous hands earn them? The products they created were sold for a fortune, but only one-hundredth, one-thousandth, or one ten-thousandth of the profit went to them. All the while the working class in China was called the "leading class!"

Joe came to class on Sunday morning with a big smile on his face and a box tied with ribbon in his hands. "A delivery man just left this for you," he announced. Tucked under the ribbon was an envelope from the company that made Ivory soap containing a letter, written in a flowery font, expressing gratitude for my choosing their product for my television demonstration. "To show our gratitude, please accept a box of our products," the letter concluded.

"Good heavens! What did you do with that ordinary soap?" Joe wondered.

"I used it to remove stains from a silk blouse." I couldn't help chuckling as I opened the box, which turned out to hold twelve extra-large bars of Ivory soap in a nice lavender plastic box with the word "Ivory" printed on it in gilt letters. A thoughtful bonus: the plastic box was waterproof so as to keep the soap dry.

Joe, who had never washed his own clothes, listened to my story about the events on Friday afternoon. "Your demonstration greatly helped not only the clothing company but the company that makes Ivory soap as well," he assured me. "Because they never would have guessed that their product could be used on such a grand mission."

Frowning, I asked, "Why do you say "grand"?

Joe calmly explained. "Silk is considered a high-class fabric. People usually dry clean it. The clothing company wants to sell silk blouses that have to be washed after every wearing, which means that the cost of dry-cleaning would soon exceed the price of the blouse. Now, not only have you demonstrated how to wash and iron silk blouses, you chose inexpensive Ivory soap to do the job, showing American women that they can afford to wear silk. Imagine how this helps the clothing company. When the river rises, so does the boat on it, in this case the indispensable Ivory soap, which has risen from common and ordinary to distinctive. It's no wonder that both companies are grateful to you. Oh yes, they should also thank Dr. Yates, whose recommendation got the ball rolling." Joe stopped and looked at me with a smile.

I felt very grateful for Dr. Yates's encouragement, but I felt some concern, too. I had honed my skills in an adverse environment under the supervision of a trained professional in a clothing factory. Could American women living in comparative leisure learn these skills, too? Joe reassured me. "Americans love to use their hands. They'll pick it up quickly if there is someone to teach them." This gave rise to a new question. "Why do Americans love to use their hands?"

Joe considered for a bit before replying. "The concept of 'Those who work with their brains rule, and those who work with their muscles are ruled' simply does not exist in America. Secondly, most Americans are descendants of immigrants. Immigrants are basically people who have left their homelands, for whatever reasons, to create a new life in this New World. Besides strong willpower, they also needed a pair of skillful hands to survive here. Hence, skilled craftsmen are generally respected. At the same time, they are proud of their ability to have achieved so much with their hands."

I snuck a glance at Joe's fine, callous-free hands and kept silent.

With a big smile, Joe told me he had acquired one skill from his father: placing a miniature model boat inside a narrow-necked glass bottle, turning an ordinary object into a work of art. "The boat is constructed folded up," he explained. "After pushing it through the bottle's neck with a pair of long, slender tweezers, the boat will resume its original shape. This is an old, traditional English skill. Father does it well, but I do it better." Joe didn't try to hide his pride.

"Someday I'll give you a present: a model of a 102-foot, 170-ton sail boat with over 5000 square feet of sail. I'll set it in a glass bottle 375-millimeters around with a 2-centimeter diameter neck. Oh, I almost forgot to mention that this boat, the 'America', will be surrounded by blue sea water dotted with white caps."

Without question, such a skill would require slender, well-cared-for hands. I could only nod in agreement.

Joe, however, had a question: why was I assigned to a clothing factory by Beijing's Office for the Placement of Educated Urban Youth Working in Rural and Mountainous Areas?

In the spring of 1976, I was thirty years old and returning to Beijing from Xinjiang. The employees at the placement office told me, "At your age and being a woman with a complicated family background, no state-owned enterprise will take you. Try a collective unit. This garment factory sounds right for you. Besides, it isn't hard labor, and the skills you learn will enable you to make your own clothes, saving you money." Thus was the universe of my possibilities delimited in a few words.

Joe zeroed in on the terms "state-owned" and "collective" and asked about the differences between state-owned and collective enterprises. I explained that small factories under the collective ownership system had to assume responsibility for their own profits and losses. The wages and benefits they offered their workers were smaller than in state-run factories. If state-run factories lost money, the government made up the losses, whereas collective ownership units would require their workers to work more or take lower wages and fewer benefits.

The factory where I used to work was a collectively owned unit which, before the Cultural Revolution, had a good business producing the elaborate costumes found in Chinese operas. During the Cultural Revolution, when only eight "model" operas could be performed, and those with just workers, peasants, and soldiers bouncing around the stage wearing simple, drab clothing, all that was left for the factory to produce was the curtain for the stage. Poverty gave rise to change. Factory managers arranged with export companies to produce suits, denim jeans, and jean jackets for the Hong Kong market. As the demand for jeans was high, the factory set up assembly lines. Master tailors would quickly cut out on big cutting boards the pieces of cloth used to make each pair of jeans. The pieces for each pair would be clipped together on hangers attached to a continuous belt that carried them to stations where employees would sew the pieces together on machines. Each pair of sewn jeans would be collected by workers from the pressing department for ironing, folding, and quality inspection. The finished goods were packed in cartons for shipping.

The clothing we made was subject to many layers of markups, but the factory's profit on a pair of jeans was quite small. High-volume manufacture was the only way to maintain an adequate income. Each worker had to sew eighteen pairs of jeans in eight hours, averaging no more than twenty-six minutes per pair. This left twelve minutes a day for lunch and bathroom breaks.

Joe was dumbfounded. I went on to tell him that the first job given to new employees was to sew stage curtains. Once these techniques were mastered with good speed, the next step was ironing. To do a good job, a worker had to be quick of eye and deft of hand. After mastering ironing skills, workers could move to the most critical job on the assembly line: sewing jeans. Only after a week or two sewing would a worker be able to complete a pair of jeans in twenty-six minutes or less and have any hope of fulfilling the daily quota in eight hours. At my age and with only one working eye, I had to exert all my energy every day just to earn my daily wage of one renminbi.

"One renminbi for eighteen pairs of jeans," Joe muttered to himself, figuring the accounts.

For spending an hour in front of a camera washing and ironing a blouse, I received five hundred dollars plus a handsome, new iron, a state-of-the-art ironing board, a dozen bars of soap, and endless gratitude. The contrast left me almost breathless with sadness. Actually, I had seen in Hong Kong jeans manufactured by our factory. While less expensive than jeans imported from the United States, they were still not that cheap. With my purse empty, I couldn't afford to buy a pair.

At our factory, a worker's monthly wage was just enough to buy one such pair of jeans; yet each worker had to sew at least 468 pairs of jeans each month. I didn't blame the factory's management. The factory director and the department heads were all working on the assembly line. The lunches they brought from home were no different from those of all the other workers. The exquisite suits they cut and sewed were not for themselves; they made for themselves and wore "Mao suits." They were exploited as much as the ordinary workers, ground up by the "socialism with Chinese characteristics" meatgrinder until they withered away.

On this day, Joe's lesson expanded beyond language, prompting him to undertake a thorough comparison of typical capitalism and so-called socialism. At the conclusion, he insisted on increasing his tutoring fee, saying, "Such a teacher is a rare find. I'd feel awful if I didn't pay you more." To which I responded, "Teaching benefits students and teachers alike. I have learned a lot from you, too." But Joe was Joe. He insisted on doubling what he had been paying. "You must not refuse; otherwise I could no longer take lessons from you." I had to accept, for I did not want to lose this friend.

As time went on, I had more and more such experiences, but not all had such happy endings. With a long weekend coming up, Dr. Yates asked if I could work some overtime on a Saturday evening. I said that of course I could. Dr. Yates said that he would bring the "job" to my apartment.

After wrestling with a computer all Saturday morning, I told Maddie I couldn't meet her at McDonalds for our usual tea and chat. Instead, I rushed home to clean the whole apartment. I even bought a bouquet of flowers which I placed in a vase on the coffee table in the living room. After an early dinner, I sipped hot tea and waited expectantly for Dr. Yates' arrival.

Dr. Yates did not come alone; a handsome, dignified-looking man came with him. In his left hand, this gentleman carried an elegant leather attaché case; in his right, was a garment bag of similar style and material. After introductions, Dr. Yates asked me to hang up the garment bag, saying, "It's his outfit." I noted that here was another character like Joe's father.

"When he's done here, he'll be going directly to the airport and then to Guangzhou via Hong Kong," Dr. Yates explained. He then handed me a thick English-Chinese dictionary of industrial terms and took his leave.

After sitting down in the living room, I handed my visitor a cup of tea and asked, "How may I help you?" He told me that, after China and the United States established diplomatic relations, American companies started exploring business opportunities in China. His company manufactured automated paper production equipment.

"The Chinese may have invented paper, but completely automated paper-making equipment is our forte," he smilingly informed me. He went on to say that, with his company's equipment, three to five workers could produce tons of paper "with no noise or air pollution. Any waste, such as wood chips, tree bark, or hemp bags, that could serve as raw material for paper could be fed into one end of the machinery and emerge as paper at the other end. I'd like to introduce to China our most advanced paper-making equipment."

Hearing that he intended to visit Guangzhou, I asked, "Do you intend to introduce your company's product at the trade fair?"

Pleased that we were already thinking along the same lines, he showed me an exquisitely printed and illustrated brochure describing his company's extraordinary machinery. One picture showed a technician inspecting a bank of gauges next to a huge machine in a gigantic, spotless workshop. The technician's uniform was snowy white, as were his shoes. His face wore a calm, almost serene, expression. Nearby, huge cylinders of paper lay on their sides as workers inspected them. The people looked like tiny Lego figures next to the rolls of paper.

"You could publish a lot of books with so much paper," I gasped in admiration. No wonder paper was so inexpensive in America, I figured. I also wondered if he wanted me to translate the brochure into Chinese.

My visitor was smart. He quickly informed me that his was a different kind of job. He took two sheets of paper from his attaché case. "This is a draft of my presentation. I'd like you to translate it into Chinese, record it, and teach me how to present it - in Chinese, of course." As if by magic, he produced a mini-tape recorder.

"Have you ever studied Chinese?" I had to ask.

"Not at all. I can't even use chopsticks," he replied with a smile.

So, in the space of a few hours, he had to grasp the four tones of spoken Chinese well enough to read a speech in Chinese. Talk about a challenge! Did he have a genius for picking up languages?

"Don't worry," he assured me. "I have a good ear and an acceptable speaking voice."

Far from reassured, I told him, "It's getting late. I'd better start by translating your presentation. I'll write each character phonetically for you to review on the plane."

"Thank you very much. I also need a copy of the presentation in Chinese without the phonetic spellings; the sponsor has requested one. And here is payment from our company for your services." He handed me a large envelope.

I picked up presentation, dictionary, and envelope with my "reward" and stood there. I thought it over a bit and spoke my mind. "This is the first time we've met, and I have to be honest with you." He was listening attentively, so I continued. "You should know one thing: no matter how convincing you are, China will not buy this machinery. Over there, everything is done with human labor. There are too many people, too many people who need jobs. Your machinery is fantastic, but it doesn't fit China's needs."

He didn't seem surprised. "Even if they don't buy anything," he replied in a straightforward manner, "we are showing them a beautiful future. Everyone has the right to pursue a beautiful future. People living in a populous country such as China should have this right, too. At least they can see how other people think, work, and live." These goals were much more than promoting machinery. I nodded and told him that I had to first concentrate on translating the speech. Settling comfortably on the sofa, he said, "I'll wait here," and a novel appeared in his hand.

Returning to my study, I went over the speech. Much to my relief, I was able to quickly find technical words in the dictionary. The large envelope was the size of a regular sheet of paper. I removed the contents: several sheets of blank paper and a check for six hundred dollars.

I had to admire the thoroughness of the gentleman waiting in my living room. Since he was promoting paper-making equipment, the paper he used for his remarks would naturally be an integral part of his presentation. I carefully examined the sheets of blank paper under the desk lamp; they shared the same watermark as the sheets on which his draft speech was printed. Oh, what gorgeous paper! What kind of pen was worthy to write on it? Many years ago, when I was in high school, Uncle Tianfeng brought me a Parker pen from the United States. That pen wrote beautifully. I left it at Grandma's house when I was sent to rural Shanxi Province. It was confiscated by Red Guards during the Cultural Revolution and never returned. After returning to the United States, I bought myself a Parker pen and some dark ink at a stationery store. Buying the pen had reminded me of mild-mannered Uncle Tianfeng. Now I could put this pen to good use. I opened the drawer where the grayish pen lay, glimmering with a soft glow, and set to work.

By the time I had translated the speech and made copies, one with Romanized pinyin and one without, it was midnight. In the living room, my novel-reading visitor seemed not to have moved at all. He stood up when I entered with the papers in hand. Rubbing his hands, he exclaimed, "Marvelous! Let's work on the pronunciation."

As we sat at the dining table, he asked me to read the speech aloud all the way through while he recorded it. I articulated each character as clearly as I could while his eyes focused on the motion of my lips. When I had finished, he turned off his tape recorder and said with a smile, "Now please read it once again at normal speed." By now I realized that the man sitting at my table had a kind of genius for languages. He could mimic any language without knowing the meaning of the words. He wasn't interested in learning Chinese but rather in using phonetics to deliver a presentation in Chinese.

I adjusted my speed, speaking like a person giving a speech instead of a teacher. He turned on the recorder again and, with a satisfied smile, focused his eyes again on my lips. When I had finished, he carefully put away his tape recorder.

"Now we're coming to grips with practicalities," he told me. "Please read and pause where you would need to take a breath. I will repeat after you." Taking up the pinyin version, he confidently signaled me to begin.

"Ladies and gentlemen (pause). Today (pause) I am pleased to have this happy opportunity to meet you…."

I was floored. Like a parrot, he imitated every sound and tone perfectly. After going through the presentation many times, he turned his attention to the pinyin, asking intelligent questions and paying special attention to the subtle differences between the sounds of "zhi," "chi," "shi" and "zi," "ci," and "si." Looking at the pinyin copy, he read it one final time with ease, ending this most unusual phonetic training. He told me that he planned to use the copy without pinyin when he was on the speakers' platform. "I'll have plenty of time to practice on the plane," he said confidently.

He was about to leave when I remembered the sheets of beautiful paper that were left-over in my study. I was going to return them, but he politely declined. "I hope you like them. Let me know if you need any kind of stationary in the future. My business card is on the last page of the brochure."

He stopped at the apartment door. "You are a remarkable language teacher," he told me. "Dr. Yates has a pair of sharp eyes to have spotted you." Embarrassed by the flattery, I asked, "Going to the airport this early?" He said he could catch some rest in the airport's red-carpet club. Then he walked down the stairs.

As I was wondering if he had to call a taxi, I heard the sound of an engine starting. Looking out the window, I saw a car slowly pulling out of the parking area, my visitor in the back seat. So, the driver had waited all that time to take him to the airport!

At the time, such a world was completely alien to me.

Back in my study, I placed the beautiful papers in my desk drawer and then lined up the illustrated brochure, the industrial dictionary, and the draft copy of the translated presentation on the desktop. I copied all the new vocabulary words and turns of phrase into my exercise book and went over them until I was satisfied. By then, it was five o'clock in the morning, almost daybreak. As Joe was coming for a class at ten, I hurriedly washed and went to bed.

My internal clock woke me around nine o'clock after exactly four hours of sleep. After a leisurely breakfast, I waited with piping hot coffee in hand, totally refreshed, for Joe to arrive.

He stared at me when he came in. "When did you go to bed?"

Dr. Yates must have told him about my overtime project. "From five a.m. to nine," I cheerfully told him. "More than enough."

He then told me that he and his father had had a serious talk with Dr. Yates, reminding him that my health was fragile. Constantly working overtime and taking extra shifts were like a snowball rolling downhill that might cause me to collapse one morning. Dr. Yates had told them, "Teresa has quite a reputation here. There's a steady stream of people asking for her services. I have refused many requests, passing on to her only the best: those that pay the most and require the least amount of time."

Joe informed me that even the Voice of America and the Johns Hopkins University's School of Advanced International Studies wanted pieces of my time. I replied with the Chinese expression "Generals will stop the advancing enemy, and sand will block the rushing water," meaning that there are ways to cope with every eventuality. "So far," I pointed out, "no enemy soldiers are in sight and no flood has occurred, so let's get to work on your lesson." Joe cracked up.

At the end of the lesson, I asked Joe what a "red-carpet club" was. In return, he wanted to hear all about the previous night's "phonetic training" experience. After I had satisfied his curiosity, he explained that a red-carpet club was no more than an airport lounge for the airlines' best customers. "Those folks fly a lot, usually buying first class tickets. The airlines naturally have to treat them well, so these lounges were created to offer some extra luxury: comfortable chairs and good food and drink with good service. If customers need to take a nap, the lounge employees will wake them in time to catch their flights. That gentleman flying to Guangzhou to promote his company's paper-making equipment chose an airport red-carpet club instead of going home – a wise decision," Joe remarked off-handedly.

"No matter now important he or she may be, no economy class passenger can use that lounge for free. But here's what's so lovely about capitalism: even if you are not a first-class ticket holder, you can still get "red-carpet" treatment and enjoy a moment of quiet comfort by paying an admission fee. Using money to buy service is perfectly reasonable," he concluded.

No parallels existed in China because there was no capitalism in China in those days. Twirling the Parker pen in my hand, my thoughts turned to gentle Uncle Tianfeng. A highly-regarded astrophysicist, he had resisted China's calls to return during the "Great Leap Forward" when China was vowing daily to surpass Britain and America in a short time. Living in the United States, Uncle Sun Tianfeng was not swayed. When informed by a person he trusted of his mother's death, he knew it was his duty as the only son to arrange her funeral. Leaving his research in America, he hurried back to China only to find his mother alive and well. He, however, instantly lost his freedom and, to seal his captivity, was pressured into marrying a young woman chosen by his work unit's leaders. When he came to visit, his attractive wife would accompany him, always wearing a smile.

He once gave me a toy box filled with colorful metal pieces and screws. With simple tools, these pieces could be assembled to form trucks, buses, tractors, tanks, cannon, armored vehicles, and other objects. I really loved this toy. I believe that my dream to become a shipbuilder started with this box filled with endless possibilities. I once asked Uncle Tianfeng why I couldn't find such a toy in China. I never forgot his reply, delivered in his Yixing dialect: "America is an industrial country."

The environment in which I grew up and the text books I studied told me only one thing: America was nothing but evil capitalism. All of China's ills were caused by this evil country. Yet Uncle Tianfeng's words were so simple that I believed them. Words of truth are powerful. These words supported me for a long time, giving me courage to face the slanders and vilification of a whole society. From the words of Uncle Tianfeng, I drew the conclusion that "My country is an industrial country, and China is not." This idea firmly rooted itself in my mind. The slogan "Catch up and surpass Britain and the United States" was nothing but the ranting of a madman. Soon after, the appearance of the golden Parker pen provided solid proof of this conviction. As a daughter of America who had returned home only a year earlier, this train of thought filled me with pride as I sat in my study outside Washington, D.C.

I began to view America with increased respect as a young girl thanks to encounters with Uncle Tianfeng and Uncle Pan Lingru, who, at that time, were newly returned to China from the United States. Uncle Tianfeng had a square, gentle face. He rarely smiled and, even when he did, his eyes evinced a deep melancholy. Seeing his gentle yet sad eyes made the twelve-year-old me very uncomfortable. Once, when his wife was with Grandma in the kitchen, I quietly asked him if there was something upsetting him. He recalled wistfully that, when he was working in Chicago, there were new discoveries every day.

"Science advances rapidly. A scientist is happiest when his work is at the forefront of this advance. When you're standing in a pool of stagnant water without any possibility of making new discoveries, just passing along information that everyone knows already, you're no longer a scientist." He did not specify the reason for his frustration, but I understood it completely. He was "passing along" information and cooperating with the government because his elderly mother and numerous family members were still living in China. Their safety depended on his enduring an unbearable situation.

Uncle Pan Lingru's situation was different. He had come back to China after learning that his wife was critically ill. He never saw his wife; instead, he saw his son standing in front of a new grave. This child was a year younger than I was, quiet and malnourished. The Chinese authorities considered Uncle Pan to be quite a catch. They were convinced that, with him, China's aviation industry would soon make giant leaps forward. Uncle Pan quickly disabused them of this notion, stating plainly that China could not build its own airplanes in the absence of a strong industrial base. And so the former VIP spent his days drinking tea and reading newspapers at a mathematical institute in the Chinese Academy of Science. He refused the government's match-making efforts and took care of his son himself. He came to visit us often. Feeling sorry for him, Grandma always cooked him delicious dishes. Another reason for Uncle Pan's visits was to give his son a chance to play with me. The funny thing was, Uncle Pan always ended up playing chess with me while his son happily accompanied Grandma in the kitchen, diligently helping to peel garlic or clean scallions.

I attended Beida Fuzhong, the prestigious senior high school affiliated with Beijing University. My school was close to Zhongguan Village, where Uncle Pan lived, so before going back to school on Sunday afternoons, I usually stopped by his place to deliver the dishes Grandma had prepared for him. Under a desk lamp with a green glass shade, Uncle Pan showed me a <u>Life</u> magazine where I saw pictures of the high-rise buildings of New York City for the first time. Uncle Pan solemnly told me, "New York is the greatest city. You are a New Yorker. You will go back to New York one day."

During the early stages of the Cultural Revolution, Uncle Tianfeng, Uncle Pan, and the smiley woman all simply disappeared. I tried inquiring about their whereabouts only to have a person at the mathematical institute reply, "Pan Lingru? I've never heard of him. I've been working here for more than ten years, but I have never heard of this person." In 1979, I even asked one of my former students working at the American Embassy in Beijing inquire about them. He received the same reply: "Nobody knows anything about a scientist named Pan Lingru. As for Dr. Sun Tianfeng, he used to teach at Beijing University, but no one can tell us what happened after that."

I was hopeful then that I would have a chance to locate them some day. Little did I know that that day would come so soon. In the summer of 1983, my husband and I arrived in Beijing to work at the American Embassy. I tried inquiring about them again, but all channels were fruitless. One day, I mentioned this to Grandma.

"It seems that Uncle Tianfeng and Uncle Pan Lingru have disappeared from the world. Only you and I still remember them."

"Whom are you talking about," Grandma asked me in all apparent sincerity.

"Uncle Sun Tianfeng and Uncle Pan Lingru of course," I replied.

"Who are they? I've never heard those names," Grandma said, still serious.

"How can you forget Uncle Pan," I asked anxiously. "His son was always following you around in the kitchen, peeling garlic and cleaning

Han Xiu

scallions for you. You asked me to go to Zhongguan Village at the beginning of the Cultural Revolution to look for him. Uncle Tianfeng was from Yixing."

Grandma's answer remained "I have never seen those two people, nor have I ever heard of them." She gently squeezed my hand, signaling me to stop asking.

One day, one of the students in my language class at the embassy told me that Sun Tianfeng and Pan Lingru had indeed worked in American research institutes, had returned to China in the 1950s, and were never heard from again by their American contacts. The Massachusetts Institute of Technology, where they had studied, and the research institutes where they had worked had been sending them invitations for the past ten years without receiving any answers. "You are one of the last people to see them," he concluded. I told my student what I knew. "The last time I saw them was during the summer of 1964, right before I was sent to the countryside. In early 1967, I had a hurried two and one-half days in Beijing during which time Grandma had me go to Zhongguan Village for news of Uncle Pan. Today, Grandma remembers everyone else but has 'forgotten' those two people." "There must be a good reason for this," my student concluded gravely.

What could this reason be? Whatever it was, it was so grave that even Grandma had to hold her tongue, keeping the truth from me. What had the Chinese authorities and the absurdity of the times done to those two scientists?

Back in 1979 though, I had other things on my mind. To prepare for my students, who came from all walks of life, as well as to broaden my own knowledge, I spent hours with English-Chinese and Chinese-English dictionaries researching the vocabularies of fields such as agriculture, textiles, herbs, technology, medicine, art, linguistics, international commerce, economics, and architecture to name a few. All these students were referred by Dr. Yates, but Joe was the person who explored with me the singular achievements made by Americans in these fields, although he was reluctant to jump to a discussion of tax brackets or Gresham's Law after immersing himself for two hours in the *Letters written home by the Venerable Zeng Guo Fan* or the works of Tang poet Bai Juyi.

When I was alone, thoughts of Uncle Pan and Uncle Tianfeng would sometimes pop into my head. I hoped there would come a day when I would meet them in the United States and tell them how much what they told me about my country had meant to me. With everyone in China condemning everything about the United States, they were the only people who gave me a glimpse of what America was really like and what kind of city New York really was.

CHAPTER 7

NATIONAL GEOGRAPHIC MAGAZINE

I t was the early spring of 1980, and the cherry trees were in full bloom across the Potomac. Busy with studying and teaching, I had no time for leisure activities. When other teachers in the Chinese section asked if I had seen the cherry blossoms, I could only shake my head no.

One afternoon, I was still busy in the classroom after the other teachers had left. There was a knock on the door followed by a greeting in a distinctly Russian accent. Looking up from my work, I saw a pair of sky-blue eyes under neatly combed chestnut-colored hair. "Is the Russian section going to show another good movie?" I asked casually. The Russian language section at FSI was a large one, and all the teachers there harbored an inveterate hatred of the Communists. I was friendly with them, and they usually notified me about films they planned to screen for their students. Unfortunately, I hardly ever had time to go.

An embarrassed reply came, "Sorry. I'm not from the Russian section."

"I'll bet Russian is your mother tongue, though. The way you pronounce your "rs" is beautiful," I was pleased to inform him. Those blue eyes beamed with energy. "You're right. My mother tongue is Russian, but I don't teach here. I work for National Geographic magazine."

Oh, America's National Geographic was an extraordinary publication. I invited him to sit down.

Blue eyes had a famous surname: Bolkonsky. Good heavens! Wasn't that the name of the handsome prince in *War and Peace*? Blue eyes smiled and gracefully waved his hand. "I'm Boris." I broke out laughing. "It's not often I get to meet a descendent of Tolstoy's prince. Maybe I should just call you 'Prince'. What can I do for you?"

It turned out that Prince was a professor at Georgetown University and a friend of Sylvia on the State Department's China Desk. The editors of National Geographic were in the process of compiling a book about China and were looking for someone with recent personal experience in Xinjiang. So far, they hadn't been able to find anyone.

"The book will be titled *Journey into China*. As the intention is to go into depth by "walking into China," it can't merely skim over the surface but must be honest and accurate. That's the hard part," he explained with a smile that did not at all reflect the difficulty he faced.

Prince explained that the book's editors were nearly at their wits' end when he thought of Sylvia. When he telephoned her at the State Department, she told him that National Geographic was in luck. There was, indeed, in Washington a person who had lived in Xinjiang from 1967 to 1976. Prince immediately asked her if this person had spent time in the Chinese gulag. Sylvia had pondered for a moment and then replied, "Close. Look her up. You can't go wrong."

"After talking to Sylvia," he continued, "it was almost quitting time, so I thought I'd try my luck by coming over here. The entire Chinese section is dark except for this classroom. My good luck seems to be holding." Prince was all smiles. Since Sylvia had promised that he couldn't go wrong, I, of course, had to give my all. But it was a book, an enormous project. Where could I find time? Seeing my reluctance, Prince hastened to explain.

"I may have given you the wrong impression. You don't have to write or compile the book; just help us discern what is true and what is false. This kind of book usually contains a large number of photographs. Your job would be of vital importance because you lived there recently. You can tell what is genuine and what isn't. National Geographic would rely on your experience and your eyes."

Considering my tightly packed schedule, I figured that the only time available would be in the evenings. But would the National Geographic people be working then? I asked Prince when I should go to the National Geographic offices.

"Now is a good time, if you're free this evening," he cheerfully replied. "Shall we go?"

"I have to go home first to feed Pele," I told him. "I was going to fix his dinner right after I got off work since my evening was free. I don't have any students or classes tonight."

"Who's Pele? He's welcome to join us." Prince refused to give up.

"Pele is my dog. He's small, but he still needs his dinner."

Prince smiled. "Well, we'll pick him up first and then go rescue National Geographic."

As one would expect from a gentleman, Prince helped me on with my trench coat. He turned on the corridor lights while he waited for me to turn off the classroom lights and close the door gently behind me. We walked down the stairs together. The security guard in the lobby bid us a friendly good evening. It looked as though Prince was a familiar visitor.

On the bus home, Prince explained that people from all walks of life helped National Geographic prepare its publications. They were all busy people, but they were more than happy to assist National Geographic because the organization was well-respected. I knew this to be true. To a certain extent, the magazine had helped me understand the world. But I had never been to its offices. "Our boss, Mr. Grosvenor, is very understanding and considerate," Prince told me. "In addition to paying his employees well, he also tries to make working conditions as convenient as possible for them. For example, some staffers have to take their children to work. Mr. Grosvenor arranged for space for the kids to do their homework or watch television. So, I see no problem bringing Pele to the office. The office even provides simple dinners, saving everyone a lot of time."

Prince and Pele were instant friends. Prince took Pele for a walk and poured him some milk, so we were soon on our way.

"But pets aren't allowed on the bus or subway," I said, wondering if it would be better to leave Pele home.

"He's been home alone for twelve hours. He's so small, no one will notice if you just tuck him in your shoulder bag," Prince suggested with a cunning smile.

What a smart dog Pele was! He sat in my black shoulder bag with just his little black nose sticking out, not making a sound. We made it downtown without a hitch. The National Geographic Society headquarters occupied a block on M Street between 16th and 17th Streets. It was unremarkable in the dark. The hall on the first floor was not large but was undeniably solemn and dignified. Shelves displayed the organization's books and magazines. Seeing them, a visitor could feel the connection to nature. We went upstairs to a spacious, well-lighted room. Prince introduced me to a number of friendly people sitting at desks. Many of them spoke English with foreign accents, which eased my mind quite a bit.

Prince placed Pele on the carpeted floor. Nose twitching, Pele immediately detected the aroma of food and sniffed vigorously, giving everyone a good chuckle. Prince and I followed Pele to an adjoining room where a round table held a neat array of edibles: salad, deep-fried chicken wings, sandwiches, sushi, as well as coffee, water, and other beverages. Three boys eating pizza caught sight of Pele and rushed toward him with happy cries. Pele swiftly jumped onto a chair, avoiding the children, and looked expectantly at Prince. Prince sat down and carefully tore a piece of meat from a chicken wing and placed it on a paper plate. Pele rubbed Prince's hand with his nose to express his thanks and started in on the chicken. Soon all three of us had finished our meals. Still reluctant to play with the boys, Pele ran back into the main office. No sooner had Prince sat down than Pele jumped into his lap and made himself comfortable, lying down and wagging his tail. I spotted a large map of Inner Mongolia on the desk and surmised this to be Prince's area of interest.

Smiling, Prince pointed to a large desk in the middle of the room and said, "That's your spot." A stack of manila envelopes sat neatly on the desk with a note of instruction on top: "Please place the usable photos in the document basket on the left and the unusable ones in the document basket on the right." Taking a closer look at the baskets, I realized that they had been carefully designed with soft linings inside to prevent any damage to photos. I sat down and took a sip of coffee. As I was about to place the mug on the desk, I noticed that the right-hand arm of the chair had a round spot for just such a mug. Placing the mug down, I discovered a lid, which I used to cover the mug, admiring the thought and professionalism that had gone into the design. Pictures, documents, and atlases had nothing to fear from careless scratches or coffee spills. Glancing around, I saw that everyone had similar chairs. As I watched, a white-haired gentleman picked up his mug, took the lid off and sipped, then placed it back as he continued to study the illustrations in front of him. It was time to get to work.

I opened the top envelope on my desk, carefully removed the photos inside, and studied them. What was this? Every one looked like something out of a <u>People's Illustrated</u> magazine, one of the Chinese government's propaganda publications: a friendly gathering of soldiers and civilians, soldiers delivering medical supplies, a Mao Zedong propaganda team distributing "little red books," Uyghur men laughing heartily and gesticulating with both hands, imams leading prayers. A phony imam without a doubt. Photo after photo went into the right-hand "unusable" basket. Soon it was full, while the left-hand side remained empty.

I heaved a sigh of relief. If all the photos were like these, this job wouldn't be much work at all. Yet, at the same time, another thought crossed my mind: barely one year after the establishment of diplomatic relations and already so much Chinese propaganda was flooding National Geographic. It made me indignant. Thank goodness I was here to check the pictures. We Americans would not be deceived so readily. A feeling of zealous pride came over me, pride in defending the intellectual integrity of National Geographic magazine.

Suddenly I felt a little strange. I raised my head and saw everyone looking at me. Even Pele, sensing something unusual in the air, was staring at me with his black eyes. I gazed around the room, not understanding the intense interest in what I was doing. Then I saw a faint smile appear in Prince's eyes, followed by more smiles around the room. At last, a man sitting across from me politely asked, "Excuse me, can't you find even one photo that is honest and genuine? Perhaps you'd like to go through them one more time?"

"That won't be necessary," I replied firmly. "I saw more than my share of this stuff when I was in China. This kind of propaganda is not suitable for National Geographic."

"Are you sure?"

"Positive." I indignantly stacked the entire pile of photos in the right-hand basket and marked in block letters "Not Usable." After writing those two simple English words, I noticed, printed in tiny letters on the envelope, the words "Xin Hua."

"Ha!" I exclaimed aloud. "New China News Agency." No wonder the photos looked so familiar. Laughter broke out, and the man across from me chuckled thoughtfully while wearing a perplexed expression. I saw Prince giving me two thumbs up and smiling mischievously.

I placed the manila envelope marked with my "not usable" comment under the right-hand basket. I opened the second manila envelope, ignoring the tiny print on it so as not to be biased, and tried to objectively evaluate the photos inside. They showed a number of strange subjects: crates for storage or transport and exotic and antique clothing and ornaments with a Middle Eastern flair. They looked old, but the bright, fresh colors suggested otherwise. The last one was a black-and-white photo showing very familiar scenery and a hastily erected structure made of dried poplar logs that looked like an animal shelter. Actually, it was a shelter for people to use in dust storms. These were often found in the hinterland of the Taklamakan Desert and were usually built close to a water source. I gazed at it for a long while, almost feeling the warmth of camels and hearing the thunderous roar of a gale rolling up the sand dunes. I seemed to have walked into the picture, into the endless darkness.

I didn't place this envelope of photos in either the right-hand or left-hand basket. Instead, I drew a large question mark in the envelope. My pen stopped as I noticed the small print at the bottom: "Loulan yizhi." I was stunned! Could this be true? The ruins of Loulan, a once-important stop on the ancient Silk Route, had never been found, let alone photographed! I felt deceived and a chill passed through me, yet I had no idea what to make of these photos. I had no way of knowing what the ruins of Loulan should look like. All I knew for sure was that the final photo in the envelope showed a sandy landscape characteristic of the middle of the Taklamakan Desert, definitely not the dark, stony ground of the eastern part of the great desert where the northern and southern Silk Roads intersected and where Loulan was supposedly located.

The footsteps of a middle-aged woman in a navy-blue suit came to a stop in front of me. Introducing herself as Mr. Grosvenor's secretary, she handed me a form requesting my name, address, telephone number, work place, and social security number. She also handed me an envelope containing a check large enough to cover my rent for a year. I signed a receipt acknowledging receipt of the money, but I was not at all happy because I was still puzzling over the photograph I had annotated with a question mark. The woman asked in a kindly voice, "After work the day after tomorrow, could you please come here? Mr. Grosvenor would like to discuss those photos with you in person." My English writing class was scheduled for that evening, but I decided to skip it. I felt obligated to give National Geographic my all on this important matter. "I'll be here as soon as I leave work," I replied.

It was after ten p.m. when people started bidding each other good night, gathering their belongings, and calling their children to go home. I stood there uncertainly, half of my mind still on the photos Mr. Grosvenor wanted to discuss in two days. Prince placed Pele in my shoulder bag and bid me good night. He seemed on the verge of saying something, but in the end, he didn't. He just took a long look at me before turning around and quickly stepping into the dark.

I had lunch with Maddie at McDonalds the next day. I handed her my writing assignment and my door key. "I have to work overtime tomorrow, and it's really inconvenient to take Pele along. Would you mind going to my apartment after class to feed him? Would you also please hand in my assignment, explain my absence to our instructor, and tell me what was covered in class and what our homework is?"

"What can be so serious?" Maddie teased. "Aren't you always the confident one, with your 'learn to know, learn as you teach?'"

"This time is different," I replied. "I have to identify a legendary place, and it's not something that can be learned anywhere." As I explained my difficulty with the task I had taken on at National Geographic, Maddie whistled a sigh of relief. "I heard that they pay generous consulting fees. At least you'll be well paid this time." I said nothing. The check was still in my handbag, and I was thinking that, if I could not tell truth from fabrication, I should return it to Mr. Grosvenor.

On the third day, I donned my most formal clothes: a black dress suit with a narrow skirt. I left water, milk, and biscuits for Pele, as well as a thick layer of newspaper on the little rug. Pele's round eyes seemed sad, as though reluctant to see me go, so I held him in my arms and told him, "Maddie will come by later to take care of you." At that, he jumped out of my arms onto the ground and hopped onto the window sill where he turned to look at me as if to say I needn't worry about him.

Outside, I looked up at my apartment window and there was Pele watching me from his perch on the window sill. Walking to the bus stop, I could still see his tiny silhouette framed in the window. I whispered to myself, "Dear, loyal friend, I sure hope this doesn't happen too often."

In class this day, I wore my blouse and skirt, hanging up my suit jacket on the coat rack. I noticed students admiring my unaccustomed outfit but told myself to concentrate on the lessons. Forty-five minutes before the end of the work day, I donned my suit jacket, closed the classroom door, and headed down the corridor to the elevator.

"Hey, got a date today?" Ms. C, another Chinese instructor, called out from her classroom in her strident voice.

"Her one and only good outfit and probably reserved for the advanced lessons on the Seventh Floor," came the envious tones of Ms. O. Indeed, when I went to tutor advanced students at the main State Department building, I usually wore this outfit because the employees there always dressed up in coats and ties. I smiled nonchalantly without slowing my pace and walked up to Dr. Yates' door and knocked.

Seeing his warm smile calmed me as I briefly related my concern about the task at National Geographic. "If you know, you know; if you don't, you don't," he bluntly told me. "Nobody in this world knows everything. National Geographic is famous for its honest approach to finding the truth. As long as you have tried your best, you don't have a thing to worry about. Why don't you go there now to give yourself a little more time?"

Catching the subway in Rosslyn, I soon arrived in downtown Washington, where the setting sun illuminated clouds of cherry blossoms in full bloom. I stopped several times during my walk to the National Geographic building to admire the pink flowers covering the branches, flowers so bright and lovely that they looked like brocade. People were always saying that spring was the most beautiful season in Washington, and I finally got to see it.

A cherry tree occupied a space in front of the entrance to the National Geographic building. It was an older tree with fallen petals covering the ground around it. Its crown bathed in the light of the setting sun, flaming like a burning bush, dazzlingly resplendent. I silently thanked it for bringing me warmth before walking into the building where a receptionist directed me to the elevator.

Mr. Grosvenor's office door was ajar. His secretary this day was wearing a dark brown suit with a golden brooch on her breast. She nodded a friendly greeting and said, "Mr. Grosvenor is waiting for you in his office."

The man standing behind the huge desk, the head of National Geographic magazine, looked to be about the same age as Dr. Yates. He was lean and tall and wore a sweater over a shirt. He looked comfortable, and he was pacing back and forth with a document in his hand. Noticing me, he put the document down and motioned to me to sit down in a chair by a side table in front of the window.

After opening pleasantries, he remarked casually, "I saw you twice last year. The first time was early in the year during Deng Xiaoping's visit in the White House Rose Garden. You were standing next to Mrs. Swift. It was a cold day. The second time was in October at the Republic of China's national day reception at the Hilton Hotel in Washington. Ambassador Xia Gongquan was the first head of the Taiwan office in Washington to host a grand national day reception since the United States severed diplomatic ties with the Republic of China. You were standing in line to greet the host. You were wearing a long, dark-green skirt and standing next to Dr. Yates and an ABC television reporter. That day, Ambassador Xia made a moving speech that allowed us a glimpse of the spirit of Taiwan: resilient and resolute, not giving in to might. It was very inspiring, but I also felt a sense of gloom."

What an incredible memory! I was an ordinary Chinese language teacher, yet he had paid attention to me.

"Many people were paying attention to you, not just me," he smiled. "You're the first American citizen stranded in China to escape from behind the Bamboo Curtain. You had no help from friends or family in the United States, but you fought for the opportunity to return here. What you did gave people in this country quite a shock. Without Dean

Swift and Dr. Yates as buffers between you and those who want to pick your brain, you'd probably be working non-stop night and day. Look how it took me a whole year before I could have a chance to work with you."

Me working with Mr. Grosvenor? What qualifications did I have to work with such a publisher? I couldn't even authenticate some pictures.

"Don't worry, we'll take our time. Don't worry about our feelings; just tell us what you know, your experiences, your ideas. That's all you need to do. Let's try something different today, maybe it will help you. You must be hungry. We'll have dinner first, and then we'll tackle each mountain."

In the cafeteria, Mr. Grosvenor warmly greeted National Geographic's specialists. I saw him talking to Prince, the two of them laughing heartily. I chose a small table in the corner, next to a plump, middle-aged lady with cropped hair, no makeup, and a bookish look. She introduced herself as Malena, an employee of the National Geographic Museum. Her British English, spoken in a low voice, was very pleasant to the ear.

After dinner, a group of us left the cafeteria together; I walked behind Malena. We did not go back to the large room of two nights earlier. Instead, we went to what looked like a conference room. We all sat around a long table while Mr. Grosvenor stood in front of a glass wall composed of a number of squares. Suddenly a huge picture of People's Liberation Army soldiers delivering "medical supplies" came up on the wall. With the picture enlarged and broken into many squares, I was able to see even more details. I felt calmer.

"Teresa, please tell us why this photo, which was supposedly taken at a rural hospital in the Xinjiang Uyghur Autonomous Region, cannot be used," Mr. Grosvenor asked in a calm voice.

"This photo could not have been taken there," I replied. "The 'Serve the People' slogan on the wall and the notice by the door to 'Close the door behind you' are written in simplified Chinese characters. Signs in a hospital for Uyghurs would be written in the Uyghur language in Uyghur traditional script; otherwise the locals could not possibly read them. Also, look at this 'villager': he's glowing with good health. No way is he a hospital patient." Laughter arose, and I knew I didn't have to continue.

That picture was followed by one of a Mao Zedong Thought propaganda team distributing the famous little red book, *Quotations from Chairman Mao*. Uyghur men were shown reaching out with raised hands and cheering lustily. On a nearby table covered with red cloth, unnoticed and ignored, were several piles of four-volume sets of selections of Mao's writings. Some Uyghur women, mouths covered with their scarves, were whispering to each other, eyes and eyebrows filled with laughter.

The conference room was dead quiet. I spoke in a quiet, confident voice. "Uyghur men use the pages of *Quotations from Chairman Mao* to roll cigarettes. The paper is of dictionary quality with just the right thinness and size. That's why the men are fighting to get the book...." My words were completely drowned out by laughter and applause.

"How about this picture of Uyghur people celebrating good times with song and dance?" I heard a touch of laughter in Mr. Grosvenor's tone.

I explained. "These people are dancing the 'Loyalty Character Dance'. The lyrics start 'Venerable Chairman Mao, the red sun in our heart'. The dance steps are a combination of peasant dances and broadcast exercise, with no resemblance whatsoever to the graceful traditions of Uyghur song and dance." From the resulting buzz came a question: "Then where do these men and women of minority tribes come from?"

"The Minority College, the East Song and Dance Troupe, local cultural ensembles." All government- or Communist Party-sponsored."

The picture was replaced by one titled "an imam leading worshippers in a prayer session." Enlarged, it revealed the sleeves of the grass-green military uniforms worn by the "worshippers." The collar of the loose robe worn by the "imam" showed a red PLA collar tab underneath. All those present in the room were intelligent people, experts and scholars. I could hear Prince chuckling.

"Look, red collar tabs!" someone exclaimed.

"I see them," called out another person. "That guy's a soldier! Ha, ha!"

I didn't say a word. I didn't have to; the deception was obvious.

"This one is indeed unusable," was Mr. Grosvenor's conclusion.

Next appeared some antique-looking chests and trunks and clothing. This time, the wall showed four photos.

"Teresa, please tell us why you doubt these photos," came the firm but gentle voice of Mr. Grosvenor.

"The ancient city of Loulan is mentioned in poems and songs of the Uyghurs, Kazaks, and Hui. No one has ever seen anything unearthed from Loulan. I cannot tell how those pictures came about, but the colors of those utensils look too bright, making me..." I faltered, unsure how to express my suspicions.

Then I heard Malena's British-accented voice, full of the confidence that comes from education and deep knowledge of her subject. "Teresa's suspicions are right on target. These utensils and clothing are loud and vulgar, just unskillful imitations." With fervor and assurance, she systematically pointed out how the imitations most likely came from Iraq, Iran, and even Turkey. She used the ancient names of those countries, specifying the dates such relics were unearthed and where they were now preserved. I noticed that a couple of them were now displayed in museums in Washington D.C.

The pictures on the wall suddenly changed, and now we were looking at pictures of genuine antiques juxtaposed with the pictures I had questioned. The contrast between the refined, graceful, genuine antiques and the coarse modern imitations was strikingly obvious. The whole room was applauding enthusiastically. I found myself applauding too, but as I did, I was also moved to tears. All I could think was "Knowledge is power. Knowledge is indeed powerful."

"As far as I know, there have been no archaeological reports about the discovery of the ruins of Loulan," Malena summarized in conclusion, even as the applause continued.

Finally, the black-and-white picture that had been perplexing me over the past two days appeared on the wall. With something less than Malena's confidence, I began to slowly analyze it out loud, square by square, for any trace of modern society.

"After Lin Biao's plane crashed, I was sent to work with a group of Uyghur men. We were to take a caravan of camels to the western part of the Taklamakan Desert, from Bachu to Moyu. The sky was clear and boundless. Suddenly the camels stopped moving south and turned eastward instead.

"Ahead, we saw an enclosure of intertwined poplar branches. The camels quickly walked into the enclosure and lay down snugly next to each other. In less than twenty minutes, the sky turned pitch-black. The wind was howling, and huge sand dunes were being blown up and flattened all around us. After the storm passed, the camels made no attempt to go on. This meant that another storm was approaching, so we decided to stay where we were. We repaired our enclosure by reconnecting the tenons that had disconnected from their mortises, retying them firmly. Uyghurs and Kazaks in the desert would all do this for the benefit of later travelers. Finding shelter from a sand storm was a matter of life and death, not something to be taken lightly."

The conference room was dead quiet. My story had slowly lifted a corner of the curtain that separated Washington. D.C. and the great desert. There was poetry in the desert's vast sky and endless plain and ferocious storms, but this wasn't the time for poetry.

Ropes made of wire, hide, or strands of raw silk twisted together might all have appeared on the ancient Silk Road. I was grateful to those experts who were patiently and quietly waiting. Perhaps they were, just as I was, peering intently at the photo with their eyes and experience, searching for the truth.

I was by now quite certain that the photo was not of ruins along the ancient Silk Road. But I needed proof. I continued scrutinizing every square of the picture on the wall. Every object in the bright sunlight cast a dark shadow. But wait! I saw something: one shadow was light gray. The object casting the shadow was flapping in the breeze. It was a rope with a knot tying two pieces of wood together. The end of the rope beyond the knot was fluttering in the air. It would have left an obvious shadow on the sand below, just as did the wood, if it were made of hide, wire, or silk – unless the rope was transparent.

"Can you enlarge that square?" I asked, pointing with my finger.

The spot where the two pieces of wood joined blossomed toward me. The rope was tied tightly, holding two dead branches firmly together. The rope seemed to flicker in the sunlight, the material composing it almost transparent.

"That's a nylon rope!" I was so nervous and excited that I blurted it out in Chinese instead of English.

Almost at the same time a clear voice came out of the dark: "Nylon rope."

"Of course, nylon rope. Look at that shiny knot." Someone jumped up to point it out.

"Oh, of course; nylon would not cast a solid shadow," chimed in yet another voice.

The picture disappeared, and the glass wall resumed its soft grayish-white color as the conference room lights came on.

"Well, now we know the truth," Mr. Grosvenor cheerfully declared.

I was standing, covering my face with both hands, unable to stop waves of tears. People crowded around me as Mr. Grosvenor looked at me thoughtfully. Malena smiled and handed me a box of tissues. I grasped her hand with my tear-soaked ones. "I don't know how to thank you, Malena." Everyone laughed.

I turned around to see, of course, Prince before me, eyes glistening with tears. I wiped my eyes with a tissue, looked at his silvery gray tie, and laughed.

"Nylon rope."

Friendly laughter was all around us. Work was done, but no one wanted to leave. The long table was crowded with people talking excitedly. Someone brought in coffee, sandwiches, and cookies, and we all sat down. I sat between Prince and Mr. Grosvenor.

After downing a mouthful of hot coffee, I got to thinking. Now that this job was done, I might not have another chance to meet Mr. Grosvenor.

"I don't mean to offend," I said, turning to him, "but you said earlier that I came back to America solely by my own efforts. This is only partly true." I saw his eyebrows rise, and everyone stopped talking to listen.

"Had it not been for the importance President Carter attached to human rights and the unremitting efforts of brave people whose names I know – David Dean, Thomas Gates, Mr. Roy, Jerome O., Frank W., John T., Sylvia – and others in the State Department whose names I don't know, no matter how resilient or determined I was, I would have been ground to dust by the cruel machine that is the Chinese government. That's why I attended that ceremony in the White House Rose

Garden more than a year ago when Assistant Secretary of State Richard Holbrooke invited me. I wanted to take the opportunity to show my respect and gratitude to President Carter." I immediately felt a great sense of relief to have gotten this off my chest.

Mr. Grosvenor nodded with a smile. "We seldom hear such a heart-felt testimonial to the State Department," he said to his colleagues. "Very good – thanks to the State Department." His words were met with smiles and friendly nods.

"Excuse me, Teresa," asked a white-haired gentleman from across the table. "You mentioned the language issue earlier. Can you tell me how many Uyghur people understand Chinese? I mean, what percentage of the Uyghur population?"

I knew the answer to this one, so I confidently answered. "Ninety-five percent of Uyghurs don't know Chinese, but almost 95 percent of Uyghurs, Kazaks, and Kyrgyz understand Russian. At least that was the situation when I left Xinjiang four years ago, in the spring of 1976."

"That's about what we thought," the white-haired questioner remarked with evident satisfaction.

"Excuse me," asked another person. "Other than the traditional Uyghur language, are there any other languages Uyghurs have to pick up?"

"In one marketplace, I heard someone call out excitedly 'Bazaar!' in non-standard Russian. Storefronts usually display signs in traditional Uyghur, the government-promoted 'new Uyghur language', which no one recognizes, simplified Chinese characters, Hanyu pinyin, and, of course, Russian. This way everyone, whether local or not, can tell what the store sells." I saw nods of agreement around the table.

"You were just talking about walking from Bachu to Moyu. We know where Moyu is, but can you tell us the approximate location of Bachu?"

"Bachu is located southeast of the Sanchakou junction, 79 degrees east longitude and 40 degrees north latitude." This reminded me of something my friend Zhang Mingzhong once said: "Sooner or later this place will be known in human history as a place of blood and tears." This was shortly after he had been released from confinement.

The person who had asked nodded and presented a photo. "We can't figure out what kind of structure this is. Perhaps you can tell us?"

It was a photo taken from space. It showed a series of what looked like stripes on a stretch of grayish-yellow land. If these stripes were houses, then it seemed that they had walls but no roofs.

"This is a housing area for reform-through-labor prisoners," I said, pointing.

"My guess was right," Prince said quietly. "That's China's Gulag."

"This picture shows part of China's Gulag," I corrected him. I saw Mr. Grosvenor's eyebrows go up again, and Prince looked uneasy. I stopped there.

"See, we still have much to learn from you," Mr. Grosvenor said deliberately. "Not only are you familiar with the region's politics, economy, customs, and traditions; you also know about its climate, geography, flora and fauna, and a lot of other things we have questions about. We'll need a lot of help from you."

"I thought I was finished when we went through those photos," I told him with a laugh.

"Oh, not yet. We really need your help." Mr. Grosvenor also started to laugh.

As soon as we were done talking, another picture appeared on the glass screen.

"It's mid-summer in southern Xinjiang," I murmured. "Near the southwest edge of Xinjiang....Typical landscape of the western part of Tielongtan....A Muslim Kyrgyz man is facing Mecca as he prays. The cliffs of the Kunlun Mountains are on his right and the Gobi flats are on his left, shimmering and dotted with the green that only appears in mid-summer. The only man-made color comes from a small maroon prayer carpet on which the man kneels. He is wearing a white skullcap and blue-striped, double-layered flannel jacket and pants. A small tin water pitcher sits near his hand."

"Do you think this photo is genuine?" asked Mr. Grosvenor.

The words came out of me without conscious thought: "This is the most honest, beautiful, and peaceful picture I've seen since I started here."

Mr. Grosvenor laughed. "You'll see a lot more honest and beautiful pictures, I promise you."

Prince wanted to introduce me to the photographer, a young man who seemed a little bashful as he walked closer. "That area is not open to foreign journalists," he told us. "I took those photos with a telephoto lens from the Pamirs."

"India still controls that area," I said. "Your guide is too cautious."

"That area's like a jigsaw puzzle," he replied with a bashful smile. "We have to be very careful."

Mr. Grosvenor stood up and asked cheerfully if I wanted a lift home. "I brought my car," Prince interjected before I could say anything. "I'll take her home." I wondered if Dr. Yates was behind such a thoughtful gesture.

As we were saying goodbye, Mr. Grosvenor said, "We'll be in touch with you soon."

'I'm at your service. I'll tell you everything I know."

"That's a promise," Mr. Grosvenor said sincerely.

As I bid Malena goodbye, she whispered in my ear, "Come to see me at the museum. I have some good things to show you." Deeply touched, I nodded my appreciation.

As Prince was starting his car, he asked, "Do you see the implications of discarding the pictures provided by the New China News Agency?"

"At worst, *Journey into China* will not get into China. National Geographic's reputation is much more important than this book," I blurted out. After a moment of silence, Prince said that, after what had happened that evening, he respected Mr. Grosvenor even more and truly admired the truth-seeking spirit of the National Geographic Society.

"Nineteen seventy-nine is an important year. Many in the West believe that the billion-strong Chinese market is finally opening up and are vying to get a share of it. They have forgotten what kind of government rules there. They can't believe that a country with '5000 years of civilization' can be as despotic, brutal, and cruel as the Soviet Union. Mr. Grosvenor resists the temptation and insists on reporting the truth. In the foreseeable future, National Geographic's journalists and photographers will encounter many restrictions and obstacles in China, which is much more serious than just banning *Journey into China*."

So, that's how it was. I was a bit sad. I couldn't possibly have known at the time, but it was not until ten years later, in 1990, that the ruins of Loulan were actually discovered. Experts from National Geographic were among the team of archaeologists that made the discovery. I imagined that Mr. Grosvenor would be extremely pleased to hear the good news. By 1990, my husband and I and our son were back in Washington, D.C. When I read about the discovery of Loulan, I dashed into my study, took up *Journey into China* published in 1982, and looked for the approximate location of Loulan on the enclosed map. As I did so, images from my time at National Geographic rushed through my mind. I was pleased by the firm integrity of National Geographic on the one hand and my honesty and persistence on the other. At the same time, I could not help feeling sad over what was happening in Xinjiang, and tears misted my eyes.

On a balmy spring evening in 1980, I was thinking of Prince as I sat in Joe's car. I recalled his double "thumbs up" to express appreciation and support and also the clear blue eyes that seemed to pierce the silence and misinformation surrounding the gulags, both Soviet and Chinese.

"When Prince stares at you, his eyes are bright as stars," Joe commented with a smile.

"His area of responsibility seems to be Inner Mongolia," I said, though I wasn't really sure.

Joe said that Prince seemed to be an expert on the gulag. He was researching China's "reform through labor" and "reform through education" systems, which was why he paid special attention to the unusual configurations in the earth's surface in the northeast, in Inner Mongolia, Qinghai, and Xinjiang.

"Prince might even have been imprisoned in the gulag,'" Joe remarked, a shadow of uneasiness passing over his face. Before I could say anything, he seemed to make up his mind. "I wish you hadn't been imprisoned. I felt a twinge in my heart when you pointed to Bachu on the map."

I patted his hand on the steering wheel. "Even ordinary people living on that land are imprisoned in a way. They don't have to be convicts or undergoing reform through labor. But I was not imprisoned, although some probably wished that I were or, better yet, gone altogether. A friend told me the precise location of Bachu, and I'd love to tell you his story."

The car was parked in Rosslyn, by the entrance to Joe's apartment building. He handed his key to the ever-attentive Tom, and we went upstairs to Joe's spotless residence. This time, I asked for coffee. Sitting at his dining table, I began to tell Joe the story of Zhang Mingzhong.

It was during the 1960s in Beijing. When I was living at 56 Shijia Alley, Zhang Mingzhong lived at number 40. We were practically neighbors but did not know each other. He was a few years older than I and had graduated from Beijing's College of Geology. In Xinjiang, I was stationed in Agricultural Division 3, 48th Regiment, Company 5; Zhang was in Company 2. Company 5 was the closest company to Maola, so on Sundays, when people from Company 2 went to the Maola market to buy items such as eggs and yoghurt, they would have to pass by Company 5.

In 1965, young people from Beijing sent to "support the border areas" traveled to Xinjiang by train. There was a near riot when they discovered they were being escorted by armed soldiers on the train. Zhang, a few years older than most, persuaded the young people to be patient and not to charge the soldiers' guns, thus preventing likely bloodshed. Many of the Beijing youth were grateful to him and started calling him Da Zhang (Big Zhang) out of respect. Every time he passed by Company 5, people would ask him all kinds of questions, including questions about national affairs and news from Beijing. Before long, we all got to know him.

Da Zhang's father died young, leaving his widow to raise Da Zhang and his younger sister by herself while working as the head nurse at Beijing's Xiehe Hospital. It wasn't easy for her. Da Zhang grew very close to his mother and very protective of his sister.

The turmoil of the Cultural Revolution destroyed President Liu Shaoqi but not his brainchild, the "Xinjiang Production and Construction Corps," whose mission - opening up wasteland and garrisoning the frontier — remained unchanged. Agricultural Division 3 was responsible for felling the poplar trees in the thousand-year-old forest around the Taklamakan Desert and opening up the cleared land for cultivation. In Xinjiang, cultivation took the form of miles-long strips of fields about four feet wide sown with corn and wheat, with the idea of turning the area into a granary for the Corps.

Southern Xinjiang's groundwater level was high and its saline-alkali soil unsuitable for agriculture. Local inhabitants, Uyghurs and Kazaks, focused on animal husbandry, devoting small areas to growing melons and vegetables, gradually improving the soil and forming green patches in southern Xinjiang. North of Maola was one such area, lush with grass.

Agricultural Division 3 was formed in Maigaiti in 1965 with three kinds of members: large numbers of young people cast out of urban areas; senior workers with good status and specialized skills, such as maintaining agricultural machinery, who were transferred from military units in northern Xinjiang and who were in charge of technical work; and demobilized soldiers in overall leadership positions. Those demobilized soldiers became the real setters of political ideology and "opening up wasteland and garrisoning the frontier" suited them just fine. Under their leadership, more than one hundred thousand people began to attack the natural barrier that contained the desert.

When I first arrived in Maola in early 1967, Company 5 lay completely concealed inside a thick forest. When I left there in the spring of 1976, Company 5 stood in an empty plain, surrounded by farmland suffering from salinization and desertification. A green patch north of Maola sat on the edge of the desert, seriously endangered.

"Those nine years were spent felling trees and digging up their roots, flattening the land, and digging and cleaning irrigation channels. We used mostly hand tools: axes, shovels, and mattocks. We seldom used sickles."

I spoke dispassionately and straightforwardly. Joe's eyes showed bewilderment.

"No wonder the Taklamakan has been expanding so rapidly," Joe muttered to himself while refilling my cup with hot coffee. "National Geographic has reported it but couldn't attribute it to a particular cause. If you told them that a hundred thousand people spent ten years on such a 'worthy project,' I'd bet most experts would be flabbergasted."

Da Zhang was one of the few people who pointed out - tactfully of course - the danger of desertification. This humble message had no chance against the official clamor to "race against time and go all out." Not only were cautionary voices stifled and the speakers forced to write self-criticisms; officialdom demanded that they throw themselves wholeheartedly into the absurd tree-felling madness so as to "perform meritorious services to atone for one's crimes." Da Zhang did just the opposite.

He continued to maintain that felling so many poplars would alter the natural ecological balance and bring disaster not only to our descendants but also to humanity in general. As a result, he was charged with the crime of disrupting the policy of "grasping the revolution and promoting production" and therefore being an active counter-revolutionary. The regiment employed the military system of establishing its own court and maintaining its own prison without any restrictions. Da Zhang was dragged to a series of different units to be criticized and beaten badly each time before finally being locked up in solitary confinement.

Seeing him in serious peril, some young people returning to Beijing to visit family went to Xiehe Hospital and told his mother of his plight. She rushed to Maola. Generally speaking, in China, when a person sent to a border region found himself in trouble, other family members would instantly "draw a clear line of demarcation," that is, sever ties in the interest of self-preservation rather than come running to the rescue. No sooner had this determined and tenacious mother arrived than she demanded to see her son immediately, catching the lawless local leadership completely by surprise.

There were two kinds of solitary confinement cells: wet and dry. During the day, Da Zhang worked making adobe bricks; the nights he spent shackled and handcuffed in knee-deep sewage. At that rate, he wasn't going to make it.

His furious mother stayed at Company 2 for three months, using her nursing skills to save her son's legs. During that time, all the people from Beijing came voluntarily to help her. They even managed to get rare antibiotics from a local hospital for her. That was when I got to know this mother. I traded a Uyghur some ration coupons for a little over ten pounds of rice and carried it from Maola to Company 2. I found her in a flimsy, half-underground shack. I watched her put some beans in a cloth bag, warm it on the stove, and place it on Da Zhang's knees, which were swollen into red, purple, and black balls. Despite this frightening sight, mother and son were cheerful.

"Thanks to everyone's help," she told me, "his kneecaps are saved."

"I'll be playing basketball in no time," Da Zhang added.

I looked at Joe and smiled. "Da Zhang and his mother were an inspiration for many people. They showed us that a mother would walk through fire and flood for her child - how powerful the word 'love' can be. During the move to simplify Chinese characters in 1956, the character 'love' was simplified by dropping the 'heart' part of the traditional character, reducing the new 'love' to something heartless. At the same time, waves of political movements were washing over the country, sowing distrust, antagonism, and hatred within the population and within families. 'Love' became nothing more than 'class friendship' and 'comradeship'. Differences in 'class' and ideological 'lines and directions' severed every healthy and good human connection. But in the midst of all this evil, a demonstration of maternal love took place. A mother traveled more than a thousand miles to the unforgiving desert to save her son who had been all but doomed as an active counter-revolutionary. The influence of this act transcended the individuals involved, for it offered a glimmer of hope in an otherwise hopeless darkness where for many years talk of 'human nature' was forbidden." Coffee mug in hand, Joe looked sad.

Although Da Zhang was punished for what he had said, his case was left unsettled. In the meantime, the mad felling of poplar trees continued apace. No matter that people were skeptical that the region could ever become a sustainable granary; their skepticism did not slow down the operation, which rapidly thinned the green protective screen surrounding the desert.

It was getting late. Joe drove me home. On the way, I asked him why Dr. Yates had urged him to go to the National Geographic building. "Was he worried my English wasn't up to handling the situation," I wondered. I wasn't expecting the reply I got.

"Some experts live in their specialized worlds out of touch with the rest of the world. They can be conceited and talk in jargon. If a listener does not understand what they're saying, it only increases their arrogance. Dr. Yates was concerned that you might come across such people, and he asked me to help if necessary." At that time, I had only been back in the United States a little while and so had not yet faced this situation. I knew of it but never gave it much thought.

I tried not to make any noise inserting my apartment key into the keyhole, but Pele still heard me and ran to the door excitedly. Maddie was asleep on the fold-out sofa bed, her text books and exercise notes on the coffee table. I carried Pele to my bed and walked into the study to review my homework. The teacher had written words of encouragement on it. I reviewed her corrections and copied them into my exercise book.

Homework completed, my thoughts wandered to the photo taken in Pamir by the young photographer. That Kyrgyz man in the photo could have been herding sheep or just a traveler on his way somewhere. When it came time to pray, he had spread out his little carpet, washed his face and hands, knelt facing Mecca, and prayed in all piety. At that moment, his heart was most likely filled with gratitude and serenity. Looking at him, I could picture the smiling face of the Kunlun and hear the breeze singing in the desert. That's how Xinjiang should be. This photo would be included in *Journey into China*, published in Washington, D.C., and my heart, too, was filled with gratitude and serenity.

Lying in the dark after turning off the light, the words of Mr. Grosvenor popped into my mind: that I was the first person to break through the Bamboo Curtain. These words prompted me to recollect how I had managed to do so.

On January 4, 1977, a week after my old U.S. passport and birth certificate were returned to me, I arrived at 85 Beichizi, the Foreign Affairs Section of the Public Security Bureau, to inquire about returning to the United States. My request was formally rejected on January 21. According to the Foreign Affairs Section's official notice, the documents in my hands had "expired and were no longer valid as far as the Chinese and American governments were concerned."

I spent an entire month secretly preparing my next attempt: locating the address of the U.S. Liaison Office in Beijing and sewing myself appropriate clothing. On February 21, I dashed into the Liaison Office's compound and met diplomats Frank W., Jerome O., David Dean, and Thomas Gates. The U.S. State Department quickly determined that my documents were valid and within six minutes confirmed my status as an American citizen. Because the Liaison Office did not issue passports, I was told to come back for my new passport in a month.

Suddenly the warm spring night in Washington turned chilly. The anxious face of David Dean appeared before my eyes as I recalled him saying, "You must remember this five-digit telephone number, and you must try to contact us." I completely understood what he did not say: that a fierce battle was about to commence. While the American government would do its best, I, a nobody living in China, would have to withstand the enormous pressure that would be placed on me by the machinery of the Chinese state.

My eyes were wide open, the five digits still clear in my mind three years later and two years after returning to the United States.

CHAPTER 8

THE JOURNALIST

Just as Mr. Grosvenor and Joe expected, all information about the southern part of Xinjiang had to be checked and verified by National Geographic magazine experts.

"It's not an easy job to clear an ancient forest. You said that the Xinjiang Production and Construction Corps had only basic tools such as shovels, axes, and mattocks. How was it possible to accomplish such a task using those tools?" The person asking this question was a well-known expert on vegetation. He even brought with him a finely detailed diagram of a poplar tree covered with branches and leaves and showing gnarled and twisted roots below ground. It was vividly drawn.

"That's a good picture," I commented. "Almost lifelike. We had to start by clearing the lower branches with axes so we would have room to place our feet. We also needed enough space to swing our axes at the thick roots. Then we used shovels and mattocks to dig out a big circle around the tree, throwing the dirt far away and eventually exposing the whole root system. We then cut the roots one by one with axes. After that, we rocked the tree vigorously back and forth using the weight of the tree itself as a lever to break the deeply buried roots. After the tree was down, we lopped off all the branches and leaves, carried the tree away from the work site, and bundled up the branches. Then we went back to the big hole and thoroughly dug up all the roots, big and small, thick and thin, and removed them from the work site. Finally, we filled the hole using shovels. This was how we removed those thousand-year-old trees whose circumference it took two men's arms to reach around."

As I spoke, I pointed to the expert's diagram with a pen. My audience of experts attentively listened and followed my hand closely, a hand with clean fingernails, no calluses on its palm, no cracked fingertips oozing blood. It was still strong though, capable of moving mountains and filling the sea. The experts frowned suspiciously.

"Do you have any tree that needs to be cut down?" I challenged with a chilly smile. "I'd be happy to show you how it's done." It was no idle boast. This skill never left me. One day, when I felt mentally drained from writing this book, I took a shovel and an axe to clear a large patch of shrubs. Cleaning up the gnarled roots, I was comforted to find that my hands still remembered what to do after forty years.

"In the United States, a machine is used to grind out the roots. The roaring machine reduces the roots to wood chips that can remain in the soil to become fertilizer..." The voices of the experts were gentler although their facial expressions remained bemused.

"That's great. Easy and ecologically sound," I replied. "It's a different story in China. It's usually more like an army corps at war, with endless numbers of workers who will not stop until the poplar forest is turned into desert." My voice shimmered with a certainty that brooked no compromise. The expert silently rolled up his diagram, then asked another question. "What about those trees? How are they being used?"

"A few were used to build underground shelters but most were burned. There were more than one hundred thousand corps members, plus their families, living in the dense forest without coal, electricity, or natural gas. Nothing. So, they cooked over burning trees and warmed themselves in winter with burning logs. With the forest gone, only firewood was left, and eventually everything was gone. The entire forest went up in smoke."

Suddenly I realized that I had been speaking in an odd manner: so abrupt and harsh. It seemed that this manner of speaking unconsciously reflected the absurdity of the situation I was describing.

"Is there any other vegetation besides poplars?" the now-totally dismayed expert asked, almost as a formality.

"Russian olives and red willows," I replied. "Russian olive bushes are thorny. We had to first use shovels to knock them down and then use axes to cut the trunks before we could dig up the roots. The Russian olive flowers were fragrant and the fruit dry and tart. It's not very tasty, but if you ate a handful you wouldn't be hungry or thirsty all day long. Uyghurs would carry some if they had to travel in an emergency. Red willows were useful, too. They were used to make the roofs of underground shelters. They were also used to pave roads. In early spring time, when the subsoil thawed but the surface soil remained frozen, motor vehicles could get stuck on mushy roads. During those times, motor vehicles could only drive on roads that we covered with red willow branches laid side-by-side. The red willow branches were tough and pliable. They were also used to tie up poplar branches into bundles."

The expert was quiet. He looked sad as he opened his notebook and began to write.

"You said you once walked from Bachu to Moyu. Why didn't you use the camels?" An elderly professor, a specialist in the deserts of the world, glanced at the card in his hand and leveled a solemn, intense look at me over the rim of his glasses.

I smiled. "There were more than ten of us and close to one hundred camels. But each camel carried a heavy load because we brought with us provisions for three months, the camels' food, plus water, tools, and large bundles of burlap sacks and white cloth."

"White cloth?" the old professor frowned.

"The Corps authorities in charge of building the highway from China to Pakistan anticipated that some road builders would perish. As they saw it, this wouldn't be a problem as long as the deceased were not buried outside the country. Their solution was to bring the bodies from Pakistan back to Chinese territory, dig a trench with a bulldozer, and bury the bodies. End of story. Since the workers of the Corps were not physically capable of crossing the Taklamakan Desert on their own, the Corps relied on members of Uyghur communes for this work. As a result, those unfortunate souls who died building the road received more careful, more tender treatment than most Chinese who died in Xinjiang. The Uyghurs would collect the broken body parts in burlap sacks, which they then wrapped in white sheets, like mummies. After being transported back to China, the bodies would be placed in graves with their heads facing north and feet facing south. The Uyghurs would recite some verses from scripture and then bury them."

"So, your trip to Moyu was to collect bodies?" The old professor's eyes were wide open. His colleague of the tree diagram raised his head from his notebook to stare at me.

"The China-Pakistan highway stretched from Xinjiang's Hetian to Rawalpindi. We went to Moyu to resupply, then continued south, skirting Hetian and heading directly towards the Big Red Willow Plain (Dahongliutan), high up in the mountains. From there to Tielongtan stretched a rugged path where many road builders had perished. They had been buried there immediately, so we didn't have to do anything. Our work started when we entered Pakistan. Armies of young people still in their teens had used crude, makeshift methods to demolish high mountain ridges. The people in charge of this project were soldiers in China's People's Liberation Army. Following the approximate directions provided by the soldiers, we located bodies and buried them. My job was to try to identify the dead, find their names and home towns."

"So that's how you are familiar with the geography west of Tielongtan," the expert whispered, almost to himself.

"Ironically, according to the Uyghurs, our burial sites were actually in the Aksai Chin region technically under the control of India after the Sino-Indian war in 1962. So, what we were doing was carrying the dead from Pakistan to India without actually bringing them back to China. This presented no problem for my Uyghur companions. The Uyghur elder leading our team would always remind us that the most important thing was to give those souls a proper send-off into eternity. Where they were buried wasn't important. In any event, they were more than a thousand miles from home."

"How long did your job last?" the old professor asked slowly in a gentle voice.

"About six months, after which the Corps recalled me. Although I was 'eating in the wind and sleeping in the dew,' as the saying went, I was far away from political movements. I would say that those six months were the most peaceful for me in Xinjiang," I said with forceful certainty. The old professor and his colleague were speechless.

Slowly I regained my composure, eventually pulling my thoughts step-by-step out of the rubble of the Kunlun Mountains to discover the presence of another person who was staring at us through glasses with thick lenses. Mr. Grosvenor's secretary hurriedly approached him and bending down told him in a soft voice, "Excuse me, but we're in the middle of something here. It's not a good time for an interview."

The stranger smiled, nodded at me, and assured the secretary, "Sorry to bother you. I'm not here to do an interview nor will I report a word of what I've heard. I'm here to set up a class schedule with my Chinese teacher."

This was how I first met Micah, a well-known reporter for the Washington <u>Post</u>. He struck me as very courteous and polite.

I discovered soon enough, though, that "courteous" and "polite" were not all he was. I was facing a very stubborn personality who would persist until he reached his goal. Micah bid good night to the old professor and his colleague, who were already gathering their things and getting ready to leave. Sitting down in front of me, he immediately got to the point. "My newspaper is posting me to Beijing in six months. During that time, I have to study Chinese with you for six hours per week. I'm only free in the evenings. Three classes per week, two hours per class at a rate of sixty dollars per class. I'll pay you every four weeks. Here's my tuition for the first four weeks." He pushed across the table a check from the Washington <u>Post</u> in the amount of $720.

Except for some trouble with the four tones of Mandarin, Micah's Chinese was quite clear and fluent. I told him, "Your spoken language is good. Are you looking for lessons in reading Chinese?"

He smiled. "What little Chinese I learned in college is definitely insufficient. I have much to learn, not just reading."

I wondered if Micah was another Joe, whose drive and capacity for independent study were strong enough that one two-hour lesson per week would be sufficient to keep him improving. But it was not possible for me to devote three evenings per week to teaching Micah.

"I'm sorry, but I can't give you three evenings per week. I can do two evenings per week at best."

"Why did you say "dui bu zhu" (sorry) instead of "dui bu qi? And 'chong qi liang' (at best) is a good expression, too," Micah noted attentively.

144

My goodness – this student was like a vacuum cleaner. I had to take him seriously. "'Dui bu zhu' is a bit of old Beijing speech with an extra hint of courtesy. As for lessons, my schedule is really full; that's why I can only give you two evenings."

"Fine," Micah said, not at all put off. "Two evenings per week and three hours each time."

Teaching Chinese all day and teaching three more hours in the evening meant that I could only study English late at night, I quickly calculated. However, I reasoned, I could still handle it if I slept less. I reminded myself to mention to Dr. Yates that my schedule for the next six months was full and that my "private school" couldn't accept any new students. So, Micah and I opened our appointment books. I took a peek at his, which also looked to be completely full. After comparing schedules, we set a time for his first lesson two days hence from eight to eleven p.m.

"I want to know everything about the Changguanlou incident," he told me, by way of providing context for our first lesson. "The whole story from beginning to end."

This started my brain spinning as I probed my memory for any information related to those three words. Nothing came up. Not to worry though – he pulled from his attaché case a copy of a "big-character poster" from the Cultural Revolution era. One look at the combative headline and I instantly caught on. It referred to something that happened in 1961 and that later became one of the "crimes" of Peng Zhen and the Beijing municipal Communist Party committee.

"'Chang'" – fourth tone. 'Guan' – first tone. 'Lou' – second tone. 'Chang' as in feeling happy. 'Guan' as in audience. 'Lou' as in a building of more than one story. It was a place in a western suburb of Beijing outside the Xizhimen and within the Beijing Zoo."

"Changguanlou," Micah repeated immediately, "in a western suburb of Beijing within the Beijing Zoo. Marvelous." His pronunciation and tones were perfect.

Micah gave me a ride home that night. As we drove into the parking area of my apartment complex, I pointed at my building. No sooner was I out of the car than he sped off, a "good night" wafting out of the car window. How different, I thought. Micah and Joe and were so different.

On the day of Micah's first lesson, Pele was bristling with anger and baring his teeth even before Micah walked through the door. As soon as I opened the door, little Pele started barking loudly at tall, big Micah. He only quieted down after I picked him up, stroked him, and cooed soothingly in his ear. Then he hopped on the sofa and stretched out with his back to Micah.

This little episode has no effect whatsoever on Micah. It was time for his lesson. Ignoring the big-character posters and vocabulary lists lying on the table, he opened his notebook and posed a question which had nothing to do with Changguanlou. My remarks at the National Geographic meeting on my experiences in southern Xinjiang had gotten him thinking.

"Please tell me why the Production and Construction Corps authorities sent you across the border into Pakistan. Presumably you were not someone they considered trustworthy, right?"

"That was a critical time. Lin Biao was originally the 'deputy commander-in-chief,' Mao's most likely successor. However, he conspired to usurp power and fell to his death at Öndörkhaan in Mongolia. That explanation might fool most people, but not the locals in northwestern Xinjiang.

"Everyone there clearly remembered that, in order to 'combat and prevent revisionism', Lin had personally ordered an anti-aircraft missile unit deployed along the Sino-Soviet border. If he really had wanted to rebel, he would have fled southeast, not north toward the gun muzzle that he had placed there himself. This was common sense understood by everyone, but no one would say it out loud for fear of facing bogus charges aimed at eliminating imaginary enemies during those unsettled times.

"Following instructions from the central government, Xinjiang at that time was on high alert for possible war. Rumors flew that the Soviet Union was just waiting for an opportunity to attack China. Although no one really believed in the movement to 'criticize Lin Biao and Confucius', everyone feared for his own life as the campaign spread rapidly throughout the country. Persons with a 'bad class background' carrying all kinds of 'political burdens' had best keep their heads down and be totally obedient and quiet.

"It was at this time that both the Xinjiang Production and Construction Corps and the local government received a request from the authorities in charge of the China-Pakistan highway project to send people to take care of certain matters. The job was not meant to attract attention, so people and transportation 'tools' were to be sent quietly through the great desert. The local government requested that the Corps provide personnel as the dead to be collected were all Han Chinese and the Uyghurs could neither tell them apart nor figure out where they came from. 'Everyone has parents who should at least be notified of their child's death' was the quite reasonable request.

"But the Corps had a problem. No one was willing to undergo the hardships of an arduous trek across the Taklamakan in the company of Uyghurs whose language and lifestyle were so different. About this time, a political cadre of our regiment was attending a Division meeting where he realized that this movement to 'criticize Lin Biao and Confucius' was a violent storm that would destroy many people. He had also just received an order to gather together all the young people of 'bad class background', creating a ready pool of targets for mass criticism assemblies. I had been at the Corps for almost four years at that point. I had been discreet in word and deed and so far had avoided disaster. But there would be no escape this time. He asked his superior for permission to send me to the Kunlun Mountains. His superior thought that, since there were active Chinese military personnel along the highway project, I could not possibly 'escape', even if I had had wings. Besides, crossing the desert was not exactly a cushy assignment. Sending me to such an awful environment could never be construed as 'taking care' of me. I might not even survive the ordeal."

Micah was hurriedly taking notes while listening, all the while marveling at the excellence of his new educational resource. The lesson moved on to phrases such as "trumped-up charges," "the sound of wind and the cry of cranes" (frightening rumors that spread rapidly), "docile and obedient," "indiscreet in word and deed," "weighing the pros and cons" (be in a difficult position), "eat in the wind and sleep in the dew" (endure the hardships of an arduous journey), "discreet in word and deed," and "difficult to escape even with wings." After thinking for a while, Micah ventured to exercise his newly learned phrases:

"For many years, I have been docile and obedient before my wife, never daring to be indiscreet in word and deed. But now I intend to rebel and escape. My wife is going all out to trump up charges, intimidating me with frightening rumors. My lawyer advised me to be discreet in word and deed. He said that, if I am not careful, my wife can make me lose everything. If that happens, I will be forced to eat in the wind and sleep in the dew. This matter puts me in a difficult position. Is there no escape in marriage even if I have wings?"

Good heavens! I almost passed out laughing. Hearing me laugh so hard, Pele raised his head, growled quietly, and decided to no longer bare his teeth at Micah. Micah also smiled, but it was a forlorn smile.

"Is this true?" I asked quietly.

"It is. My lawyer said that I can successfully rebel and escape. I will not fall to my death, nor will I have to nervously prepare for war anymore," he replied solemnly. Then I returned to Micah's original question.

"During the early spring of 1976, before I left Xinjiang, the political cadre of our 48th Regiment told me that in the late 1960s and early 1970s bundles of damaging documentation regarding me had been received by the Political and Law section of the Corps. During the frenzy of a political movement, that material could easily have gotten me killed. So, sending me away to the Kunlun Mountains at that time could have represented punishment. But it also forestalled people from leveling accusations and rendered the damaging material temporarily useless.

"I was puzzled why this political cadre, normally as ferocious as wolves and tigers, was suddenly displaying compassion. One thing he said seemed to come from his heart: 'The Lin Biao issue is most disheartening.' No one could have found fault with this statement, which could, however, be interpreted in two ways. The first interpretation was righteous indignation: Chairman Mao was so good to Lin as to appoint him his successor and still Lin decided to rebel. The second interpretation was that Old Mao is just plain spiteful: Even as loyal a follower as Lin could become a victim and have his bones scattered over the countryside.

"My usual response to anything political cadres said was to just listen and not say a word, even though my heart was filled with skepticism.

Nevertheless, his momentary mood kept me out of reach for six months from a political movement that could have killed me. I had dodged a potentially fatal bullet."

Micah listened carefully. Then he raised a new question. "When you reached the Free World, arriving in Pakistan, did you think about escaping from China?" Indeed, a Uyghur youth said the same thing to me. During the long journey with those Uyghur men, they naturally heard my story, and it piqued their interest.

"When I arrived at the Maralwexi Commune in the Fifth Company's donkey cart with my bed roll, the Uyghurs assembled there ready to set off on the mission were flabbergasted. 'A girl?' A flood of foul language ensued. My comprehension of the Uyghur language by that time wasn't bad, so I gathered that they were condemning the Corps as inhuman. I responded with a smile and greeted them one by one. The elderly leader of the group came over in a friendly manner to inspect my gear. Seeing my homemade hand-sewn cloth shoes, he had someone bring me a pair of boots of the sort worn by Uyghur boys. I deftly put them on, slipping into one boot the dagger I had brought with me. The dagger was from near-by Yingjisha County, which was famous for them. 'Wonderful!' the Uyghurs exclaimed approvingly.

"That very afternoon we walked a long way, past the 48th Regiment. We pitched our tents before dark and built a bonfire in the lee of a sand dune. To the north of our camp was the reform-through-labor prison known as the First Construction Detachment, while to our south lay the vast desert. At the group leader's behest, a young Uyghur handed me a sheep's-wool blanket to keep my bedding dry and me warm during the night. Using my rudimentary Uyghur plus Russian, I talked about many things with those kind-hearted people."

"You don't look like the Han people, nor do you look like us. Where are you from?"

"From the west."

"West is good; east is not. Where in the west? Mecca?"

"Farther than Mecca, much farther west."

"Farther than Mecca? America? Where in America?"

"New York, a city in the northeast part of America."

The men held their thumbs up, declaring, "New York, a good place! Radio Moscow and the Voice of America have both broadcast stories, music, and songs about New York."

Amidst a chorus of "Wonderful!", a long-necked Uyghur lute began to play, soon joined by a dombra and tambourine as I became one of them. After a number of Uyghur and Kazak songs they urged, "Sing one, sing a song from your hometown!"

Songs from my hometown? What did they sound like? Tears welled up in my eyes. "I left New York when I was eighteen months old. I don't know any songs from my hometown."

Lute, dombra, and tambourine fell silent, leaving only the crackling sound of red willow wood in the fire and the rustling of the moving sand dunes. Regaining my composure, I recalled one song I might sing for these kind-hearted people. It wasn't from my hometown, but somewhere close to it. I began to sing:

Then come sit by my side if you love me
Do not hasten to bid me adieu
Just remember the Red River Valley
And the lass that has loved you so true.

Almost at once, instruments started playing with male voices adding harmony. It turned out they were quite familiar with this Canadian folk song. As time passed, we went on to singing Russian folk songs: *Moscow Nights, Katyusha, A Small Path, The Little Birch Tree,* and many others.

At daybreak the next morning, we breakfasted on flatbread and yoghurt before packing up and heading south. After walking for about an hour, the two large dogs accompanying our party suddenly stopped, looked at our leader, and whimpered. The old man summoned two young men to walk over to the dogs for a closer look. I hurried over, too, to see part of a garment peeking out from the edge of a sand dune. The two young men quickly pulled the owner of the garment out of the sand. His feet had no shoes; those were probably sunk deep in the sand dune. There looked to be recent wounds from shackles on both of his ankles. Both hands were covered with scars, with dark purple bruises on his wrists from handcuffs. This was someone who had tried to escape. His face held a hint of a smile. I looked north toward where the First Construction Detachment was. Dead silence. The men also looked north then started to work.

Mattocks carved elegant silvery curves in the morning light as the young men quickly dug a deep grave on a north-south axis, ramming the earth at the bottom of the grave. With a shiny shovel, another young man smoothed out the dirt around the grave. The old man ordered a check of the dead man's pockets for any bit of writing. There was none: the dead man was wearing prison clothes that had no pockets. The old man heaved a deep sigh. Facing west, he sat down, crossed his legs, closed his eyes, and solemnly started to chant. As he was doing this, the other men carefully wrapped the body in white cloth, neatly tucking in the corners and ends. Several pairs of hands gently raised the corpse and placed it in the grave, head to the north and feet to the south. Mattocks flashed again and the grave disappeared, leaving only a slightly darker rectangular shape in the sand. The old man ceased his chanting and summoned me. "Say a few words that this person could have understood."

I walked up beside the old man silhouetted against a still-rising sun. Imitating him, I sat down, crossed my legs, closed my eyes, and said, "I don't know who you were. I don't know your name or where you came from. But I do know you suffered wrongs and humiliation. You cherished freedom. The desert and the blue sky are protecting you now. No longer are you confined or starved or put to hard labor. You are free. All of us here will treat you as our brother and walk with you part of the way as you leave us. Be safe and peaceful on your journey."

Opening my eyes, I saw compassion in the faces of my companions. The sunlight gave the uneven sand a smooth look, and the ever-moving grains of sand rustled softly as they slithered across the ground. Soon the burial site would disappear completely. Without looking back, we continued to travel south under a cloudless blue sky.

Throughout our journey, those pious men prayed five times each day. They did not all gather together to do so but rather formed small groups. Each man would spread out his own small carpet, clean his hands and face, face Mecca, and recite his prayers in a low voice. Whenever this happened, I, too, would sit facing west and pray to all the gods in heaven to protect those kind-hearted people. One evening, the old man smiled and asked me what I was mumbling five times a day. I told him the truth. Everyone laughed, full of goodwill. The old man patted my hand and said cordially, "Allah will protect you, too." I was so pleased to hear that that I replied loudly, "How wonderful! Thank you indeed." The men laughed heartily, the old man until tears rolled down his cheeks.

"Eventually we arrived at the border with Pakistan. In the distance, Americans were helping Pakistan to build a railroad. We could not see anyone, just the shining rails and huge, slow-moving bulldozers on top of which fluttered the Stars and Stripes. Closer to us were Chinese road builders crowded together using shovels, pickaxes, and steel drills on the rocky ground.

"We were moving broken rocks, trying to collect shattered limbs from under the stones and match them with the rest of their owners' bodies. A Uyghur youth nodded significantly toward the border and whispered to me, 'The people you're looking for are over there. We'll help you get there, then you can go home.' I turned around and saw the other Uyghur men solemnly nodding, silently agreeing to help me. Collecting my emotions and, for one final time, taking a long look at the American flag fluttering in the sunlight, I walked away. Later, when no one else was around, I told them that I did not have any documents proving my American citizenship, so walking toward my country's flag was not the solution."

"We all trust you," the young man spoke again. "Why won't your people trust you?"

"I never forgot what Grandma told me. When we three met for the first time, Rev. Hubbard's son-in-law handed her my birth certificate and passport and cautioned, 'These are the most important documents she has. They prove her American citizenship. Please be sure to keep them safely.'"

"Came 1964, I was sent to the countryside and could not take them with me. There was a passport with a green cover and three identical copies of my birth certificate. During the Cultural Revolution, our house was ransacked by Red Guards, and many of our possessions were confiscated along with my documents. They were nowhere to be found."

Micah thought for a while then asked, "When you were in the Kunlun Mountains, did you ever believe that you might one day find your birth certificate and passport?"

In 1972, in the rocky wastes of the Karakoram and Kunlun Mountains, I had no idea if I would ever leave Xinjiang or reclaim my confiscated birth certificate and passport. I had no idea that one day I would walk into the U.S. Liaison Office in Beijing, present my documents to an American diplomat who would validate them in six minutes, and receive an offer of all the help the Liaison Office could provide. I had no idea that one day I would stand again on American soil and even return to New York City, my hometown, and live there and look down from my twentieth-floor living room to closely examine every street I could see. No, on that day in the embrace of the Kunlun Mountains, I only looked longingly at the colorful flag in the distance before walking steadily back to my friends, determined to wait patiently. Four years later, I was able to leave Xinjiang, still carrying my Yingjisha dagger. Two years after that, I was able to return to America, bringing only a sick and damaged body.

Micah declared at this point that it was time to take a break. He immediately put down his pen and walked to the center of the living room where he dropped to the floor and started doing push-ups. Pele watched him with great curiosity until I picked him up and took him outside for a quick walk.

Over the following hour or so, Micah and I talked about this boring "Changguanlou Incident." If I hadn't seen his copy of that combative big-character poster, unwanted people like me would never have known what those "national leaders" were up to. To be honest, before this time, I had never heard of Changguanlou. It wasn't a famous old tower like the Huanghelou or Yueyanglou. So what could it be?

The "incident" happened in November 1961 – during the three-year Great Famine. The Chinese people were starving. I had just entered the high school attached to Beijing University, where the dormitory food of watery soup and little else could hardly fill my stomach. Thanks to Grandma's "little yellow fish," we were able to buy extra provisions, such as crackers, which kept up my strength.

It was during this time that the Beijing municipal Communist Party committee first secretary and concurrent mayor of Beijing, Peng Zhen, with the support of President Liu Shaoqi, convened key members of the municipal committee such as Deng Tuo, Li Qi, Song Shuo, and Zhang Wensong at the Beijing Zoo's Changguanlou to secretly examine all the records and instructions given by the central government, as well as by Mao Zedong himself, to local officials throughout the country down to the county level from 1958 to 1961.

The big-character poster labeled this action "quibbling" and rejection of the "Three Red Banners" with the aim of subverting the correct leadership of the "great leader" (Mao, of course). The poster charged that the meeting sought to prepare material for a "Khrushchev-style secret report" (referring to a 1956 speech highly critical of the rule of Joseph Stalin).

The poster highlighted the "seriousness of the international and domestic situations." The Soviet Union had set in place its modern-day revisionist system and Khrushchev, Kennedy, Nehru, and Tito had formed an "anti-China band." Domestically, the "Three-Year Natural Calamity" (the famine) had created a misconception among class enemies of all descriptions - landlords, the rich, anti-government elements, bad characters, and rightists, along with all kinds of "monsters and demons" - that the time had come for them to reclaim their lost pre-revolutionary "paradise." Meanwhile, the "Jiang Gang," entrenched on the island of Taiwan, was ready to make their move.

Talking to Micah about this vicious, spiteful poster, my mind veered to thinking about Grandma. She was far from alone in being robbed by the new regime of loved ones, fortune, and basically everything. Did these people really wish to revolt in the early 1960s? I doubt it. They were lucky just to survive. Grandma's most fervent wish was to keep me from starving, and her greatest pleasure was in seeing me not go hungry. That was the extent of her desire. In 1977, when I stepped into the U.S. Liaison Office, she realized that my situation was not hopeless and that perhaps I did not have to spend my life working in a Chinese garment factory until I went blind. After all, there were countries in the world that were not intimidated by the malignant power of the Chinese government. This was when Grandma's wisdom and courage shone brightest. With no hesitancy, she set her frail shoulders firmly in her granddaughter's corner, fending off attacks from that government. Her central message to me was this: "Don't worry about me. I'm already eighty years old. What can they do to me? The important thing is you. You must not give up. If you do, there will be no hope for you." Under her fearless umbrella, I naturally stopped worrying about my own safety. A tyrannical government can't intimidate a person who is not afraid for family members and not afraid of death or life imprisonment.

Micah's poster dripped venom. "In June 1961," it read, "Peng Zhen and another biggest capitalist-roader in the party then in power (i.e. Deng Xiaoping) launched an investigation in the Beijing suburb of Shunyi. At the same time, the biggest capitalist-roader in the party in power (i.e. Liu Shaoqi) arrived in Hunan to understand (i.e. investigate) issues involving the people's communes."

Micah's patience ran out. Frowning, he said, "What kind of language is this? There can only be one 'biggest.' How can there be a second one?"

"This poster came out during the early phase of the Cultural Revolution," I explained. "Do you think you're reading normal Chinese prose? This is Chinese created during an unusual time; it's a short-lived mutation. Trust me: this kind of language could not last long. It was doomed to die, leaving behind not even ashes."

Even worse was another big-character poster claiming that "For 17 years, from 1949 to 1966, the anti-Party, anti-socialism, anti-Mao Zedong Thought crimes committed by the evil tyrant Peng Zhen in Beijing were too numerous to record. Conspiring with the Chinese Khrushchev, they plotted to usurp the Party and the country, subvert the proletarian dictatorship, restore capitalism, and other evil deeds." The Changguanlou anti-revolutionary incident was only one of their more apparent and exposed plots.

Micah raised his head from his notebook and asked, "The Beijing municipal Party committee first secretary and concurrent mayor of Beijing; does this mean the power of the Party and the administrative power of the government were both held in the hands of one person?" I nodded.

"What does 'documents transmitted to the county level' mean?"

I told him that he would often encounter this and similar phrases. It meant that a governmental or Party policy document was sent as far down the administrative chain as county-level cadres, or within the military, as far as regimental-level cadres. Officials and cadres below that level, such as those in communes, production brigades, and squads, as well as ordinary Party members, would not receive the actual document but rather "the spirit of the document." During the transmission process, leaders at various levels would usually add their interpretations of what the document meant or intended, so that by the time the matter was made known to the general public, it could have been distorted beyond recognition. Similarly, by the time a document setting an objective reached common soldiers, it could have been reduced to a slogan or a simple command.

"What are the 'Three Red Banners'?" Micah wanted to know next.

"The General Line for Socialist Construction, The Great Leap Forward, People's communes," I rattled off, continuing almost automatically, "The General Line for Socialist Construction: Construct Socialism by going all out, aiming high, and achieving more, faster, better, and more economical results."

"How long ago did you leave there? You remember those empty slogans so clearly." Micah was amazed.

To be honest, in a society where everyone was required to sing the same tune over and over, a lot of official dogma was pounded into the deepest recesses of memory whether one agreed with it or not. I could probably recite this stuff twenty years from now. It pleased me that Micah's first reaction was "empty slogans." A hopeful sign. I prompted him to consider the implications of what he had read. "What serious problems do you see in those 'empty slogans'?"

Micah responded instantly. "The Changguanlou investigations at most suggested that the 'Three Red Banners' policy had failed. However, they never progressed beyond words to become a bomb that could unseat Mao." What a quick study, I thought with pleasure. He even fit in the "at most" grammatical construction I had just taught him.

"That was true. But by 1965, with Mao controlling the Party, government, and military, he felt that the time was ripe for a counteroffensive. In order to start a political movement to oust Liu Shaoqi and Deng

Xiaoping, he began to spread the word indirectly - through the media and meetings - that revisionism had appeared within the Party and that it could lead to the loss of the fruits that the Communist revolution had won with lives and bloodshed. At first, Mao made no progress toward eliminating his opponents. Peng Zhen completely ignored the repeated indications of Mao's displeasure, pretending not to hear them. Mao had no choice but to go to Shanghai. It was November 1965 when Yao Wenyuan's long, critical article entitled 'Hai Rei Dismissed from Office' marked the beginning of the Cultural Revolution, which reached its peak in June 1966 when Peng Zhen was dismissed from office. You could say that what happened at Changguanlou triggered Mao's hatred of his opponents. To ensure the stability of his dynasty, he had to eradicate his rivals using the Cultural Revolution – his trump card."

"So, we can conclude from this small incident, just as some people said, that the Cultural Revolution was in fact a power struggle within the Party as well as a tragedy for Chinese culture," Micah summed up accurately.

While we were on this topic, I taught him a few unusual terms and slogans he should remember: "February Outline," "February Note," "Destroy the Four Olds (old ideas, old culture, old customs, old habits) and Cultivate the Four News," "Criticize Lin and Confucius," and "Respect Legalism and Criticize Confucianism," and some others. These Cultural Revolution-era terms were aimed directly at subverting traditional culture.

By now, Micah must have been approaching educational overload because he loudly announced, "Class dismissed!" Before he left, he promised to bring me a book next time. He also presented me an example of a petition from a Chinese citizen to the authorities seeking justice, saying that he wanted to discuss petitions mailed to the authorities and petitions presented in person at his next session.

Piece of cake, I thought to myself.

After Micah left, I refused to waste any more time on that repulsive thing called the "Cultural Revolution." I opened an English-language edition of the correspondence between Vincent Van Gogh and his brother Theo. The brothers' tender and considerate love for each other deeply touched me. Simple words and sincere feelings so beautifully written. The letters were precious to me not so much because they recorded the life and thoughts of an artistic genius but more because they provided assurance that beautiful human relationships did exist in the world. Contempt, hatred, killing, false charges, and conspiracy were not all that the world offered. Most of all, such beauty in some places did not require a disguise but could reveal itself openly. What happiness! Although Van Gogh never sold a painting in his lifetime, although he suffered from depression and ultimately cut short his own life, he was still fortunate in that one important respect, I concluded after reading the letters. And so the evening's lesson did not sadden me despite plunging me into unwelcome recollections of the past. I had to remind myself that now I was in a place where human relationships needed no disguise and could be openly offered and accepted.

While waiting for Joe that weekend, I prepared a vocabulary list for Micah's next lesson. Joe walked jauntily through the door, cast an eye on the papers spread on the table, and asked, "What's this stuff: 'place of detention', 'local detention center', 'waiting to petition waiting room', 'waiting room for those whose petitions have been accepted', 'strike hard movement', 'prison cell', 'head prisoner'"? Finally, he noticed "prison common room" and asked, "For whom are you preparing these vocabulary words? They seem very difficult." I told him about Micah, my unusual student.

I was surprised to discover a soft look in Joe's eyes, a look that reminded me of those looks from the Uyghur men. My stare embarrassed him. He smiled. "Micah is Jewish, but his wife is not. So, his family won't object if he decides to leave her. But..." he hesitated for a moment, "now he is head over heels in love with a Chinese girl. They're talking about marriage. Now, not only does his family object to a marriage, the girl's parents are completely opposed as well. The Chinese parents have a sound reason for their objection: they don't think the marriage will last."

"Why not? Just because it would be an interracial marriage?" I was curious.

Joe – the man who knew everything and everyone! He really seemed to understand Micah.

"Not that," he calmly explained. "The problem is that Micah is an eternal searcher. He lives to search for truth, and his work is everything. Just imagine: would it be easy to live with such a person?" Noticing that I made no comment, Joe started to talk about the Micah he knew. "Micah is a top-notch journalist. Everything he reports is supported by ironclad evidence. He is a good choice to go to Beijing as a correspondent for the Post. He is proficient in Chinese." Glancing at the vocabulary list on the table, Joe continued. "Having a Chinese wife might fool the authorities for a while, making them think he's one of those 'panda-huggers'. But it won't be long before they discover that he can be fearsome. In a country filled with lies, when an absolutely truthful person charges in...."

Listening to Joe's analysis, I was suddenly filled with pride. I would not allow yesterday's nightmares to plague me. I was determined to help Micah master all that short-lived, hateful vocabulary so that he could understand the reality of Chinese society.

Joe, however, wasn't so sure that the Cultural Revolution-era parlance of distorted politics and twisted society would be short-lived. He reasoned that, since it had played such a central role in so many people's life-or-death struggles, it would sink deeply into popular consciousness and be reflected in literary works and, to a certain extent, alter patterns of speech, writing, and even thinking. It could be so long-lived as to subvert the tender and graceful traditional style of Chinese writing and language, turning it into something totally different. He went so far as to predict that, by the end of the twentieth century, people would be able to distinguish easily which written pieces came from Taiwan and which from mainland China, beyond the obvious difference created by the use of simplified characters on the mainland. The most frightening prospect was that the wording and syntax created by a totalitarian government could eventually debase the literary spirit of the Chinese language.

So, this was how Joe saw the relationship between literature and living. With a smile, he slid the vocabulary list in front of me. "Now you can tell me what kind of story is behind all those phrases."

It was a tragic story of a broken family and death. The writer of the petition was a lonely old woman. Before 1949, she and her husband owned a bookstore in Wuhan. In addition to books, they also sold copybooks for calligraphy, pens and ink, and stationery. In the 1950s, the government took over the bookstore, and the couple's class status was determined to be "small business owner." They were allowed to stay on at the new, expanded bookstore, now called "Xinhua Bookstore," as janitors. Their only son worked at a publishing company. In 1957, he said that "traditional characters should not be abandoned and that publishing of old books should resume." For this, he was labeled a "rightist" and in 1960 starved to death at the reform-through-labor farm at Jiabiangou in Gansu Province. That same year, her husband died and her daughter-in-law remarried and moved away, leaving behind a boy and girl. During the early stage of the Cultural Revolution, the girl was sent to a farm in the countryside where she was raped by the leader of a People's Liberation Army propaganda team propagating Mao Zedong Thought who then turned around and accused her of corrupting a military officer. After being dragged to numerous public criticism sessions where she was beaten black and blue, she hanged herself in a cow barn. The boy had just entered high school when the schools were closed due to the Cultural Revolution. Jobless, branded with bad class status, and friendless with no one to talk things over with, he went straight to the farm as soon as he heard what had happened to his sister. No sooner had he arrived than he was tied up and thrown in prison, charged with the crime of "attacking the PLA propaganda team," in other words, being an active counter-revolutionary.

Life in prison could be easier when there was a "head prisoner." A prisoner who obeyed the rules and did not challenge the head prisoner's authority could survive. However, this sixteen-year-old was tossed into the prison's general population where there was no "head prisoner." It was a place of constant, fierce struggle and pestilential atmosphere where anything could happen to prisoners, sometimes with the connivance of prison officials. For reasons unknown, the boy died in a brawl – stabbed - for which no one was held responsible. Now the old had to bury the young. The old woman was the only family member left alive.

After the Cultural Revolution, not being able to walk, this old woman could not petition for justice in person. So she wrote and sent a petition to the city of Wuhan's "Office of Petitions by Letter" requesting that the publishing company redress her son's case, penalize the military officer in active service who had raped her granddaughter, discipline the Communist Party committee members on the farm who had set up a private court, and punish the "King of Hell" and "his little devils" who had murdered her grandson in prison. This letter of blood and tears provided plenty of details: times, places, events, perpetrators' names and work units were all listed. Each letter was numbered. The letter Micah brought as teaching material was numbered 96.

This lonely old soul wrote letter after letter, mailing one per week. Who could have known that one of her letters would find its way overseas and fall into the hands of a tenacious foreign journalist? I even imagined Micah, six months after arriving in Beijing, being able to bring about the realization of the old lady's dream. The Chinese authorities might smilingly say to him, "Those wrong, false, and misjudged cases were all the fault of the vicious 'Gang of Four.' We have already implemented policies to redress all the mishandled cases and pay retroactive wages." They might point to this as a resolved case to preclude further inquiries.

Sure enough, eight or nine months after Micah's arrival in Beijing, news came that he had been injured and hospitalized, causing an uproar in the foreign media. According to a report in the Washington <u>Post</u>, the paper's special correspondent was hurried along by police on the streets of Beijing as he was trying to read petitions spread out on the sidewalk by out-of-town petitioners. When the correspondent tried to reason with the officer, he was beaten up. An English reporter saw what happened and called the American embassy. An American diplomat quickly arrived at the scene and took Micah away. For the time being, he was out of danger. The American embassy had lodged a complaint with the Chinese Ministry of Foreign Affairs.

My heart ached on reading this news. Not long afterwards, I received a letter from Micah sent via diplomatic pouch. Waxing humorous, he reported that he was still alive and that his Chinese continued to improve. "Not even a gun butt can knock it out," he wrote. He added that he wished I could be in Beijing because the Chinese teachers arranged through the Chinese government were all "little spies, but you, my dear teacher, what you told me is the truth, the real Red China." After reading his letter, I immediately wrote back, bidding him to be careful and avoid direct confrontation with the police.

Of course, Joe and I could never have expected what was to come. Joe wasn't very interested in politics, but he did make one prediction. "If Micah sends you a book, it will be Alexander Solzhenitsyn's *Gulag Archipelago*." "Oh," I responded. "Is Micah an expert on the Soviet Union?" Joe nodded. "Micah is one of Washington's top Sovietologists." This reminded me of Prince and his blue eyes. Micah must have heard of me through Prince.

"I'm more interested in your trip to the Kunlun Mountains." Joe had already changed the subject. "Can you tell me how you handled the problem of privacy as a girl traveling with a group of Uyghur men?" Joe hesitated, as though realizing that he was also a male. "I mean, if you don't mind. You don't really have to answer me. I'm just curious...." he added in seeming embarrassment.

"Actually, we resolved the problem before setting out. A young Uyghur woman, the daughter-in-law of our group's leader, brought me a large, beautiful white dog. She told me that the dog's name was Nina, adding that, if I had to leave the group to relieve myself, all I had to do was call Nina, stroke her head, and she would lead me to a spot where no one could see me. If someone approached, she would stop him and bark to alert me. How wonderful! I was touched by her thoughtfulness. I bent down, looking Nina in the eye, and stroked her ears. She gazed back at me, her head pressed against the back of my hand as if to set my mind at ease. Then she quietly turned around to face another large grayish-white dog, a male, standing there dignified and solemn.

'Misha is Nina's mate. They will both go with you. They are our most experienced herding dogs. You can trust them,' the young woman said with a smile, and she bid me goodbye.

"As expected, Nina was always by my side. If I had to relieve myself, I would stroke Nina's head, and she would lead me away. At the same time, Misha would bark to alert the others that they should continue on their way but at a slower pace. When Nina and I returned, the group would not be too far ahead of us, so we didn't have to race to catch up. The men were extra careful with me in the group. If they had to relieve themselves, Nina would lead me forward, leaving the men behind. In a few minutes, they would catch up with long strides, laughing and talking. In this way, nothing embarrassing ever happened during those six months."

Joe was totally amazed, commenting, "In many situations, the relationship between man and animals can be telepathic and effective." It was much more than that. A good story came to mind, and I began telling it to him in dramatic fashion.

Felling all those poplar trees had another major consequence. For centuries, the dense forest had served as the natural habitat of forest wolves. Around the Production and Construction Corps, we often heard the gunshots of wolf hunters, swaggering members of the armed militia. It was said that they cooked and ate the wolves they killed, afterwards complaining about the meat's foul taste.

Uyghurs, Kazaks, and Kyrgyz would not eat wolves, dogs, camels, or, especially horses. They urged me to never eat them either, saying, "They are our friends." So, even though every family had rifles, they would never be used against wolves nor would the wolves ever attack their friends' flocks.

One evening after we had set up camp and started a fire, Nina and I emerged from behind a sand dune to rejoin the group. All of a sudden Nina froze, the fur all over her body bristling. I froze, too, and cautiously looked around. My breathing became short and rapid. Three wolves had emerged from the other side of the sand dune and were slowly approaching the campfire. Camels stopped chewing, turning their heads in unison to watch the approaching wolves. Voices ceased singing, and musical instruments fell silent. Misha stood protectively in front of the fire, his bristling fur forming a golden ring against the firelight. Nina glanced at me and dashed off, kicking up a cloud of sand. In a flash, she was standing beside Misha, both ready to defend against an attack.

The three wolves stopped advancing; they even lowered their heads. I saw Nina and Misha turn slightly, making way for the visitors. Our guide, the elderly Uyghur, smilingly waved at the wolves, who slowly crept toward him, whimpering. In the firelight, I could clearly see the hind leg of the wolf in the middle was dragging a frightful steel trap.

The wounded leg dripped blood onto the sand, where it formed a line of tiny holes. I quietly moved toward the fire to sit by the old man who by now was using both hands to pry apart the terrible jaws of the trap. When the trap was off, the old man gently raised the wolf's broken leg, carefully examining it in the firelight. Then he told me to cut a straight red willow branch no more than twenty centimeters long. Dry red willow branches were just by my feet, for we were burning them in our campfire. I took out my knife to shave the branch flat and smooth. I knew that this splint was what the wolf needed. While I worked, the old man took some medicine from the cloth satchel he usually carried over his shoulder and carefully applied it to the wound. He then took the splint from my hand and tightly bound it to the wolf's leg, signaling to me to stabilize the splint with a strip of hemp cloth. This was the first and only time I ever touched the body of a wolf. I could feel it shaking, obviously in great pain, but it uttered not a sound. The old man smiled and nodded, pleased at my firm yet careful efforts. At this point, I finally looked eye to eye at the wolf. Its eyes were brimming with tears!

The old man was going on about how long the wolves must have walked to find us. The wounded wolf slowly stood up and tried to walk a few steps, then stood steadily. All three wolves simultaneously lowered their heads as they faced the old man, who raised both of his hands to signal acceptance of their gratitude. As the wolves backed away to leave, pieces of mutton flew from the group of Uyghur men, landing beside the wolves.

On this night, under a full moon in the dead silence of the desert, the songs of wolves could be heard. Rough and bold, drawn-out and lingering they circled around earth and sky. My eyes, wide open, watched the three raised heads as their songs mingled with answering songs from the distance. The old man threw that terrible instrument of torture into the fire, where it gradually lost its shape and its ability to do harm.

Warming his hands at the fire, the old man told me softly, "They are noble animals who understand gratitude. We are honored to be able to do something for them, an opportunity afforded us by Allah. From now on, you don't have to be afraid of wolves should you come across them in the desert. They will be your loyal and reliable friends for life."

Learning that I would have those friends for life left me filled with heartwarming emotions. The old man had offered me an opportunity to use my own hands to save a wounded wolf. I felt that, not only the wolves, but also the old man and the kind Uyghur men in our group were my friends for life, forever loyal and reliable. Oh, and of course there were Misha and Nina and even our camels; they were all my friends. Suddenly I felt so rich, so accepted and recognized that I could not hold back the tears that already covered my face. In the dark, a bass voice started singing a sad song. I softly harmonized and soon many voices joined in. In the lingering notes I could hear the free harmony of the wolves. For many years afterwards, the memory of this full moon night brought me a sense of real warmth.

"Fantastic! Even more beautiful than *Scheherazade*." Joe was all misty-eyed.

In the early spring of 1976, I was summoned to regimental head-quarters. Our company's political commissar, whose devilish face usually radiated unadulterated evil, brought me the order and showed a rare smile as he considerately suggested, "Why don't you go by horse? Headquarters isn't close." At regimental headquarters, a cadre in the Political and Law section (responsible for internal security) handed me a slip of paper, commenting, "No one can say how long Deng Xiaoping will remain in power." This note from his office must have traveled a long time before it arrived at Third Division. The upper and lower parts of the slip had been cut off, leaving only one line: "This person is not suitable to remain in Xinjiang." After reading it, I silently returned it to the cadre. Seeing no sign that I was overjoyed, he probably figured that I had connections with higher-ups in Deng's office. This made him anxious and cautious, so he swallowed his questions and took me to the Personnel Section to go through the formalities of changing residency. Still silent, I thought back twelve years when another slip of paper reading "This student is not suitable for admission" crushed my dream of a college education and discarded me to the remotest corner of China. Now, "This person is not suitable to remain in Xinjiang" was sending me back to Beijing. I didn't care why. It was always good to be back with Grandma.

The formalities proceeded swiftly. The faces of the people in charge were not wearing their usual expressions of disapproval by which they signaled their "exalted" positions. Instead, they became friendly. I responded coolly and without much expression. One woman said, "How fortunate it is to be sent back to Beijing." I just looked at her until she turned away in embarrassment. Only two months earlier, she had come to our Fifth Company to extol the great significance of "taking root at the frontier," driving us unmarried men and women from our mud brick houses to underground dungeons to make room for newly-wed couples - literal support for the policy promoted by leaders at various levels of the Production and Construction Corps. Back then, she had been standing at the entrance of the Company office gesticulating as I pulled a hand-cart filled with my luggage, books, and tools, my back bent horizontal as I passed her, and she hadn't even glanced at me. Now I told her, "Nine years ago I moved from inner China to an underground dungeon, and now I'm moving from the dungeon back to inner China. I've come full circle." She just looked at me, words failing her.

The cadre at the Political and Law Section said to me in a gentle voice, "Go back to your company to pack your things and come back here tomorrow afternoon. You can stay a night in the visitor quarters, and the next day we will have a car going to the depot at Daheyan." His words carried an unspoken order: "Don't stop on your way to the depot and don't talk to anyone about this."

It was getting dark as I rode Old Black in the dusk with my change of residence document and 360 renminbi of severance pay tucked in my pocket. At the rate trees were being felled, within a year this place would be a desert. I felt more sad than happy.

Suddenly Old Black – an experienced denizen of this area – began to neigh, and the mane on his neck stood up. I turned my head and saw not far from us a large gray wolf running parallel to our course. I saw a friendly face, so I patted Old Black's neck and told him, "It's just a good friend saying goodbye," which seemed to reassure him. His breathing returned to normal, and we continued to move steadily forward. The wolf stopped as we neared the company headquarters, but I could still see his dark shadow as I walked into the Fifth Company's living quarters. I waved at him and whispered, "Goodbye, friend." As though he had heard me, he turned and disappeared into the darkness.

Class was over. Before Joe left, he urged me to tell the story to Micah, who would never be able to hear it from anyone else. Later on, he might even develop an interest in studying issues relating to China's minority groups. I smiled and sent Joe on his way. Then Pele and I went for a walk as my mind lingered over that brief period on the eve of my departure, a short but very meaningful night.

My permit to change residence stirred up a small storm of excitement in the boundless reaches of desert. Uyghurs who passed by our company quickly learned of my impending departure.

On this cold spring night, I assembled my collection of books to give them away to the young girls who shared my dungeon. The books whose paper covers promised *How to Cultivate Different Varieties of Corn* were really a four-volume edition of *Jean-Christophe* by Romain Rolland. The girl who received it carefully placed it in a wooden chest. A thin volume of Pushkin's *Eugene Onegin* was wrapped in a gray paper cover that read *A Brochure on the Prevention of Diseases in Cotton and Wheat.* The recipient carefully wrapped it in a pillow case and hid it under a folded cotton jacket. I kept Eliot's The *Waste Land,* which I had had no chance to return it to its owner. Another keeper was the *Inferno* of Dante's *Divine Comedy.* I placed those two books at the bottom of my cloth bag with two sets of clothing on top. Then I rolled up my bedding and sent it to the home of an old worker with three children but only one set of bedding. As for the tools that had served me well over the years, I gave them to a sickly girlfriend. Good tools would save her a lot of energy. My kitchenware went to a woman who dug licorice root, as did my much-patched clothing; she could use them to make shoes. It was late at night when I finally squeezed into the bed with the other girls and slept briefly.

The next day was a Sunday, market day at Maola. The girls were hesitant about shopping for food there. "Just go," I urged them. "The canteen is short of food now. Go see the locals for something to eat."

Opening the door, I found Nina and Misha waiting outside wagging their tails. Close by were three horse-drawn carts drawn up in a line, driven by the old Uyghur man, his son, and daughter-in-law. They waved when they saw me. I handed a cardboard box to the old man's daughter-in-law. It contained my sweaters and scarves, along with my knitting needles, steel needles, and yarns. The beautiful young woman accepted my gift with a smile and presented me with an embroidered cloth shoulder bag, some soft and puffy naan, yoghurt in a porcelain jar, and a small bag of sweet, dry wild olives.

My Uyghur friends, young and old, waited patiently for me to say my goodbyes. As I climbed into the first cart, the old man asked, "Is this all you have to take?" Brandishing my new embroidered cloth bag, I replied with a smile, "Plus this bag of treasures!" Everyone laughed.

Amidst the laughter, the carts began to move, stirring up a thin cloud of grayish-yellow dust from the empty expanse of the Fifth Company's parade ground, where only a shiny red placard bearing the obligatory quotation from Chairman Mao stood glimmering in the sunlight. People, young and old wearing their Sunday outfits, stood expressionlessly around their living quarters with dust covering their feet to watch the carts depart. In the background, the wind carried the voice of the company commander telling someone, "How fortunate it is to be an only child! Why else would she be called back to Beijing?"

So that was the cover story put out by the Corps about my departure. Now I had a clue. It was squeezing one last bit of utility out of me: to promote the One-Child Policy.

The old Uyghur man spoke many kind words to me on our way to the depot. His most important sentence was "Go west, and then keep going until you are home."

On a quiet afternoon in 1981 in Arlington, not far from the Capitol, the face of the old man appeared clearly before my eyes. Pointing with his horse whip towards the setting sun, he voiced this advice most seriously. All the Uyghur men and women in our party nodded their heads in solemn agreement. I patted the Yingjisha dagger at my waist and told my friends equally solemnly, "I will go home, and I will never forget you."

I didn't know much about what lay ahead, but the one thing I did know was that I would be embarking on the difficult journey home. But first I had to go east.

By 1981, I was really home. I had no idea that, twenty years later, I would be speaking up for my beloved Uyghur brothers and sisters before the U.S. Congress, bearing witness to their missing freedom, their stolen land and homes, and the grievous suffering inflicted on them. This testimony was the most significant product of my nine-year stay in Xinjiang. I could not have predicted this back in 1981, but I could recount in detail the last night I spent at the 48th Regiment back in 1976.

The horse-drawn carts stopped near the 48th Regiment office. After our goodbyes, my Uyghur friends remained in the cart while Nina led me to the headquarters office and then left. As the creaking of the departing horse carts gradually faded, I collected myself before walking calmly inside. The cadre from the Political and Law Section personally escorted me to the visitor quarters where he unlocked a door in the farthest corner of the building. The brick chimney wall in the room was still warm. Against the chimney wall stood a three-drawer bureau. A desk held a tall pile of papers while a single bed with a full set of bedding occupied a corner by the chimney wall.

"I'll get you dinner in a while," the cadre promised. "According to regulations," he noted, pointing to the papers on the desk, "we should have destroyed all this material in your file. However, the reason behind your being relocated is rather unusual." I knew that he was referring to the origin of that slip of paper. Remaining silent, I watched him closely.

"All these documents were written on carbon paper, so the originating unit in Beijing also has copies. You have one night to review them so you can mentally prepare yourself." Seeing me still quiet, he continued in a helpful manner. "There is a small door behind the chimney wall that leads to a bathroom." At this point, I expressed thanks, which seemed to please him. "This material shouldn't be seen by anyone else. Please don't be upset that I must lock the door from the outside." I smiled and told him not to worry. With an answering smile, he left the room but was back within ten minutes with some rice and a few dishes as well as a thermos of hot water. Then I heard him once more locking the door from the outside.

I opened the file to see handwriting I had known since my childhood referring to "the worthy progeny of American imperialism" and "the true colors of the so-called 'good student.'" The writer wondered "why did she join the riflery team? Who is her real target when she aims her small-bore rifle?"; "Corrupting the sons and daughters of revolutionary cadres, what evil intentions is she harboring?"

I closed the file, ate dinner and finished my soup, visited the bathroom, and washed my hands. Then I sat down to read every word of the hatred spewed onto paper by the woman who had given birth to me. I took care not to touch my lips with the hand that turned the pages, for I truly believed that the words contained poison- deadly poison.

As I read on, I discovered that this huge pile of documents from the Beijing People's Theater also contained denunciations of other individuals. One document stated that the famous playwright Tao Jin had often tinkered with a radio transmitter at the student dormitory when he was studying film theory in New York. The writer claimed to have evidence that Tao Jin had been recruited by the CIA while a student in New York to become "the enemy of the Chinese people." What a horrific frame-up! Tao Jin, a handsome film actor and a creative movie director, would never have imagined in his wildest dreams that someone would fabricate such a charge. I remembered him proudly telling me when I was young about his skill in repairing radios and how, as a poor student in New York, he had earned pocket money by fixing radios for people. He even fixed my small radio which had been producing more static than music. Uncle Tao Jin would have been completely blindsided if pressed to confess his relationship with foreign spy organizations. This slander guaranteed that he would suffer greatly. Deep into the night I struggled to read on.

Early next morning, the cadre unlocked the door to bring me a bowl of cornmeal porridge, a steamed twisted flour roll, and a plate of pickled vegetables. While I was having my breakfast, he stuffed all the documents on the table into the firebox at the base of the chimney wall and tossed in a match. A bright fire started, and soon only a layer of ash remained.

The cadre opened the door in answer to a knock. A voice outside said, "The car is here, and the driver is eager to get going." I picked up my satchel and the embroidered cloth bag, bid the cadre goodbye, and marched out of there with long strides.

An old Dodge truck was parked outside. It was empty – a rare sight. The driver nodded at me, and I climbed into the cab. Soldiers nearby in green army uniforms with red collar tabs were exchanging greetings with thermoses and tea cups in hand. The driver took a look at me and said with a smile, "You get to move back to Beijing so smoothly. Does this have anything to do with Nixon's visit to China?" I looked back at him and asked, "May I know your name? How long will it take to drive to Daheyan?" He replied, "My name is Wei. With no other stops, we'll get there in four days for sure." Shaking vigorously, the truck had already passed the headquarters office of the 48th Regiment.

Joe's prediction turned out to be half right: Micah did bring two copies of *The Gulag Archipelago*. However, during our ensuing lessons, he didn't show particular interest in issues relating to China's minority groups. Rather, he focused on the problem of the One-Child Policy.

The two copies of *Gulag* that he brought were in Russian and English. How I wished that I could keep the Russian copy which held Solzhenitsyn's own original words. However, with limited time and energy, I chose to keep the English copy. As I looked up words in the dictionary, I made Micah a useful vocabulary list, pages and pages of Marxist-Leninist jargon that was both familiarly depressing and repressive.

We eventually came across the term "dignity." Micah asked, "How does a person retain his dignity in the face of absolutely crushing oppression?"

That is a very difficult thing to do. Although I lived in China for thirty years, I never wrote a self-criticism or denunciation while, for various reasons, people all around me were doing so. This kind of writing destroyed family bonds and caused people to lose all self-respect and self-confidence. Just imagine: when a person poured out a flood of invective against his elders, his family, his loved ones, his friends, and even himself, what dignity had he left? But no one asked me to write such things. I believed that they felt I was born with my "sin." Only when I was young and living at home was I made to write such things by the woman who hated me to the very marrow of her bones. I started boarding at school when I was fourteen or fifteen, and three years later went to work in rural, mountainous areas. In 1976, I was relocated back to Beijing and lived at home. By that time, she was appalled by my presence and by the way I looked. She had no idea what I had gone through during those twelve years away. But my contemptuous look and my strong hands and arms kept her from baring her fangs and claws in front of me. All she could do was act as an informer. So, I could say that no organization or leader had ever made me write a single word of self-criticism or denounce my grandmother, my father, or anyone else. This situation simply meant that all of society knew that I was beyond help and not worth "saving." As a result, I retained a measure of dignity. I could use my silence to resist the discrimination I faced whereas many, many people were deprived of the right to remain silent. Even so, living in a society that disregarded human dignity, there were still times when the remaining shreds of dignity faced assault.

Returning to Beijing in the spring of 1976, I had to register my residency at the local police station, where I was handed a card on which my name, address, and age were written. At that time, I was twenty-nine years old, not quite thirty. People at the police station solemnly told me to take this card to the Shijia Alley neighborhood office. I did as I was told. After seeing my card, a man there told me to go to the planned parenthood office. "I'm single and have nothing to do with planned parenthood," I said, to which he replied, "Planned parenthood is national policy. It applies to everyone." I had no choice but to go there.

Posted on the wall of the planned parenthood office was a huge chart on which were written the names of all the neighborhood females capable of becoming pregnant, along with additional information: address, age, marital status, with or without children, children's birth dates, sterilization record, abortion record, any symptoms of pregnancy, contraception measures, contraceptive ring implanted or not, records of removing contraceptive rings without permission, and time of last monthly period. This last item was underlined in red. A fierce-looking middle-aged woman took my card and wrote my name, address and age on the huge chart. As I mechanically answered her questions one by one, she diligently entered my answers on the chart. My last sentence to her was "I had my period yesterday." Satisfied, she filled in the date. She then began to extol the virtues of the single-child pledge and sterilization, both of which came with rewards. Before she could finish, I turned around and strode quickly out of the office.

Micah looked at me with a stupefied expression on his face and even stopped jotting down notes. He wrestled with his thoughts for a bit and came up with a question. "I wonder what this 'contraceptive ring' is?" Although tempted to reply that it was akin to that barbarous trap on the leg of the forest wolf, I restrained myself. Instead, I simply told him, "I've never seen one. But it's metal, and once it is placed in the uterus a fertilized egg cannot attach itself to the womb. It's a very effective method of contraception." With pain written all over his face, Micah asked, "Does the ring cause complications for the woman?" Before I could reply, he chuckled cynically and added, "I suppose that, in light of the One-Child Policy, the comfort and health of women are hardly considerations." He had seen clearly and thought the matter through so thoroughly that I did not have to say anything.

I eventually was assigned to work at a garment factory. At the end of the first day of work, as everybody was rushing out the door, I stayed to clean my machine with some cloth remnants. The assistant floor supervisor, Master Li, came over and spoke to me in a soft voice. "You're single, so in theory I shouldn't bother you with this form. But, in this factory, everyone has to fill one out unless a woman has already reached menopause...." Her face was red with embarrassment. From my previous experience at the neighborhood office, I could understand her dilemma, and I appreciated her bringing it up when no one else was around. I replied with a smile. "Master Li, it's just filling out a form, isn't it? I'll do it right now." I filled out the one-child pledge form, signed it, and handed it back to her in a matter of two minutes. All smiles, she carefully put the form away, cooing, "So reasonable. You are educated after all." And she chattily continued, "Many workers, especially those young female newcomers, are most reluctant to complete the form. They say, 'I'm not married yet; I don't even have a boyfriend. Isn't it unreasonable to expect me to pledge to have only one child?'" She had to work hard to convince them. Turning to me, she said, "What's so hard about it? You're not signing your life away!" I smiled at her but made no reply.

Since I intended to leave China, filling out the one-child pledge was not a problem for me. But for the young female workers who had to live there the rest of their lives, promising not to bear a second child even before they got married wasn't so simple. What were they going to do if they got married, gave birth to an unhealthy baby, and then found they were not allowed to have another child? This could lead to serious trouble with in-laws; their husbands might ask for a divorce, and they'd be the ones to suffer in the end. For these understood but unspoken reasons, many young women stubbornly resisted the pressure, refusing to promise to have no more than one child. Privately they whispered to me, "Elder sister, we really don't have the courage to sign that pledge. What if, say, in the future we give birth to a daughter and our mother-in-law insists on having a grandson and pressures our husband to divorce us and remarry? He might then have a son. But for us, with a girl, who will marry us? Having a daughter from a previous marriage is a dead-end street for us!"

But in China, the implementation of policies is closely related to endless repression. Threatened with unemployment or dismissal, the female workers had to give in for the sake of earning a living. Master Li eventually collected all the forms and turned them in to the eastern district's planned parenthood office.

Perhaps it was stories such as this that made Micah detest the One-Child Policy; or perhaps he had already thoroughly researched the subject. Whatever sparked his interest, he did a lot of field research on the One-Child Policy during his stay in Beijing. I also supplied him with some actual cases. In the mid-1980s, shortly after Micah and his wife left China, the Washington <u>Post</u> published the most thoroughly researched in-depth report in the Western world on the One-Child Policy, its abuse of human rights, and the suffering it inflicted on Chinese women. The reporter behind the story was none other than Micah.

Reminiscing about the benefits of teaching and learning with Micah would always bring me back to 1977. After I stepped into the U.S. Liaison Office for the first time, Grandma gave me her full support while my mother collaborated with the Public Security Bureau to inform on me. She meticulously recorded the names of all my classmates and friends who had contact with me and had possibly supported me. I believed at the time that many people might have thought that I had already been thrown in jail.

On March 21, the day I was supposed to pick up my new passport, the route from my home to the U.S. Liaison Office was infested with police, making it practically impossible to get through. I had no choice but to go to work as usual. Soon, officers from the Public Security Bureau arrived there demanding loudly that I promise never again to get in touch in any way with the U.S. Liaison Office. Faced with blank paper, I swiftly wrote two letters: one to Premier Hua Guofeng and another to Foreign Minister Huang Hua, denouncing this barbaric and dishonest action. That was the first time I had ever written a letter of appeal in China; the first time, claiming that "It is not a crime to be patriotic."

This was how I defended my personal dignity in the face of such high-handed treatment.

On March 28, I discovered an old telephone, installed during the Japanese occupation in Beijing's Xidan district, that was connected to the office of the consul at the U.S. Liaison Office. Early the next morning, I made my roundabout way to the Liaison Office in Jianguomenwai by way of Miyun. The consul was waiting at the gate of the U.S. Liaison Office with my new passport. It was in my hands for less than one day. That same evening, I was seized by the police, who also confiscated my documents, launching the next round of our bitter struggle. But I understood that the American government was confident about winning. It was now protecting an American citizen with a valid passport. It would do so with all its will and skill. All I had to do was face down the Chinese government without yielding an inch.

CHAPTER 9

MR. MOORE

Today, I would be meeting a federal government security officer. Dr. Yates had informed me two days earlier that he would come to my classroom after work. When he duly appeared at my wide-open door, I cordially invited him in. He was neatly dressed in suit and tie.

Closing the door as he greeted me, he flashed a badge identifying him as the security officer Dr. Yates had spoken of. Instead of sitting right down, he remained standing to examine a poster hanging on the inside of the door. The poster displayed 444 American flags – one taped on each day from 1979 to 1981 - the period when American diplomats stationed at the embassy in Iran were held hostage. Every day during that crisis, my students and I would paste another flag on the poster with heavy hearts, hoping our colleagues would be released and come home. Our hoping went on for over a year, a total of 444 days. The poster had been up for quite a while, but I was reluctant to take it down. In a colorful way it represented our shared wish, concern, and conviction that they would come home. Our government, our military, and our citizens would all do their best to secure their safe release. Standing in front of the flags, my visitor was quietly pondering.

"You haven't taken those flags down," he finally observed, turning around to sit down.

"Such incidents will happen again," I replied. "Maybe not taking hostages; maybe some other outrage, such as a bombing." He looked at me calmly, as if encouraging me to go on. "My experiences over a very long time have made me very sensitive to danger. Even distant danger would fill me with worry. This is why I don't believe that this hostage incident is a one-time event, nor do I think that the crisis is over." I felt embarrassed to have blurted out so much, as if showing off in front of an expert.

The security officer listened to me intently before saying, "It's very important to be alert to potential danger. To be honest, I wish more Americans were."

Of course, my emotions were involved as well. I could not forget the distress and yearning I felt in my heart back in January 1977 when I saw the Stars and Stripes fluttering under the blue sky near Ritan Park in Beijing. I also could not forget that on February 21, when I finally walked into the U.S. Liaison Office, how Mr. O. listened to my appeal in front of that flag. By the time I was done, our eyes were red. I could no longer control myself, and tears covered my face.

In 1981, I was finally able to speak my mind openly and calmly. "I see American diplomats every day. I know their credentials, experiences, family situations. I even know who's remodeling the interior of his house and who's building a new deck. I also know their temperaments, their language abilities, their strengths and weaknesses. But what I know best is that they all share a common conviction and have their feet planted solidly on the ground. Let me put it this way: I often feel that they are soldiers in suits, ready to give their all to this country: their wisdom, ability, health, even their lives."

The security officer continued to listen closely then nodded. "Dr. Swift, Dr. Yates, and some of your students all described you as the most positive, enthusiastic teacher and one who really cares about her students. I know about your background. My purpose in meeting you today is to discuss a special student, Mr. Moore. You might have already heard his name."

A month or so earlier, during a routine staff meeting, Ms. O., a senior teacher, had vehemently opposed allowing a student carrying a gun into the classroom. The student's name was Moore. Everyone piped up, wanting to know the details. Thumping her chest, Ms. O. loudly proclaimed, "I was scared out of my wits. This person walked into my classroom, and when he draped his trench coat across the back of a chair something went 'clank.' This gave me a scare, so I asked what the sound was. He said it was nothing. How could it be nothing? So, I kept on asking. He reluctantly reached into the coat pocket and pulled out – a pistol!" Ms. O. emphatically expressed her opinion: "Does Mr. Moore work for the CIA or FBI? No matter. He should not be allowed into a classroom of the Chinese section of FSI." Keeping his face expressionless and saying nothing, Dr. Yates waved his hand to signal the end of the meeting.

Micah had finished his evening sessions with me the week before, leaving me time for other matters. I guessed that Dr. Yates would arrange for Mr. Moore to take lessons at my home. What I did not expect was that a security officer had to interview me first.

The security officer sat before me with a smile on his face. "I can tell you that, for many years, Mr. Moore has worked with great success on the dangerous front lines of the war against illegal drugs. His job means that his personal safety is always at risk, and his experience and vigilance are his best protection. As your student, he would have to learn to listen and understand but not to speak. Preferably, he would not be able to speak a word of Chinese but could understand it when spoken. So in class, he would speak English and you would speak Chinese. Would this format work for you?" he inquired.

"Why not," I replied. In my heart I hoped that his lessons would take up less time than Micah's so that I could have more time to read novels in English or perhaps to sleep an extra hour. "Two evenings a week with two hours for each lesson should be enough," the security officer said. Oh, that's great, I thought thankfully. I was also pleasantly surprised when I heard how much I would be paid – even more than the Washington <u>Post</u> and <u>National Geographic</u>. The security officer smiled again. "You're not worried about your own safety, teaching such a student?" This was the first time in the United States that someone had asked me whether I might feel insecure. I replied almost without thinking. "Coming from a most unsafe place, I know a bit about self-preservation."

Such as?" The security officer was curious.

"A person without desire is a strong person. If someone is not greedy, not taking short cuts, not out to win fame and fortune at any cost, he will not even consider committing a crime. Such a person is relatively safe to be around," I concluded calmly.

The security officer nodded in agreement, then asked, "You just mentioned the word 'crime.' As a formality, I have to ask if you have a criminal record." Seeing my astounded expression, he added, "Any parking or traffic tickets?" He opened his notebook, ready to record my answer.

I shook my head. "I've never gotten a ticket. But once I carried my dog, Pele, in my handbag and took the subway to the National Geographic building...." I figured it was best to come clean about that even though my "illegal behavior" was never discovered.

The security officer beamed. "Is your handbag very big?"

"Oh, it's not big," I told him. "My dog is very small." I demonstrated with my hands and couldn't help laughing.

The security officer closed his notebook and stood up. "Glad to have such a pleasant experience. It's very interesting talking to you. Mr. Moore will get in touch with Dr. Yates to set up a schedule for his lessons. One last thing: it would be best if you didn't mention to anyone that Mr. Moore is your student." Just as he was leaving, he said, "I'm driving. Do you need a ride home?"

I thanked him for the offer but declined, telling him that I would be teaching at the Johns Hopkins University's School of Advanced International Studies that evening. He bid me a polite goodbye and disappeared down the corridor.

My things packed in my bag and my mind at ease, I went downstairs to the McDonald's where I bought a fish filet sandwich, an order of French fries, a small apple turnover, and a large coffee. Sitting there, I took a volume of the Ming Dynasty novel *Jin Ping Mei* from my bag and started reading. The dissertation of one of my Johns Hopkins doctoral candidates concerned one of the book's main characters, Wu Yueniang, and her significance in the family and in society. As Maddie had predicted, I was learning while teaching. The complete original version of the four-volume set, bought by mail from Hong Kong, was a book I had never read before. It was unexpectedly good, a complete re-creation of life at the time written in simple, honest prose. Even more unexpected was that a young American sinologist provided the opportunity for me to fill this major gap in my knowledge of Chinese literary classics.

Mr. Moore was very courteous even before we met. He first asked Dr. Yates to check with me about the most convenient times for me to conduct his lessons. As for himself, "Any evening is fine, even on holidays." This flexibility was really convenient for me. With Micah, weekends and holidays were out – they were his sacrosanct personal time.

"Mr. Moore is divorced and has an adult daughter. He lives alone in a small apartment in downtown Washington," Dr. Yates explained. I remained silent. Americans treasured their privacy. It was fine if they wanted to tell me their stories, but I would never push them to do so.

Mr. Moore was scheduled to arrive on a Friday evening at nine o'clock. At five minutes before nine, I was standing quietly in front of my living room window looking down at the parking area. An old black Honda sedan slowly pulled into a parking space under a street light. A man of medium height in a wrinkled trench coat of indeterminate color emerged from the car and immediately turned up his collar against the wind. He locked the car and, swinging his arms, marched toward my building.

The doorbell rang. It was Mr. Moore. He looked so ordinary. No one would pay him the slightest attention if he were to show up in a supermarket. His hair was graying and his face was wrinkled. His grayish eyes were filled with smiles. I invited him in and offered to hang up his coat. He stepped in, but, before he could take off his coat, Pele excitedly dashed up and ran around him in circles, his version of a passionate welcome.

Mr. Moore squatted to pick Pele up and, stroking his head, said affectionally, "You must be the famous Pele, hiding in Teresa's handbag to ride the subway." He spoke so tenderly, as though he were someone coming home after a long trip to chat about the old days with his dog. Lying on his shoulder, Pele radiated contentment.

The ardent welcoming ceremony ended, and Mr. Moore placed Pele on the sofa. He then took off his coat and handed it to me. He was wearing a much-worn plaid shirt of the type often seen on blue-collar workers under an old woolen sweater. Tiny woolen pills dotted the sweater's sleeves. The knees of his blue jeans were turning white with wear. His shoes had walked through ten thousand crags and floods. Their original color, whether black or dark brown, was no longer discernable. The contrast with the business attire worn by the security officer who had visited me caused me to smile. Touching the trench coat, I could feel the outline of a pistol. I handed the trench coat back to him. He appeared surprised for a second and then smiled. "I heard that you weren't afraid of them."

"That's not the issue," I replied. "This pistol isn't a toy. It's better to put it in a safe place." Mr. Moore took the pistol out of the pocket and handed it to me, butt first. I took it. It felt heavy in my hand. I put it in the drawer of the side table closest to the dining table where it joined some postcards and stamps.

"When did you start handling guns?" Mr. Moore asked as soon as I had put the pistol away.

I talked to him about the Soviet physical education system, which focused on "run, jump, throw" track and field events as well as target shooting. I started senior high school in September 1961, a time when China was still following Soviet models in many respects. I was fifteen years old then. Beijing University paid close attention to the physical education system in its attached high school, anticipating that those high school students would become tomorrow's Beijing University students. If any athletic talent could be discovered among them, this would give Beijing University an edge over other universities, especially local rival Qinghua University, in collegiate competitions.

For political reasons, I couldn't get into team events such as basketball and volleyball. Long-distance running was my favorite sport, but I was never allowed to take part in relay races. In other words, I was always competing as an individual, and target shooting was typically a singles competition. But unlike long-distance running, a target shooter had to use a gun, and even a small-bore rifle could inflict casualties. Could I join the shooting team with my background of having an American serviceman for a father? Of course, I would not express an opinion. It was fine with me if the authorities wanted me to join the team and equally fine if I were rejected. It was rumored that the people in charge had a heated argument over the matter. They finally decided to give me a chance. If I out-performed everyone else, they would consider accepting me. One reason I was given this chance was that no other high-school girls wanted to join the shooting team. Other girls considered lying on the ground to be not only dirty but unsightly as well. By default, I became the female representative of the university's attached high school. At this point, Mr. Moore chuckled. "Unlike the other girls, you weren't afraid to be dirty or unsightly." I laughed too, saying, "One can't have too many skills."

I was extremely patient, lying on the ground under the blazing sun while other contestants were dripping with sweat. I felt totally calm as I stared unblinkingly at the target. Other shooters had to close their left eyes and, over time, the eye muscles became tense. I didn't have this problem because my left eye was a lazy eye, so I didn't have to close it. People like me must be born target shooters. My results that day were outstanding, surpassing by far the other participants, all of whom were males. The university's shooting team coach told my high school Communist Party committee secretary, "I definitely want this student. She's a natural at target shooting." Thereafter, I had plenty of opportunities to lie quietly, left hand supporting a rifle barrel, and practice taking aim. Which, in turn, gave my mother a good excuse to enthusiastically impugn my motives: why was I so dedicated to this practice, taking aim with such concentration? In my heart, who was I really aiming the rifle at? She wrote this all down in vivid detail for the benefit of the authorities' file on me.

At this point, Mr. Moore smiled and walked over to the telephone. Picking it up, he took a look and announced, "It's clean. No bug." I laughed and figured that he probably knew everything about bugging telephones. Resuming his seat, Mr. Moore asked, "So, was all that practice at the shooting range useful?"

Was it ever! I arrived in Xinjiang in early 1967, a few months before my twenty-first birthday. Within a month, I figured out that, if I wanted to survive, I could not depend on food from the company mess. I went to the bazaar in Maola where I bought yoghurt, pulled mutton, and dry cheese, items whose gamy taste most Han Chinese found repulsive. But we were performing hard labor and could not endure days of starvation. I had to find more nutritious food. I diligently studied the Uyghur tongue and made some Uyghur friends. When I went to the bazaar, I avoided people from the Corps, borrowed a horse and a rifle from my Uyghur friends, and headed to the forest to hunt rabbits. The poplar forest at that time was still quite thick, and the wild rabbits that lived there were big and fat – really magnificent creatures.

I tied up the horse where the grass was lush so it could graze. Then I found a spot, set up my rifle, and waited for the rabbits. This was much simpler than practicing target shooting in high school. In less than half an hour, I got my rabbit. Using materials at hand, I covered it with mud, built a fire with dried wood, and roasted it in the fire. When I knocked off the mud, it came off with the fur and skin. What a savory dinner – I called it "beggar rabbit." When I was finished, I picked up the rifle, hopped on the horse, and happily rode back to Maola. When my Uyghur friends found that I had only used one bullet, they raised their eyebrows in surprise. "Did you get a rabbit?" they wanted to know. "I did, and it's already eaten," I honestly replied. That always gave them a hearty laugh.

Mr. Moore also got a good laugh from the story. "Waiting for a rabbit by a tree, amazing indeed." In fact, such days were few. First of all, it was difficult to get away from people from the Corps since there were so many of them. Secondly, the company was felling the poplar forest very quickly. The animals that used to live in the forest had to move elsewhere. Rabbits became fewer and fewer. A few years later, I would sometimes buy chickens from Uyghurs to make "beggar chicken" instead of "beggar rabbit." Still later, even the Uyghurs' lives became difficult. Chickens became scarce in the bazaar, and I had to settle for buying a few eggs to assuage my hunger. I was drifting farther and farther from keeping my promise to myself to "eat enough and keep warm."

During a break in our lesson, Mr. Moore put on his trench coat and beckoned Pele, who instantly jumped up on him. Off they went, out the door and downstairs. Looking out the living room window, I saw Mr. Moore light a cigarette by the building entrance while Pele scampered on the lawn. The cigarette tip glowed in the dark, but suddenly Pele was not in sight. My heart started palpitating. Mr. Moore's work must have cost a lot of bad people piles of money and made him many enemies. My apartment complex was located near highways that radiated in many directions, and the management didn't provide much in the way of security. If Mr. Moore's enemies found him, what should I do? The important thing was that his pistol was not with him but in the drawer of the side table. I felt extremely nervous, but just at that moment I heard Pele howl. I dashed toward the side table and opened the drawer where the pistol was lying peacefully on a small pile of postcards. I could tell that it had been well cared for because it shone with a soft glow. I was reaching down to pick it up when there came a light knock on the door accompanied by happy yelps from Pele. Mr. Moore was fine! I pressed my hand against my thumping heart, pushed the drawer closed with my knee, and rushed to open the door.

Mr. Moore's piercing eyes looked me up and down. He gently put Pele down on the floor, removed his trench coat and hung it up, and asked, "Why are you so nervous? You look like you've seen a ghost." I calmed myself down and replied, "I grew up in a chimney where everyone around me smoked. Smoking indoors is not a problem. If you have to stand downstairs in the dark just to smoke a cigarette, I'd rather you smoked right here. This way you'd be safer, and I'd be less worried."

Mr. Moore pulled out a chair to sit down and said in a friendly voice, "You're worried about my safety?" I nodded. "You've cost a lot of people a lot of money and probably put some of them in jail. Those people must hate you, and they do terrible things...." Mr. Moore laughed kindly. "Aren't you afraid that I might bring trouble to your door?"

"I'm not afraid. I just don't want you to get into trouble because of my carelessness." I looked directly into his soft grayish eyes. Sensing my mood, Pele scampered over, jumped into his lap, and stared at him with wide open eyes. Faced with our joint concern, Mr. Moore started to talk about his life.

Never in his wildest dreams had he imagined that Pele and I would be so concerned about him on his first day of lessons. He was deeply touched. He had a wife and a daughter, a beautiful wife and a pretty daughter. But his wife could not bear the thought of him bringing a pistol home. Because of that, he always stored it out of sight in his study when he came home. Yet his wife remained extremely nervous, almost obsessed, about it. It finally happened one day: a car drove by and an automatic weapon sprayed bullets into his house. All three family members were home but not near any windows, so no one was hurt. "The main damage was a broken tall case clock," he said. But the incident devastated his wife. She filed for divorce and was awarded custody of their child. Further, she demanded that he remove himself completely from their lives, except for monthly alimony payments. "I live my life looking at pictures of my child. I get pictures of her every year on her birthday. Last year she turned thirty. She's married, and I am a grandfather."

Mr. Moore took out his wallet and pulled out a photo showing a couple with blonde hair and blue eyes smiling as they cuddled their little prince. "You'd think it would be all right to bring a birthday present to her house, wouldn't you? So that day I dressed up and had an assistant drive me over there. With a big box in one hand, I rang the doorbell. My son-in-law opened the door, and immediately his face turned cold. Then my daughter walked into the room. She went crazy when she saw me. She pushed me and the present out the door so forcefully that the ribbons around the box came loose and the silver fox coat inside spilled onto the lawn."

Mr. Moore's story deeply saddened me. The woolen pills on the sleeves of his sweater suddenly appeared irritatingly noticeable. Following my look, he glanced at his sleeves and looked at me kindly. "I dress casually not for financial reasons but because my job requires it. I don't have to live frugally, so I can afford to give my child a silver fox coat. But I didn't expect you to react to this story the way you did." I thought a while and replied, "Family love is one of the most precious things on earth. If my father were alive and had to live a dangerous life for a good cause, I would have faced anything at his side. I would have risked my life to support him and never let him fight alone." I was on the verge of tears before I finished my sentence.

Mr. Moore was embarrassingly eager to defend his daughter. "People aren't to blame for wanting peaceful lives. Given the nature of my job, it's little wonder people might want to keep their distance from me." At that point, my curiosity got the better of me. "If you moved off the front line of the war on drugs and led a peaceful life, mightn't your family change their minds and come back to you?" To my surprise, Mr. Moore proudly replied, "You're a natural target shooter. I'm a natural drug buster. We won't be quitting for quite a while!"

This evening, the farewell was affectionate and cozy. Pele wouldn't leave Mr. Moore's lap for the longest time, nose sniffing continuously as if smelling something extremely aromatic. Mr. Moore told him tenderly, "You must have been a chain smoker in a previous life." As if in total agreement, Pele lay there contentedly, not moving a hair.

Eventually Mr. Moore bid us goodnight and headed downstairs. Pele squatted on the window sill while I stood in front of the window. We both watched Mr. Moore drive his beat-up Honda slowly out of the parking area and then turned away. That night, Pele was really exhausted, so he went straight to bed, skipping his usual ball game. This left me more time to read and do my own homework assignment.

A few days later, Joe walked into the apartment and sniffed. "Good heavens! Have you learned how to prepare French cuisine? Smells great!" I had just finished eating a big meal called "Provencal rabbit." Pele was chewing a leg bone with gusto but managed to nod his head as if in greeting.

"No way could I do that," I replied. "A student of mine had a restaurant send it to me, and he was thoughtful enough to warn me to give Pele only the big bones, lest he choke." I showed Joe the order slip from the restaurant. He took a look at the name of the restaurant and whistled. "This place is famous! Your thoughtful and generous student must be Mr. Moore. What good story did you tell him that moved him so much that he sent you such a spectacular dinner?" Observing that I was silent, clever Joe added, "Don't worry. Dr. Yates and I are the only ones who know that Mr. Moore takes lessons from you here."

But there was another reason for my silence. Such delectable cuisine! Was it from Provence? I had no idea. I had just looked up Provence in the dictionary. Provence was a famous area in southern France.

Joe was embarrassed. "When it comes to cuisine, my Chinese vocabulary is far from adequate. Herbes de Provence are famous. Is 'Provencal Rabbit' prepared with herbs, spices, or culinary grass? I'm not sure which word is closer." Seeing that I wished to pursue the topic, Joe continued to explain. "'Herbes de Provence' basically is a mixture that includes basil, thyme, fennel seeds, and lavender flowers and, of course, savory things, too. How should I put it? They are not just aromatic but also somewhat salty." Joe wrote down those words as he spoke them. I looked them up in the dictionary and thought that this was a completely new world to me. Those words represented ingredients that could be used in cooking! But their appearance, unique flavors, and combination with other ingredients to create savory dishes were totally beyond my ken. After returning to the United States three years earlier, my vocabulary and knowledge had increased considerably in the realms of politics, economics, literature, defense, science, technology, even industry and medicine. After all, I had been teaching diplomats and soldiers. But when it came to cuisine, whether eastern or western, the subject seemed far removed from someone like me who had, for the longest time, lived on the verge of starvation. The distance between "beggar rabbit" and "Provencal rabbit" was farther than the distance between Earth and the moon. So, I remained silent, although my facial expression probably reflected the sadness I felt.

Joe continued to explain tactfully. "While the savory taste of food can come from other ingredients, it can also come from salt. But there are many kinds of salt: Cyprus black sea salt, Australian pink salt, Japanese sea salt laced with kelp flavoring, Himalayan red salt, and others. There are lots of different kinds of rock salt as well. Provencal gourmets even use precious truffles to create a unique kind of truffle salt, the quintessential seasoning salt."

I listened intently without really grasping everything Joe said while I filled my tiny slip of paper with Chinese and English terms. As I placed it in my notebook, I was grateful to Mr. Moore and Joe for opening, even by happenstance, a door into a new field of knowledge. That people must be fed is a basic principle. Yet in a country adhering to Mao's calls to "replace insufficient grain and oil with melons and vegetables" and "eat solid food during the busy growing season and gruel during slack times," foreign cuisine was seldom on anyone's mind and even Chinese cuisine was substandard or lost altogether. I secretly told myself that one day, when my schedule was not so crowded, I must explore this world of fine cuisine. I must understand the uses of various herbs. I must taste all the different kinds of salt, and I must create the most delectable dinners for my friends and family. Collecting my thoughts, I thanked Joe for opening a window although I still had to find the spare time to enter such a beautiful world.

Actually, during the first lesson with Mr. Moore, talk of food had led to a discussion of attitudes towards weapons, such as guns. How I waited by a tree for a rabbit with a rifle was a story of survival. What was preposterous was the PLA strategy of "turning the reserve into the vanguard." This concept intrigued Joe, so I began to tell him the story. Of course, two cups of tea – ordinary Lipton teabags-- had to be brewed first.

There was a reason I was called back from the rocky terrain of the Kunlun Mountains. At that time, preparations for war in Xinjiang had escalated. With the exception of the elderly, children, the sick, pregnant women, and new mothers, everyone in the Corps, active and inactive, and all militia members were ordered to the border with the Soviet Union, completely throwing existing military arrangements into disarray. Unit cohesion, whether a company, battalion, or division, was discarded as people streamed in to take up positions with strangers in various trenches. For how long? Nobody knew.

The PLA passed out rifles at the front line. Not small-bore pieces but .38 caliber rifles left behind by the Japanese in 1945. They were so rusty that the bolts couldn't be drawn. No ammunition was issued. As the enthusiasts got busy scrubbing their rifles, I closed my eyes and basked in the warm sun. In a crisis, this .38 caliber antique with a stuck bolt would be less useful than a fireplace poker. What was the point of scrubbing it? Red flags and slogans everywhere proclaimed "Fear neither hardship nor death." Already a veteran of difficult situations at the age of twenty-five, I just quietly and calmly awaited what life or rather what "higher authorities" had in store for me.

After rocking along in a truck with strangers for three days followed by a whole day of walking with bedrolls on our backs, we settled down at our assigned position before sunset. Standing next to me was a teenaged girl about one head shorter than I was. She was so skinny that the only thing you noticed was a pair of big eyes on her perplexed face. I waited until "the higher authorities" had departed before I started to dig a trench with my shovel. Afraid to lag behind, the girl also picked up a shovel and began to dig, picking up a shovelful of dirt only to drop half of it. Seeing that her arms were as thin as hemp stalks, I didn't have the heart to criticize. So instead I asked her, "What's your name?" She looked at me, lowered her head and said softly, "Not allowed to tell." My heart skipped a beat. In a gentle voice I asked her, "Which division are you from?" "Not allowed to tell," came the reply. I was becoming a bit impatient. Nobody knew how long we had to stay in that place. Sharing a trench with someone who was afraid to say anything and too weak to truss a chicken would make the days ahead difficult for me.

I stopped shoveling to look around while there was still daylight. The people digging the trench line with us were all wearing the blue and black garb of common folks, which, in the Corps, meant that they came from the best class origins but with the least political influence. One hundred meters behind us, the grass-green-clad "primary militia" were jabbering away in the Shanghainese dialect. Another hundred meters behind them were the red collar tabs with red star insignias glittering in the sunlight. My goodness! PLA troops dressed in full gear, with pitched camps and even majestic-looking tanks lined up two to three hundred meters behind us. I looked at my .38 caliber rifle and couldn't help chuckling. I got to thinking. "Combating and preventing revisionism" was aimed at the USSR. But where was the Soviet army? I turned around to look. Good heavens! Neatly dressed Russian soldiers in high boots were taking the tarpaulins off big guns! They were so close to us – no more than 150 meters at most. A row of Katyusha rockets with depressed muzzles looked like black holes from where I stood. I realized at this moment that we actually were in the front line, deliberately positioned to give the appearance of strength while ensuring that we would be the first casualties should the Soviets attack. Suddenly I heard muffled sobbing. It was my trench-mate, who had just reached the same conclusion. With both hands covering her mouth, her thin body shaking uncontrollably, she was staring in terror at the Katyushas. Feeling sorry for her, I offered consolation by proposing action. "Come on, don't cry. Let's hurry up and dig a hole, otherwise we'll have no shelter to sleep in." She cried as she dug, repeating over and over, "I'll never see my grandma and grandpa again." Nevertheless, she put all her strength and energy behind her shovel so, shovelful by shovelful, we soon created a waist-deep trench.

When we had finished, her face took on an empty, faraway look, as though preparing to bid farewell to the world. I tried another tack.

"Have you ever heard of a parabola?" I asked. She shook her head, eyes wide. I told her to look at the gun muzzles. "At such close range, the shells from those muzzles cannot possibly fall on our heads." I described an arc in the air with my hand as I explained. "If there are really shells flying, they should fall at least one or two hundred meters behind us. In other words, we are closest to the muzzles but also safest from their shells." At that, she stopped shaking, and a smile broke out on her dirt-and-sweat-caked face.

As night approached, the sky filled with stars. I spread out the plastic sheet she had used to wrap her pack over the bottom of our hole. We could then open our packs and semi-recline on them. Then we stuck our two rifles into the soil to serve as tent poles, attaching the plastic sheet that had wrapped my pack to form a sort of roof. With this structure, we hoped to keep out cold drafts and survive the chilly night.

As soon as her pack was opened, the girl pulled out and held tightly to her chest a tiny stuffed toy bear. She sat there looking at me nervously. "My grandpa brought me this when he came back from abroad. Its name is Teddy." Teddy was apparently not on the list of "forbidden" subjects. This reminded me of pictures of American children clasping this kind of soft, fluffy toy that I had seen in a Life magazine at Uncle Pan's home in Zhongguan Village. "Don't worry," I told her. "Teddy will be fine." She calmed down, her eyes shimmering in the half-light.

Dinner came late that day. Heralded by shouting far behind us, the mess staff came up with pots on shoulder poles and flashlights; they stopped fifty meters behind us. In front of us, we could hear Soviet soldiers noisily working their rifle bolts.

I led the girl over to where the mess staff had dropped their loads. There were a few people around us from the 48th Regiment, but the majority were strangers. Even so, we were all in the same situation so we acknowledged each other with nods and remained quiet. Lukewarm soup made of soy sauce and cabbage was ladled into our bowls. Each of us also received one small, ice-cold cone of steamed cornmeal bread. I noticed the girl's bowl was exquisitely enameled but could only hold half a ladle of soup, so I asked the people around us, "Does anyone have an extra bowl? This girl's bowl is way too small. Thank you for your trouble." I was hoping that, by speaking in the Beijing dialect, I might attract the attention of another person from Beijing. Sure enough, someone squeezed over and handed me a mess tin that was just right for this place. It had a hole drilled in the rim from which hung a metal tag. The tag had a white background and bore the three characters "Ma Xiaoliu" in black paint. I took a look at this youth named Ma: strongly built, good-looking face, a hemp rope tied around his waist, obviously someone who had seen a few things. Without saying much, he would understand. So I smiled and said, "Thanks!" He also smiled, replying, "Don't mention it." Then he turned around and left. At this point, I felt the piercing look of the cook in his grass-green uniform, so I led the girl back to our hole.

The night was quiet. The girl was half-starved. She finished the soup quickly. "We'll be lucky to get two meals a day out here," I told her. "Eat slowly. We don't know when our next meal will be." She obediently started to chew and swallow more slowly. After finishing, she asked, "What should I wash the bowl with?"

"Listen," I told her. "We'll be lucky if we get one bowl of water a day here. We have no water for washing, so just cover the bowl with a towel and that will have to do. She took a small towel from her pack and used it to cover the bowl. As she did so, she felt the metal tag with her finger and said, "This Ma Xiaoliu was pretty smart to attach this tag to his bowl so it can't get lost." I didn't say anything. Ma Xiaoliu must have come from an even harsher environment. Only in places of administrative detention or reform-through-labor units would a person guard his most important possessions, especially this eating utensil, so carefully. The girl asked, "Why did he tie a hemp rope around his waist?" "Nothing beats a rope around the waist for warmth at night!" I told her. "Around here, one wears a leather jacket in the morning and thin cotton clothing at noon, but at night, winter or summer, it's always freezing cold. Ma Xiaoliu is prepared for this climate."

The cold came fast indeed. Clutching her bear tightly, the girl huddled under her blanket and shivered so much her teeth rattled. Unable to sleep because of the cold, I got to thinking that the girl, from her accent, must have come from Beijing. If her grandfather had returned from abroad, how about her parents? I asked, "Where are your parents?" Half asleep, she replied, "In the mountains in Sichuan." No sooner had she finished than she sat up and started to whimper. "I'm not supposed to tell." I patted her reassuringly, saying, "Relax, it will be all right."

This reminded me of the boy who had lent me a copy of Eliot's *The Waste Land*. He had been living in Beijing with his grandmother while his parents worked in a high-security factory far away. He wasn't able to see his parents for long stretches of time. This girl's situation seemed similar. Her parents or grandparents must have been persecuted during the Cultural Revolution, leaving this innocent child to be sent from under her grandparents' protective wings to a real-life wasteland.

The night passed quietly; important events would wait until the next day. The sun rose quickly the next morning. I emerged from under the plastic sheet, which was frozen stiff with a thick layer of frost on top. All around me colorful plastic sheets were spread out to dry in the sun, making quite an interesting patchwork sight. Not long afterwards, accordion music could be heard. Ha! Soviet soldiers in long overcoats were dancing to the music to warm themselves up. A little way behind them, cooking fires sent smoke and steam into the cold air, accompanied by enticing aromas.

Still clinging tightly to her bear, the girl idly watched the dancing foreign soldiers. I told her, "Pretty soon those folks behind us might come to inspect our trenches. You'd better hide your bear." The girl obediently hid the bear in her blanket. I noticed a triangular hole in the bear's stomach where the stuffing could be clearly seen. "Did the Red Guards poke him with a bayonet?" I asked. Tears rolled down the girl's cheeks, and she nodded. "It will be all right. I'll sew him up for you when this is over." The girl started smiling even before her tears were dry.

As I expected, it wasn't long before some military big-shot and his retinue walked in our direction. Core members of the militia started applauding and shouting slogans such as "Salute our senior officer." At this very moment, loudspeakers from the Soviet lines broadcast a Chinese-language warning: "Active duty Chinese military personnel, please return to your camp immediately. If you continue to advance towards the border, it will be considered a military provocation, and Soviet border forces will respond with force." As the announcement blared across the front lines, the dancing Soviet soldiers were no longer visible, most likely waiting under cover in combat readiness. The Chinese soldiers behind us turned around and walked back in silence. The noisy members of the militia also quieted down. I couldn't help chuckling, and I said to the girl, "Now that the scare is over, bring out your bear so I can mend it."

I had been carrying my sewing kit ever since leaving Beijing for the Shanxi countryside. As my sewing skills improved, the size and contents of the sewing kit increased. Handing me the toy bear, the girl gently consoled it: "It won't hurt. It will take just a little while." Then she focused on watching me perform the surgery. A hole had been forcibly poked through the stuffed animal. I found a spool of dark brown thread and sewed up the hole with small stitches of double threads until the chest was neat and smooth. Then I turned it over and sewed up the back in a similar fashion. By the time I was cutting off the thread, the girl was smiling happily. Watching her carefully hide the little bear under her blanket reminded me of Uncle Pan's child, the well-behaved boy who would sit on a stool peeling onions and scallions for Grandma. When he was in her kitchen, the happy expression on his face made Grandma's heart ache. I wondered where he was now.

As my mind wandered, the cries of the water-carriers sounded behind us. Our ration was much less than I expected: everyone got one mugful of water for drinking, tooth-brushing, and washing. I told the girl, "We must not waste a single drop. If you want to see your grandma and grandpa again, you must not waste any precious water." The girl carefully carried her mug, covered it after taking a tiny sip, and placed it in a safe place.

Joe picked up the tea cup and asked, "Eight ounces of water a day? For how long?"

"Three months – ninety-one days." Because water and food were so scarce, their rate of consumption was very low, even though we had dug a large trench to serve as a latrine.

The second day seemed extremely long. Even after finishing two meals, the sun still hung high in the sky. The most unbearable torment came from the direction of the Soviet army: the aromas of meat, chicken, and savory soup wafting towards us. Tears welled up in the girl's eyes. She bit her lip and turned her back to the Soviet soldiers. I took out the sole of a cloth shoe and started stitching swiftly. At least I wouldn't waste all my time.

"Nobody in my family knows how to sew. My grandma and mother can't even sew buttons on. The maid sews them on when they fall off," the girl said slowly. "Now that the maid is gone, I wonder what they are going to do?" I assembled a small sewing kit for her, saying, "It's not hard to learn how to sew buttons. In the present situation, it will be useful if you could sew a little." The girl took the kit and put it under the blanket with her stuffed bear.

It finally turned dark - an extremely cold night. The Soviet soldiers started a large bonfire which, though far away, still seemed to bring us a sense of warmth. Accompanied by an accordion, they started to sing. All the songs were familiar to me. I was really tempted to sing along. When a few baritones began singing *Katyusha*, I sat up in my trench and joined in. This started everyone singing aloud, men and women, many in the original Russian lyrics. The girl glanced at me with a surprised look. Before we could finish the song, active duty PLA officers and members of the core militia rushed towards us with their guns shouting, "No singing allowed! No singing allowed!" Well, this caused the Soviet soldiers to immediately raise their guns and start shooting. Their bullets, landing right in front of the unmusical soldiers, stopped their forward movement. Instead, they roared a torrent of abuse. No sound came from our trenches. After a few minutes, the shouters got tired of shouting and retreated, taking their guns with them. The Soviet accordion once again played the opening bars of *Katyusha,* and this time around I didn't wait nor did anyone else. As soon as the accordion introduction ended, we all started to sing. Our voices reverberated in the sky, blending with the voices of the Soviet soldiers. When the song came to an end, the Soviet soldiers all shouted bravo, and we were silent. The next song started, and we all sang along again. What a precious experience this was, joyfully singing familiar Russian folk songs all night in a mixed-voice chorus along the Soviet-Chinese border.

Everyone seemed to know at that time that we were the unwanted, to be used as cannon fodder and human shields. Our lives were worthless in this absurd "anti-revisionism" movement launched by the Chinese government. Our hearty singing this night was nothing but a cry wrung from the helplessness of our soon-to-be-over lives in this world.

After daybreak, a kitchen worker walked up to us with a somber face and fierce words. "Who sang last night? Leniency to those who confess and severity to those who refuse!" Everyone ignored him. "If you sing again tonight, your old debts and new debts will be settled all at once," he threatened angrily.

The Soviets seemed to have gained a clear understanding of feelings on our side. Loudspeakers broadcasting famous Russian folk tunes sung in the magnificent voices of Russian singers replaced the simple accordion. What an open-air concert indeed! The lyrics of *Moscow Nights* were so deeply imprinted in my heart that I softly began to sing along. When I listened closely, I could hear other men and women on our side softly singing along, too. The booming broadcast drowned out our singing.

Suddenly the opening bars of Tchaikovsky's Fourth Symphony pierced through the dark night like a sharp sword, and my tears fell onto my chapped hands. Since being sent to the countryside in 1964, I had lost all contact with classical music, and, since the beginning of the Cultural Revolution, all we heard were the so-called "model" works such as *The White-Haired Girl*, and *The Red Detachment of Women*. All traditional music, both Chinese and foreign, disappeared. It had been a long time, dear Tchaikovsky! As an added plus, the performance was by the Leningrad Philharmonic Orchestra. The exquisite sound of the horn echoed the heartfelt aspirations of the composer, of all of us. The tragic force of the music was tearing up hearts starving for some happiness. The girl watched me, transfixed. She probably couldn't understand why this tough-as-nails elder sister was brought to tears.

All of a sudden, we heard gunfire not far behind us. Under cover of darkness, active duty Chinese soldiers must have crept up behind us to shoot at their target – the Soviet loudspeaker. The Soviet soldiers immediately fired back. Crackling and whizzing shots fell behind us. In this crossfire, the comforting theory of parabolas no longer held true. I grabbed the girl and covered her with my body. Soon the gunfire dwindled and moved farther way, and I let her up.

Every now and then gunshots could be heard coming from the Soviet side, as if in warning. There was no movement behind us. In the dead silence of night, I figured that the loudspeaker had been destroyed. Who would have thought that, after a burst of static, the *Nutcracker Suite* would explode through the air, whereupon the girl quietly clapped her hands?

Joe suddenly stared at me. "You know, your story shatters some people's assumptions. In the United States, in the West, people always felt under tremendous pressure from the Soviet Union. In the early 1970s, when Kissinger secretly visited China, his aim was to join with China to contain the Soviets. In the eyes of many Westerners, the Soviet Union is the devil, whereas China, though under cruel Communist rule, is seen as different from the Soviet Union because of its 5000 years of civilization."

"Lenin and Stalin did much evil, killing many innocent people," I replied scornfully. "But at least they did not suppress Pushkin, ban performances of Tchaikovsky's works, or eliminate the Orthodox Church. The Chinese Communists went wild destroying the ancient culture. In their view, Confucius committed monstrous crimes; even the poet Li Bai came in for condemnation. Playing the Chinese zither, seen as a symbol of the landlord class, was banned. Any thought other than Communist belief had to be exposed and eradicated. What kind of ancient, civilized country could this be? Sooner or later, Westerners will realize that the Chinese Communists are even more horrifying than the Bolsheviks. Only by then it will be too late. As for Kissinger and his secret visit to China, did he give any thought at all to the suffering Chinese people? Do you know, during the Vietnam War, how many Chinese were hoping that the Americans would fight all the way into China? Compared to the Chinese Communists, who have no regard for human life, the American army is quite humane." Joe looked serious and remained quiet.

"Nevertheless," I continued pleasantly, "I have to thank you for reminding me. I now realize that those three months in the trenches could really have been a show put on for American consumption to indicate that the Soviets were the sworn enemies of the Chinese Communists.

The Corps and the military vigorously translated into action the intentions of their political leaders. Along the way, we, the unwanted, were conveniently placed on the front line. Any accidents while polishing the guns would see us sacrificed. That would be killing two birds with one stone, wouldn't it?" Joe looked really sad.

Time passed slowly in the trenches, with only the evening "concerts" providing brief spells of enjoyment. Without water for bathing, we were extremely filthy. Fortunately, I had a fine-toothed comb from Shanxi. Older women there didn't wash their hair often. What they usually did was carefully comb their hair under the sun. This comb was now put to good use against the lice we lived with. It really helped stop the itching.

Around dawn one morning and without any warning, the PLA soldiers far behind us lifted a red banner reading "Celebrate the great victory in the fight against revisionism!" Amidst a deafening roar of shouted slogans, they prepared to move out. The militia members were packing up, too, hoisting their baggage onto their shoulders. With flags flying and patriotic songs on their lips, they prepared to follow the PLA. As for our group of men and women on the actual front lines, we all were really glad to see the end of this ordeal. Without formations, without songs, we swiftly packed up and silently marched away with spirited strides from the holes where we had spent three months. I turned around and saw Soviet soldiers walking out of their earthworks and standing there to see us off.

Although we marched hard trying to catch up, we still missed seeing the magnificent sight of those anti-revisionism "heroes" climbing into trucks decked in red silk. What was waiting for us were dusty trucks, where we turned in our ancient rifles and waited for roll call. Before she left, the girl did not forget to return the bowl to Ma Xiaoliu. "Thank you, Big Brother Ma," she said brightly. He received the bowl with a smile and then hopped into his appointed truck. The girl looked at me. "Thank you, Big Sister." After a moment's hesitation she whispered, "My last name is Qian." I told her, "After arriving at your place, take a shower, change into clean clothes, and do not wash these dirty clothes; they're full of lice. Just burn them." Before I could finish, someone hollered to the girl to get in the truck. Then my name was called. The girl, Ma

Xiaoliu, and I climbed into three different trucks. I left Xinjiang five years later and never saw or heard from them again.

Back at my company, everything was quiet. Returning to the dungeon, I ran into Yuan Lin, a woman from Beijing whose feigned illnesses kept her from work a good deal of the time. She gaped at me as though she had seen a ghost. "They all said you wouldn't make it back," she finally said. "Many people wanted to take your things. I tied up your clothing and bedding; otherwise, you probably wouldn't even have your bed board." Indeed, there was my bundled clothing and bedding on my bed attached to a rope tied to one of the legs of Yuan Lin's bed.

"Where is everybody?" I asked.

"Celebrating the big victory at Corps headquarters. I heard it will last three days. Why don't you hurry over to the canteen for water so you can wash your hair and shower?" With buckets on a shoulder pole, I ran to the canteen. Seeing me, the cook said, "Everyone is back, and I figured you should be back, too. I've been saving water for you every day. Take all you need." Beaming with delight, I thanked him and ran back with my hot water. With Yuan Lin sitting by the door knitting and acting as lookout, I joyfully washed off three months of filth. I placed the dirty clothes and blanket in an empty bucket and carried them to the kitchen, where I fed them into the burning stove.

Yuan Lin and I lay comfortably in our bunks as we chatted. Oh, my God! The loudspeakers outside began to squawk, followed by the blare of automobile horns and a hubbub of voices. Feet stomped past the windows of our dungeon as their owners disputed who should get first, second, or third-class merit citations.

"People fighting alongside Old Chairman Mao on the front lines still had water for washing up," Yuan Lin remarked conversationally. "They didn't look like you, so filthy that you have to burn your clothing and blanket. Weren't you with a rear service unit? How did you get so dirty?"

I swore bitterly to myself. Rear service? When was that? It was a total fabrication. I was a human shield, cannon fodder, and even deprived of water, damn it! Thinking of that Qian girl's face, so dirty she looked like a spotted cat, her neck like a car axle, and her black hands made me fume. "Don't get angry," Yuan Lin said soothingly. "Don't get angry, it's not worth it. Don't get angry with them." She was right. I had to suppress my rage and indignation. I understood that I could not say that there had been no battle. I couldn't say anything about first line, second line, or third line. I definitely could not say anything about the singing. This reminded me of the girl who kept saying, "Not allowed to say." I told myself that there would come a day, sooner or later, when I would say all the "cannot says" and tell all the "not allowed to tell" stories to the whole world.

And here I was, ten years later in Washington, D.C., recounting those stories to Joe, who asked with a brooding look, "Could that girl who did not know about parabolas be related to nuclear physicist Qian Sanqiang?" I could only admit that I did not know. All I knew was that she, I, and Ma Xiaoliu would never be cited in the ensuing awards ceremony, nor would we be included in any of the celebrations. What did please me was that the awards ceremony was held during the day, sparing us from working in the fields. I couldn't care less about disputes over the merits of the awardees, for my heart was filled with Tchaikovsky as I deftly stitched shoe soles.

Surprisingly, forty years later, when artist and human rights supporter Ai Weiwei was allowed to post bail after three months of imprisonment and faced the national and international media, all he would say was "It's unsuitable to talk about it." Reading that news revived the contempt I felt for those who attempt to enforce silence to cover up their misdeeds and abuses. Someday, I hoped, all these "not allowed to say," "cannot say," and now "not suitable to say" would at last be able to be said.

Hearing the story of the rear service troops turning into front line troops, Mr. Moore shook his head and sighed. "Poor kids...." This included me, the Qian girl, Ma Xiaoliu, and all the young men and women singing in the trenches. We were silent for quite a while, then Mr. Moore said, "One expression in your story – 'the unwanted' – reminds me of something that happened recently. A Jewish organization tracked down somewhere in Central America a German military doctor who had worked in a Nazi concentration camp. His name was Dietrich. Although quite old and frail, he was nevertheless put in a wheelchair and pushed into court to face trial. In court, he calmly confessed to all the charges.

Finally, the judge asked him if he had anything to say. He thought for a while, then replied, 'Yes. I did perform abortions on female Jews at the camp, terminating their pregnancies. If I had not done so, all those women along with their babies would have been slaughtered or sent to the gas chamber, for they were the unwanted. They would not have been spared. I eliminated their fetuses and, as a result, some of those women survived until the end of the war. I do not wish absolution – my crimes are too horrific. I can only accept my punishment. I am just pointing out a fact.' After he had spoken, he remained seated, quietly awaiting his fate."

"What happened afterwards?" I asked in a hoarse voice.

"There is no afterwards," Mr. Moore answered calmly. "That very evening he died of heart failure. Since he had lived and practiced medicine in that small Central American village for decades, his grateful neighbors buried him there."

After a long pause, Mr. Moore looked at me closely. "Don't tell me you had something to do with this doctor."

"This is just coincidence. I fractured my right arm when I was two years old. It was probably he who fixed my arm with a stainless-steel pin. That was in the spring of 1949, shortly before Shanghai fell into the hands of the Communists, a time when he was trying to flee." This was all I knew.

"And then," Mr. Moore prodded gently.

"And then my right arm regained strength and remained strong, which has helped me through many difficult times," I said with a wry smile.

It was at this very moment that I quietly locked up Dr. D's story in my memory bank for good. I would no longer take his grayish image for that of Santa Claus.

CHAPTER 10

ME AND J

D r. Yates retired in the summer of 1981, and Dr. Sheehan replaced him as head of the East Asian Language Department at the Foreign Service Institute. Far from being a fashion plate, he usually wore casual shirts and coats. He was informal and easygoing, creating a more relaxed atmosphere in the Chinese section.

Soon afterwards, a class of new students arrived. As with past classes, these experienced diplomats didn't know Chinese, but they commanded enough knowledge in almost every other discipline to act as professors to their "teachers." I never considered myself a "teacher" - someone in a class apart who generously dispensed knowledge - for I believed that the education process benefitted those who taught as well as those who learned.

The first day passed smoothly, with students and teachers getting along well. After classes, when the students had left with their homework assignments, the instructors sat down together to choose Chinese names for the students, discuss their language abilities, and arrange classes. One student had a rather long last name: "Buczacki;" someone ventured that the name was East European. Following normal practice, instructors suggested different characters representing a "bo" sound for a surname. I didn't think any of their ideas was ideal. As for a first name, I thought "Zuoqi" really sounded genteel – not a bad choice. This student was tall and polite and didn't flaunt his academic credentials, leaving me with the impression that he was a gentle and courteous person.

After some hesitation, Dr. Sheehan expressed his opinion, which gave me a bit of a shock: "Johns Hopkins University is famous as an academic institution of original thinkers. Mr. Buczacki earned undergraduate and graduate degrees there. For five years, he had a full scholarship. As soon as he graduated, he was hired by the State Department and assigned abroad at the age of twenty-three. A student like this will be a challenge for an instructor." The instructors around me all wore serious expressions. I didn't say anything.

"We have to find a young, energetic instructor to take extra care of this student," Dr. Sheehan concluded. Looking around the table, his eyes met mine. "How about this," he said. "Teresa will take primary responsibility for him." This clearly was not a request, so I nodded. "No problem." When class schedules were set, this student in fact ended up spending more time in my classroom. I did not consider this an issue. How could a bright student be a problem?

FSI did not allow students to speak English from the moment they stepped through the door. The second day of class was the only exception. Upon receiving their foreign-language names, which usually approximated the pronunciation of their actual names, they could use English to understand what their names meant. If they expressed dissatisfaction with the names chosen for them, instructors were obligated to find names that satisfied them because after leaving language training they would have to use these names in the countries where they were assigned. Disliking one's name was out of the question.

In different combinations of characters, the character "bo" could indicate thickness, frailty, lightness, shallowness, poor farmland, or sharp-tongued. Oh no, those wouldn't do. Untalented, poor pay, philandering, slighting, scorn, favoritism? No, those were even worse. Twilight, rapid decline, enjoy it while it lasts? Nope. Mint? Most inadequate.

I simplified the whole matter by explaining that "Bo" was simply a Chinese surname. This Mr. Buczacki looked at me with a smile, offering no objection. As an international relations major in college, he understood the realities of China and of course knew who Communist Party leader Bo Yibo was. No point in arguing about a family name shared by thousands of people, I figured he reasoned.

"Zuo" was easy to understand. It simply meant "to assist."

Now the character "qi" raised an issue. Uniformity? No. Respecting the husband? Definitely not. A hundred flowers blossoming, running neck and neck? They all sounded bad. A liberal arts scholar would probably prefer "only one stands out." The country of Qi during the Zhou dynasty? Too serious, not good. Suddenly I remembered the "qi" character used by the legendary Monkey King, Sun Wu Kong, to proclaim his greatness, and I blurted out the name.

This brought a smile from Mr. Buczacki. He must like the Monkey King.

So, in one smooth stroke, Mr. Buczacki became Mr. Bo Zuoqi. Harmony reigned in the classroom. Every morning we exchanged greetings of "Good morning, teacher," "Good morning, Mr. Bo" and every afternoon "Good-bye, teacher," "Good-bye, Mr. Bo."

Rocking with laughter, Joe asked, "How did you ever think of calling the Monkey King to the rescue?" I then asked him about the university's reputation for original thinking and was surprised to hear him agreeing with what Dr. Sheehan had said, that anyone who had studied at Johns Hopkins for five years could not be ordinary. Teachers might find themselves baffled by their questions. I mentioned my lovely graduate students, whereupon Joe pointed out with a smile that they were studying at Johns Hopkins to earn doctorates in Chinese literature. They had all received undergraduate and graduate degrees, probably elsewhere. Such was not the case with Mr. Bo. This was vintage Joe: always able to highlight the key difference in just a few words. Soon I completely forgot the subject.

The cafeteria at the State Department was a crossroads where one could come across unexpected people and happenings. One day, I went to the main State Department building to give a lesson to an advanced-level student. As I came down the stairs after class, I passed by the jam-packed cafeteria. I was starving and it was lunchtime, so I got in line and bought myself a sandwich and a cup of coffee. Finding a small table unoccupied, I sat down, pulled out Shen Congwen's *Border Town*, and started to read as I ate.

Before long I heard a voice asking politely, "May I sit here?" I hurriedly raised my head, pulled the table closer to me to give the new arrival room, and offhandedly responded, "Please." The man wore a suit and tie, as did almost every other man in the cafeteria, by all appearances another

State Department employee. He sat down right across from me holding an attaché case in his arms. Looking at each other, I saw the corner of his mouth turned up in an unconvincing attempt at a smile belied by a cold look in his brown eyes. Never had I met such an unfriendly look on first acquaintance since returning to the United States. I immediately retracted my welcoming smile and sat ready for combat,

The man clicked open his attaché case and plucked out a business card, which he pushed towards me. Like an arrowhead, his two long, slender fingers pointed at a surname that I was least interested in ever seeing. My hands were as cold as the icy look in my eyes. My expression must have looked ghastly as I stared at this son of an American diplomat who had been stationed in China during the Second World War. I remained silent, and my silence seemed to surprise him; the corner of his mouth skewed even more. Pausing briefly, he blurted out what he had prepared to say. "There is one thing I don't understand. Someone..."

His use of "someone" told me right away that he was choking on the name of a person he despised – my mother. And I knew what he was about to say.

"Someone told me in person that she raised you, my father's child, as the daughter of another man. What does this mean?" I shot back immediately. "That same someone also stated that, when your father was in Yan'an, a Communist leader said to him, 'Next time when you visit Yan'an please bring your wife along.' Your father's answer was 'I don't have a wife, just a lover, Ms. So-and-so.' As far as I know, you and your mother were living in Chongqing. Isn't your mother your father's wife? What did this someone mean by saying this?" I stared hard at him, not expecting him to answer. He started to wilt.

"Lies! All lies!" came the automatic, vehement response.

As long as he understood this, I had nothing more to say. Just then I noticed three people standing behind him: Mr. Bo and two of my other students. I hadn't noticed them sitting nearby, and they looked ready to pounce on the man across from me should our confrontation escalate.

I pushed the business card back to him and said, "Your father called me in 1978. His Chinese is not at all fluent." This clearly was news to the person across from me.

"What did he say?"

"Just sending his regards," I replied scornfully.

Retrieving his business card, the man stood up, only then noticing the "Three Musketeers" behind him. He turned around and hurried away.

The three students pulled chairs over to sit in front of me. "Are you all right?" asked Mr. Bo in English. At this point, I could not think of a Chinese word that he could understand to describe my gloomy mood. I was tongue-tied. Immediately he sought to comfort me. "This is not FSI. You can speak English." The other two students chuckled, and I loosened up. One student casually asked, "Three years ago when the 'old friend' of the Chinese Communists phoned you, was it just to send regards?" Indeed, when I heard him on the phone, I didn't feel like talking. He muttered for a while and hung up. But there was another old leftist, Anna, who called from Santa Barbara and kept urging me to move to the west coast lest I be "used" by people in Washington. One student muttered, "They sure move fast. You'd only just arrived in Washington." Mr. Bo asserted, "The Chinese government must have notified them." This got us all laughing.

Seeing that I was feeling much better, two of the students got up and left. Mr. Bo accompanied me to the shuttle bus stop at the door of the State Department. On the way to Rosslyn, Mr. Bo cheerfully talked about a lot of things, such as new movies and concerts. I could feel that he was trying to cheer me up. I could not help feeling grateful.

"Every person has only one father. Blood is blood and cannot be undone or denied." Hearing me relate the incident in the State Department cafeteria, Joe broke his silence with these words as he was packing up his books. "To obtain their ends, totalitarian governments and people with personal agendas think that high-handed means and lies can change facts and sever natural family ties."

I felt that he had something to tell me, so I asked him to go on. "Liars, for their own ends, fabricate different stories for different occasions and audiences. But facts undercut them, resulting in gaping contradictions and inconsistencies in their tales. When your mother, the 'someone' in the incident you just mentioned, was in New Haven in 1947, she used to brag about her relationships with Chinese Communist dignitaries, especially

Zhou Enlai. She even told young American students that, a few years earlier during the war against Japan, Zhou had arranged for her live with a left-leaning American diplomat in Chongqing. She said this at a time when the KMT government and the Communists were engaged in a civil war. But this diplomat, this 'old friend' of the Chinese Communists, was in a sad situation after being investigated by the American government. The students who heard this, among whom were the Swifts, thought that this woman was out of her mind, so they remained noncommittal and kept their opinions to themselves."

I was stunned speechless for a moment, after which I managed to say, "In other words, they lived together before the American diplomat visited Yan'an. The reports he sent to the U.S. State Department were what the Communists wanted him to see as 'facts'. Or it's possible that he was forced to write what the Communists wanted him to write because Zhou Enlai had a hold on him."

"This 'old friend' arrived in China during Nixon's visit there, believing that Mao Zedong would meet him. He waited and waited, but Mao ignored him, considering him unworthy. Eventually, Zhou saw him instead. Of course, the Communists were unwilling to let this 'old friend' meet his former short-time 'live-in lover' to reminisce about the old days. After all, the whole business was unspeakable. Dr. Swift and Dr. Yates didn't want to upset you, so they never mentioned this messy business to you," Joe concluded in a clear voice.

Fortunately, Grandma had told me long ago about my father. When I was very young, my mother told me that I was the daughter of that old leftist, which exasperated Grandma.

"During the 'Loyalty and Honesty Movement', you admitted in writing that the child's father was Mr. Han," she said to my mother. "Why are you lying to your child?" My mother replied, "Mr. Han is an enemy of the Chinese people. It won't do any of us any good if I admit this publicly now."

"What Mr. Han did was support China in resisting the Japanese invasion," Grandma retorted. "How can he be an enemy of the Chinese people? That leftist supported rebels and deceived his own country, his own family. What scum!" They were quarrelling vociferously. In the end,

Grandma simply hung up a photo of my father in trim military uniform in my bedroom.

As for me, I became a target in society early on as an "evil element of American imperialism." For exactly this reason, I quickly forgot about that leftist because he was not related to me in any way. My mother, in any event, had helped the Communists at a key moment and also gotten an American diplomat into hot water. Zhou did not forget her. Not only did he compel the eminent writer Lao She to invite her to return to China, he also met her at parties held at international clubs and European and American university alumni associations.

In 1964, I graduated from high school, totally oblivious to the perilous political climate in China. I was pleased with my performance on the college entrance examination. Never having attended an adult dance before, I went to Beijing's International Club in my school uniform -- black skirt and white blouse -- not to watch a movie but to dance. Shaking her head and wagging her behind in Zhou's direction, my mother had adulation written all over her face. Looking at me, Zhou asked her, "Is this the kid?" "Yes, indeed," she replied, humbly extending her hand and wearing a suggestive expression. Ignoring her, Zhou asked me, "Slow foxtrot, okay?" Hearing his words, the orchestra broke into a slow foxtrot, and I followed the lead of this expert ballroom dancer. This was the only time I was so close to him that no one else could hear us. I asked him a question.

"Premier, what do you think of the leftists in the West?" I had in mind at that time people such as Edgar Snow, Anna Louise Strong, Han Suyin, Sidney Rittenberg, and Sidney Shapiro, all of whom I considered untrustworthy. I was eager to hear how Zhou viewed them. His candid reply to a seventeen-year-old left me tongue-tied.

"They are weak." He wore a pleased smile, a triumphant smile. Fifty years later, I can still picture that self-assured, confident smile.

The dance was over shortly. Zhou released my hand, looking somewhat preoccupied.

"Soon you will receive your rejection letter," he told me. "Pretty soon you will be sent to the countryside." Joe stared at me intently.

Before this moment, I had never associated my being sent to the countryside with this dance or with my question and Zhou's reply. Now that I thought about it more deeply, I saw that, from Zhou's point of view, a budding original thinker who would pose a serious question to someone in authority had to be promptly bludgeoned into silence before her thoughts matured and her questions become louder and more insistent.

"The high school asked me to make a clean break with my father, that is, to denounce him. I refused. I had almost believed that this was the main reason why I was sent to the countryside. Of course, my mother's passionate desire to curry favor with the Communist Party by sending her only child to the countryside was another reason. Her eagerness to get rid of me made many people realize that talk of her 'raising her daughter as the daughter of that leftist' was a total lie. She simply and wholeheartedly did not want me around anymore."

After this conversation, no one, including Joe, my students, or my friends, ever mentioned this subject again. That is until 1999, when my husband, J, and I were about to return to the U.S. from Athens, where we had been posted to the embassy for three years.

One day, a letter from Gladys Swift arrived. By then, her husband, Dr. Swift, had passed away, and she had sold their home of many decades to move to northern Virginia where she could be closer to her children. Gladys wrote, *I hate to say anything disparaging about other people, but I cannot bear not to tell you this. Shortly after you were born, your mother told us that you were the child of a "famous person" in the State Department who had a wife and three children. A year later, she completely forgot that she had told us that and asked us to go to New York City to pick you up at your father's home. It was then that we learned that your father was an army officer. Earlier this year, the "famous person" died, which reminded me of her lie, and I thought you should know about it. I am getting old. My poor memory keeps me searching for keys and glasses all the time, but things that happened long ago remain deeply rooted in my mind. I often thought that the one thing we should not have done was to take you back to China in 1948. If you had stayed in New York, you could have lived with your father after his return to the U.S. How nice that would have been!*

After reading her letter, I was at a loss how to respond. J replied instead. An experienced diplomat, he wrote to Gladys that our new house was in northern Virginia, enclosed our address, and said we looked forward to meeting her there. When we finally met her there, the nice elderly lady happily showed us photos of her grandchildren. We talked about cooking, gardening, and sewing without touching on the past, as if it had never happened.

But all those things that happened in 1981 with this tall Mr. Bo left me with a favorable impression of him. Calmly and quietly, he had comforted me. "This is not FSI. You can speak English." I could feel his consideration and flexibility. So when those new students started to pick up the language and say a few complete sentences, his questions never failed to astonish me.

One afternoon, after the last class and all the students except Mr. Bo had left, he asked me, "Teacher, would you like to go to Taiwan?" The sentence was basically correct, but the wording was not quite right. He should have used words such as "wish," "want," or "be willing," not "like." He hadn't learned that vocabulary yet, so this was not his fault. I cheerfully replied, "Sure!" He formally bid me good-bye and walked away in a lighthearted way.

I asked Joe, "How is Taiwan?"

"A top-notch place," he replied. He had studied briefly at Furen University in Taipei and had loved everything there. His most often-used characterizations were "sincere and friendly." A good place with good people, it seemed. His tone was one hundred percent positive. "You will never see so many passionate, kind, and hard-working people in one place anywhere else in the world."

During the Cultural Revolution, when books were burnt everywhere in China and traditional culture was constantly under attack, Grandma had also said, "Thank heaven we still have Taiwan!" Joe agreed. "Your grandmother was right! To say that 'Chinese culture still exists in Taiwan' is absolutely correct."

In the evening, when I had finished my assignments, I chatted with Pele. "How about going to Taiwan for a look?" Pele did not seem excited by the idea and after a long look at me closed his eyes. He was too tired, I thought; just let him sleep. I never noticed the sad look in his eyes.

Within a few months, the students' command of Chinese had progressed considerably. It was another afternoon after classes were over when I was in the copier room preparing teaching materials for students in the advanced class. Mr. Bo popped his head through the door and asked politely, "Teacher, would you be willing to work in Beijing?" I was very pleased to hear his complete sentence with no mistakes and with perfect pronunciation.

"What kind of work?" I asked.

"Teaching Chinese at the American Embassy," came the immediate reply.

I wanted to say, "Why, that would be fantastic!" Grandma was already eighty-four years old, and I had not seen her for three and one-half years. Wouldn't it be nice if I could work at the embassy while taking care of her? I thought for a moment and replied simply, "Sure!" Mr. Bo smiled and walked away with a spring in his step.

Later, my heart became heavy as I thought the question over. Could I take Pele with me to a foreign country if I really had a chance to travel? I was in somewhat of a daze when a colorful figure appeared before my eyes. It was a teacher from Sri Lanka, come to the copier room to xerox some teaching materials. She was a senior instructor, experienced and knowledgeable. I asked her politely if she knew anything about taking a dog overseas. She replied that it all depended on the destination. In a rich, democratic country, people would know how to care for pets. Dogs from foreign countries would be quarantined while they underwent physical exams to make sure they were not carrying any infectious diseases before being released to their owners. But, she said solemnly, holding up a warning finger, "Dogs are sensitive animals. Staying in quarantine inflicts psychological wounds. While large dogs suffer less damage, small dogs usually don't take it very well. The experience leaves them with a permanent change in temperament."

The destination was mainland China in the 1980s. How could they know how to treat a small dog well? If Pele should fall into the hands of a vicious handler, what could I do?

That day, I rushed home to hold Pele in my arms. He immediately sensed my fear, and it showed in the deep melancholy in his eyes. My heart ached to see this. I started speculating that Mr. Bo was just practicing his Chinese rather than really trying to help me change jobs. Or perhaps he was planning to suggest the switch to the State Department, which might not even consider it. I recalled that, earlier in the year, a senior diplomat in charge of the Voice of America's Chinese service had taken a demo recording I had made to the station and offered me a job there with excellent pay. Dr. Yates left it up to me to decide whether to accept the offer. The salary offered by the VOA was good, but how could I just leave when the State Department, in the persons of Dr. Swift and Dr. Yates, was treating me so well, and the students were so lovely? I decided to stay at FSI, and, as a result, I came across a group of excellent students. Although Dr. Yates had retired, Dr. Sheehan was also a good boss who even said to me in private, "Dr. Yates' keeping you here makes my job so much easier." He said this with such evident satisfaction that it almost embarrassed me.

My mind was swirling with so many thoughts. "Anyway, it will be a long time before anything happens," I told Pele, who still looked at me with unconcealed sadness. He perked up when he saw Mr. Moore or Joe, which puzzled me. Joe noticed this, too, and asked, "How come Pele seems so distant from you today?"

I related Mr. Bo's suggestion about a possible move and about the potential problems of taking Pele to China. I saw Pele's sad look reflected in Joe's eyes. Stroking Pele, he remained silent for quite a while. Then he said, "Dr. Yates retired only six months ago, and things have already changed so much." Before I could fathom what he meant, he continued, "It would be good if you could be close to your grandma....You shouldn't risk Pele, though. Leave him with me. I'll think of something. There must be a way. That is, if you really have to move." Tears of sadness dampened my cheeks. Pele stared at me with his round eyes. Joe turned around to smile. "Perhaps it's just idle talk." He looked at Pele who shook his head, prompting Joe to look grave again.

It turned out not to be idle talk at all. Mr. Bo frequently invited me to dinner, to concerts, to movies, all of which I declined. I told him that I had to attend a class at a certain university, had to tutor a student at home, had to go to Johns Hopkins for the final stages of my students' dissertations. He always replied politely, "That's all right. We'll do it some other time." It seemed to me as though the things I had to do kept snowballing, with me getting busier and busier. When could "some other time" be?

Until one day he said to me, "You have eight students at Johns Hopkins. They must have all received the degrees they were working for. Let's go celebrate." But I was unwilling to go out to dinner with him. So, I suggested, "Let's make dumplings at home. I learned how to make food with flour in Shanxi, but I can't cook anything else." He hesitated, then with his eyes wide open, he asked, "You'll have worked all day, and you can still make dumplings?"

"I have a puppy at home," I replied. "He'll be happy if I'm home early." Mr. Bo paused for a moment and then agreed.

Driving in his unsightly Toyota sedan, we went to buy ground pork, Chinese cabbage, and green scallions. When we saw ready-made dumpling skins, he considerately asked, "Shall we get a bag of these?" "Homemade tastes better," I replied, causing him to smile. Before we left the store, he inquired about Pele's size and preferences and ended up buying him a small bag of pricey dogfood and a beautiful little ball as well.

When we arrived at my apartment, Pele greeted us with what was for him a restrained welcome. Mr. Bo cheerfully prepared Pele's food and water while I kneaded the dough for the dumpling skins. Pele politely nibbled on the food and then picked up his leash in his mouth and carried it over to Mr. Bo. "Oh, so you want to take a walk?" he asked pleasantly, swiftly attaching the leash. This had never happened before. What a difference this was compared to Pele jumping right into Mr. Moore's arms.

They went downstairs. I looked out the window as I kneaded the dough. Wow! As soon as they walked out the door, they met the queenly Mary. Mr. Bo and Mary's owner greeted each other and began chatting. Snow-white Mary and dark, shiny Pele walked side-by-side in front of them, with Mary strolling leisurely and complacently while Pele pranced with dignity on the grass. Oh, good heavens! Could this be the same Pele as the passionate pursuer of old? Another surprise.

The evening proceeded smoothly. The dumplings were delicious. Not only did Mr. Bo use chopsticks skillfully, he also liked the vinegar sauce that I had prepared. "I can't believe that vinegar goes so well with dumplings." "Not only is it tasty," I pointed out. "It's also healthier." I noticed Pele sitting quietly on the windowsill, missing Mr. Moore perhaps.

We already knew a lot about each other from class. He knew that I had a grandmother living in Beijing. I knew that his parents, younger brother, and two younger sisters all lived in northern Connecticut. Our attention shifted to the wall-to-wall bookshelf. He was overwhelmed by the whole wall of books in Chinese, a "wall" he could not possibly penetrate. Among my students, only Joe and the graduate students at Johns Hopkins could pick up a book from the collection and start reading easily. After all, the diplomats at FSI were on a two-year crash course in Chinese. They had no problem dealing with subjects relevant to their work, such as politics and economics, but reading classical and contemporary literature was almost impossible for them. Squarely facing this unfamiliar world, Mr. Bo was neither intimidated nor curious. He just carried on wearing a warm smile.

Our good byes at the end of the evening were conducted diplomatically, with Pele courteously wagging his tail. Mr. Bo complimented him. "Pele is such a well-trained dog." He left with, "Good night, Teacher."

As soon as he left, Pele seemed so exhausted from a whole evening of restrained behavior that he immediately fell asleep on the carpet. I picked him up and placed him gently on the bed, wondering what could be on his mind. Why was he so well-behaved? Was he trying to make a good impression on Mr. Bo? Trying to persuade him to let him travel with us? Transferring wasn't in Mr. Bo's hands, but those of the State Department and, ultimately in mine and mine alone. The point was, I couldn't bear to have Pele confined in a Chinese veterinary facility for "inspection." My heart ached at the very thought.

In the following days, Pele seemed to want to be extra close with Joe and Mr. Moore. Watching him follow them everywhere, I began to wonder what kind of soul animated Pele. Did he figure that, while it would be great if he could go with me, if he couldn't either Joe or Mr. Moore would take him in? Either way would be fine with him. Or perhaps he was just trying to soothe my aching heart, not wanting me to worry about him. Could a four-year-old dog be so wise as to understand my situation? I shook my head, relegating these thoughts to the back of my mind while I concentrated on my daily tasks.

Towards the end of April, students at FSI were anxiously preparing for their final exams and the move to Taiwan for their second year of language instruction. Most walked in a rush, yet Mr. Bo remained his calm self. One day he invited me to lunch in the little cafe downstairs, and I accepted. I was concentrating on using my knife and fork to deal with the food when suddenly I heard him say, "Shall we get married? May 8 is a good date." Without knowing why, May 8 had floated through my mind. Was there something special about that date? So, I asked, "Why May 8?"

He calmly smiled. "After getting married on May 8, we can ask the State Department to apply for your Taiwan visa. After we get the visa, we'll have to pack and decide which things have to be shipped by sea to Taiwan and which things should go by air freight. Then I have to get my house ready to rent, and you have to give notice to terminate the lease on your apartment. Of course, I still have to finish classes at FSI and pass my final exam. You, too, have to finish work here. All these things have to be done within one month if we are to arrive in time for me to begin classes in Taiwan. So, our wedding date can't be later than May 8. And we have to do certain things before that date. This weekend, we'll have to order wedding rings, which usually takes a week to ten days. You may have to get a wedding dress, which means allowing a few days for the seamstress. Of course, we'll have to go to Connecticut to invite my parents and siblings to our wedding...." This was the first and only time I noticed that my knife and fork were shimmering with a cold light that ran all the way up to the ceiling.

Still smiling, he continued. "This afternoon I have to attend a regional research conference in another building. That will take about two hours. It will be around four o'clock by the time I get back to your office, so you have three hours to consider. What do you think?" At the end of his sentence, he calmly finished the food on his plate and then courteously stood up. I nodded at him. Staring at all the colors on my plate, I moved my knife and fork mechanically; bit by bit I slowly finished my lunch.

Back in my classroom, I received a phone call from the student in my advanced class asking to be excused from class because he had to go to the White House. This gave me time to close my door and think things over. Getting married instead of accepting a temporary transfer meant that my days from then on would be spent traveling to many countries with an American diplomat. I couldn't take FSI and Johns Hopkins along with me. Not only would I no longer teach Chinese and Chinese literature, I would probably have to learn some other languages. The four years immediately before me stood out clearly: one year in Taipei followed by three years in Beijing. What would come after was unknown. What would I do in the future?

Looking at the pens and papers on the desk, I felt for the first time that writing in Chinese might be my life-long work – what gave meaning to my existence. It presented one possibility.

Then, I thought, what was this marriage based on? Mr. Bo and I understood each other quite well after ten months of classes. I had never bought into the Cinderella story, but Jane Austen was wise. She said that the foundation of creating feelings for each other came from gratitude and respect, which, in this case, we both had. Yet Cupid's arrow had not struck. Instead, there was a firm sense of trust. I trusted this calm and considerate Mr. Bo. Now the biggest problem was Pele. My heart ached when I thought of him.

Time passed in the blink of an eye. I heard a light knocking on the door. "Please come in." It was indeed Mr. Bo, with a radiant face.

"I worry about Pele."

"I'll ask around. I'm sure we'll find a solution," he replied immediately. He paused for a moment, looked at me intently, and softly asked, "Shall we go dancing on Saturday night, just to celebrate?"

I shook my head. "I can't. I have to teach."

He thought for a while, then said, "Besides caring about your students, do you teach so much because you need the money?"

I got really nervous hearing this. "That isn't your concern."

He smiled. "There are many kinds of marriage. I prefer the kind where husband and wife share everything. In other words, my money is your money." To which I immediately responded, "Then how about my money?" He laughed. "Your money is still yours."

Good heavens! This logic was completely contrary to that of the Chinese Communists' "Mine is mine, and yours is mine, too" which had always been the practice of those in authority abusing the common people. How marvelous was this Mr. Bo, who thought the exact opposite? In my heart, I shouted "Bravo!" and my attitude naturally turned warmer. Right away and completely unexpectedly, he took out a checkbook and asked, "How much do you need to pay off all your credit card bills?"

I hurriedly calculated mentally: Sears, Bank of America – close to two thousand dollars. When I told him, he calmly wrote me a check for two thousand dollars, then said, "All right. Now can we go dancing this Saturday?" I was still clueless.

"What kind of dance?"

Radiating energy, he replied, "Polka!" I became anxious. "What should I wear?"

With his hands he described a big circle around me. "A round cotton skirt." Wasn't that what Maddie wore all the time? I could do this. "Fine," I replied happily.

He stood up. "I'd better hurry to the personnel office before they close to see about Pele." As he walked to the door, he turned around. "Do you want one or two?"

"One or two what?" I asked, puzzled.

"Rings. Do you want one or two?"

Seeing my blank look, he patiently explained. "The engagement ring has a diamond and the wedding ring is usually a plain gold ring. People usually wear the plain ring all the time. Some people like to wear them alone while others like to wear both at the same time...." He explained with the help of gestures to make sure I understood.

I understood right away. The wedding ring was worn all the time, including dish-washing time. Soaking a diamond in dishwater? I replied with certainty: "I want two rings."

He hurried away with a smile on his face. I noticed that the leisurely, calm Mr. Bo seemed to be, temporarily at least, a being of the past.

When I told my private students that I was going to get married, they not only immediately offered congratulations, they also voluntarily cancelled all their lessons. The Johns Hopkins graduate school said with regret, "We were going to renew your contract, but we wish you the best of luck. Remember us if you come back."

I couldn't bid such a cursory farewell to Joe and Mr. Moore. I continued with their classes until I moved out of my apartment. When he learned of Mr. Bo's proposal, Mr. Moore looked at me earnestly, took out a business card, and wrote a telephone number on the back. "If this guy doesn't treat you well, if you want to come back to Washington, just call this number and I will take care of everything. I am your family. This is a permanent phone number; you can always reach me." Staring at the card, I finally grasped just how senior his government position was, and looking at the hand-written number moved me to tears. I finally had family here. While I never used this number in the subsequent decades, I still felt the warmth of Mr. Moore, whose love was no less than that of a father for his daughter.

I asked Maddie to take care of Pele for a while. A big, round sky-blue skirt trimmed with white lace was lying on the bed. Maddie's face wore a pensive expression. "Teresa, let me give you a piece of advice. Sooner or later, you will find out that this thing called money is indispensable and will bring you happiness and well-being. Especially for women, life without money is no life at all. I really don't get you. Instead of fortune, you choose to wander around with a government worker."

I didn't tell her that earlier I had walked into a dress shop in Rosslyn and told the amiable dressmaker, "I need a white dress; not a long gown because I want to be able to wear it after the wedding." Well accustomed to dealing with customers, the dressmaker did not embarrass me but smiled and said, "Congratulations! For such an important event, let's choose a better-quality fabric. What do you think of this French silk cloth?" I touched the fabric, feeling its softness and elasticity. I nodded. I also picked a pattern. For the first time in my life, I was having a dress custom-made. When I tried to tell J -- no longer Mr. Bo -- about this, he smilingly put his finger on his lips. "The bride's wedding dress is top secret; it's bad luck to reveal it to the groom before the wedding."

So, I just genially replied to Maddie, "Money can never be enough by itself. We are still young. We can use our hands to create our lives together, and this can be joyful and fortunate." I paused before continuing. "J has furniture – dining table and chairs, plus a sofa in the living room. Besides, the State Department will provide us with furniture while we are posted overseas. There's no point in storing all my furniture. Why don't you take whatever you can use?"

Joe's reaction was completely different. When he heard that Mr. Bo was now J, he just murmured a Chinese literary reference to the effect of "Lost through negligence," which left me bemused.

He went on to tell me that there was no perfect solution for Pele. Being quarantined twice within one year would definitely not be good for him. Then he asked, "What are you going to do after four years? Will Pele be traveling around with you everywhere you go?" Pele looked at him and then looked at me. I stretched out my arms, but he jumped into Joe's arms instead and quietly rested his head on Joe's shoulder. Joe was on the verge of tears. "Pele, you're a really good friend, so trusting. Teresa will travel far away, but our lives here have to go on." This reminded me of Joe's gray-colored apartment, which got me worried.

"Don't tell me you are going to take care of Pele."

He shook his head. "I'll probably go to California. I will find Pele a good family to care for him before I go."

Joe was just speaking the truth. Immediately I thought of his father. My leaving would probably occasion the departure of both father and son from Washington. My heart was filled with remorse. Joe had no intention to offer consolation. Instead, he mentioned the book *The Injustice to Dou E*. "Keep it," I told him. "My Grandma will be happy to know that it is with you." Joe looked straight in my eyes. "I will always keep this book with me. After all, you're my best Chinese teacher. I'm thinking that perhaps I should start learning Latin, Hebrew, or ancient Greek."

I was so sad that words failed me.

The silence lasted for a while. Joe eventually said, "You know how to find me. I'll be there for you any time you need me." Hearing these words. I could no longer hold back my tears. "As for Arlington Cemetery, I'll take care of it. Red tulips, right?" Finally, he cracked a smile.

"No. White ones are better," I replied lightly.

The polka dance evening was great. Many students came, and they all enthusiastically invited me to dance. Stepping onto the shiny dance floor with colorful lamps hanging above, dancers happily swirled, following the delightful rhythm of the music, proving that there was more to life than working hard.

Classes at FSI became increasingly intense as final exams loomed, but I no longer went to McDonald's for lunch. J introduced me to Rosslyn's restaurants, one by one. Our favorite was an Italian café whose meatball and cheese submarine sandwiches were the world's tastiest. They became the standard against which we judged all such sandwiches. Many years later, we went to Italy but never found a better sandwich there. During breaks before and after lunch, we also discussed serious issues.

One day, he cautiously raised the issue of religion. Having been brought up and resident in an atheistic country, I was pretty much ignorant about religion. So, I just listened as he talked. His grandparents were Ukrainians of the Eastern Orthodox faith who, when they came to America, turned to Roman Catholicism in the absence of Orthodox churches where they resided. Born in the United States, J's parents were also Catholics. As for J's generation, "God is in my heart. I seldom go to church except for Christmas and Easter. But I love religious art, and I love to visit churches around the world." I listened carefully, planting his words firmly in my mind. Yet I didn't understand what all this had to do with me.

He quickly came to the point. "Catholicism is against birth control. If you don't want many children, we'd better not get married in a Catholic church. We can get married in a justice of the peace's office. This would be all right with my parents." I got to thinking. Grandma didn't believe in God, so a civil ceremony would be acceptable to her. But I wanted to make myself clear.

"Getting married by a justice of the peace is not a problem. Indeed, I don't want many children, but I do want one. I want to give him or her a good childhood. I definitely don't want whatever time we spend in Beijing to cast a shadow over his or her heart. So, I want our stay in Beijing to be as brief as possible. We can only have a child during our last year in Beijing."

This shook J. "By that time, you'll be close to forty years old. Are you sure you want to do it this way?" I nodded. I told him that the child was much more important than I. I was certain that this was the most reasonable plan. My resolution still surprised J, but the matter was not of immediate concern, so we dropped the subject. With my mind set, I planned carefully, consulted my doctor, and took all necessary precautions. As planned, our son was born in Beijing. He left China when he was eight months old, started speaking and learned to walk in New York City, and grew up wrapped in unfailing love and parental attention. All this came later.

As for religion, I always wondered why humans thought they needed a mediator, such as a priest, abbot, pastor, or imam. Why couldn't people communicate directly with God? I kept this question in my heart without discussing it with anyone, not even with J. It was not until 1996, when I went to Delphi and Mount Olympus in Greece, that I realized the gods I could get close to and communicate with were right there. From then on, I found true tranquility.

In 1982, I was exhausted and confused by feelings of happiness, bewilderment, doubt, and restlessness. On a spring weekend, we squeezed time out of our busy schedules to drive to Connecticut.

On the drive up from Washington, the Manhattan skyline gradually emerged on the right: my city, my New York. After leaving thirty-four years earlier, I finally saw you again in person, not in a magazine or movie theater. J slowed down the car and said apologetically, "Sorry we can't stop. We're pressed for time. Otherwise, we'd stop here for a while to take a good look at this great city." I replied, "It doesn't have to be now. Sooner or later we will live here, and I'll have a chance to explore every street and alley." He asked doubtfully, "Are you sure?" "Quite sure," I responded. Sure enough, four years later we moved with our son to Manhattan.

Within a few minutes of our warm greeting at J's parents' home in Connecticut, the conversation turned to politics. It was only then that I discovered that the whole family favored the Republican Party, with J the only Democrat. In 1982, the President in the White House was none other than Republican Ronald Reagan; it was a golden era for Republicans. Father and son, brother and brother, all they talked about was politics. J patiently but vigorously expressed his own and Democratic views on current issues which promptly encountered resistance from the whole family. With much expectation, my in-laws-to-be asked, "Teresa, which side are you on?" I replied honestly, "I'm a Republican." My future in-laws cheered, and then they asked me why I chose to become a Republican. I explained how I joined the party.

Shortly after starting to work at FSI in 1978, a man walked into my classroom asking if I would like to join the Republican Party. Cautiously, I asked, "What kind of party is it?" He patiently explained. "There are two main political parties: Republican and Democratic."

Still cautious, I asked, "What do they do?" "The main purpose of the Republican Party," he said, "is to oppose Communism."

"You don't have to go on," I told him. "I'll join." He handed me a card where I filled in my name. I assumed that the next step would be to pay a fee. He shook his head and smiled. "No such thing as party dues. During a campaign, if you are willing to contribute some money, that would be fine. If not, that would be all right, too, as long as you vote." He looked at me and said in a pleasant voice, "If the Democratic candidate is more to your liking, you can certainly vote for the Democrat. America is a democracy." So that was how it was! I tucked away this much-cherished card and became a Republican.

Beaming with joy, my future in-laws welcomed me with great enthusiasm. I looked at J, who did not show much emotion but remarked with a smile, "The Democratic Party would never tolerate a Communist system either. You'll find out in time that the policies of these two parties can change. Principles associated with Democrats for a long time can become Republican principles and vice versa."

I thought of Joe, whom I had known for four years. During that time, we had never talked about politics or religion, for our world was literature. This realization left me with a sense of missed opportunity and loss.

After a while, J took out an ordinary tin of tobacco, filled a pipe, and walked into the backyard, where he sat on a wicker lounge chair facing the green lawn. He lit the pipe and smoked contentedly, sending a pleasant aroma into the air around him while gazing at the school building behind the fence as if in thought. A mystery novel lay in his lap.

The school was an elementary school that all four children had attended. When he was very young, J had worked in the surrounding tobacco fields during the summers to earn pocket money. Everyone was eager to relate funny stories about J when he was young. A green apple in the fruit platter on the dining table caught my eye. I quietly picked it up, sliced it, and took three slices to put into J's tobacco tin. This surprised everyone, and they asked, "How did you know that green apple slices will keep the tobacco moist?" I replied, "I once saw a student in his office place green apple slices in his tobacco tin." While I was explaining this, a thought came to mind. For our first Christmas together, I would give him a fine-looking tobacco humidor and an exquisite pipe.

The wedding was held on May 8. The next day was Monday. J walked into my classroom and greeted me as usual: "Good morning, Teacher." "Good morning, Mr. Bo," I replied with a straight face. "Did you have a good weekend, Teacher?" he continued. "Quite good," I responded. The other students roared with laughter.

Later, J and I walked to Dr. Sheehan's office to inform him that we would be leaving FSI together. "Teresa, I asked you to take a little extra care of him," he said in mock exasperation. "I didn't ask you to marry him!" Seeing me laugh, he turned to J and continued, "Do you know you're taking away our best teacher?" J calmly replied, "To learn a language, of course one must find the best teacher." Shaking with laughter, Dr. Sheehan said, "It sure is hard dealing with an outstanding student from Johns Hopkins." As we left, Dr. Sheehan said to me in all sincerity, "Please continue to teach at the embassy after you arrive in Beijing." Equally sincerely, I said that I would, causing him to break out in a smile of satisfaction.

Just as Joe had predicted, there turned out to be no good way to arrange for Pele to travel with us. The safest course was to keep him in the United States. Separation from Pele became inevitable. My sorrow was beyond words.

One day, Joe drove to my almost-empty home bringing good news. An old friend of his father, one-half of a most reliable couple, had just lost his dog to old age. They were eager to find a puppy to fill the void in their hearts. Pele would arrive at their house, his new home, this very day. Pele's baggage was already in the car. I held him closely then gently placed him on the passenger seat. I told myself that I would change my plan and take him with me no matter what if he jumped out of the car. But he didn't budge, just looked at me quietly. Without saying a word, Joe walked over to close the door on Pele's side. He placed in my hands a box inside of which was a glass bottle holding a model of the sailing ship "America" on a rolling sea.

The car started to roll. Joe slowly rolled up the window. Pele suddenly jumped up, his front paws scratching at the window glass, and started barking sharply and urgently. Tears rolled from my cheeks onto the elegant box in my hands.

I was devastated. I didn't have the courage to step into my apartment knowing Pele wouldn't be there to greet me. J appeared just in time. His blue Toyota sold, he was driving a rental car. Holding "America" in my hands, I got into the car, and we headed for a hotel.

I knew that future years would see me caught up in continuous moving, dealing with rental car companies, and living in hotels. But "America" would always be with me as a keepsake from Joe. After all, Joe was the most outstanding student I had ever taught.

CHAPTER 11

READY FOR LAUNCH

Could this be real? There, written in beautiful traditional Chinese characters, not missing a stroke, was "International Airport." Store signs all bore attractive, enticing names: "The Best Market," "Blossoming Department Store," "Elegant Studio," "Reliable Construction," "Lovely Woman Fashion," "Leave Only When Full" restaurant, "Short of Cash" noodles, "Best Bakery" – the list went on. As I gazed around in enchanted awe, I couldn't help muttering to myself, "Good heavens: stewed pork rice, rice noodles, cuttlefish rice congee, even Shandong-style steamed buns!" Some of the locals claimed that store signs in Taipei were too numerous and rather unsightly, to which I replied, "Not at all, not at all." I was hungry to see more.

On our arrival in Taipei, the American Institute in Taiwan assigned us a Western-style house formerly occupied by members of the American military advisory group. At that time, all our mail had to be delivered via diplomatic pouch. That very night, I wrote a letter to Grandma relating my excellent initial impression of Taipei. Her reply came shortly. She urged me to buy a small piece of jade and tie it to "Mr. Bo's" pocket watch. "Doesn't he carry his pocket watch every day? Tying a piece of jade to it will keep him safe. The quality of the jade is not so important. Do this right away before you come back to Beijing." Grandma, always calm and steady, sounded an unusually urgent note in her letter. This got me thinking. She came from a home with all females. Since her husband passed away in 1937, there had not been a man in the house for a good forty-five years. To her, this Mr. Bo had to be very precious. With this realization, I immediately took action.

On my first shopping trip into the city, I asked a salesman where I could buy a book that showed how to make decorative Chinese knots. He politely escorted me to a side street where a sign board reading "Yuying Crafts" could be seen hanging outside a small shop full of yarn, knitting and embroidery tools, Chinese knots, and other crafting materials. There were how-to books, materials, tools, even classes! I decided to learn how to make Chinese knots by studying the how-to books. After purchasing the materials and a book, I asked Ms. Xiu Ying, the shop's proprietor, "Where can I find a small piece of jade? I want to tie it with a knot onto my husband's pocket watch." She told me that her older brother ran a small jade shop inside the upscale Lai Lai Hotel downtown. "I'll give my brother a call so he can bring some suitable pieces to your residence," she offered. I told her I lived on Yangming Mountain at the end of Kaixuan Road, right next to the Chinese Culture University.

That very evening, as J was doing his homework, a man rode up to our house on a motorcycle. Wearing a white shirt and blue pants, he carried only a canvas satchel inside of which were many small red velvet bags. "My sister said," he began, "that you want to make a Chinese knot to attach to your husband's pocket watch. For that, the jade should be small and exquisite." He sounded professional and sincere, very different from the stereotype of a merchant. He placed several lovely jade articles, shimmering with a soft glow, on a piece of black velvet. I had my eyes on a small ruyi (an elongated S-shaped object) with a cute gecko on it. Most importantly, it had a tiny hole at one end where I could attach a Chinese knot. "New jade," my visitor said with a smile. "The quality and craftsmanship are both quite good."

After buying the ruyi, I immediately dove into my project. This was a beginning, the first of the ornaments and articles of clothing I would make for J. The book I bought from Xiu Ying was most helpful. Following its diagrams, I finished making a Shi Quan knot, a symbol of good fortune. The other end was a button knot which I had learned from Grandma. She always made her own button knots for her cotton jackets and, as she worked, she also taught me how to make them. It was way past midnight when I finished. Not at all sleepy, I spread out a piece of paper to write a letter to Grandma reporting that there was already a small jade ruyi on J's pocket watch.

In the morning, J was so pleasantly surprised that he kept on asking, "What does this mean?"

"May everything go as you wish, with peace, happiness, health, and longevity. This is my grandmother's and my wish for you." From then on, for more than thirty years, this small ruyi has always been with J.

The Chinese language school on Yangming Mountain was a branch of the main FSI in Washington. Naturally, I was invited to teach there. But since there was so much to see and learn in Taiwan in only one precious year, I turned down the invitation.

A big, beautiful tree grew in my front yard, and only a wall separated my house from the Chinese Culture University, a wall with a big hole resembling a moon door. Young men and women, students at the university, often came through it to sit under the tree on our nicely trimmed lawn while they ate their lunch and quietly chatted. I always felt warm inside seeing them so relaxed and happy. I had no wish to disturb them. That "moon door" also beckoned me to pass through, and I took two courses as a one-year student at the university. Not only did I learn a lot in class, I also had an opportunity to befriend several well-known Taiwanese writers and publishers. I was extremely fortunate to have started my writing career there.

Compared to my non-stop life in Washington, the year in Taipei could be considered relaxed and leisurely. I thought to use this rare opportunity to learn some cooking, especially after I had the good fortune to see Ms. Fu Pei Mei on television. The ingredients she used were clearly displayed, and she explained each step as she demonstrated it with great precision and clarity. Each show was a solid half-hour class. I wrote down the recipes in my notebook and immediately took a bus down the mountain, straight to the Shilin market.

Shopping list in hand, I bought the items on it one by one. After buying celery and bell peppers, the shopkeeper generously handed me a couple of scallions. "Take them. You'll need them when cooking." Seeing she was inclined to be helpful, I decided to consult her. "Where can I get pressed tofu?" She pointed the way and, following her directions, I arrived at a huge booth where I saw the most spectacular exhibition of soy products. I couldn't help but recall that for so many years soy products in China were available only with ration coupons and in limited amounts and varieties. But here was a completely different world! Bamboo steamers held all kinds of tofu, and large platters displayed thin tofu, tofu skin knots, pressed tofu, fragrant pressed tofu, shredded pressed tofu, steamed gluten, fried tofu, puffed tofu, and large tofu skin. That was the first time I ever saw a complete piece of large tofu skin. It was so soft and fluffy, golden and fragrant - so tempting! The middle-aged shopkeeper noticed that I couldn't take my eyes off the tofu skin. "Use it to stir-fry vegetables; roll shredded pork or shredded bamboo shoots in it, they're all good," he suggested. "It's also good just to simmer it with soy sauce." I was so happy that I bought tofu, pressed tofu, and tofu skin. Shopping cart stacked with bags, large and small, I cheerfully returned home.

That evening I cut the tofu skin into small pieces, simmered them in shrimp roe sauce, and placed them on the dinner table. J enjoyed it so much that he never forgot the tofu skin from Shilin, claiming that it outshone every other delicacy. For a whole year, I became a frequent customer at that tofu shop. Every time I went shopping in Shilin, I would stop by and chat with the shopkeeper and his wife for a while before leaving with a big piece of tofu skin. Thirty years later, J still cherished the memory of Shilin's tofu skin. Even in Paris, the city of haute cuisine, he would still say he missed Shilin's tofu skin. I, on the other hand, missed the kindness and warmth of Taiwan's markets, which are unmatched anywhere in the world. They are at the top of my list of best places.

Bookstores, especially Taiwan's bookstores, are another thing I could not live without. Having experienced oppression and cultural desolation in mainland China, I found that Taiwan's lively literary scene proved the truth of Joe's heart-felt praise of Taiwan. What a beautiful sight it was to see readers of all ages quietly perusing and choosing books. No one looked at me in surprise as I joined them. But, as soon as I spoke, I met smiling faces. "Wow. Your Chinese is excellent! Did you learn it at Furen University?" Joe had learned his Chinese at Furen, so I nodded, adding, "I also study at the Chinese Culture University," which was usually greeted with "Oh, indeed," and nods of comprehension.

Good times passed quickly. The spring of 1983 arrived with flowers blooming splendidly on Yangming Mountain. Some of the FSI students had already finished their lessons and moved on to their new posts.

One balmy afternoon, Mr. Chen, the man who mowed our lawn, brought his father to see me. Mr. Chen senior had started out mowing these same lawns when young. Now he was a senior manager for administrative services of the American Institute in Taiwan, to which FSI's language school on Yangming Mountain was attached. When we first moved into our house, he attentively directed workers to hang new curtains. My general impression was that this father-son team was constantly seeing off departing personnel and welcoming new arrivals with enthusiasm, care, and consideration. Seeing them reminded me that we were soon to leave.

As though sensing my feelings, Mr. Chen senior said, "No, you will still be here for a while. It will be a month or two before you move on." He continued, "A family recently left here for Hong Kong. The vacant house has been cleaned. Before a new family moves in, you might like to go there to take a look. General Han once lived there."

I was stunned. Mr. Chen senior opened his document folder and took out a framed photo wrapped in cloth. I immediately spotted the gentle smile and the familiar casual military uniform. Standing next to the big, tall American officer was a person who looked like Mr. Chen junior. "That's my father," Mr. Chen junior explained. "The photo was taken twenty years ago."

"As soon as you arrived," Mr. Chen senior continued the narrative, "we noticed your resemblance to the General. The house was occupied then by a family with children, so it wasn't possible for you to view it. Now that it is vacant, we have cleaned it and restored the living room to its original look. The General didn't like too much furniture, so the living room has only two small sofas without even a coffee table between them. His dog, 'Captain,' was big and followed him everywhere. Too much furniture would have made it hard for him to turn around." Mr. Chen senior set out these details with much feeling.

The photo showed a large, solemn-looking canine protectively sitting at the General's left side and coming up almost to the senior Mr. Chen's shoulder. That had to be "Captain."

"The dog was supposedly from Denmark. Its huge size was rather scary. It didn't bark or bite, though, and over time adults and children got used to it," the junior Chen explained.

"Is the General your father?" Mr. Chen senior softly asked. "That was our guess."

I nodded. "How long did he live here?"

"Four whole years, in the same house. He was away on official business quite often, always taking Captain with him. He would leave the key with me so we could clean the house and open the windows to get fresh air in," Mr. Chen senior explained.

My vision blurred. "What was he like?"

Mr. Chen senior smiled. "He never got angry with us; with us he always wore a smile. I heard that during meetings of the military advisory group, he often blew his top and slapped the table. If you want, you can keep the photo."

I handed the photo back to him. "You keep it as something to remember him by. Thank you for taking care of him for so long." I could feel that my reply pleased Mr. Chen senior. He nodded and put the photo back in his document folder, took out a set of keys, and led me to see the house.

The three of us slowly walked down the hill, following, I imagined, in the same footsteps the General had taken for walks. But no. Mr. Chen senior told me that the General, in fact, did not take this road for walks. He would walk downhill from his house to Lin Yutang's White Cloud Mountain Villa and then turn around and walk back uphill. He had some problem with his legs, probably stemming from an old wound; walking uphill was supposed to help with rehabilitation.

The General's old house was about a five-minute walk from mine, and was built in the exact same style: one floor, brick exterior with a large picture window, and car port. It sat on the corner of a small road which I would pass by when I walked to Gezhi Road. There were two trees in the front yard, not big, but luxuriant.

Mr. Chen senior opened the door for me. Usually, a recently cleaned house such as this one would have a strong odor of cleaning agents. In this house, however, there lingered the scent of flowers. Standing by the door, Mr. Chen senior said, "He liked wild ginger flowers. He would buy them whenever he could. Only when he couldn't get them would he make do with Casablanca lilies."

On a small table under the window sat a vase of wild ginger flowers in full bloom. Snow-white petals pressed against the full-length white curtains like a relief, reminding me of those white tulips against the white tombstone. From here to there, a short journey, a short passage of time.

In Mr. Chen senior's photo, the General's right elbow leaned on the fireplace mantel as he held a pipe in his hand. His sideburns were gray. I could imagine him standing here during the winter with one hand touching the mantel as he gazed at the crackling flames in the fireplace.

Opportunities to use a fireplace in Taipei, with its sub-tropical climate, would be few; but fireplace and mantel were indispensable in New York. Probably he would just stand there watching Captain most of the time. So here was the place where he could quietly read and think. Inhaling the fragrance of the flowers, he could allow his thoughts to leave work and fly to faraway places. I sat on the small sofa, reached out my left hand as if to feel Captain's body. I could sense him watching me with concern, just like Pele used to. Tears rolled down my cheek.

Walking out the door, I found the Chens quietly waiting for me. I thanked them profusely. Mr. Chen senior locked the front door before we said goodbye.

I followed the street to reach the main road, walking downhill until I reached the White Cloud Mountain Villa. There, I turned around to retrace my steps going uphill. As the slope became steeper, I could feel the pressure on my knees. Both legs began to shake. Sharp pain brought on by my serious arthritis caused me to break out in a sweat.

"Next time, instead of walking all the way to the White Cloud Mountain Villa, perhaps you could just walk to that middle school," suggested a gentle voice in my mind. I imagined I saw Captain looking at me with concern before he turned around and started heading uphill gallantly in front of me. I followed closely, forgetting my bodily discomfort, and before long Guanghua Road appeared right ahead. Now I understood how he walked back home twenty years ago without using his cane.

This night, scorched with pain as if split by a hatchet, I could not move my legs at all. As I lay in bed, the pain kept me from falling asleep. I told myself that I would not walk that far again; I would turn around at the middle school. Despite the pain, I was happy because I figured that, if he could walk such a long stretch of uphill road, his wounded leg must not have been as bad as my arthritis. That was good, very good indeed, so at last I could close my eyes and slip into dreamless sleep.

The next day, Joe's letter arrived - such beautiful penmanship, whatever the language.

I can finally give you a report on Pele's situation. I'm sure you remember that reliable old couple. After only a week, they found that they could not handle Pele's energy; their former dog had been quiet, well-behaved, and hardly moved. They accepted a vet's suggestion to neuter him. The vet said that Pele would be more sedate after the surgery. Fortunately, the wife loves to chat. She mentioned this to my father on the phone the night before the procedure. I was just getting ready to move when I heard this news. I ran over there and saved Pele from the knife. The good news is that a college friend of mine had just gotten married and bought a house and was looking for a lively puppy. I strongly recommended Pele for the position. The best news is that Pele will soon be a father. My friend also adopted a lovely female dog named Honey, and she and Pele hit it off immediately. Now he keeps busy circling Honey all day long. I'm sure he will be a conscientious father, and it shouldn't take long for him to have his own team of World Cup champions.

As for me, my story is much less exciting than Pele's. I moved to San Francisco six months ago. My father's company is based in southern California, but I live in the north. I understand that my father's business will one day be mine, but I'm really not interested in business. Fortunately, it won't be difficult to assemble a management team I can entrust everything to. So far, business is booming. I really don't have anything to complain about.

Hebrew is not as difficult as people claim. Besides, there are a lot of ancient books and records to research, so I spend a lot of time in the library. I didn't find myself a teacher. I absolutely don't want any language teacher. You certainly know the reason better than I.

I really hope that you like the model of the "America" I gave you. My father said that it was the best one I'd ever made. San Francisco is not that

far away from you, with only the small Pacific Ocean in between. I'd be
happy to welcome you anytime here, where birds chirp and flowers release
their fragrance.

At the end of the letter, Joe did not forget to send his regards to J, as a gentleman would.

I took out some beautiful Taiwan stationery to reply to Joe's letter. I told him all the wonderful things I had found in Taiwan and declared that someday I would return there to live for a few more years. I told him about stepping into the house my father had occupied, seeing his gentle smile and Captain's look of concern, and Mr. Chen senior's care for them. I wrote about following his walking trail and discovering that his leg wound may not have been as serious as I had thought; for that I felt relieved. I had found out that not only could he smile gently, but that he could also lose his temper and slap the table. How wonderful! I told him about Captain, probably the tallest dog in the world, yet his eyes were exactly like Pele's. Oh yes, and the General loved wild ginger flowers, a special kind of flower from Taiwan – white as snow with a strong fragrance. As I had guessed, he loved white flowers.

I also told him that I loved his model of the "America" and displayed it proudly in our home; for now, though, I was not going to take it across the Pacific, but rather across the Taiwan Strait. I did not know what I would encounter on the other side, but I knew that this time around this "unwanted one" was much stronger, braver, and smarter than she had been five and one-half years ago. I could overcome any obstacle and meet any challenge. Of course, I would convey his regards to Grandma. I concluded by saying that I would write to him from the other side. The letter was disorganized and messy, but he was Joe; he would understand every word I wrote.

The "America," sitting in its bottle on the mantelpiece under the warm Taiwan sun, looked ready to launch. In my mind, it had already set sail.

The End

CHRONOLOGY OF SIGNIFICANT EVENTS

IN CHINA: 1947-1979

1945-49	Chinese Civil War
1949	Chinese Communists take power. Land reform in the countryside. Mass killings of landowners
1949-1950	Thought Reform Movement targets intellectuals. People are required to write personal histories and encouraged to inform on others.
1950-53	Korean War. Americans in China are interned in concentration camps. General hostility to Americans
Early 1950-51	Movement to Suppress Counter-revolutionaries. People are required to write personal histories in order to identify persons associated with the former Kuomintang (KMT) government. More than 800,000 persons are killed.
1951-52	Three Againsts, Five Againsts Movement targets non-KMT democratic elements and capitalists
1953-56	Collectivization of private businesses
1956	Hundred Flowers Campaign. Briefly welcomes criticism of the Communist Party and government, but criticism of Mao brings this period of liberalization to an end.
1957	Anti-Rightist Campaign. Chinese intellectuals are targeted for suppression in order to control dissent. 1-3 million persons are persecuted.
1958-62	Great Leap Forward. China attempts to industrialize quickly.
1958	Land is organized into people's communes
Late 1950s	Sino-Soviet rift opens
1959-61	Great Three-Year Famine. 30-40 million people starve to death.
1964	Socialist Education Campaign. Attaches political and class labels to individuals, resulting in persecution of those with "bad class background."
1964-1978	Millions of young people from urban areas are sent to the countryside.
1966-76	Cultural Revolution. Results in an estimated 3 million deaths.
1971	Lin Biao, Mao's heir-apparent, dies in plane crash after an alleged coup attempt
1971	China-USSR border tensions
1972	President Nixon visits China
1974-78	U.S. Liaison Office operates in Beijing
1979	U.S. and China establish diplomatic relations

ACKNOWLEDGEMENTS

Many thanks to Thomas Appich, Judith Strotz, and Andrew Buczacki for reviewing this translation and offering valuable comments and suggestions.

Thanks also to Asian Culture Publishing Co., Ltd. of Taipei, Taiwan and to Mr. Chi-Shun Yang for permission to use his award-winning cover design, which also graced the original Chinese-language edition of this book.

ABOUT THE AUTHOR

Han Xiu is the pen name of Teresa Buczacki. The daughter of a United States Army officer and a Chinese student, she was born in New York City but lived in Mainland China for most of her life before the age of thirty-two. She returned to the United States in 1978 and began teaching Chinese at the U.S. Department of State's Foreign Service Institute and Chinese literature to doctoral students at The Johns Hopkins University's School of Advanced International Studies in Washington, D.C. She has published more than forty-five works of fiction and non-fiction in Taiwan and China. *The Unwanted*, first published in 2012, is her third novel and the second to be translated into English. She lives with her husband in Virginia.

ABOUT THE TRANSLATORS

Katherine Lu retired from a Chinese literary magazine in 2008 after seventeen years as its director. She received her MA degree in English from the University of Iowa. Choosing to be a stay-at-home mom, she held several part-time positions including item writer for ACT, test specialist at Riverside Publishing Company, and translator for various organizations. She has been married to her soulmate, Chia-Hsing, for over fifty years. Together they focus on protecting the environment.

Jeffrey Buczacki retired from the U.S. Department of State after twenty-nine years as a Foreign Service Officer. His postings included Kinshasa, New Delhi, Beijing, Kaohsiung (Taiwan), and Athens. He and the author have been married for thirty-eight years.

Made in the USA
Middletown, DE
26 August 2022

72331682R00136